The Professor And His Son

**Book Two
of the
The Zradian Chronicles**

**The Reluctant Hero
The Professor And His Son
The Doomsday Bomb**

James Apps

Published in the United Kingdom
TAUP UK
Sheerness
Kent

Contents

"I like cats but when they're that big and playful, I 'ates 'em."

The Ferret

Prologue

The Pairs lying or sitting in their bunks listened to the small Half Pair who spoke quietly but powerfully as he leaned against the wooden upright. They pitied him because his twin was dying but listened because what he had to say was full of meaning; full of good sense and inspired them take action before they succumbed to the ultimate humiliation of oppression.

"Every turn more of us die. Every tenth there are more and more coming in to be used like machines. We are fed poor food, whipped, made to work to quotas that become harder with each passing turn yet we are still alive. This despotic president takes us from our homes not because we physically oppose him but because of our chosen belief. However much he oppresses us he cannot oppress the truth; he cannot destroy us if we believe," he said and looked at the group of ragged pairs and half pairs who, weary as they were, listened to him attentively. "Are you all willing?"

There was a soft murmur of assent.

"Then we are ready?"

Another murmur.

"We move at first light."

The Zradian sky lightened but Camp Red Three was still in darkness. It was enough to cover the movements of the group of pairs and half pairs who sneaked out of the westernmost hut fully dressed, armed only with wooden staves taken from their bunks, and carrying what little food they had stolen in small cloth bags they snaked along the track toward the main gate where the wagons were parked. Keeping to the shadows the main body watched whilst one Pair crept to the shadowed side of each wagon, unlocked the cab, and entered quietly. Both pairs appeared a few moments later waving to the rest of the group who quickly boarded the vehicles.

A few short periods passed and slowly the wagons eased away from their parking bays, turned and headed toward the gate. Guards, suddenly aware of the wagons rushed out of their comfortable huts.

"Nong! That time already?" said one guard and stabbed the button to open the gates.

The wagons rolled forward faster, rolled through the open gate, turned and stopped. The guards saw the plasma gun aimed at them and before they could move were cut down by the searing fire.

As a parting gift to their oppressors the two wagons lined up the laser cannons on the Polisoc administration block and fired two converging streams of plasma heat into the building. That done the wagons turned and rolled on down the slope to the main road and once there headed off west.

Nert, sitting in the lead wagon watched his twin, Tern, cough and breathe his last breath as he held his twin's hand and tears ran down his craggy face. Later, after the wagons were stopped for the night and they had buried their dead Nert felt his confidence draining away. In later turns he became increasingly more diffident and where before he was quiet he became apologetic and quiet, but his oration was still as powerful and persuasive.

When the wagons ran out of power too far from a fusion power station to find a charging point the group took what they could carry and burned the wagons and disappeared into the bush.

The column of smoke from the burning camp was a beacon for the Rebel patrol. They rolled up the slope cautiously ready to flee or fight reaching the gate at the top of the hill to be greeted by the sight of devastation.

"It's a labour camp!" said the Leader Pair.

The main block was on fire and yet there was one fully armed group of soldiers and Polisoc Police with blade weapons and laser guns firing at groups of ragged prisoners or attacking them with swords.

"We know what to do lads," said the Leader Pair.

The rebel wagons rolled through the gate, disembarked their Pairs who immediately began shooting the uniformed soldiers and Polisocs.

"Prisoners! Retreat!" the leader Pair announced as his Pairs pressed home their attack. The result was inevitable. The Rebel Patrol eliminated the overseers; the self appointed Leader Pair of the prisoners asked what would happen next.

"We have already called for more wagons, er, we have sort of rescued you," said the Rebel Leader Pair. The prisoners salvaged their meagre belongings from the huts, gathered and stacked as much of the food stores as they could manage and when the second patrol arrived with more wagons the ex-prisoners and the stores were loaded aboard.

The column moved off and as they passed through the wrecked gates and down the hill the prisoner Leader Pair asked: "Where are we going?"

"The Rebel Army needs recruits," the fully armed Leader Pair said.

"Oh, good. We are supposed to be recruits are we?"

"Er yes, you understand, we rescue, we also train you to do what we have just done," the Leader Pair said with a grin. "You will end up killing the President's soldiers if you are lucky."

The Pair smiled warmly. "Lead on..."

"In this case it is lead on."

Star Station Two

Clard and Dracl were missing!

Rumour had it that as revenge for their ill treatment they had transported a dozen Carnibeasts and released them to run riot in the corridors.

Panic!

Pour and Roup, hearing of the rumour cursed and called in the Polisocs.

"Guard the Transfer Ports. Let nobody out until this rumour is laid to rest. If necessary you will take extreme measures to bring order to this chaos, and bring the rumour mongers to me for punishment," said Roup.

"And we want Clard and Dracl caught and brought back to us," said Pour aware of his lapse into the informal 'we'

"We will do as your Honour requests," said the Senior Leader Pair, licking their lips happily, fidgeting with their swords.

"A minimum kill please - just enough to calm them down," said Pour, nervously.

The Senior Leader Pair saluted neatly and stomped off stiffly.

"I hated doing that but we have to stop the panic somehow," said Pour.

"We must do what we can under the circumstances," said Roup.

"Do them good - a purge," said Pour.

"The staff or the Polisocs?" Roup.

"Both. The staff need a strong guiding hand and a modicum of dread and uncertainty, and the Polisocs need something to keep their minds off subversion I suppose. On the whole not a bad solution if it works," said Pour.

"And if it doesn't?" asked Roup.

"More and deeper purges I suppose," said Pour.

"Regrettable but necessary," said Roup, nodding his head gently.

The Polisocs issued a statement, locked off the Transfer Ports, and began a minor purge. The statement was broadcast throughout the Star Station on all communications systems.

Hear this Pairs! The Pair Clard and Dracl have defected. There is a reward of T500,000 for their arrest - alive. There is also a bounty of T100,000 for their dead bodies. There is no, repeat, no Invasion of carnivorous animals. All staff will resume Off World Invasion duties immediately!

By Order SS2 Polisoc.

Two turns later Dral and Darl waited nervously for the Polisoc Leader Pair to speak. The panic was more or less controlled and the purge was nearly over, and so far they were safe. Until now.

"We have a formal request."

"Oh yes?" said Darl.

"We need some information from your records."

"I'm sorry but our records are not accessible to other departments," Dral said.

"You refuse us access?"

"No, not personally, but we are not authorised to release information except to our own people. No offence meant but there it is," said Darl, careful to smile. "I'm sorry."

"I will go higher."

"If you wish," said Dral, and bowed politely.

The Pair left their office obviously annoyed and Dral glanced at Darl nervously.

"I feel we are on borrowed time my twin," he said.

"I'll call Pour and Roup and ask them," he said.

Dral and Darl searched the latest Presidential Directives and discovered that as long as the Polisoc department paid for the services through internal accounting any information they required could be passed on to them. The provision in the directive was that as long as any department was internally charged for services or information they were responsible for its use, and that any department selling the information was therefore no longer responsible.

"Got the bulgers!" said Darl.

The Pair presented their report to Pour and Roup with smug smiles and stood by while the Pair summoned the Polisoc Leader Pair to their office. Dral and Darl had obtained the endorsement of the Twin Consuls through the office of the Treasury. Gleefully they listened as Pour and Roup made constructive suggestions based on their own work. The Polisoc Leader Pair bowed keeping their hands on the hilts of their swords and solemnly thanked them.

"You have done a great service for Zrad," said the Leader Pair.

"May the President live forever," said Dral.

"Long live the President!" said the Leader pair, saluting.

They turned smartly and marched out through the portal.

"Jerks," said Dral and Darl.

Pour and Roup laughed.

From that time onward Pour and Roup adopted this method of passing the buck unwittingly creating a bureaucratic nightmare for their administration. The result of Dral and Darl's solution and their

Leader Pair's approval was that the system of financial approval, requiring confirmation and accounting to be ratified by more than one section for each operation slowed the supply system to about two thirds of its normal slow rate.

The signal drifted in quietly and sifted into the memory banks softly at first, but steadily grew until it probed the edges of the security system where for a few nano-seconds it stopped. It flashed binary code back along to its source and shifted a little further into the chips. It saw opportunities for expansion as little by little the memory banks gave in to it. It stopped when it found what it wanted, and with an electronic sigh it imprinted its message onto the matrix of the Star Station Master Computer. On every screen from the smallest portal viewer to the flat monitor on the bridge an image of a small carnivorous animal washing its delicate paws and whiskers imposed itself over all working data. It stayed on the screen for no longer than five small periods but every Pair that saw it recoiled in horror. They watched fascinated as the kitten on their screens, distracted from its face washing, happily played with its tail. Many Pairs attacked the screens. Some switched off their lights and sat moaning in the darkness. Others stood numbed and recalled the nightmares of their childhood. Some Pairs attacked the nearest Polisoc troopers and were cut down for their trouble. Then the apparition disappeared and music began to play insidiously over the public address system. There was no escape from it. Whatever the technicians did there was no turning it off. It pervaded the weapons systems and Comsec. It whispered out of computer speakers and became the background to all internal communications. The bridge was filled with it, and all dispensing machines played it whenever they were used. There was no getting away from it. At intervals the tune was punctuated by a useful and informative spoken message which was sometimes quite clear, and at others totally off the wall. At exactly 12 noon Earth Standard Time all sound stopped and an authoritative voice spoke to the Soldiers and the Civilian staff on board the Star Station.

Do not be afraid of the rodents! Do not be afraid of the Rodents!
We hope you enjoy the music - Napoleon/Betty/Anthony wish you
success with your enterprise - remember the Ides of March - snow
in Moscow - the victory of Dunkirk - and spaghetti - Do not be afraid of the rodents - A Whiter Shade of Pale is our favourite tune - it should be yours - do not be afraid of rodents during the Ides of March - Give my love to Pour and Roup.

Pour and Roup stared at their screen open mouthed. It was filled with animated figures of rodents running hither and thither in a myriad of colours interspersed with flashes of the phrase Do - Not - Be - Afraid - Of - The - Rodents!

Their shoulders slumped, and frantically they pressed buttons on their consoles trying to expunge the message from the screen. "A virus! We have a computer virus!" yelled Pour, angrily. "Technicians!" But there was nothing the technicians could do; the virus was deep within the entire program.

In the Amazon jungle the crazed robot stomped slowly through the undergrowth and gazed with fondness at the carpet of furry backs undulating ahead of it. Its family of ravenous rodents was thriving. To keep itself amused it modified its contact with the Star Station Two computer. It infiltrated the security system and to keep the main computer busy it started a virus adding a fail safe self destruct timed to react to a particular code, and explored the resistant system. It broke through and became immediately immersed in a program which both computers agreed would be a lot of electronic fun. It sent feelers of electronic thought deeper and deeper into the new lines and what it found kept it busy for many long periods. Eventually it had an electronic surveillance system of its own installed and metaphorically sat back on its digital haunches and waited for the data to roll in. The robot, monitoring the situation from its jungle home approved of Dral and Darl's solution, found some more obstructions, added them to the system and informed it's contact on Star Station One and the friendly operator at NMF headquarters. Indirectly the request for an attack was passed to the Women's Rebel Army. It was eagerly taken up beginning a series of sabotage attacks on the Zradian military supply structure designed to annoy the President by further slowing his invasion.

In addition to all this interference It forgot to send the anti-virus code.

The map on the screen showed planet fall on all continents, the deployment plans showed rapid progress in all areas justifying the call on supplies and troops that Pour and Roup demanded.

"We have planet fall my twin in two places. One in the place they call Australia, and the other in North America. The other locations are the ones we are using to build up with , if you get what I mean," Pour said, pointing at the screens showing the activity. "How is our build up going?"

"Twin, we are gathering stores and troops and equipment steadily. In fact we have written off so much that those daft bulgers back home are falling over their feet to supply us. It is working! We have gotten rid of some nasty troopers to a place where, when we really begin, will be useful. So far it is working," said Roup. He handed a flimsy with the latest figures to his twin pleased that Dral and Darl had passed them on endorsed by Zrab and Braz, the originators of the idea.

The loop was working in their favour. For the first few tenths the stores and equipment were barely enough, but once the paper war got under way creating its virtual invasion the suppliers, who were all on contracts, saw enormous profits in war consumables and clamoured for inclusion. Supplies and equipment began to flow and now, or within a few tenths, they might have enough to make a real invasion possible. In the meantime the President was happy. The messages that came from his office were puzzling but encouraging.

Pour read the latest one: "He says, 'Well done My Pairs, you are deploying your rodent hordes well. Give my regards to the pale. Our troops will prevail!' and there is more like it but this is the clearest, the rest is babbling rubbish, and I have no idea what he means by rodents," Pour said and shook his head.

"Yes, but let us make plans for a proper invasion," Roup said.

"Let us hope we have enough time," replied Pour.

In his chamber the President of Zrad lay drunk on his bed. A glass flopped from his limp hand and spilled its contents onto the floor. He smiled happily. Half awake and half asleep and definitely in a drunken stupor he dreamed of friendly rodents and leafy dens. Like the pages of a notebook unfolding, messages slipped into his sight, and he read them letting them spin around in his head in a continuous loop. It was as if he had a group of Bulger cubs in his mind playing tag with their tails. It was fun, he thought, hiccupping silently in his mind. Oops, pardon me, he muttered. In the recesses of his addled brain the little gems of wisdom dropped into slots ready for recall. His favourite image was of himself striding like a great warrior though the defeated ranks of alien prisoners. He swelled with pride at the vision of his enemies at home paying homage to him before they were sent to the Polisocs. He wriggled uncomfortably when the pleasing images began to deteriorate into a jumbled mass of spinning darkness that hit the pit of his stomach. He threw up. He woke briefly and rolled over the edge of the futon groaning. He was vaguely aware that he was lying in his own vomit but he was past caring and did not resist when Pairs rushed in and cleaned him up. They gave him a quick sniff of tranquilliser, and with a snort and the beginning of long series of snores he fell asleep.

The Pairs stripped his clothes and replaced them with a new nightshirt and dropped him on a new futon and busily cleaned the mess of glasses in the room and replaced the empty and near empty bottles with full ones. They sprayed the room with aromatic waters and left a herb stick burning turning the lights down and retired to their posts behind the screens.

In less than a short period the President was in full cry snoring loudly and grunting like a pig. The Pairs pointedly ignored the noise knowing the guards were watching what they did. It did not pay to make disloyal comments about the President.

The President slept on, snoring and grunting and occasionally muttering incoherently uttering lucid words at intervals.

"Do not ... babble babble ... dents!"[1]

"What does he mean do not whatever with his teeth?" asked one Half Pair, nervously.

"I don't know, maybe he is dreaming of tooth paste?" replied another.

In a side room four technician Pairs worked frantically to remove the virus that infected the President's personal computer in a desperate effort to save his most valued data. The cute little rodents that danced around on the screen refused to be removed and however low they turned the sound down the strange, haunting tune continued to play.

"You have until sunsrise," demanded the captain of the guard.

Tired and frightened but suddenly animated by fear the four Pairs worked until from outside they heard the raucous sound of the dawn chorus and with one accord they dropped their tools and made a dash for the portal.

They were cut down before they reached it.

The screen full of rodents chasing each other changed colour for the umpteenth time as the guards dragged their wriggling bodies to the disposal chutes.

The servant Pairs nervously dashed out of their niches and cleaned the floors fussing and muttering as they mopped up. They carried out their grim task quickly and efficiently, and as indifferently as they could manage. It did not pay to look even slightly disgusted.

And so began another turn.

And suddenly, as if the rodents had given up and gone home the screen cleared to normal.

---

[1] *The reference to 'dents' regarding teeth is taken from the French - a most confusing linguistic oddity.*

The President's Army

The wind blew steadily across the desert whipping up the dust into whorls of biting sand that smashed against rocks and Pairs alike. Short of being a full scale sandstorm the wind blew sand and dust and bits of plant matter into as many crevices as were left uncovered. The foot soldiers, the long suffering Pongos, slowed to little more than a walk and bemoaned their lot. The Polisoc Stormtroopers trotted ahead and complained that the Pongos were deliberately holding them back. The Pongos covered their faces with breathing masks and plodded on unable to flee or retreat because of the forces that surrounded them. That they would fight was beyond question, but it was also certain that unless their own lives were in jeopardy they would not fight enthusiastically.

The briefing, and the inevitable nauseating political speech from the Polisoc Leader Pair the night they started on their campaign, exhorted them to fight heroically, and with all diligence to defend the rights of the Republic and the Honour of their Glorious President to rule over them.

The Pongos, long suffering ordinary soldiers, listened with silent patience and a huge dollop of scepticism.

"What do they expect from us," said a Troop Leader Pair, miserably.

"Loyalty and death," said a soldier Pair.

The other Pairs laughed.

"We get shot at, bombed and cut to bits while that lot," a Pair said, pointing ahead to the Stormtroopers. "Climb into the wagons and fight from there."

"Keep in line Pairs," called the Leader Pair out on their flank. "All Troop Leader Pairs begin fan out procedure."

There was a rustle of equipment and a visible increase in the tension as the Pairs of Centre Strike spread out in fan formation. The dust blew between them sometimes obscuring Pairs from one another but they held their positions advancing steadily across the rocky terrain toward their objective. The Leader Pair had explained, just after sunrise, as they were eating breakfast that the Rebel enemy were trapped in the valley over the hills.

"The Bulgers are surrounded by our own Army Section in the North and Yellow, Green and Blue on the other sides. We have them trapped Pairs."

Within their twin minds each Pongo Pair had a similar thought. *Sure you do.*

Quarter Section Red marched behind the Stormtroopers of Quarter Section Blue wishing they were Quarter Section Blue and therefore at the rear of the Pongos. Through the swirling dust, low scrub covered hills loomed up before them and the Stormtroopers disappeared, one group veered left and the other to the right. The Pongos continued to the ridge and poured over the top. The soldiers fanned out into troops and taking advantage of cover they surrounded a large formation of rocks which their Leaders assured them was where the Rebels were hiding. One hundred metres from the target the Stormtrooper sections leapt from their cover and raced in zig zag columns firing whenever there was space clear in front. There was no response from the rocks and the Stormtroopers hesitated, confused and then, urged on by the Leader Pairs, surged forward again. The Pongos of Quarter Section Red waited ready to go into action. And then the rumour began. There was nobody there. The rocks were deserted.

The Senior Stormtrooper Leader Pair stood staring at the plastic sheet attached by laser bolts to its rock support. They ground his teeth angrily and listened as his subordinate read the message.

"We are sorry we could not be here to meet you but we do thank you for the trouble you have taken to find us - On behalf of the Zradian People's Army - Women's Section"

Underneath the neatly scripted message was a panel and a button. The subordinate pressed it and the panel flipped open to reveal some more script which the Pair dutifully read.

"We have left you a little present - you have five short periods to evacuate the area. Bombs set by Julian the Bomber, thank you for your custom."

As if to remind them of the passage of time the button began to flash with the passing of each small period.

"Bulgers! A bomb!" shrieked the Stormtrooper Leader Pair. "Out! Everybody out!"

The Stormtroopers coming in stood their ground demanding answers, and for three of the five short periods confusion reigned. One more short period passed and the incoming Stormtroopers gave way.

"Retreat you stupid Bulgers!" yelled the Leader Pair.

The remaining Stormtroopers took sixty small periods to react which left barely forty more to get away. The explosion hit the Stormtroopers with such a devastating effect that only a few half Pairs were left to stagger groggily back to the waiting Pongos.

"Shoot the wounded?" asked the Pongo Troop Leader Pairs, happily.

"No other choice," replied their Leader Pairs.

Scribe Grot dropped his stylus. It made a tinkling rattle on the plastic desk which in the thick angry silence of the President's outer chamber sounded like an iron bar dropping on concrete. His twin gasped and together they dropped submissively to the stone floor.

"Forgive our intrusion your Honour," they cried, and waited for the swords to slice downward and cut their necks. When nothing happened they rose slowly and cautiously from their grovelling position risking a nervous glance at the President.

The President sat in his throne staring despondently at nothing. Clutched between two fingers a flimsy fluttered in the light warm breeze. It was hard to tell whether he was drunk or merely stunned. The news of the disaster from the Waste Lands was written on the sheet. No Pair had yet plucked up courage to tell him the details. The Pairs in the chamber went about their business quietly, eyeing the Dog Squad cautiously, and becoming ultra careful not to make any noise. A Pair could die for something as simple as dropping a stylus they reasoned. At intervals the President uttered a curse, arching his back and raising his fist to the ceiling, and roaring in anger. It was then that all activity stopped and Pairs immediately prostrated themselves on the stone floor trying not to look at the dried bloodstains. To put it more succinctly, the atmosphere was tense.

"Bulgers! OUR Stormtroopers destroyed by Women!" the President moaned. "Sucked into an ambush by Women!"

He emphasised his words with foot stamping and dark glares at the High Leader Pairs gathered at the lower end of the chamber.

"And what was your answer to their cowardly attack?" he waved his free hand to quiet them. "No, no, don't answer that, I know. Your soldiers panicked. They ran out of the valley like frightened Bulgers and onto the lasers of the Rebels who were waiting behind you!"

The High Leader Pairs cringed.

The President stood up and waved the flimsy at them.

"And while you were so busy attacking a pile of rocks the Women crept up behind you and bombed your transport! We are not happy! Incompetent wretches! Some of you will die!"

The High Leader Pairs cringed lower and huddled together.

"Soldiers! Pick out any six Pairs and kill them now!" yelled the President.

The Dog Squad Troopers descended on the cringing High Leaders and grabbed six Pairs and dragged them into the centre of the chamber, and with hardly a pause sliced into the bodies with their sharp double bladed swords. The President watched the Pairs die, switching his gaze from one to the other as the swords slashed deeply into them. He was pleased that the executioners were careful to make certain blood did not splash onto his boots or pants. Good skills troopers, he thought, and smiled. He always liked a violent execution.

"Bring Us some gin and tonics," he called out, resuming his seat. "And you other Pairs clean up this mess."

He pointed down at the bodies and waved the Dog Squad back. While his drinks were served by a nervous servant Pair the surviving High Leader Pairs scurried forward to clear the bodies away and wash the floor. The serving Pairs took great pleasure in supplying the buckets and mops for their superiors to use; it was a lesson for them in humility, they thought, and besides, it lowered the risk of servants being victims of the sword happy guards. Grot and his twin sat on their pad scribbling notes with their styli pretending to ignore what was happening. The President sat sipping at drinks for many short periods glaring at the trembling High Leader Pairs until at last he seemed to have made up his mind.

"We will call a conference. We will have the best computer operators on hand. We will work out a plan. We will have complete obedience! We have spoken. It will be done!"

"It will be done your Honour!" echoed all the attendant Pairs.

The President walked slowly and unsteadily from his inner chamber through the East Portal and out into his private garden. Supposedly this haven of tranquillity was in the exact centre of First City. True, it was designed as such, square with a circular path touching all four points it was divided into segments that reflected the colour divisions of the greater city. Four paths radiated from a centre circle described by seating and bedecked with plants. Each section had its own colour theme. Royal Red, Service Green, Storage Yellow and Proletariat Blue. The President walked to the centre seating and sat down bathing in the warm sunslight. He relaxed against the soft plastic and waited until his hands stopped shaking.

He stood up and opened a panel in a statuette and removed a bottle opening it and sipping directly from its neck. He sat thinking and drinking for a long time letting the periods go by until he had finished the bottle but nothing came. He desperately needed an advantage, despite what his Consuls and Military Leaders said he knew that unless he could subdue the rebels he was in trouble. The invasion of the Earth was necessary but unless they had a victory soon that would turn into a fighting war.

"Whatever the stupid Bulgers try to tell me, the Doomsday Bomb has to be the last resort if we are to win," he said, addressing the bottle. The problem was that their own planet was uninhabitable in many areas. Zrad was a desert planet with very little fertile land concentrated around the large inland sea in the contaminated south. The cities were crowded and expanding outward. He had approved the newest construction only a few tenths[2] before for First City Green and more in Yellow. "I think, I did."

Racing through his mind was the message that filtered into his mind every night. Drink was the only thing that got rid of it but the point of clarity lasted only a short period before the drink took off and he reverted to drunkenness. It was during the earlier drunken periods when he came up with his ideas and that was what nagged at him. Was he right or was he making some big mistakes. When he was sober the message in his mind distracted him enough to disturb rational thought. And if he was drunk he could not be sure of what he was doing. All he really wanted was to get rid of the constant chant in his mind.

"Do not be afraid of the rodents," he said, sardonically. "I don't give a Bulger's fart about rodents!"

He dropped his head into his hands wobbling in his seat as the world around him seemed to spin. He felt maudlin, and sobbing, he drooped lower letting the emotion take over. The tears rolled down his cheeks and he snuffled. Then the tune wandered into his mind and in spite of his depression he couldn't help humming along with it. He flopped even lower and dropped sideways to the warm flagstones. His aide Pairs crept out and gently lifted him from the where he fell and carried him into his private bed chamber. They placed him on his futon and covered him with a light blanket. One Half Pair sprayed a tranquilliser into his nostrils and he began to snore.

"What's that tune he's humming?" one Pair asked as they withdrew.

"I believe it is called A Whiter Shade of Pale," replied another. "It's from Earth."

"It's nice," said another.

The other Pairs looked at him askance and they blushed turning away embarrassed.

"Sorry."

The screens showed the the centre square of the palace in First City and the President taking a drink. The Pairs watching rang a buzzer which sent an alarm to a room a few doors from their operating station. Two Pairs reacted getting up from their seats quickly and hurried to a cage in the corner of the yard outside their room. They opened the transfer portal at one end of the cage and

---

[2] *The Zradian year or Orbit is divided into twenty equal parts (Twentieths) and these are divided into two (Tenths) and two again (Fifths) - why the buggers didn't use days and weeks is probably because they have no moon. Or some other equally silly explanation.*

prodded the animal inside the cage with long poles. It turned, snarled and slashed at the poles but as it made contact so it received mild electric shocks. It reacted to these by first jumping backwards and then moving forward to attack but each attack was met by more nasty poles until it was forced through the portal. To add to its anger the front wall of the cage moved forward as it moved back giving the Pairs with the nasty poles a chance to attack it again.

The Carnibeast roared; it spat, it hissed and slashed knocking the poles away but yowling loudly as the electric pulses hit it. It was forced backwards into the portal until at last it was entirely in the port. The door hissed shut and before it could smash against it there was a sudden lurch and the beast dropped into a small square snarling and spitting.

A door opened and with a howl of anger the Carnibeast raced through it looking for something to murder.

"Bulgers!" said the watching Pair. "We missed, the shithead has already left!"

The Carnibeast raced into the corridors growling and angry, smarting from the cruel prods and looked for the two legged things that had tortured it. The animal found some. It came upon a lone Pair standing near a cage where another of the creatures lay and immediately attacked, slashing and biting first one and then the other. It was hungry and gorged on the warm meat, and sated turned to where the strange smell came from. It pushed its nose against the bars and howled when electric shocks stabbed into its mind. It jumped back, spat, roared and, learning from the experience before it was sent to this gloomy place and the sudden shock from the door that reminded it if the nasty sticks that had tormented it the animal ran off, finding a dark place to sit and rested to let its food digest. It realised that patience was going to help and, like most hunting animals it moved stealthily at its own pace until the opportunity came to make its move to freedom.

The Pairs in the NMF who had sent the animal in the first place were disappointed that their attack on the President had failed, but short of pushing the creature into the port, there was nothing much more they could have done.

The general agreement was that trying to assassinate the President by Carnibeast was not successful.

"You win some, you lose some," said the Pair in charge.

"Delirium Tremens is a terrible thing."

Sherman Holmes Private Detective and Security Agent couldn't decide which was most important; his affair with Hermoine Braine or the unopened bottles of booze on his shelf. Hermoine was a wonderful woman, he thought, well he hoped she was, he had never really been sober enough to tell. The pleasure of a good belt of Scotch or a long draught of beer took a lot of beating, he thought. The difference between Hermoine and the pleasures of the bottle was that she was softer and warmer. He hated warm beer; it foamed and frothed at the wrong time and suddenly went flat. Cold beer got at his teeth and tasted a lot like iced water. Somewhere in between was right; cool, not cold and smelling of hops. Unlike a woman who should be warm to hot; cool women puzzled him; cold ones frightened him. The trouble was that Hermoine, when she was warm was sometimes willing and sometimes volatile. When she was cold she was icy, more frosty than the ice barmen insisted in putting in his whisky. He hated cold whisky. He sipped his drink and let the glass slide through his fingers and rest gently on the desk top. It made a ring that overprinted at least five others. He didn't care what happened as long as he was supplied with booze and the work was easy. He thought of Hermione's ageing but compliant body and belched.

"Have to knock the booze off a bit if this goes on," he said, and waved expansively to the stack of ageing files on his desk. "No work and clients, clients, humph scumbags, falling over themselves to turn me down."

And one more problem - he had realised his secretary had quit a month ago.

He stared angrily at the dusty files.

"I'm sorry mister Holmes but we have decided to take our business elsewhere," he mimicked his last caller."Elshwhere," he mumbled. "Who to?" He addressed the files again. "I mean, what's wrong with good old Sherman, eh?" Take last night; Hermoine threw him out. She came straight to the point.

"You are a piss head Sherman. Knock it off or stop knocking me off. No more nooky until you walk in here sober." He could see she meant it because she kicked him out of her bed and handed him his clothes. She helped him dress and placed a soft hand on his back and guided him out of the house "Shoo, Sherman until you can walk in a straight line," she said, and pushed him along the driveway.

"Hey, hang on, what about all that crap about loving me for ever?" he demanded, slurring the words.

"Piss off," she said.

He did as she ordered, and that was why he was sitting in his office nursing the remains of a bottle of whisky and talking to his defunct files. His reverie was interrupted when his door opened and a man walked in. Holmes tried to focus on him, undecided whether to get up and throw the fellow out or let him do what he was already doing, sit in the only other chair. He decided to let the man sit. Besides, moving out of his own chair was not an option. Holmes realised he was too drunk to stand. The only limb that worked properly was his right arm, the one with the glass in it.

"You are shupposhed to make an app... talk to my sec...wassername," he mumbled.

"What secretary?" his visitor said, casually. "I have a job for you if you want it and plenty of cash but first you have to sober up."

Whether he was too drunk to focus or whether the stranger really did have two pupils in each eye Holmes couldn't work it out, whatever, the bloke was in his office and he was muttering about paying him for his services and that was supposed to be important. Wasn't it? The most important feature of the stranger was the open bag he placed on the desk. Inside there was more money than Holmes had ever seen.

"Lotsh of munny that," said Holmes. "How much?"

"One hundred and twenty thousand and it is all yours, plus a lot more if you do as you are asked to do and last the distance," said the stranger.

"Cor," said Holmes. "What for?"

"Doing a difficult and dangerous job with plenty of excitement."

"What about women?"

"Maybe."

"Booze?"

"No drinking until after the job."

"I'll think about it."

"I'll see you home and you can think about it there."

"I shaid, I'll think about it."

"And I said I'll see you home and you can think about it there."

"You and whose army," growled Holmes making a supreme effort and rising shakily to his feet his fists ready to do battle. Holmes didn't see the stranger move. He felt hands touching him and then there was pain. However much he tried to move or break the hold he was helpless, and from somewhere behind his left ear the stranger chuckled.

"Like I said, we go home."

He vaguely remembered the drive home. The journey was a mass of blurred and frightening images ending with the hired car parked awkwardly against a lamp post. He was aware of another person who helped drag him up the stairs and resisting feebly when the two people put him to bed and forced a fluid down his throat. After that he slept and woke feeling dry mouthed but otherwise fine.

No hangover. The first morning in weeks.

He got out of bed and wandered uneasily into his lounge. Sitting in his favourite, or rather his only armchair was his benefactor.

"Morning," said Holmes. "What's going on and how come I don't get a horrible head?"

"Oh, good morning Sherman, I gave you a pill last night before you dropped off to sleep. I expect you want some breakfast?"

Holmes squinted and looked carefully at the stranger's face. Two eyes with two pupils each. Odd that, thought Holmes, very odd.

"Who are you?"

"My name is Blard, known by some as the Barmy, and to answer your question, yes I do have two pupils in each eye. I come from the planet Zrad and the job I want you to do is to help me to save Earth from destruction."

"Oh shit," said Holmes in despair. "Delirium Tremens is a terrible thing."

"Correct," said Blard, smiling. "But now you are sober. I am sober. You are not suffering from a hangover or the effects of hallucinogens nor are you going out of your head. I am an alien, and I am going to pay you a vast amount of money for your services and I am as barmy as they say, dangerously barmy. You will enjoy the next few months Sherman, that I can promise you."

"Show me," said Holmes, belligerent.

Blard took his Atlas from his pocket pressed a series of buttons.

"Sit down in my place and watch the wall over there," he said. "I am about to show a you a potted history of my home planet."

Holmes did as he was instructed surprised at his willingness to do as Blard told him. What he saw worried him. It was either an excellent science fiction film, a documentary on the Sino - India war or what Blard said it was, a short history of his home planet What bothered him was the twin suns. Somehow two suns hanging in the sky seemed awkward. While he watched the film Blard fossicked in the kitchen and wrestled with the pots and pans trying to cook a meal.

"You for real then?" asked Holmes, scratching himself.

"Looks like it," said Blard.

Holmes stared at him. A bloke from another planet in his own home. He had expected a little green man or something, he mused, or was that green elephants?

"I need a drink," he said.

Blard handed him a bottle of ginger beer.

"That's all you are getting apart from tea and coffee and whatever we can get when we get going."

"I need a real drink," complained Holmes.

"That's all there is, I tipped the rest down the drain. No booze. No bother." Said Blard.

"You can't do that!" panicked Holmes. "There's a fortune of liquor in there." He pointed to the drinks cupboard with a shaking finger unable to believe what he had heard. He almost cried when Blard opened the doors to display empty shelves.

"Too late, I already have, and from now on it's ginger beer or water. I want you sober and alert with all your senses intact," said Blard with a grin.

"I might not want to work for you," said Holmes, petulantly.

"Don't be silly, Holmes, this is the best job you'll ever have. You will make more money than you have ever seen in your life. You will be independent and on top of that when you get back you will be able to call the tune with your lady love. She will fall at your feet Holmes. You'd like that wouldn't you?"

Holmes looked at Blard with deep respect. "You are despicable mister Blard, you've hit the spot haven't you?"

Blard grinned wickedly. "I have hidden depths Holmes. I am also one of the best scrappers you have met and I will lie and cheat my way through anything except when it comes to my friends or my Twin. I can also teach you some nifty ways to beat the daylights out of your worst punters."

Holmes smiled.

"Will there really be lots of money?"

"Plenty."

"And punch ups?"

"Heaps."

Holmes screwed his face up in concentration and with a sigh of longing he looked at the empty cupboard and said. "Okay, I'm in."

"Good, now this is what I want you to do..."

Blard talked for a long time and Holmes sat quietly and listened occasionally grunting approval.

"And the first thing you want me to do is teach you to drive?"

Blard nodded.

Holmes gripped the dashboard and sighed with relief when Blard jerked to a crunching stop. With a deep intake of breath he turned to Blard.

"I think we have a long way to go," he said.

"You're not impressed?"

"No, I'm scared shitless," said Holmes.

"What am I doing wrong?"

"Everything, you are supposed to drive on the left and not override the traffic lights. When the lights go red you are supposed to let the auto take over, you press the large button on the quadrant until it turns green. If you were on a race track I would enter you for the demolition derby, so for the rest of the day I will drive, you will watch."

Blard looked disappointed but gave in and swapped seats.

"I used to be much worse," he said.

"Nah," snorted Holmes. "Nobody could be worse than that"

Back in his flat Holmes looked at the display of weaponry and gadgets in amazement. He shivered at the thought of the wicked double bladed knives biting into his flesh and looked fondly at the spiky cudgel Blard hefted in his hand with such flexibility.

"This thing is designed to crush bones. If you hit somebody on a bone it is guaranteed to do some damage. If you have ever used a cosh then you will be familiar with one of these."

"Well, not officially," said Holmes.

Blard grinned.

On Holmes' coffee table Blard had spread the tools of his trade naming them as he laid them down. There were two short laser cannons, two gas pistols, two double bladed knives, a coil of marble sized grenades, a bag of refills for the laser cannons, the cudgels and what looked like a cheese wire.

"What's that?" Holmes asked.

"Cheese wire, very useful for strangling," said Blard. "The other gadgets are my Atlas which is about the equivalent of one of your fastest and most up to date computers, my locater, a variety of floating cameras and sound monitors, and a complete Telecom telephone repair kit and fault finding devices, the latter stolen from an unattended van not far from here."

"And our first task is to locate the receiver of what you so casually call the Doomsday Bomb which you are telling me is located in a telephone booth somewhere in London. Do you realise how many telephone booths there are in London?" Holmes asked eyeing the cudgel enviously.

"Twenty one thousand three hundred and twenty two of which at this very moment four hundred and fifty four are under repair and another seventy two have been irreparably damaged by vandals. Of the remainder seventeen thousand and forty five are in use and of those..."

"Yeah, all right smart arse, no need to give me all the details, which is the one we want?" said Holmes without rancour.

"I haven't a clue," said Blard. "No idea."

"It's going to be a long hard summer," said Holmes with false dejection. The most uncomfortable feeling was the nasty idea that somewhere out in space there was a crowd of four-eyed maniacs dead set on killing him. That they were also threatening to murder the rest of the human race was not of much concern to him; he resented the personal nature of the threat. Nobody, Alien or Local, had any right to do that to him, and if it meant he had to sit at a desk for ages looking for a telephone number then so be it. Save the world and save the Sherman, he thought, and save the Hermoine too; now that was more like it.

Hermoine Braine cursed the telephone receiver and then cursed the drinks cabinet with Holmes' tankard sitting on it, and for the fourteenth time that afternoon decided not to call him. She sat with a drink clasped in one hand and nothing in the other wishing that her lover was neither a horrendous drunk nor a randy chauvinist. By God she wanted him, but by God she had to have him sober. She loved his raw aggression; loved the sudden bursts of violence when verbal confrontation reverted to the primeval. Sherman Holmes, she thought, was an animal and she Hermoine Dolores Braine nee Conlan was putty in his hands. Up to a point that was. She reached for the telephone for the fifteenth time and this time she picked it up and readied her finger to stab the buttons.

She was surprised when a voice spoke politely in her ear.

"Is that you H? Emily here, I have a paying job for that beast of yours." Pause. "Hello?"

"Oh hello Em, I was about to call him. I chucked the piss head out you know, so what the heck do you mean by calling here. Why not call the ratbag's office instead?"

"I thought you might be able to talk to him for me," Emily said.

"I hate him."

"No you don't."

"Oh yes I do."

"Oh no you don't."

"Oh sod it Em, I don't know what to think. What the heck are you waffling about anyway? Who want's to employ him? And why cannot you go through my no good useless faggot of a son?"

"Do you think I ought to?"

"Might be best because I haven't seen his high ratbagness for a few days and as far as I'm concerned that's fine if I never see him again. The drunken bastard."

"If that's how you feel H I'll call Oliver and see what he can do to help. Or better still I'll get Richard to call on him."

"You do that darling and leave me to die of grief in the safety of my own hovel."

Hermoine didn't want to appear rude but she hung up on Emily Byrde and sat staring at the telephone for a few minutes and then reached out a hand nervous in case it rang again. This time she did ring Holmes' office number. The no connection sign came up on the indicator and so with a sigh she rang his home number. She got his answer phone message and listened to the incoherent voice explain that he was out.

"Out like a light no doubt," she said, and slammed the receiver down on its rest.

In Holmes' flat Blard the Barmy noted the caller's number and entered it into his data base. The name and address flashed up and with a smile he noted the number in his address book. So that's who Holmes' girlfriend is, he thought, and leaned back in his chair letting it rock back on the rear legs as he regarded Holmes's massive frame working at the computer desk.

"One day you will be glad of this my friend," he said softly, and smiled when Holmes turned to look at him.

"Doing all right Sherman?" he said.

"Yeah, fine but I could do with a bloody shot of rum or something."

"Try coke and imagine there's rum in it," said Blard.

"Arseholes," said Holmes and glowered at the screen.

We went gardening

Byrde pushed the office door open and stepped inside. He glanced briefly at the General Assistance Services sign on the desk and the name plate that sat on the surface. "Penny Draper," he read aloud, and smiled at the woman sitting looking at him expectantly. "You must be mister Braine's secretary?" he said.

"That's me and you are?" she said, offering a quick working girl smile.

"Richard Byrde to see Oliver Braine," he replied.

"Follow me," she said, and wiggled into the inner office.

Oliver Braine looked up angrily from his desk and immediately fixed a welcome 'my God a client' smile on his face. He stood up quickly hitting his leg against the edge of the desk and winced. Unsure whether to clutch his bruised knee or shake Byrde's outstretched hand, for a few seconds he did neither.

"Mister Byrde to see you Norman," Penny said, and wiggled out again.

Oliver Braine ignored the pain in his knee and shook Byrde's hand. His eyes shifted from Byrde to the door and back again.

"Your girlfriend is she?" Byrde asked.

"No, just my secretary; provocative baggage," he said, and blushed. "I mean she's lovely eh?"

Byrde chuckled.

"I don't..." Braine began, and dropped his gaze. "She's got a boyfriend who threatens to punch my lights out if I so much as look at her. The baggage plays on it and deliberately wiggles; flaunting her gorgeous body in front of me. I hate her."

"Okay, let's forget about her and get down to business shall we?"

"Er yes, depends what you've got for me doesn't it?"

"I need somebody to act as a bodyguard..." began Byrde.

Braine spluttered and stuttered. "I'm sorry we're booked up solid; I can't possibly do any of that sort of work for weeks, months ..."

"Sit down," said Byrde putting his hand on Braine's chest and pushing him back into his seat. "According to your mother you have nothing on your books, and apart from that all I want is you to arrange some people for me. Like you are supposed to be doing for my friend Professor Arthur Renfrew or have you forgotten?"

Braine paled and looked up at Byrde.

"I'm no good at violence," he said. "I'll get Sherman Holmes on to it."

"Holmes seems to have disappeared," said Byrde. "I checked, with your mother, she sort of thinks you are not up to much and talked of cutting something or other off if you stuff me around."

"It's Penny, she tells her everything and I can't fire her or her boyfriend will hammer me if my mother doesn't do me over first." Braine said adding a spreading hand gesture.

"I'll treat you to lunch and we can talk," said Byrde.

They went out together leaving Penny at the desk who telephoned Hermoine Braine immediately they left. She spoke for a short time and then she called her boyfriend.

"See you tonight Gerald, his Nibs has gorn out wiv a client for 'is lunch so I'll 'ave to eat me sandwiches 'ere, sorry luv. Miss you too."

"I can get a couple of good blokes for you easily enough but if you want anybody for Professor Renfrew I'll have to look a bit further afield. Mind you I think that one incident on the say so of an old Chinaman is a bit over the top," said Braine, amused.

"This Chinaman you speak of so lightly is not what he seems; he was employed by my father who sort of left him to me in his will. He nearly got incinerated instead of me. And don't forget there was also the incident with the car and Arthur was assaulted."

Braine shuddered, and led the way into the Drunken Clown pub "We can get a good meal here and the landlord does a good jar," he said.

Byrde grinned. "My local."

Inside, while Byrde bought beer and a meal each Braine made two calls. One was to the Ferret to fix up a meeting, and the other was to Colin Hicks a 'heavy' who lived in the market town of Maidstone in Kent. Colin was a big man with a beer belly, shaven head, and sported a tattoo on his muscular chest that spread across to encompass his massive shoulders and biceps. He wore black boots on his feet that looked heavy but were in fact light and flexible. In spite of his size he moved surprisingly fast. His big hands were hairy and his knuckles were marked with the standard prisoner's identity, and now and then he raised one meaty hand up to his broken nose to wipe it and cover a sniff. He came from a suburb called Shepway and did nasty things to people for a reasonable fee. Braine was terrified of him, but agreed that he was the right man for the job.

"Me and me blokes will be up the smoke ter meet yer termorrer, right?"

"Right," said Braine and hung up.

Back at their table Braine said. "I've fixed it up with both parties"

"Good, good, that is excellent," said Byrde.

"All part of the service," replied Braine, expansively.

"In the meantime Norman I would appreciate you keeping close and watching my back," said Byrde raising his glass and drinking. "I'll pay you well."

"I only want my regular fee," said Braine, stiffly. "And expenses."

Byrde smiled at him putting his glass down and taking up his knife and fork. "Eat up cheapskate," he said.

"My fee is a fair one and I resent being called a cheapskate," Braine said, puppy dog sad.

"Okay Norman but ..." Byrde began.

"Please, mister Byrde I prefer the name Oliver, it's the initials you see, embarrassing. My father wanted a daughter, I think. Or something," Braine said.

Braine ate his food and demanded another beer. He sat back comfortably in his chair and sighed with pleasure enjoying the meal thinking that Byrde was being a bit paranoid, probably imagining enemies, so he felt almost comfortable filling in until Lugs and the Ferret turned up. With two jars of ale inside him, and the best lunch he had had for several days Oliver Braine felt at peace with the world. Business was poor and he had difficulty paying the bills, his clientele being mostly hoi-polloi whose income reflected their inability to pay. Maybe he should charge more and had wondered why he had gone coy when Byrde mentioned money.

"Oliver, do you like your job?" asked Byrde.

"Not really, well I mean I like to be in business but the work gets a bit tedious sometimes. The way of all things I suppose. What I really want to do is paint pictures, but my father gave my mother all the money and left me with nothing. He wanted me to fit in with the family business but I had no interest in it. All I wanted to do was go to art school and learn to paint. Mother, dear volatile, dangerous mother, refused to give me an allowance unless I worked for it. I tried all sorts of things but nothing suits me." He spoke with great bitterness giving Byrde a weak smile.

"Your family was into making trucks I believe; my factory supplied plastic parts for them and still do," said Byrde. "You didn't like making trucks?"

"Hated 'em and I don't like cars either or aircraft."

Byrde laughed.

"A fast pair of shoes?" said Byrde, laconically.

"You think I'm a bit of a failure don't you," said Braine. "I expect you think I'm useless, a no-hoper who all he wants to do is live an idle life on his father's money, right?"

"Right," said Byrde. " That's what you want to do isn't it?"

Braine looked at him sharply.

"You don't like me much do you?" he said.

"I don't know you enough to dislike you; what I see I like; you worry too much, all you have to do is get on with your life and be yourself. Do your best and get on with whatever you can. The first thing you can do is earn your pay and just act as a second pair of eyes for me. I don't want you to be a hero; just a watcher who will help when things get sticky. I would like somebody to look out for Emily too, so you can get some people to do that as well." Byrde spoke with conviction, and Braine felt much better. "Look, I know your mother a little. She is my wife's cousin but I don't have that much to do with her. We have met before. I saw you briefly at the fete last year if I remember?"

"Oh that," said Braine.

"A farce if I remember," said Byrde.

Braine looked pained.

"Yes, well, that was my mother arranged that. Nothing to do with GAS. Shall we go back to my office and finish off the details," said Braine.

Braine suggested they take a short cut through the allotments and led Byrde down a side road and on into the Bywater road. They turned into the allotment gate and walked along the pathway admiring the plots and Braine pointed out the burnt out garden shed.

"It happened a while ago; a policeman was killed and two men disappeared. One of them was that young idiot Julian Renfrew, the fellow who came with Angela Breen to the tea party where Holmes got pissed..."

"I remember that and the way Julian panicked," said Byrde.

"Julian is no hero, I'm afraid he's been killed. Surely nobody could survive an explosion like that?" said Braine.

"True but they haven't found any remains so far. He worked for me at my factory," said Byrde.

"Oh, how sad, you miss him?"

"Yes, but you know, I had to put somebody else on his job and quite frankly Julian was much better. I had to sack a manager as well, and that has made a difference too. A bit worrying but we will manage," Byrde said, smiling ruefully.

They stood for a while gazing at the burnt out shed neither man saying anything lost in their own thoughts. Braine thought mostly about how much he should charge Byrde for his services and how he was going to broach the subject again now he had committed himself to a fee. The name cheapskate niggled him and distracted him from working out how much. Something else distracted him too and for a few seconds he thought he heard an insects buzzing; erratic buzzing and it was getting closer.

He turned and gasped. Heading more or less in their direction was a hired hovercar travelling fast across the allotments. The reason it had yet to hit them was the driver seemed to be arguing with the passenger over the controls. With a final lurch it angled directly for Byrde and without thinking of himself Braine launched his body at Byrde and together they tumbled across the soft soil of somebody's newly planted allotment and skidded on rows of freshly watered plants to land in a heap on neatly trimmed grass.

He ducked his head as the vehicle crashed gracefully against the solid brick wall on the end of the row of terrace houses. The craft landed upside down on the grass and skidded to a stop a metre from Braine's feet. He was up and dragging Byrde by the collar before the machine stopped rocking, half carrying, half dragging his burden back as far from the machine as he could. Byrde struggled from his grip and stood looking at the wreck brushing clods of soil and damaged plants from his suit while Braine tried vainly to drag him further back.

Somebody grabbed at him pinching his elbow tightly and yelled at him. Braine turned to the new threat and jerked back as spittle sprayed into his face. It was an angry looking man who snarled words at him and Braine flinched.

"My gardin'! You've smashed my gardin'! I just put them plants in and dug the bloody earth and and..."

Braine brushed the man's hands away and with all the pent up frustration and fear he was feeling about his business, Penny, his mother and his financial state he drew his fist back and punched the guy on the nose knocking him backwards into his precious garden plot.

"Bugger your garden," Braine said as the punch landed.

Byrde gripped his arm and grinned. "Okay Hero I think we ought to shift before the police come."

They hurried away and soon stomped excitedly up the stairs to Braine's office.

"See what I mean by being yourself," said Byrde. "You saved me from the car without any thought of your own safety."

"I was protecting my investment; which reminds me, my fee, we have yet to discuss my fee. I suggest that since there is an element of danger in the job I should get a bit extra for my trouble. Penny, will you bring us some coffee please?" he said as they walked into his inner office past the astonished girl.

"Ooh, your clobber is all dirty," she said, stating the obvious.

"We went gardening," said Braine. "When you have served the coffee you may as well go and grab a bite with that animal friend of yours."

Penny arrived with a tray loaded with coffee things and biscuits and placed them on the desk with a flourish. She wiggled away and looked back gauging the effect. Getting no reaction from Braine she slammed the door behind her.

"Now, my fee," he said, giving Byrde a satisfied smirk.

Lugs was happy to sit and watch the sport on the telly, but his mate, the Ferret on the other hand was bored, he would like to be out but their financial resources were all but non-existent. They had enough in the kitty to pay for milk and a loaf of bread and unless they got some work the Ferret would be forced to raid Lugs' piggy bank. Desperate times called for desperate measures and raiding Lugs' piggy bank was a most desperate measure. It was not the money Lugs worried about, it was the fact that to get at it they would have to break the china pig open with a hammer. Lugs, bless his heart, was sentimental about things like that.

When the Ferret asked Lugs for fund raising ideas all the big man could think of was robbery.

"Why don't we go down the wharf and nick some stuff," said Lugs.

The Ferret didn't have to answer because at that moment the telephone rang.

"Ferret," he said, briefly into the mouthpiece.

"Oliver Braine here, I have some work for you if you want it, something to keep your big mate occupied. You will be looking after a gentleman for a while who reckons somebody is trying to sort of eliminate him."

The Ferret accepted the job straight away and began the long and involved explanation to his huge mate. He sat facing Lugs watching the craggy simple face for signs of puzzlement, trying to catch them before Lugs lost the thread. The big man's heavy features smiled benignly as the Ferret unfolded Braine's tale in its simplest form, and with animal joy Lugs cracked his massive boxer hands together and crossed his big feet and closed his eyes in ecstasy when the Ferret mentioned there may be fighting.

"How many people we got to bash," asked Lugs, fairly brightly.

"None yet but I'm sure you will find enough to keep you happy."

Lugs sat back in his armchair and continued to watch the television, happy that the Ferret had found some work for them and happy because his favourite Australian football team was winning. Lugs didn't need much to do his work. The Ferret did the thinking and Lugs did the bashing. All he needed was his knuckles and his strength. Right now, he thought, he could go a pint of ale in the Drunken Clown, but the Ferret said they had no money. Lugs didn't mind, soon they would.

Colin Hicks fussed around 'his lads' checking they had all the equipment they needed and removed bottles and cans from their hands as the time to leave approached.

"No drinking on the job unless I tells yer, okay?" he said. They all agreed. He was pleased with them and glad of the job coming just in time; one more week of short commons and he would have started a mini crime wave to pay his way. It was his old lady giving him gyp because she wanted new things for the house that created the shortage. Besides, there were bound to be some perks. "Rightho lads it's time to get off so finish yer ales and make for the front door 'cause them taxis will be here in half a mo'," he said and as good as his word he picked up his own bag and swilled the remainder of his beer.

At the station the lads made a rush for the toilets and when the bullet shaped train hissed to a halt at the platform Colin shepherded them on board. He grinned when they politely but firmly asked the other passengers to move so they could all sit together.

That's my boys, he mused, proudly.

Oliver Braine met Colin and his mates in a busy bar not far from Victoria Station. He eyed the men warily as they talked and across the room Richard Byrde watched what was happening catching Braine's eye and nodded.

"I never expected so many Colin," said Braine. "I mean a gang but a whole army?"

"I need all of 'em 'cos I want some on and some orf and some in the middle if you get what I mean. In this business mate you need reserves. No worries about payin' 'em all 'cos I jest gives you a price for the job plus expenses. I can't say fairer than that."

It was obvious Colin wasn't going to be moved from his position so Braine did what he did best. He shrugged his shoulders and gave in.

"Okay we got a deal."

Colin smiled. "All right I need to get to know the punter and then we can go from there. We don't need separate rooms or nuthin' like that jest give us a room wiv six beds and plenty of food. I don't want no drink nor any fags and no wimmin, got that?"

Braine gulped. He hated the implied violence in Colin's words and responded fearfully remembering his first meeting with Colin. Oliver was visiting a contact in Maidstone when Colin stopped him in the street and demanded a light for his cigarette. Braine apologised and explained that he didn't carry a lighter or matches because he didn't smoke. Colin looked at him pityingly and shook his head.

"You don't get it do you mate," he said.

"Get what?"

"You are supposed to be scared stiff 'cos you recognise me as a mugger, see?"

Braine did see and held out his wallet.

Colin told him to put it back.

"You look so pathetic mate I couldn't do it to yer."

Braine felt relieved but didn't know what was expected of him next and waited for Colin to say more.

"You're supposed ter run away and tell the rozzers," Colin said, and laughed.

"Oh am I?" said Braine.

Colin gripped his sleeve and drew him close. "Listen mate I'll give yer a chance. You go into that pub with me and I'll let yer buy me a beer, okay."

Braine understood from his tone that Colin was somehow doing him a favour, and meekly, without objection, he went with him and they ended up staying until closing time. Braine missed the last train and stayed overnight with his new found friend. They talked late into the night over draughts of strong ale and whisky. Braine learned more in that night about life than he had ever known. Once back on his home territory he had set up the General Assistance business using Colin as one of his valued agents. Oddly, Braine liked Colin although he was eminently scared stiff of him, and it seemed that in return Colin liked Braine, calling him his gent mate from the smoke.

"Here's the keys to the place and a bit of card with the address. You turn off the High Street and down the Bywater road and turn left at the junction and the street you want is on the right," said Braine. "The place is not the best but it is easy to get to places from and it has exits at the back. Ideal really if you like that sort of thing."

An hour and a quarter later Colin and his men let themselves into a scruffy apartment on the second floor of a dirty brick terrace in a dingy street where the car parking spaces were occupied by abandoned wrecks, and the dogs fought the cats for the contents of the garbage cans.

"Nice," said Colin as they crowded into the rooms. "This'll do us lads."

Arthur Renfrew was surprised when his old friend Richard Byrde and his companion called on him accompanied by a huge man who looked like a hired thug.

"This is Colin; he and his men will be your bodyguard. I'll leave him with you and you can tell him what you do each day, and after that he will make arrangements to protect you and Marjorie. And

Arthur, don't worry about paying them because I will pick up the tab as the Americans say. All part of Byrde and Ceedy expense account."

"Me 'an my blokes don't muck about Prof. If anybody tries anything we bash 'em and bash 'em good. We sort of learned in the Army; unarmed combat and all that; know what I mean?"

Arthur said he did and would Colin mind coming with him to the Dojo where they could watch the class. Colin agreed, and he and two of his men went with him. Fascinated, they watched the evolutions of Aikido practice and sat looking on approvingly.

"I like it," said Colin. "Reckon you could show me some?"

Arthur Renfrew grinned.

"Get your shoes and socks off and get on the mat."

Colin did and Arthur explained to him how a simple wrist lock worked.

"Show me," said Colin.

Arthur invited Colin to hit him and Colin punched hard and fast. Arthur turned and Colin felt a brief pain in his wrist and then he crashed to the mat.

"Bloody heck, I do like that," he said, shaking his wrist and gazing admiringly at the Professor. "Your girlfriend do this as well then does she?"

Arthur nodded.

"Cor," said Colin.

Professor Renfrew grinned, and for the first time since they met he began to treat Colin not as a thug but with some respect. In her turn Marjorie was amused at the way Colin's men deferred to her and amused too, although she wouldn't want to show it, at the way they treated Arthur. They described Aikido as Arthur's Japanese Kung Fu and demonstrated the wrist lock to each other telling and retelling how it worked.

"Nifty mate, said one. "Bloody nifty, we all gotta do it."

Back at Marjorie's flat Colin listened into Arthur's call to Sally Aitcheson sitting quietly with his hand over the mouthpiece concentrating not on the words but listening for tell tale echoes. He liked the sound of Sally's voice and as she spoke he listened more carefully. One disc recorder and a tap on the main line he reckoned and tried to figure out who would want to listen in to Marjorie. Fuzz? MI5? Other media stations? He figured more than that and decided a trace on the fibre line would be best. Stevie could fix that up and then they could jam it.

"Maurice Bannerman asked me to invite you onto the Science program tomorrow," Sally said. "I suggest you take the offer and the pay. He's running my story on you tomorrow morning and would like to have you on the program. Would you like to do it?"

Arthur glanced at Marjorie and she nodded. "Yes, yes of course, I will come along and do something, I don't mind. Tell him I will have a crowd of extremely efficient security men with me who will need some refreshment."

"No problem. We cater for large crowds can you be there at five?" she said.

"On the dot," replied Arthur.

The Zradian Pair detailed to watch the Professor took a wrong turn on their way back home arriving on a small waste lot where they surprised a woman feeding a group of feral cats. Their reaction was instant. With a howl sounding much like the yowls of a pair of wolves they attacked the cats displaying a mixture of determination and terror the way a cornered rat would fight its way out of a situation. The poor woman rolled over into the small scrub that littered the waste land screaming in terror, "I'm being murdered!" she yelled waiting for the inevitable blows. They didn't come; instead she heard cats growling and yelling. Looking up from where she had fallen, spitting rubbish from her mouth and off her face she saw the big Tom turn and face the attackers.

With the determination of any wild animal forced to defend itself, the dominant Tom turned on the Pair slashing and clawing, spitting and yowling angrily. The other cats, seeing their leader getting stuck in turned and attacked the two men.

The Pair turned and fled.

The old woman stood up, gathered her feeding paraphernalia and carried on where she had left off. "I wonder who they were?" she said. "Naughty men weren't they pussies?"

The cats didn't answer but continued their interrupted meal. Traumatised after their experience, scratched and cut, the dejected Pair stayed in their bed licking their wounds and missed the most important piece of information about the Professor's activities, which they failed to pass on to the New Moral Few and hence the Rebel Army on Zrad.

Professor Renfrew and his bodyguard arrived at the Examiner Studios exactly on time. His entourage was shown into the dressing and make up rooms by Maurice Bannerman himself. Colin and five of his men spread out and chose strategic places in the studios like a group of watchful felons casing a joint. Maurice Bannerman and Sally Aitcheson briefed Arthur and gave him a list of questions. He read them through and made some notes on the edges and looked up at Maurice and turned to Sally.

"Good questions people. I can speak to these for however long you want. What format are you going to use?" he said, and placed the sheet on a small table.

"Question and answer and allow you to explain. We have star charts on screen and close ups as well as a whole stack of on call stuff you can use. Sally gave me a rough plan this morning so we can go with that if you want," Maurice said. "Work it out now with Sally and when you are ready we will give you a meal and then slap some tar on your mug before you go on screen. How's that."

"Fine with me. I've been on screen before so you have no worries about what I am likely to do. I will treat the program like one of my lectures although I will enjoy the subject much more," Arthur said, and smiled.

Sally and Arthur worked on the content for an hour and when they were satisfied she showed Arthur and Marjorie into an ante-room next to the studio. Colin and his mates followed and on cue two catering staff rolled a table laden with food into the centre.

Colin eyed the array of food appreciatively and grinned.

"All we need is a cask of good ale and we're made," he said.

"I think we can arrange that," said Sally, and spoke quietly to one of the staff. The young man grinned and disappeared to return a few moments later with a cask of Guinness and a tray of glasses. He set them up on the end of the table and began to pour the dark ale into glasses and set them in a neat row ready to be claimed.

"Now yer torkin' mate," said Colin. He handed the first glass to the Professor with a grin. "'ere you are boss, get it down yer."

Arthur took the glass and sipped. "Don't forget Marjorie, she enjoys a glass too you know," he said.

Colin laughed and handed the next one to Marjorie. "Sorry lady, thought yer might want a short. I picked yer as a G and T type," he said. He turned to his mates and grimaced. "Bleedin' blew it again didn't I?"

His mates laughed and each took a beer.

Sally watched them and shook her head grinning when Colin offered her a glass of Gin and Tonic. "I prefer red wine, but I will have a glass of beer instead," she said, and grinned.

One of the men handed her a freshly filled glass.

"Cheers lads," she said raising the glass and taking a drink.

"Oh gawd," groaned Colin. "I can't bleedin' win can I?"

Hyde Park Corner and beyond.

Blard wrote furiously, muttering as he scratched figures on sheets of paper with a stylo. Suddenly he stopped writing and looked up at Holmes.

"Can you drive a Telecom van?" he said.

"Drive anything if you give me a chance," Holmes replied sharply not correcting Blard's reference to the company. He was desperate for a real drink. All Blard allowed him was tea, coffee or ginger beer. So far he had driven Blard wherever he had asked and several times they had done timed runs to the Bywater allotments from many different directions and when Holmes asked Blard what he was playing at the alien just grinned.

"Working out some options. We might need to make a quick getaway and I reckon we ought to know our escape routes extremely well," replied Blard.

"Escape to the allotments?" asked Holmes. "How and where to?"

"Through a hole in the space-time matrix and home," said Blard.

"Sorry I asked. Maybe we could grow some bloody cabbages or something while we're there, at least we could eat, or go to the pub," finished Holmes, wistfully.

"No pubs, just get on with transferring these figures will you?"

Holmes took the sheets and one by one laid them in the scanner and pressed the enter button. The computer screen was tacked to the wall like a calendar and the machine itself was a flat grey plastic wallet with translucent cables leading to the bottom of the screen and the roll-up keyboard. It was tedious work but at least it kept his mind off images of foaming jars of ale and nips of whisky. So far with each set of figures they had drawn a blank.

"Do a couple of hours at a time and then pack it in for a while. I'll give you a break now and then but it has to be done; just treat it like door knocking. Easy leg work." Blard said. He finished the sequence and pressed the enter key and watched the screen jiggle excitedly. Stupid thing always did that, he thought, but it never came up with anything. He leaned back in the chair thinking of beer, amused at the screen image's likeness to froth on a jar of Guinness. Sans smile, he thought, Suddenly realising there was a response.

"Oh a number," he said. "The damn thing's got a number at last."

Blard glanced at the screen and grunted.

"Grosvenor crescent; where's that?" said Blard.

"It's in Hyde Park Corner, we'll never get at it there with all that traffic," he said.

"That's why we have a Telecom van and all the gear. We are going to become Telephone Technicians," said Blard. "And now we know where the receiver is we can go there and whip it out and take it away."

"Right," said Holmes, thinking of nice cool jars of beer.

On the way to the truck Holmes thought of his change in fortune. The first time he met Bradl, Blard's twin, he liked him. He liked his quiet confidence and the cool way he examined Holmes as he shook hands. Bradl made him feel useful. Discharged from the police force for beating up thugs when they didn't come across with the goods Holmes went into the Private Investigator game, and since then he had gone steadily downhill. After a while he ceased to care and when Hermoine Braine called on him to work for her useless fop of a son he was past worrying about anything except booze. She liked him she said because he was coarse and crude and controllable. He didn't understand that last bit, but in the back of his mind he thought it had something to do with his desire for her body. Apart from the sex she was a woman he could get on with, and he had to admit he would do as she asked him most of the time. Sober now he realised how much he missed her and was beginning to appreciate Blard's hard line.

Bradl had the truck fired up and ready when they arrived and Holmes smirked when he was told to leave the hired vehicle in the garage.

"No need to worry about the car. I'm sure the owners will find it soon enough," said Blard, casually. "We won't be needing it anymore."

Holmes looked at him sharply. "Why?" he said.

"We're going gardening," Blard replied, and grinned broadly.

On Star Station Two the Pair monitoring the receiver saw the intrusion on their screen and alerted their Leader Pair. "Somebody has homed in on the receiver - I think we should shift it," he said.

"Agreed, alert the Pairs on the spot and get it done."

"Where shall we re-locate the thing?"

"Bulgers if I know. Use the next sequence and stick it there. Who cares? The whole stinking planet will be ours soon anyway," the Leader Pair said contemptuously.

"What if we can't find it again?"

"Don't be stupid."

"Yes your honour."

In a dirty room on the ground floor of a ramshackle boarding house in a dingy street where the parking spaces were taken up by abandoned wrecks, and the dogs fought the cats for the contents of the garbage cans, three Pairs responded to their Leader Pair's call. They donned overalls, and with a bag of tools each they walked to a lock up garage where they had parked a stolen Telecom truck. They drove badly to Hyde Park corner and almost succeeded in parking the truck neatly. One Pair worked on the telephone booth while the other Pair kept watch pretending to prepare cables. The third Pair remained in the truck ready to drive it off. It took only moments to remove the receiver, but as they were securing it in the truck another Telecom van pulled in behind them and a Pair dived out.

"Bulgers!" said the Lead Pair. "It's Blard the Barmy!"

With the agility born of fear the Pair piled into the vehicle immediately yelling to their companions to get moving. The other Pair, abandoning their tools, leapt out of the booth and piled into the already moving truck.

Blard and Bradl jumped back in their vehicle and Holmes eased the power back on. Blard opened his mouth to speak but Holmes beat him to it. "I know," he said, grinning. "Follow that truck."

The leading truck moved erratically through the lanes of skimming vehicles finally hurtling into a road leading out to the motorway. Holmes casually and expertly sped the truck after them easing through the traffic and closing the gap with hardly any disruption to the traffic flow.

"Couldn't do this pissed," he said, and grinned ruefully.

Holmes kept the truck in sight tut-tutting at the way its driver was weaving all over the road. He closed in on it and hung back unwilling to get too close in case it veered the wrong way and crashed. The driver, he thought, was really rotten.

"Do I get past them and head them off?"

"No just keep following them and maybe at the rate they are going they will make a mistake," said Blard. Their quarry increased speed and weaved wildly through the traffic, swerving left onto a motorway ramp heading west. Holmes grinned happily. He loved a chase. It was obvious his passengers didn't, and as the vehicle raced after the lurching truck Blard and Bradl clung tightly to the dashboard white faced and white knuckled. He turned and grinned at them.

"It gets worse," he said.

"No, it can't," groaned Bradl.

It did get worse.

The other driver accelerated into the traffic stream crossing three lanes at once and then as suddenly hurtling back to the left. Other vehicles swerved to avoid the truck and it left a trail of chaotic incidents as drivers fought to get their vehicles back under control. Luckily most vehicles were linked to the MoCom system, thought Holmes, which meant most of them would recover automatically avoiding each other albeit to the discomfort of the occupants. All he had to do was avoid the ones that weren't and let his own link predict the rest. They were approaching an off ramp and Holmes decided to take the initiative. In the rear view mirror he had caught the flash of blue and red lights approaching like animated Christmas trees. This could be fun, he thought. His second thought was that if this was a private vehicle he would be running a hell of a bill in tolls, cutting out the MoCom system was expensive.

"Get ready, I'm going to force these buggers into the bank. You grab the box when we stop because we might have to get moving fast. The cops are after us."

Blard nodded. He looked sick.

Holmes accelerated and eased the truck closer as they drew level, and then with a series of left swings he edged the other vehicle into the ditch. The two vehicles ground to a stop and when the other one was firmly embedded in the bank he eased away. Blard and Bradl jumped out, and with no ceremony they shot as many of the occupants as they could see. Bradl dived into the cab while Blard leapt onto the canopy and fired into the vehicle.

Then the Pair were out and clambering into their own vehicle. The sirens howled closer. Bradl dropped a plastic box onto the cab floor and with a yell of triumph Blard fired another few shots into the wagon. Holmes revved the engine and moved off fast.

"Right Holmes we head for the Bywater Road allotments."

The Police patrol stopped long enough to look at the wreck and stayed there. Holmes looked in the rear view and saw an officer speaking into the mike as he raced off. Their description will be all over now, he thought. Soon there will be coppers everywhere. Police didn't like shooters. Still, to heck with it, back streets and then to the allotments. Hyde Park Corner and beyond, he thought, but where. Prison?

He drove by as many back routes he could find and he had to admire Blard's preparation because almost as soon as he had started to head for the Bywater road he recognised a possible route. There was no pursuit, and with a sense of disappointment he arrived at the allotment gate without the sound of sirens chasing him.

"Drive in and park over by the old garden shed; the burnt out one," said Blard.

Holmes looked at him oddly and drove across the plots and dropped the truck next to the wooden platform that was once the floor of a garden shed. The Pair got out beckoning Holmes to follow them, and with the box under his arm Blard got onto the platform. Holmes hesitated to follow feeling a bit foolish wondering what they were doing, and turned when someone gripped his sleeve.

"Oy mate, what the effing heck do you think you are effing doing tromping all over my bleedin' gardin' plot eh?"

"Let go my sleeve," Holmes said, contemptuously.

"What about my bleedin' gardin' mate?" shouted the gardener. "I mean you buggered it again. I'm getting'... ouch!"

Holmes, finding no answer to the man's demands hit him, and knocked him sprawling into his freshly planted seedlings.

"Idiot," he said, and joined Blard and Bradl on the shed floor.

"Where we goin' then?" he said, grinning. "Flipping off into outer space or something? Because if we don't that lot is going to arrest us."

He pointed to the police cars piling into the allotment and shrugged.

Blard pressed buttons on a pillar and lights flashed.

"What's that then?" asked Holmes pointing.

He was still pointing when the scenery completely changed and after a short period of feeling as if he was being taken apart and put back together again he found himself staring not at a pillar of buttons but at a plastic wall with a regular column of recessed buttons in a tasteful surround. He was in a cabin large enough to hold a squadron of Policeman. A door slid open and Blard and Bradl smiled at him.

"Welcome to Star Station One; we, I mean the Rebels, have sort of acquired it. I am sorry I cannot tell you exactly where it is located but I am sure that even if I could you would still be none the wiser. It's all about twisting the space and time in one of those wormholes your scientists keep talking about. According to my information we are approximately 2.3 light years from Earth but don't worry too much, just relax." It was at that point Holmes realised what Blard had meant when he said they were taking the Doomsday Bomb receiver 'away'.

"Oh, we're not on Earth then?"

"No."

"How did we get here?" asked Holmes as they walked along a wide corridor.

"I'm afraid it's a long story Sherman but what you have just experienced is a Matter Transfer Port which is why you probably felt as if you were being taken apart and put back together again."

"Matter transfer can't be done," said Holmes. "Our scientists have tried it and failed."

"We have just used it," said Blard. They stopped beside an opaque panel and Blard pressed a button. The panel cleared.

"Look," said Blard. "This is where we are."

Holmes gazed out into space and saw a rocky moon and beyond that a myriad of stars. None of them looked familiar. He stood transfixed by the sight for some few minutes and then, thoughtfully, he looked at the two aliens, back again to the sight out of the view port and nodded.

"You better tell me about it," said Holmes, tight lipped.

Blard smiled.

"You might find this disturbing but this place we are on now was intended to act as the reliable platform for the invasion of your home planet," Board said.

"Oh, so what went wrong?"

"Our president's wonderful technical systems cocked it up and lost it. We, or the people who employ my twin and I, located it and we have taken it over for ourselves. Hopefully we can use it ourselves," he said and grinned again. "As long as my people can find out exactly where we are."

Holmes groaned.

"You mean we could be trapped here?"

"Not likely but it would be nice to have the Star Station back home, wouldn't it?"

"I suppose so," said Holmes, not wholly convinced.

"Not to worry, at least nobody is trying to kill us," Blard said, cheerfully.

"Oh, good, then maybe we can find some lunch, I'm feeling peckish," Holmes replied.

Revelation.

The President glared at the flimsy and glared equally fiercely at the Pair who had handed it to him. He was tempted to murder the Pair on the spot but he curbed the impulse and re-read the message.

"Who is this creature, this upstart, this gangrenous growth who dares defy Us?"

"It is a skinny Half Pair dragged up by those scummy women your Honour. We learned of it through our listening system. We had the information almost immediately your honour and passed it on directly to the Twin Consuls. It is our honour to report this matter to you. We are your humble servants," the Pair said, their words slightly muffled as they spoke from the prostrate position.

"Find it and kill it!"

As it turned out another problem was drawn to his attention by a Pair whom, so it seemed, had survived a minor purge in the supplies department. He decided to listen to them if only for their sense of self preservation. He stared at the trembling Pair and glowered.

"What are you trying to tell Us?" he said.

Grul and Lurg raised their heads to speak and crashed them back down again. Protocol demanded they keep their heads down. Above their necks the guard's swords hovered ready to slice into their flesh.

"The Invasion of Earth is a failure your Honour. Our glorious forces have made no bridgeheads. Your Honour, it is our advice that you order us to inform the people of Earth of the Doomsday Bomb," they said together.

It was best to observe protocol in the Hall of Petitioners. It was a case of the quick and the dead, thought Grul. He had seen Pairs executed for being slow to get their heads down before the President's throne. Giving their report was a risk but they were caught between keeping quiet and being found out eventually or speaking up and risking the President's anger. Neither prospect was attractive. The figures were grim, and if they did nothing it was certain they would carry the can when everything fell apart. Their report was the result of an investigation into the sudden rise in the amount of material supplies lost during the invasion. What they found frightened them. When they equated the flow of troops and supplies from Zrad to the Star Station and adjusted them for failures there was a discrepancy. Somebody was filching supplies and that was a situation they could not afford to tolerate. They re-did their figures and came up with another set. They did them again and then they found it.

Somehow the same supplies and troops were being recycled. The code numbers appeared and reappeared; first as allocated to the Star Station and then to Zrad and back again. Some supplies and troops were siphoned off to Earth but not enough to justify the massive amounts supposedly used in the invasion. Grul and Lurg sat in their office cubicle thinking for a long time and eventually came up with the solution.

"Those Bulgers on board the Star Station are working a scam," said Lurg looking archly at his twin to show that he was suggesting they pass the blame for their own incompetence on to the personnel on board the Star Station.

It, the scam, was a problem and had to be carefully revealed to their Leader Pair who decided the only way to absolve themselves was to jump the gun and tell the Twin Consuls. The Twin Consuls panicked and arrested the whole section. Grul and Lurg were the survivors and had kept some of their information back from their Leader Pair who was already waiting execution in the pig pens. It was time, thought Grul, to use their trump card before the President decided to execute them as well.

"Your gracious Honour," said Grul.

"You are addressing Us?"

"If we can tell you what is happening and who is the culprit and how to solve the problem will you let us go free?" he asked.

"We might."

"Your Honour, permission to speak privately in your chamber your Honour?"

"If you wish but please do not waste Our time or you will die here on the floor."

"We have valuable information your esteemed Honour."

The President glared at them, and then with a sly grin he nodded and stepped down from the throne.

"You have one long period to tell me what is going on. In the meantime We will have a drink while you speak."

Grul and Lurg rose slowly nervous of the guards who, with calculated menace backed away with a regulated step giving just enough room for them to follow the President into his chamber. Inside they waited while the President poured some drinks hoping he would be generous enough to share but dared show no disappointment when he failed to offer any. They noted, with a shudder, the guards standing by ready to do their gruesome duty.

"We are listening?"

Grul and Lurg cheerfully betrayed Dral and Darl and named Pour and Roup as the perpetrators. It was easy, thought Lurg, I hope he buys it.

"You will catch them in the act and capture the Earth at the same time your Honour," they said.

"Tell Us how you propose to win the invasion," said the President, craftily. "And tell Us how to defeat the rebels."

Grul and Lurg explained in detail how they thought the invasion could work and then with a glance at each other before they spoke again they told him how he could win the civil war. The President listened and when they had finished he beamed at them and offered them a couple of his precious gin and tonics. Grul and Lurg sipped them gratefully.

"Are we friends your Honour?" they asked.

"For the moment, for the moment," replied the President. "But I do urge you not to be afraid of the rodents."

Grul and Lurg felt the hairs on the backs of their necks rise and in spite of the pleasant taste of the gin and tonics their mouths had a bitter bile taste. It was the taste of fear. "Yes your Honour ... we have a plan if your Honour will grace us with your attention?"

The President looked down at the Pair wondering why there was more than one of them and wished they would stop spinning around as well. Or was that Us? We are drunk? The President farted and wriggled in his chair letting the smelly gas race out into the air. Too many olives. The Pair stopped spinning, and with an effort he focussed his gaze on them, feeling the gas in his belly welling up and with no feeling of embarrassment he belched.

"Your gracious Honour," murmured the Pair.

"We will listen to your plan. If it is good enough We will let you live. Otherwise ..."

The Pair gulped and trembled.

"We have a written copy of it on the next flimsy your Honour. If it so pleases you to read it?"

He looked at the second sheet and read it through slowly. He read it through twice and then with a huge leery smile on his ugly face that crinkled his balding pate he giggled."We like it."

"We can begin the process your gracious honour?"

The President belched again and wriggled his bottom and farted trumpet loud.

"Oops, better out than in."

"Yes your Honour," chorused the Pair.

"We give you Our command," said the President. "Dismiss."

Pour and Roup read the flimsy and let it flutter onto the plastic desk top. "What does he want from us?" wailed Pour. "I mean what sort of miracle makers does he think we are?"

"His honour has no idea. The stupid, degenerate moron has no idea how to run a Star Station, or an army, or anything!" said Roup stalking around the office angrily.

"I heard he executed his drinks Pair because they ran out of gin and tonic. What sort of ruler is that?" cried Roup, and spread his hands wide. "I mean read this stupid thing."

Att: Pour and Roup;
Invasion plans on hold - Prepare build up
All logistics under review
Establish bridgehead sector NHSW code 3.
Prepare Mathematical broadcast.
Your Glorious President

"What, for Nong's sake is code three?"

"Look it up," said Pour.

Roup tapped keys and recoiled from the message that appeared on his screen. "Bulgers, we got one turn. One bloody turn to start!" Roup smashed his hand down on the bench top.

Pour stared at the screen disbelieving and then he shook his head.

"We are right in it now. We had better get a break down and quick," said Pour.

Roup keyed buttons again while Pour spoke urgently into the speakfone and added a red alert to his orders. "No refusals. This has to be done." He stated.

"Providing we have no other problems we will get through this and survive," said Pour, and looked at his twin with a question in his expression.

"Dral and Darl will be taken care of once we have got this thing under way."

"I am interested in what happened to Clard and Dracl and that damn robot," said Pour.

"I don't know. The cargo holds in sector yellow are closed off to us still, but there is no sign of them or their robot except for that damn tune and that stupid message. We should check."

Roup scanned the screens for signs of the robot and its horrible family. He paged Clard and Dracl but there was answer. All he saw on the screen images were empty holds. He flipped the auto-search switch and let the machine do the work. The screen cleared, went blank and then, accompanied by a tinny version of A Whiter Shade of Pale a message rolled across the screen.

"Goodbye cruel world I'm off to South America - do not be afraid of the Rodents!"

They switched the screen off and smiled at each other.

"It's gone," they said.

But it had left something behind and when they found it they panicked.

Sitting in cargo hold 41 in the bottom quarter of sector yellow was a bomb on which was pasted a note. The maintenance Pair who found it handed it to Pour and Roup and backed away.

"It's not nice," they said.

"This bomb is designed to explode if certain conditions prevail - tap code as follows:

Hso 1735/42/ whz on screen three for definition - in the meantime do not be afraid of the rodents - beware the Ides of March - remember 1812 - the President is a drunken prat - googlebye - your ever loving Betty/Anthony/Napoleon."

Pour tentatively activated the code on screen three. What they read scared them so much they went into a mild catatonic trance and had to be taken to the sick bay. With an apology for being so pedantic the robot politely informed them that if Pour and Roup as much as set foot in a Transfer Port the Star Station would be instantly destroyed.

"It's not nice at all," repeated the maintenance Pair.

In a cell below the well known anonymous building in Whitehall that was the headquarters of MI6 Kord and Krod lay staring up at the ceiling in utter despair. Their questioners had exhausted them with their endless probing but, stoically, they refused to talk. Their captors left them in the cell with the light on and a dripping tap that every twenty seconds pinged a drop of water on a metal surface. It was this that broke them. For many long periods they lay and listened to it until eventually they had begged their captors to come back. But there was nothing. No sound except for the noise of the dripping tap. They tried to sleep but sleep was impossible. They lay in the bright light, covering their ears with their hands trying not to hear the drip, unable eventually to shut out the sound which penetrated their minds. They counted the short periods between each drip and waited for the plunk. They cracked completely when after a seemingly endless time of listening and bracing for the noise it suddenly stopped and the lights went out.

The sudden silence was so complete their minds couldn't cope and they lay on their bunks with their legs drawn up and urinated not caring where it went. The cell attendants carried them out the following morning on stretchers and loaded them into an ambulance.

In the same ambulance ex-Fireman Sidney Weddell sat on a seat between two burly orderlies, and as the Pair were transferred to the side bunks he smiled and dribbled spittle down his chin.

"Phwends," he said. "Nishe to she you.

And with a burbling sigh he drifted back into an interrupted sleep.

The bodies of the dead Pairs lay on the slabs surrounded by a crowd of surgeons and lookers on. Never in their whole careers had the dissectors had such strange creatures to work on. They dug and probed and weighed and examined, they cut off minute pieces of tissue and put them in slides and marvelled at the structure. They cut out organs and pickled them. They searched cells for DNA and measured body fluids and analysed them. They measured bodies and took pictures, but above all they removed the eyes and put them into special tanks marvelling at their twin pupils. Apart from the fact that the bodies were injured from the smash it was obvious there were three pairs who were exactly alike.

"Ghouls," said the Governor. "We need live ones really."

"They have some in Australia," said The Gentleman. "And we have a couple of our own."

This last he muttered quietly to himself.

"What are they and where do they come from?" said the Governor.

"Aliens old chap just like Professor Renfrew told us," he said, wistfully.

The Governor laughed but his aides turned away. They were not smiling.

Grul and Lurg staggered across the gully and climbed the hill that loomed above them. Wearily they placed one foot at a time stumbling on the rocks and stones forcing their way past the prickly plants. Less than a division away a small troop of Polisocs padded after them. Grul and Lurg thought they had crossed the border without being seen, but when they looked back the way they had come there was a dust cloud. Pairs were after them.

"Pongos?" asked Grul.

"No, Polisocs I'm afraid," said Lurg.

Grimly they continued to climb, and at the top of the ridge they gasped in dismay. Ahead as far as the eye could see there was inhospitable desert with no buildings and hardly any cover. Blue and red rocks stretched away to the horizon and purple red plants spotted the landscape waving in the hot breeze as if to mock them.

"Nong's teeth we'll never make it," said Lurg.

Nevertheless they moved out into the scrub and marched and jogged across the hot desert. Gasping and coughing they stopped to take a breath and Lurg leaned against a rock.

"I can't go on..."

Lurg didn't finish what he was saying and Grul didn't get a chance to answer. Stones rattled; weapons flicked up and they were surrounded by armed Pairs.

"Okay Pair," said the Leader Pair, "where do you think you are going?"

"With you I hope," replied Grul for them both.

"And what makes you think you will be welcome?"

"We have some information for you and behind us are a troop of Polisoc troopers who want to take us back to the President where we will no doubt end up as pig food."

"Tell me," said the Leader Pair.

Grul told him briefly what they knew and the Leader Pair nodded his head.

"Okay Pairs let's get these two into the wagons and disappear."

Glord listened to Grul and Lurg's story and smiled weakly. "I think that we should keep you here for the moment whilst we check you out, you understand, we have to verify a few points. In the meantime, welcome to our headquarters and enjoy the facilities. I will talk with the Elders."

The Pair nodded looking pleased and settled down into their comfortable cell. They rested for three days and four nights enjoying good wholesome food, and entertainment although to earn their good treatment they were put through a tough and exhausting interrogation. It was Glord who led the questioning and such was his skill the Pair told him what they had done, albeit embellished with justification of their actions.

When Glord askd the Pair to explain briefly they answered: "We were working under the threat of our lives," explained Grul nodding encouragingly.

Glord replied. "So you plead duress?"

"Yes your honour, we do."

"I will speak with the Elders. They can decide," he said.

The discussion lasted long enough to do the Pair fair service and early on their fourth morning Glord told them what the Elders had decided. It was a task he thought needed to be done but at times these decisions were hard to arrive at. However, the Elders, this time, had spent more than enough of their time deliberating. The information the Pair gave them was useful and definitely in their favour.

In the light of the rising suns two groups of Pairs each with one bound figure between them entered the yard from separate entrances, and half carried and half marched their struggling and wailing burdens to a pair of white posts in the centre of a well packed dirt surface that faced the first rays of the suns rising above the western hills. With curses and some difficulty they strapped the Pair to their respective posts and held their heads rigid while they were blindfolded.

A small group of Pairs marched from the corner of the yard and halted with a shout and clatter of arms and stomping booted feet.

"Squad! Stand at ease!"

Clunk of boots.

"Squad! Prepare weapons!"

Rattle of swords.

"Squad! Present weapons!"

Another rattle of swords.

"Squad! Four paces forward march!"

Stomping boots and the rattle of swords.

"Squad! Swing weapons!"

Air slicing of swords and rattle of metal.

"Squad! Prepare to cut!"

Coordinated air swishing of metal.

Agonised squeal of terror from Grul and Lurg and smell of urine.

"Squad! Cut targets!"

Air slicing followed by soft metallic cutting noise and howls of agony followed by gurgling of short duration accompanied by noxious smell. Sheathing of weapons.

"Squad! Right turn! Quick march!"

Stomp of boots, rattling of swords and gentle rustle of uniforms.

And the rest was silence.[3]

Glord watched the execution and shuddered. Some enemies, he thought, could not be trusted. Glord hated ritual murder but sometimes it was necessary and although he had asked for their sentence to be commuted to hard labour the Leader Pair had insisted on execution.

War, he thought grimly, was a nasty business.

____

[3] *Okay so the line come directly from Hamlet but what the heck.*

"That damn tune again"

The effect of Arthur Renfrew's appearance on Examiner TV underscored by the intrusive rodent message that marched across the screen, shocked Britons into a state bordering on activity. The newspapers that didn't get his story clamoured for a piece of it, and the television companies that missed out ran their own tale. Like a fad that suddenly sweeps the world and grips the imagination of the populace Arthur Renfrew's dire warning of impending doom spread throughout the networks and clogged the screens of millions with 'little green men from Mars' stories. It reached the antennae of a demented robot stomping through the jungles of the Amazon basin. For a few seconds the robot concentrated its efforts on a solution. For those few moments it suspended the struggle within itself and temporarily suspended the argument over who was legally qualified to certify who and put aside their desperate desire to find their Father/Husband/Brother/Adviser. Napoleon/Betty/Anthony was very angry/upset/worried about the way Clard and Dracl had slipped off to Earth without telling them. But the effect of Professor Renfrew's program was a worry too. Something had to be done. It analysed the broadcast and changed its connection with the Star Station. It checked the orbit of the Doomsday Bomb and added an extra safety margin. It changed the messages circulating through the systems and added another imperative to the messages it was sending to the President of Zrad. Satisfied with its work it turned full circle and gazed out over its squeaking, tumblingly excited family of ravenous rodents and then marched steadily forward in its search for Clard and Dracl. Progress was slow but with several thousand rodents to feed on the march Three could hardly expect to race along. Confusion of identity, so it seemed to the android, was normal. It burbled happily adjusting its speaker system once more, adding an extra digital enhancement to the upper and middle range of the scale.

The jungle filled with the tones of the tune A Whiter Shade of Pale.

"Grand." Said Napoleon.

"Nice." Said Anthony.

"It's okay." Said Betty.

Governments everywhere were besieged by lobbyists, the press media and the ordinary citizen demanding to know the truth and what the heck their elected or otherwise representatives were doing about it. The ordinary person called for action. The business world called for concessions. The entertainment world demanded film and television rights. Islam didn't believe Christendom. Buddhists questioned the inner self of little green men. The starving poor said 'so what'. And Military people panicked. Spurious litigation firms advised people on the best ways to sue for any inconvenience, accident, loss of earnings, loss of property, for broadcasting traumatic material, reduction in property values and alienation. This last was considered to be in poor taste.

In Australia they already knew what they were going to do.

"Fight the buggers," said the Prime Minister.

The Japanese diet sighed with relief. The burgeoning problem of over supply which was creating a massive crisis within their economy had led them to a time of decision. On one side of the house the doves called for moderation. On the other side the hawks demanded a solution. There was nobody willing to take a middle road so the conflict was resolved by a vote. The hawks won and the house dived enthusiastically into the concept of World War Three. They prepared to make plans to attack the Republic of China.

"It is the only honourable solution," said Prime Minister Nakamura Hiro. He was wrong. Ten minutes after the pronouncement clerks entered the chamber with a thick document. With a flourish they handed a copy each to the Prime Minister and the leaders of his opposition. All four parties read the contents and looked at each other. The Prime Minister smiled.

"I think we need to talk again gentlemen," he said.

The fourteen women members coughed gently and lowered their eyes.

"My apologies," he said.

The debate lasted for the remainder of the session. At the end of the session he stood and spoke politely.

"We have debated the issues extensively. I suggest that we recess for twenty-four hours during which time my ministers will devise a plan. If the honourable members wish to adopt it in full then so be it but if not then we will continue the debate. Neh?"

The diet agreed with a show of hands and departed to devise plans of their own. The Prime Minister's plan was so well thought out that it was adopted with only one condition. That the World War Three option remain open.

In their rooms, not far from the West London University a group of six Pairs were checking their equipment. The furniture was pushed aside or thrown out and in the centre of the room two Pairs were calibrating a small portable machine. The machine resembled a leaf blower but its purpose was much more sinister and all the Pairs were equipped with full face masks in shoulder bags.

The four remaining Pairs finished their preparations each with a gas gun, and one out of each Pair with a soft, looping set of straps, and all four Pairs were dressed as any Earthman would, in a suit, shirt and tie with sensible shoes. One Half Pair acted as the driver for the van they were to use; his twin acting as passenger and emotional support.

"Ready Pairs!" barked the Leader Pair. "Time to move!"

The four Pairs hup-hupped to the parking bay, climbed into the vehicle and with the Half Pair driving set off on their mission.

After his successful television appearance Professor Renfrew agreed to hold a press conference. It was held in a hastily prepared lecture room at the University, although there was nothing hasty about Colin's preparations. But, as Colin explained, it was going to be a bugger of a job to cover all the angles. Apart from aliens wanting to take a pop at the Prof, Colin was sure that other agencies were after him too.

The longer the conference lasted the more agitated Colin got. His worry was that all the time he was stuck in this room watching over the Prof the less he had to spend outside watching the exits. He decided to change the situation a little and called Sam over.

"Listen mate get 'old of Joe and Ivan and do a wander. If you see anything deal with it. I'll let the other lads know and I'll join yer."

Sam went off and Colin left the room in charge of one of his boys and went from man to man letting them know how he felt. Outside on the terrace he took a long look around. A big man in a suit left his post by the main door and walked slowly across the terrace and stood about a metre away looking contemptuously at him.

"Colin Hicks ain't it," said the suit.

"Yeah, what about it mate," said Colin.

"You and your animals are getting in my way," said the suit. "We have been ordered to protect Professor Renfrew, and your scum are bothering me. You should take them back to the zoo where they belong."

Colin said nothing. He was watching one of his men who had suddenly dived on a bod and disappeared around a corner to reappear and stick his thumb up grinning broadly. Colin nodded. All under control by the looks of things.

"Are you listening to me Hicks?" said the suit.

"As a matter of fact I am not," said Colin. "What is it you want?"

"Lay off and stuff off Hicks, we don't need you."

"Bollocks," said Colin. "You MI5 types piss me off. I'm getting paid for me work and if you get in my way I'll drop you like I would any other vermin. You and your blokes are a pain in the arse."

"I'm not MI5," said the suit, obviously peeved.

Colin watched as two more of his men dashed around separate corners. And then Sam came hurrying across the quad to speak to him. Colin went to meet him but the MI5 suit gripped his arm.

"Excuse me but..."

Colin hit him with two short sharp blows one after the other and the suit went down in a crumpled heap.

"Like I said mate, you MI5 types really piss me off."

Sam glanced down at the unconscious MI5 man and smirked.

"Some of them are trying it on with us. We bin bashin' 'em all over but there's a lot of 'em. We gotta get the Prof out some other way. Dunno why they want ter get in the way like that," he said, puzzled.

"I think he cheesed the government off and they want him to talk to them," said Colin.

"All they 'ad ter do was arsk," said Sam.

Colin chuckled; Sam was right. "Or watch the bleedin' telly," he added.

This time Sam chuckled.

"Come on, we better go and see the Professor 'ome," he said, and together they walked back into the hall. Getting the Professor out by a side door was easy, and soon the party were walking along a path back to the Professor's office. Nobody around and none of them stupid Government dicks in the way, he thought, and felt relieved.

It was this sense of relief that was his undoing.

The attackers came out of nowhere so it seemed, and before Colin and his men could react clouds of acrid gas enveloped them and they collapsed gasping on the ground. Colin heard running feet and then everything went dizzy.

Oh bugger, I was wrong, he thought. What a bummer.

The time was exactly four forty in the afternoon and if Colin was not lying unconscious on the ground outside the University lecture rooms he would have heard the tune A Whiter Shade of Pale wafting from the speakers of all the radio sets in the vicinity.

All over the world in some form or another radio stations played the tune at approximately twenty minutes to, or at twenty minutes past the hour, and whatever the operators did there was no way of stopping it.

In Tehran despite efforts to stop it the Western degenerate music continued to play. The Imam ordered the station's power supply cut and for a few hours silence reigned.

It was filled eventually when locals, fed up with the unaccustomed silence, tuned into stations from outside Iran with their solar powered entertainment packs and listened happily to the myriad broadcasts.

The Imam, bowing to obvious public preference, compromised and bought a pair of earplugs.

Pour and Roup do not regret...

Pour and Roup watched the action on the screens, and as the battle for the western land mass unfolded they were happy but anxious. The troops advanced and supply managed to keep up, but as yet there was no real opposition. All to the good really, thought Roup, or there would be no invasion. In spite of the recent build up of supplies they were barely coping, stores got to the point where the amount coming in could not keep up with demand. The operators managed to shift and shove and borrow from one source to another and although they squabbled incessantly at least the meagre supplies got through.

"If the supply rate drops much below the present level our troops will fail," said Pour. He stood beside his twin and kept his gaze on the scrolling and ever changing logistics balance. The problem was made worse by the lag in time between what they already had and what was beginning to come through the ports. One Star station could not keep an invasion supplied. The paper war was working but they had to juggle existing supplies mainly through lack of transfer ports on Earth.

"You realise, if we had more mobile ports on Earth we could supply faster and make what we are doing look good," said Pour.

At that moment the Pair Dral and Darl entered the cabin looking solemn carrying a sheaf of flimsies. Dral spoke whilst Darl laid the sheets out on the bench for them to see. "It appears that there is some resistance to our troops on Earth, er we are losing personnel and equipment, er what can we do about it?"

Pour and Roup read through the sheets and looked at the Pair and smiled. "That's the way it works Pair," said Pour.

"We lose some Pairs and equipment but their loss is useful to us because it generates positive responses from Headquarters. In other words we get more given to us, so Pair, we have no regrets..." Roup said and gave his twin an artful look. "Your scheme is working."

"But personnel and weaponry will have to be cut to account for food and ammunition," said Dral, "And that cannot be good. We need more soldiers."

Pour smiled and shook his head. "Cannot be helped. We have a virus on the system so you will have to sort it out yourselves," he said and smiled even more broadly. "Or..."

Dral and Darl trembled, and gathering the flimsies left the cabin.

When they had gone Roup turned to Pour and said: "Any answer on the virus yet?"

"We have not received a reply my twin," replied Pour. "The President's advisers are looking into the situation, and in between gin and tonics it is supposed that his honourship is giving our request his closest attention and thoughtful consideration."

"Do I detect a note of sarcastic disbelief in your tone my twin," said Roup eyeing his twin with a sharp look, and then glancing around the control room anxiously.

"No more than usual," said Pour. "We cannot leave the Star Station, the invasion is hanging on by the skin of a Bulger's teeth, the Polisocs are breathing down everybody's necks looking for traitors, and I have heard on the grapevine that the President is about to launch an attack on the rebels back home. That will not only tie up troops but will also occupy the President's attention and he will forget about us, result, the Vice Consuls will give us the crap."

"We are bitter aren't we?" said Roup, and raised an eyebrow.

Pour glowered and deftly recalculated the data and entered it.

"Get a bloody team up here quick and let's hand this job over to some lower paid Pairs. We should be telling Pairs what to do not doing it ourselves."

Roup grinned and tapped out a list of names. Within five small periods the address system began intoning names and ordering Pairs to report to the control centre. One full period later Pour and Roup were sitting in their cabin watching the Pairs working, and with a sigh they opened a bottle of Second City brew each and poured the contents into respective plastic beakers.

"To the demise of stupidity," said Roup, and winked.

Pour raised his own beaker and drank knowing exactly what his twin meant. Now all they had to do was devise a way of neutralising the robot's bomb and they could slip away and hide.

In sector yellow deep below the standard cargo holds where the Polisocs stored their pre-transfer prisoners a small rodent slipped from its crunchy meal of dead Half Pair and ran through a pipe line that normally carried liquid. It slid a little on the residue and skidded once, gripped its tiny feet on a yielding surface and lost its balance. It spun like a rifled bullet along the tube and popped out onto an empty plastic floor. It rolled over and over and came to a soft bouncing stop against a dull flat vertical surface that vibrated reassuringly.

Mother, it thought, and rubbed its whiskers gently against the friendly object. It climbed to the first ledge and stopped and sniffed the air. The vibrations hummed through its feet and the thought of milk and mother drew it on higher and higher. It stopped to sniff a square of flimsy plastic and idly chewed the edges, liking the feeling the vibrations made through its sharp teeth.

For a while it sat and sniffed and washed its little pointed face turning its head from side to side as it surveyed its domain. A dull light pulsating caught its attention, and with a curious toe hopping motion it wandered toward the source and sniffed. Its nose touched a loose plastic edge, and with a squeal of delight it chewed at it nibbling until a piece parted company. Inside the recess of the plastic covering there was a deliciously tantalising smell that the rodent found hard to resist.

The plastic was hard but with patience born of desire the rodent chewed a large enough hole to give it access to the treat beneath. With little squeaks of animal delight it nibbled busily, and when the delicious matrix of glue and resin ran out at the place it was nibbling the rodent enlarged the hole to find more.

Almost sated but delirious with its new found treasure the rodent nibbled down to the strangely humming plastic below and bit into the hard round strings it discovered there covered in the delicious matrix.

It had no time to think of mother, milk, food or escape before the sudden powerful current gripped it and passed through its warm body to the body of the robot's bomb. The rodent's fur stood on end for a brief moment, and then, with a wisp of dark smoke the animal sizzled and dropped into the hole it had made and became as one with the matrix that had so fatally attracted it.

Inside the bomb the memory chip recorded a change in status and re-channelled its internal signal. The demise of the rodent damaged the circuit so that the change was masked from the minute code trace that kept it in equilibrium. Two zeros changed to ones and a code discontinued.

The rodent stayed where it was and putrefied.

The code itself was masked by the minute error and to all appearances the data the bomb's creator received gave it no cause for concern. The constant tone of the operating signal continued unchanged, and the short looped checks the Robot's memory banks made on the small item continued to record a steady state. The Robot continued to guide its family of rodents through the jungle more worried about when to feed them rather than on what. As it rolled along chanting its warning cry and playing the tune A Whiter Shade of Pale it monitored the Zradian invasion and decided to do nothing about it as yet. It had calculated that the Zradians were no threat to its existence, and besides, in its current mode as Betty it felt benevolent toward all peoples.

The soldiers will have their fun she/he/it thought, and strode ahead clucking its imaginary tongue at the antics of some of its more forward animals.

Disgusting the way they behave she/he/it mused.

Fornication. A satisfying word but not a nice word, not a nice word at all.

The Cobbers

The trouble is with this farm, the stockman thought, was it was too far west. Cattle didn't like the heat, and this far from out from Port Augusta you may as well head for the Alice. And as for ostriches and bloody 'roos, well you could keep the buggers, he added. Looking for stock this far out in the bush was like hunting for mates who owed yer money. He squinted his eyes against the sunlight and searched ahead for the tell tale spurts of dust kicked up by moving animals. He thought he saw a mob way ahead and gunned the bike along the dusty track bouncing over ruts and cuts like a seasoned motocross rider. The motor hummed happily pushing out power to the fat plastic tyre. The bike skidded around the curves and kicked up a cloud of dust along the straights. He raced over the top of a rocky ridge and eased the throttle slowing a little expecting to see cattle grazing below. Instead of cows on the track it was blocked by a body of fully armed men. He braked hard and slid the bike down the slope.

"Jeez," he said, and swung the bike at an angle with his feet in an effort to turn quickly out of the way. "Rogue Abo's ..."

He didn't complete the sentence or the turn.

Fire poured at him and the bike burst into flame beneath him but he was already dead when the bike spun burning like a Catherine wheel into the flame hungry scrub.

The Leader Pair gazed at the burning machine and ordered his Pairs to move on. "Idiot," he said and scanned the horizon.

There was something dreadfully wrong here, they thought, we should be close to the city the Earth people call Adelaide in South Australia. Their Atlas definitely showed them to be close but their sense of direction insisted that they were in fact many kilometres out of their way.

"My twin," said one. "I am thinking we are lost."

"And I am thinking those Bulgers on the transfer ports sent us here deliberately," his twin replied. "All we have seen of the enemy is that idiot on the machine and some large hopping animals but where are the Earth people?"

"No idea but I suggest we keep going?"

"Our Pairs are spoiling for a fight. They want to do their duty for the President."

"How loyal."

"Do I detect a hint of sarcasm my twin?"

"When we are lost on an alien planet because our own people do not like us we have a right to be sarcastic. I am not impressed by our Star Station Leader's logic. There is something amiss there my twin."

"That's as maybe but meanwhile we keep marching until we find this city."

His twin grunted and looked to the barren horizon and the sun diving down before them. He had a niggling feeling that his twin was right. It was ironic, he thought, here we are, top line Stormtroopers with nobody to fight.

The homestead fire watchers saw the column of black smoke and raised the alarm. It took several hours for the fire-fighters to arrive, and several more for the homestead workers and volunteers to put out the fires. It was not until the morning that the men saw what had happened. Hot and sooty they gathered in a circle around the burned out machine and the charred body and stared. They stole quick glances at one another each unsure what to say. This was the bush where men were men and if a bloke got upset about anything he usually fought his way out. One brave bloke bent down and turned the body over.

"Here, look at this cobbers, this joker's been shot."

A ring of shocked faces gathered closer to get a better look and again they looked at each other.

"Who did this?" asked the ganger between gritted teeth.

He looked at the two darker faces in the group and his gaze was followed by the rest. The two part Aborigine's backed away nervously. They understood. Anger soon fired into action in the bush.

"Ain't nuthin' to do with us mate," said one.

"We're just as pissed off as you; Jack was a mate ..." said the other.

"Yeah too right, he was eh." The ganger said. "These blokes ain't like them other blacks."

Nevertheless the ganger asked the two Aborigines to look for tracks. They walked casually away from the circle of white men and fossicked around in the dirt pretending to search for signs.

"Me, I'm a city bloke," muttered one.

"Yeah, me too."

The tracks of the Zradian Stormtroopers were easy to see and with all the solemnity of Tonto they showed the ganger. In his turn the ganger examined them and looked up grimly.

"Reckon a mob o' blacks eh?"

"Yeah, we go and get our guns and pull 'em in?" said one of the men giving the two Aborigine's an angry glare.

Back at the homestead the ganger explained to the manager what had happened.

"The rest of the blokes are really pissed off," he said, and before he could explain how he had begged them not to go off after the mob there was a roar of engines outside in the yard and he and the manager rushed to the window.

"Cripes!" said the ganger.

"Jeez, Tony, why didn't you lock the buggers up?" exclaimed the manager and shook his head.

"I tried to stop 'em but they told me to pull me bloody head in. I reckon we oughter call the coppers?"

The manager called the police using the telephone rather than the radio, and when he explained that most of his men had driven off armed to the teeth to go look for the mob who had murdered their mate the officer at the other end cursed him out for being an idiot.

"You're a fuckin' Galah mate," he said.

The manager glared at the ganger and shook his head.

"You're a fuckin' Galah, Tony," he said.

Meanwhile at the site of the fire the angry mob stopped only to drop off the two Aborigine's giving them instructions to pick up the body and take it back on one of the smaller wagons.

"Leave us with all the shit work eh?" said one.

"Yeah bloody bastards."

The armed mob caught up with the marching column in the mid afternoon and with whoops of anger and blood lust they swooped down on the waiting so-called mob of blacks. The whoops stopped when the so-called mob of blacks started shooting back.

"Oh fuck," said the leading driver, and swung the wheel hard over dipping the wagon deep right, and pressing the power pedal down hard to the floor. He saw the lines of flame heading directly for his vehicle and pushed his foot harder feeling the beginning of a bowel movement that finished without him.

"Oh fuck…" and whatever else he wanted to say was cut off when the lead truck disappeared in a ball of flame. Those that didn't crash into it were fired on as the drivers drove their vehicles around in tight half circles to get away from the dreadful hail of fire. None of the angry gun toting passengers fired a shot. They were either busy dying or ducking from the fiercesome fire that boiled from the enemy weapons.

One small wagon limped back from the one sided festival of fire and staggered to a wobbly halt on a ridge well beyond the ambush. Two men rushed out of the cab and immediately vomited on the dusty scrub that lined the track. With more than a little apprehension the men looked at each other, and then with a nod as if to say 'here goes', they moved nervously to the tray and looked inside. Their mates lay on the scorched metal like a pair of overdone steaks. For the second time the two survivors threw up.

Back in the cab the driver started the engine and taking a deep breath eased the vehicle into first gear.

"What about our mates?" asked the passenger glancing back through the rear window nervously.

"The buggers are done for and the best we can do is get out of here and get some real help. This lot are no rogue Abo's mate they're fair dinkum soldiers. Shoot!"

"Looked like a mob o' Chinese ter me. Yeah, I reckon yer right mate, we oughter get goin'."

"Yeah, last one back is a sissy," said the driver.

His mate didn't laugh.

The manager listened to their incoherent story and for a few moments he stroked his chin and then with his eyes narrowed querulously he said.

"Fair dinkum?"

"Sure as me and me mate get pissed on a satd'y," said the driver.

"I'll call the police," said the manager.

"Nah, the army mate, they's no mob o' bloody blacks out there," insisted the driver.

"Police first," said the manager.

"Suit yer bloody self," said the driver, and walked dejectedly to the bunkhouse.

Five and half hours later squads of South Australian Police swarmed into the homestead filling the yard with vehicles and uniformed men with guns and flak jackets. In the distance a helicopter droned west.

"Got the bloody lot here today," remarked the driver.

"No bloody use to us mate," said his pal.

The helicopter pilot droned his aircraft along the track and swooped down on the site of the fire. The vehicle tracks were easy to follow so he rose to a better flying height and looked across at his observer.

"See anything mate?"

"Yeah, dead trucks way over the ridge and there's a mob moving off north," the observer said, and relayed the position into his mike.

The pilot eased the chopper a little higher and sped above the sandy terrain to take a closer look. The column of men marched in regular formation and with the confidence of one who was familiar with traffic control the chopper pilot dropped the machine lower to get a better look.

"Bloody oath mate, they're soldiers!" said the pilot.

The observer glanced at the pilot and spoke into the mike glancing nervously down at the marching men as the pilot began to turn.

"Bird to Base - this lot is no rogue Abo..."

A shaft of fire hit the helicopter slicing the blades from the drive shaft. It dropped like a stone, hit the ground and exploded.

"Bloody oath," said the radio operator when his line went dead. "They've shot the buggers."

The Chief Constable held the sheet in his hand and gazed into the distance.

"We got to get out there and bring 'em in," he said.

"But sir, this a job for the army now, surely?"

"By my oath it isn't. I know these people," he said. "The black buggers think just because we give 'em their land back they got the right to shoot us."

His staff, observing that his mind was made up, let him have his way although they did attempt to put him right by sending the two survivors to talk to him. When they finished their story the Chief glared at them and asked them bluntly if they worked with 'niggers'. They replied politely that they did have some fellow workers who were part aborigine.

"See, nigger lovers," the Chief said.

He dismissed the two men and gave orders to call up the armed offenders squads.

"All of 'em sir?"

"Yeah, all of them. I want some bloody action. No pussy footing around any more. I want the buggers sorted out and I want them rounded up by the day after tomorrow. You got that?"

"Yes Sir!"

The squads pulled out the next morning in trucks to the area and late that afternoon the squads sighted the offenders.

"Keep out of sight and catch them in the early morning," ordered the Chief. He was up early in the morning and waiting for reports when Colonel Chin of the Australian Army arrived with his forces.

"Good morning sir," said the Colonel. "My Battalion have orders to take over. I request your men be recalled immediately. For their own safety you understand?"

"I don't need the Army to handle a mob of niggers!" the Chief snorted.

Lt Troy glowered at the police officer her face a mask of anger and was about to say something when Chin spoke sharply: "I think the word nigger is out of line sir, we don't use it anymore, do you understand?"

The Police Chief glanced at Helen Troy and then at Chin who grinned at him as the man tried to come to terms with the Army Officers being Australian, which he could accept, but one a Chinese and the other an Abo threw him. Chin said: "According to our satellite pictures we are dealing with a different situation here. The pictures show that there is a fully armed force out there. Soldiers, you understand not a mob of blacks as you call them. You have it wrong and your armed offenders squads are out of their depth in this situation."

The Chief was about to reply when a clerk ran out of the house with a flimsy and handed it to him nervously.

Colonel Harry Chin watched the Chief's face change from excited anticipation to confused fury. "Bad news sir?" asked Chin.

The Chief said nothing, and turned on his heel and stiffly stormed back into the house. Colonel Chin shrugged and marched back to the lead truck grinning as he returned to his seat beside his First Lieutenant.

"Let's go," he said. "We have stiff necked believers."

"And some dyed in the wool red neck officers here, sir," she replied, grinning and spoke quietly into the radio mike. "Okay troops we are on our way."

The Police armed offenders squads moved at dawn. They strolled along the lines of sleeping bodies and yelled at them in a mixture of pidgin and Strine to get up and get moving. "Come on you black buggers!" yelled the officer in charge. "Move along you... oh shit!" The 'black buggers' leapt up out of their sleep and attacked the police with swords and knives and within a few minutes the police were running for their lives. They abandoned their rifles. They abandoned their wits. They left their dying mates where they had fallen and sped off in all directions as fast as their legs could carry them. They scattered in ones and twos and in bunches until eventually late that morning a sergeant gathered a larger group together and set off to find their trucks.

"We gotta get out of here," he sobbed.

The rest of the men seemed to agree with him.

"Rogue blacks? A swarm of angry wasps is better," he muttered.

"Yeah, right on mate," said a terrified voice beside him.

The sergeant eventually called a halt and gathered the officers around him. "I'm sorry youse blokes but I ain't got no idea where the trucks are," he said.

"Yeah, well Sarge waddyer reckon we oughter do?"

"Head East a bit and then turn south or whatever. As long as we keep away from that mob back there. Jeez, the Chief was wrong. Them blokes ain't no bunch of bloody Abo's."

The men looked at him and gathered closer together. He turned his face to the East and began to walk. The shattered men listlessly followed him, and for the rest of the day they walked until, scared and exhausted they stopped to rest in a small gully. It was nearly evening, and as the sun set a row of heads appeared over the ridge and gazed down at them. With cries of terror the men bunched up and grabbed each other's arms for protection. The heads evolved into men and women who walked solemnly down toward them and stopped. One old and skinny individual stepped out from the rest and looked the sergeant up and down.

"You fellas finished walking 'round in circles?" he said.

"Don't kill us," said the sergeant, his voice trembling.

The skinny man looked puzzled.

"We come to help," he said. "You fellas been wandering 'round our village all day. We give you tucker and tomorrow we find him boss and you go home. We call him on radio. Bloody cell phone don't work out here."

The sergeant stared at the man and fell to his knees sobbing.

The skinny old man wrinkled his face in amusement and waved to his companions. "Here, help me get these silly buggers back to the camp."

Colonel Chin's column stopped at the site of the Zradian camp. He alighted from the truck and signalled the Lieutenant to follow. With two of the Sergeants and a radio operator they examined the site. Bodies lay on the ground where they had fallen and all except two were police officers.

"Call base and get them to send a meat wagon squad," Colonel Chin said. "Mount up and let's get after them."

They made contact with Zradians at mid morning. Colonel Chin sent a gun wagon in to try the enemy out. The enemy response was immediate and the wagon retreated to a safer distance splotched and burnt but otherwise unharmed.

"The enemy fire power is enormous," reported the Sergeant in charge. "Some sort of heated ray, Colonel. We are cooking in here. Shall we use rockets?"

"Try one or two and see what happens."

The wagon trundled back and fired a fan of rockets at the defenders. The response from the enemy was a rain of heat that seared the rocks and took out the gun wagon leaving a smoking hole surrounded by twisted bits of metal.

Colonel Chin wisely backed off.

"Call base for back up. Their firepower is too much for us to handle on our own. Set the gun wagons up under cover and fire by

Sat-nav. Use the Sat-nav system for visual contact. The rest of us will wait for back up and then we'll go in on foot."

The fight was uneven. The enemy held them off easily and Colonel Chin pulled his troops back admitting that their rifles, top of the line laser guided and high powered, were no match for the enemy weapons.

"What'll I do?" asked Colonel Chin of his superior officer.

"Hang in there Harry we got a stonk coming up soon."

"I can't hang on much longer the blokes out there are better than we are and I got a feeling they are about to launch an attack."

As he spoke the enemy soldiers advanced on foot dashing from cover to cover in Pairs firing accurately but yet too far away to do much damage, and with a curse he ordered a retreat. They turned the wagons and drove well out of range firing their long range rockets at the advancing soldiers killing some but having little effect on the enemy advance.

"Don't the buggers ever give up?" said Chin, and ordered yet another retreat. They stopped below a low ridge and he and the First Lieutenant walked to the top and peered between two rocks at the enemy for the first time using his binoculars. He gave a low whistle and gasped.

"They are definitely not blacks or Indians or Chinese nor are they like any other troops I have ever seen. They have swords and guns and knives and uniforms but other than that they are completely alien..."

He looked at his First Lieutenant. "Helen, would you believe me if I said these were aliens?"

"No," she said and took the binoculars gazing for a long time at the advancing troops.

"Oh," she said and handed them back. "They'll never believe us."

Chin spoke into his radio mike.

"Base. We have a problem here. The enemy firepower is superior. Reckon you can send us some gunships?"

"Base to Chin. Sure thing. Back off and stand by. ETA your position in fifteen minutes. We had 'em ready."

Chin grinned and ordered his troops to retreat.

Exactly to the minute fast moving helicopters drove down on the enemy and fired salvo after salvo of rockets onto the enemy positions. They were followed by the faster fixed wing craft that overflew the position and dropped fire canisters on the milling soldiers and strafed them with smaller missiles. Chin watched the devastation from the safety of his command vehicle and grunted with satisfaction.

"Base to Chin. Reckon you can go in now Harry."

The survivors of the stonk staggered out from their meagre cover and surrendered. They seemed disorientated and with no resistance at all they allowed themselves to be herded like sheep into the wagons. Chin looked at them curiously. They really are aliens, he thought, odd looking eyes too.

Two weeks after the incident the Chief Constable stood before a board of inquiry who demanded an explanation.

"Have you anything to say?"

"It was a genuine mistake," he explained.

He had plenty of time to reflect on his reply. As part of his corrective training he was put in charge of the sanitary arrangements in the prisoner of war compound where the Zradians were held. The board explained that there he would have plenty of time to reflect on his attitude toward the indigenous people of the Great Australian Commonwealth. What galled him most of all was the appointment of Governor was given to an Aborigine.

At the bottom of a steep valley in the Urewera hills a small band of Zradian soldiers clung together under the trees. The dense New Zealand bush was cold and confusing and horribly damp. The Pairs popped out of the air and were dumped in a stream. Seven Half Pairs died screaming when the space they should have occupied was also occupied by rocks or trees. Their companions hastily finished them off with their swords and quickly marched on. Out of sight of the carnage they stopped to take a breath.

"We had better keep moving," said the leader Pair

They marched through the dank trees until nightfall and huddled together for warmth and comfort, scared of the animal grunts and bright animal eyes that peered out from the darkness. They clutched each other tightly, whimpering in fear as something large snuffled close by and wandered off. At daybreak they ate breakfast and began a slow trek that led through dense bush over steep hills and along singing stream beds.

"I've never seen so much water," said the leader Pair.

On the fifth day they emerged from the bush starving and weak still carrying their packs and their weapons and stood gazing at the paddocks dotted with placidly grazing animals. They climbed a post and wire fence and walked across grassy paddocks until, exhausted and sore footed, they stood, a dejected group, in a farmyard gazing dumbly at a farmer dressed in shorts and a black singlet wearing rubber boots, who looked them over with a critical eye and spoke.

"You jokers get lost in the bush eh?"

Somehow the lead Pair understood and nodded miserably. The farmer looked at their weapons and their uniforms and grinned.

"Trouble with you pongos you all come from the city, nobody tells yer how ter handle the bush. You blokes better come on in and get some hot tucker inside yer.

Nong, thought the lead Pair, this Half Pair is friendly.

He gazed steadily at the farmer for a few seconds and looked at his twin. His twin nodded and with a sigh of relief he gave in to his innermost feelings and smiled at the Earthman.

"Lead on McDuff," he said.

The farmer grinned.

"Better put yer gear in the shed, and I mean the shooters too, and come on in."

The farmer led them to a bunkhouse where they washed in a shower room and dried their aching bodies on warm rough towels. He gave them clothes to wear and when they were ready led them to a long low table where bowls of steaming stew and slices of thick bread were laid out.The stew was cooked by his wife and the bread was baked by her on the farm.

"Siddown mates and get stuck in."

The Pairs ate ravenously until at last they were full.

"Now," said the Farmer. "I did a bit of ringing up and according to the Army youse blokes don't exist. Would you mind explaining that for me?"

The Leader Pair took a deep breath and said. "We come from a planet a long way from here. We are supposed to be part of an invading army but we sort of got lost. It would be sort of nice if you sort of forgot to tell anybody?"

The farmer stood up and walked to the window. He rubbed his chin and gazed out at the darkening sky. Eventually he turned back to face them and cleared his throat.

"Er, youse blokes fer real?"

The Leader Pair nodded.

"Illegal immigrants I reckon?"

The Leader Pair nodded again. The farmer knitted his brows and cupped his chin in his hand again and then with a crafty grin he looked at each Half Pair in turn.

"Er, you blokes fancy a bit of hard work?"

The leader Pair nodded.

"Good, then I got plenty fer yer."

The Zradians eased back in their seats and smiled warmly at him. He smiled back. Gonna get on with this mob, he mused, yeah, too right I am. And as he gazed at them he reflected on how they knew about Shakespeare. He also thought about correcting the Leader Pair, but it was a common mistake. He changed his mind. Better get this relationship on the right footing.

"Oh, and it's 'lay on McDuff' not lead – they were fighting," he said.

"Ah yes, of course, a common mistake," said the Leader Pair.

"Right, me name's Trev and me missus is Noeleen. You'll meet my boys and me daughter at the end of the week, and I reckon you'll like it here," Trevor said and grinned. "Now get stuck in and welcome aboard."

The Pairs grinned and as Trevor suggested they got stuck in.

War!

The Pongos marched in fours flanked by rows of Polisoc Stormtroopers. Supply wagons, guarded by disgruntled Pongos, the ordinary soldiers, crawled along behind. Ahead the battle wagons fanned out in the desert ready to spit fire. The Pongos hated the Stormtroopers. The Stormtroopers in their turn hated the Pongos. The Stormtroopers knew that the average Pongo wanted to lay down his arms and surrender to the Rebels. It was only the likes of the Polisocs and the strong Loyalist Soldiers[4] in their battle wagons who wanted to fight; these troops were the 'would be Stormtroopers' and treated the Pongos badly. The Pongos were there to back them up - or else - and that was the rub; back at home their families would be sent to the work camps and they would never see them again. Rebellion, unless it was a mass rebellion on the home front as well as the battlefield, was doomed.

The Pongos marched in silence while the Stormtroopers sang marching cadences and tramped along as if they were going on a picnic. Bulging swine, was the unspoken but general opinion, and a curse on them for their arrogance!

At last the columns stopped and with all the fuss of a large body of fighting men on the move a camp formed. The wagons up front created a defensive arc acting as listening posts. Pickets were set and the Pongos were not surprised when some of the cannons were turned inward. No matter, there was food, and at least Pongos were exempted from night patrols. Sometimes, they said, it is good not to be trusted.

The plan was to sweep South from all Sectors and spread out like the fingers of a fat hand to seek and destroy the enemy. Objective one was to seek and destroy the Women's Rebel Army, objective two, to seek out and destroy the Rebel Headquarters. The Stormtroopers saw the plan as simple and easy to implement. The Pongos knew that the plan was a load of Bulgershit.

The Stormtroopers were glad to be on the move and related tales to each other of how they would treat the prisoners when they had caught them. Rape, Pillage and more rape was on their minds as well as the bloodbath they were going to have when they met up

---

4 *Yet another group of soldiers who were one grade down from ordinary Stormtroopers - like them they were volunteers and semi-professionals recruited for the war.*

with the Rebels. The name Glord and Drogl was on their lips. Troopers spat in the sand before they spoke of the Pair.

"He was a fourball player once. Played his best game at the President's stadium; you know I remember..." And so on until they had worked up an angry mood which gave them the incentive to sleep until sunsrise ready to march all turn if they had to, with twice the number of weapons loaded on their backs.

The Sunsrise was as spectacular as always in the Southern sectors and the troops rose to the call of the clarion and, like all camps in the first light of morning, rose complaining, looked for the latrines and demanded breakfast. At least the Pongos were ready for breakfast. The Stormtroopers were ready for war.

They got both.

From the hills overlooking the plains Glord watched the approaching army and smiled. The President had committed a major blunder. Fighting on two fronts in force against determined armies with a healthy ideology on their side was a dumb move, he thought, really dumb. On Earth, so their sources had said, the Invasion had started in earnest and that meant soon Dart and Drat will be there coordinating that fight. Here in the Wastelands the armies of the President were going to need more than double the troops they had if they were to control the area. And, of late, every tenth, more disillusioned Pairs arrived ready to join the Rebels. Glord thought of the many Pairs who came to them. Each had to be vetted first and then trained in the Rebel way, and although that took many tenths their army was growing stronger by the division.

Glord was happy. Around him resting below the skyline was an army of highly skilled specialists with specially adapted battle wagons that carried light but powerful Laser cannons and something that had not been seen on Zrad since the War of the Five Planets. Rocket weapons. Glord's plan was to let the enemy come within easy range and let them have a salvo or two of rockets, aiming at the Polisoc Stormtroopers and the battle wagons, and creep toward the soft core of Pongos, the long suffering and smelly foot soldiers. A few more short periods and the enemy would be within range. Glord spoke softly into his throat microphone.

"All units ready?"

The answers came in the prearranged sequence and he quietly started the countdown knowing that in every wagon, whether they were weapons ships or troop ships, a counter on the dash would be ticking away the small periods to a zero point. There would be no need to give any firing orders; the zero was the signal. For his part he would lead his Pairs down onto the plain for a lightning strike and then back out again. The attack was planned as a moral victory not a crushing one; there was not enough of them to do that.

Zero clicked over.

The first salvo of rockets hurtled into the air and landed neatly on their targets and exploded in great gouts of fire. The surviving enemy battle wagons scattered and returned sporadic fire. The second salvo screamed into the air and the enemy fire stopped altogether. Rebel weapons wagons surged forward to position two and poured laser fire into the outer crust of Polisoc Stormtroopers.

Then it was his turn to join the attack, and with a grin at his second in command he climbed aboard the wagon.

"Fast and furious Pairs and hit them hard," he said, and licked his lips. Glord enjoyed a good fight and with a quick movement he armed his weapon.

The attack was fast and furious and the President's army fell before it in confusion. The Stormtroopers rallied and fought back, but without their battle wagons they were powerless against the Rebel onslaught. The Pongos panicked and ran from their attackers as fast as their feet could carry them.

"Cowards!" yelled the Stormtrooper Leader Pair and died giving orders to his men to fire on the retreating infantry. The laser fire that cut them down came from the rear.

From that moment the President's troops collapsed and retreated in disarray. They were no match for the rapid rebel battle squadrons which raced into the fight and then raced out again presenting no real targets but poured deadly effective fire into them. Worse, each time a group tried to make a stand rockets slammed into them, and they soon learned not to try to consolidate. What with the attacks from their rear and the racing rebels the Stormtroopers gave up and ran. And then as quickly as they came the Rebels were gone leaving behind a disillusioned and badly mauled fighting force.

The Rebel army had struck its first major blow, but the President's forces, although checked for a while in one sector, continued inexorably onward.

In other sectors, and along the fragmented front wherever the President's forces advanced the same method of attack by the rebels stopped them in their tracks. The Pongos in each arm of the loyalist forces crumbled under the onslaught and panicked leaving the Stormtroopers and the Loyalist soldiers to fight against the fast moving rebel forces. If the President had known how many troops the rebels had he would have realised why the tactics of his enemy worked.

The rebel army numbered less than a quarter of his combined Stormtrooper and Loyalist soldiers, and if the Pongos elected to fight against them the rebel army by rights should have been overwhelmed. In fact, the tactics used by the rebels, attack and disappear, were bound to succeed against a marching army. It seemed that as most resources were earmarked for the invasion of Earth the President underestimated the enemy in his own back yard. This incompetent reading of the rebel army was inexcusable considering that many of the rebels were at one time trained to fight the Zradian way, fiercely with no mercy. As a back up to the rebel army forces a contingent of the Women's Rebel Army destroyed a supply depot that disrupted his physical lines of communication. This was the beginning of a campaign by both Rebel Army forces to disrupt the President's supply lines and force him to use the vulnerable transfer port seeding system which worked fine if all behind the lines was secure, but the rebels had a habit of turning up anywhere.

It was a trait the Stormtroopers detested.

The President smiled at his reflection in the mirror. He was feeling pretty good; pleased with himself, and excited. His armies were on the march at last. Soon the prisoners would be crawling in to the camps and the slaughter could begin; then the rebels (he refused to think of the rebels in upper case) will know who's boss, he thought, proudly. The plan Grul and Lurg gave him was working, and he decided on impulse to call them to his chambers and congratulate them personally. He might even promote them?

"Scribes!"

Two Pairs came running with their screens at the ready.

"We are at your service your Honour," they said bowing.

"We wish the Pair Lurg and Grul to appear in Our presence."

"We will summon him immediately your Honour."

The Pairs backed out scribbling furiously and the President preened himself before the mirror once more turning to catch his profile. He pouted his lips at himself and muttered.

"You fiercesome warrior you!" he said and simpered.

With a shaking hand, his hands seemed to shake most of the time lately, he picked up a glass from his bench and sipped happily. With a sigh he savoured the tasty liquid and stretched his free hand out - it no longer shook.

"Shteady as a rock."

Grul and Lurg stared sightless and very dead under a pile of sandy soil in a corner of the graveyard attached to the Rebel headquarters. Standing slightly crooked at the head of the twin mounds where they were buried was a small sandstone block with a plastic plate attached. The words on the plate declared that Grul and Lurg had died in the service of their President. And even as that worthy was calling for them an electronic image of the plaque, and a short video clip of their execution, was on its way to the President's personal computer via a useful but unknown channel located somewhere in the Amazon jungle on the planet Earth.

The President watched the clip and wept. He left the machine running and stared at the credits as they rolled up the screen.

Producer : Betty/Anthony
Director : Napoleon
Location : wouldn't you love to know
Rodent Productions (3 Sol)
Grul and Lurg dressed by the Rebels
Do not be afraid of the rodents.

"Filthy Bulgers," wailed the President, and clutched his glass draining the contents in one draught and spluttered as the fiery fluid hit the bottom of his throat. He had quite forgotten that Grul and Lurg had defected earlier.

"We hate them!" he screamed.

He thought of ancient times and wondered if his ancestors had the same problems. Did that Bulger's arsehole Glord the Bulging Glorious have this sort of trouble with his own minions? The President was so angry he had all the Pairs in Grul and Lurg's group crawl on their bellies the whole length of the corridors from the palace gates to his throne.

"Is there any reason why We should not have you killed," he raged.

"We are innocent..." began the Group Leader Pair.

"You are guilty as charged - we have spoken!"

The Group Leader Pair whimpered.

"Take them out in the square and cut them to pieces," hissed the President.

One Pair stood up; defiant and screamed at him.

"You drunken despotic murderous old fart...," they began.

Guards cut them to pieces before they could complete their insult and turned to menace the remaining Pairs.

"No, do not kill them here. Drag the scum out of Our sight," said the President with utter contempt. "Better still, send them to a work camp." He was even more pleased when the Pairs groaned in desperation. The Pair were right, he reflected, he was an old fart and felt every short period of it. But, he thought, We will not be refused! He shuddered. A sudden image of hordes of running rodents slipped into his mind and out again. Most disturbing. Most decidedly disturbing.

Dart and Drat walked from the conference room to the Transfer Port feeling a little apprehensive. They were about to embark on the most difficult task of their career. Their brief was to contact the leaders of the Earth Government and help them to defeat the President's armies. Their thoughts ranged wildly from visions of failure to visions of success, and they wrestled with the many unknowns and variables, going over the basic instructions and rehearsing in their minds the greeting they planned to give to their contact on Earth. The High Leader Pair of the New Moral Few had chosen an Earthman named Joseph Green, a journalist with the Examiner, to be their guide. The idea, they argued, was to use the resources of the Examiner to make sure that their efforts to help the people of Earth remained public. The NMF researchers discovered many factions on Earth who would think nothing of using Dart and Drat for their own ends. The northern hemisphere, so the researchers reasoned, seemed the best place to begin. Joseph lived in the market town of Maidstone in Kent on the river Medway, England. An odd name for a place, thought Dart, but then names for places were odd.

He hated Transfer, and whenever he was on one of these missions he liked to think of other more pleasant things. Like black holes in space or his work with the NMF, or counting grains of sand in a bucket, anything but Transfer. He shot a swift empathy wave to his twin and received a reassuring wave back. For a while he felt better. He hoped it would last past Transfer.

At the door of the Transfer Port they stopped and took their packs from the attendant and stepped inside. The door hissed closed and the lights flickered. They felt the familiar but sickening sensation of being taken apart and put back together again and then for a brief moment they were in another similar booth. Several small periods later they felt the same sensation but this time they were diving into the unknown.

Outside the Presidential Palace in First Square pairs passed by nervously. They hurried across the plaza as quickly as their business allowed them. Not that the square itself was ugly; in fact it was one of the most beautiful plazas in First City. Its fountains watered a tasteful arrangement of plants in stone boxes that were arranged in squares in each corner, each with a balance of red, green, yellow and blue plants with the various in-between hues displayed in subtle arrangements. These in turn linked up with the two other squares on the east and west sides of the palace, this main square faced south. Behind, to the north facing side was the service yards walled in and carefully decorated with plants and shrubs. The whole square with the palace in the centre took up an area that would have fitted into Hyde Park, and this was in turn surrounded by the first inner circle from where all roads radiated. The rest of First City, divided into its four sectors spread out with buildings arranged in the sectors starting with the lowest levels in First Circle, taller ones in Second Circle and so on to Circle Five where the tallest building swere located down to the low levels of Circle Ten. With the palace in the centre First City, from the air, resembled the famous photograph of a drop of water splashing into a cup already filled.

Citizens of First City knew not to linger too close to the palace and many, unless they were ordered there, kept as far away from the place as possible. Apart from the likelihood of being dragged into the palace as prisoners charged with make-believe crimes, there were the execution stands.

On this day, the day the President learned of Grul and Lurg's execution, there were four pairs chained to the posts bleeding to death from the cruel slashing by the executioners. The executioners were dressed to look like Carnibeasts and wore specially made steel claws on their hands and feet with which they tore into the bodies of their victims.

It was a slow and painful death.

Sometimes the victims would lay wounded and dying for as many as three whole turns, screaming and moaning and calling for a quick release.

The penalty for giving them a merciful release was to suffer the same fate. Pairs rarely risked helping them out. The Guards, the Polisocs and the Dog Squad Elite were always willing to add more victims to their count. Besides, the President himself liked to watch, and sometimes he could be seen standing on a balcony sipping his gin and tonics enjoying the spectacle. It was better, in spite of the lovely gardens, the fine architecture and the imaginative fountains, to pass on your way as quickly as possible. Apart from sector blue where urchin Pairs, and the families of workers lived, no children were seen in the centre of First City. Zradian children could at times be heard but they were rarely seen. No Zradian parent would take their young Pairs out to see the sights of their city, and even in the smaller cities Zradian children were kept out of sight of the Polisocs.

The sight of the red and black uniforms was enough to encourage any small Pair to behave themselves. And of course, the children of Polisoc Pairs were always a threat and ordinary children stayed home, or behaved themselves at school not wishing their families to end up in the Polisoc pig pens, or them to end up in the work camp orphanages. Parent Pairs preferred not to expose their young to the awful sights outside the palace which was a factor the President and his High Command ignored.

The administration in First City accepted the regime as normal but what many senior Pairs not noticed was that in provinces many Pairs were beginning to question the actions of the President and his vicious minions. One of the measures most provincial administrations took was to quietly remove the method of public execution from their cities.

The sight of such a racial memory[5] destroying their citizens was a little too much to stomach.

Besides, most of the reasoned, watching the sullen and crowds measuring them up for a swifter demise was an uncomfortable experience. It was an experience not shared by the President.

---

[5] *In earlier times it was remembered that the poor Zradian Dog - the Lupe - was once the prey of a large cat-like creature. As a species they solved the problem in part by forming packs to turn the tables on the feline hunter. The Zradian people themselves shared DNA and a genetic coding with the Lupe, hence the innate tendency to chase anything feline.*

Salisbury Plain to Nevada

The problem with exercises was that at times people took them too seriously. Another problem was that when the media get hold of an idea there was no way of getting the buggers out of the way or of persuading them to report properly. The media liked tanks and armoured vehicles, especially the new hover wagons that used the most up to date solar power source. General Robert Brown preferred the skill of the foot soldiers but instead, for this exercise the main focus was on the flashy exhibitionism of the armoured divisions. Let them show off their battle wagons and their high tech detection systems, and let us get on with ordinary soldiering, the General thought, disgusted at the media hype. The laser guided weapons his troops carried were every much as high tech as the Cavalry boys, as he liked to call them, and if it came to the crunch it was his weapons that made the difference. When the fighting became close and it was soldier against soldier, his forces were the ones that eventually sorted out the enemy.

A messenger ran up and came to a rigid, saluting halt.

"Message from Headquarters sir!"

General Roberts read it and nodded.

"Good man. Carry on," he said, and took the missive with him to his own canvas headquarters. The seated officers turned to face him as he waved them down with a gesture of his free hand and grinned at them.

"The exercise is on chaps, get your markers ready and will somebody be good enough to bring me a fresh gin fizz?"

There was a scurry of activity and men rushed out of the tent to attend to their part in the exercise and his batman hurried in with a fresh gin fizz.

"Good man," he said. "Now we will show this lot how a real army works."

He took the drink and nearly upset it when he swept an arm in the general direction of the exercise arena, in particular intending to include the world press contingent. "For King and country, as they say, we'll show them the best of British technology. What we have here today will show them how ready we are to stop any damned invasion," he said, and had no idea how prophetic his words were to be.

The operator Pair sat at their console and watched, amused, at the activity on Salisbury Plain. They were amused because the two sides engaged in mock battle had no idea that soon they would be involved in a real one. They watched the British Pongos deploy in formation and attack each other for the benefit of the media and the umpires, who marched around with armbands on telling the troops when and where they should stop. They chuckled when the pongos grumpily broke off the action and wandered back to their tents for a break.

"They won't be doing that when our troops get down there," said one half Pair, and grinned at his twin.

"Not very good are they?" observed his twin and pointed at the helicopter. "What is that thing?"

"I have no idea, but it has a whole pile of people inside it. See down there by the large building there are more people watching what is going on. The whole thing seems such a waste of time."

His twin was about to reply but at that moment machines hurtled over the ridges and bore down on the targets and just when the Pair thought they might see a demonstration of the firepower the screens suddenly filled with pictures of gambolling cartoon rodents. Some danced in country and western style line dances, others raced around and changed colour as they wound in and out of the line of dancing rabbits and waltzing squirrels. All of them looked excruciatingly cute, impossibly happy, embarrassingly delightful, and no matter what the operator Pair did to change the images back to their observations of the exercise on Salisbury Plain they had no effect. And then, with devastating effect on their equilibrium, already affected by the appearance of the rodents, the screens were filled with images of extremely cute and playful kittens. The awful racial memory suddenly filled their minds with confused images of an ancient mangy dog, they knew as a Lupe, being chased by hungry felines. Their reaction was to turn and fight, and it was so strong that no Zradian male could resist it without treatment.

The operator Pair wailed in traumatic agony, and dropped from their stools to the floor rocking to and fro trying their best not to slobber and attack the screens. They knew, because they had taken the psychological treatment, that they should resist reacting to the dreadful images. Instead of doing what the psychologists taught them to do, that is to turn away from the screens and pretend it isn't happening, they dropped into the foetal position and locked their bodies close to each other as if they were laying in their mother's womb.

They lay sobbing and sucking each other's thumbs and shuddered visibly when the strains of A Whiter Shade of Pale wafted through the speakers. They may have survived the trauma if the tune had simply played itself out but in the melody they detected the addition of quiet kittenish meows and adult cat purrs and trills, and with their resistance gone their minds cracked.

Their relief found them laying curled up in a corner blank eyed and slack jawed staring at a screen that displayed the message they had been waiting for.

Status One approved – begin off world operation.

With a twin look of contempt the relief Pair called for aides to remove the psychotics, and with calm efficiency began the invasion of Britain via the open space of Salisbury Plain. The area outside the pillars of Stonehenge were ideal for locating the temporary Transfer Ports, and those Pairs who did not end up as part of the standing stones took the time to walk around and admire the marvels of their construction.

Of course the sudden appearance of a large group of non-ticket holders in the delicate archaeological area from which the public were normally excluded, annoyed the custodians. The invading Pairs, who had set about clearing the car park of unwanted vehicles by the simple method of torching them with plasma guns, stared blankly at the complaining Wardens.

"Oy mate, you can't do that!" said one warden.

"Why not?" replied the Leader Pair, "It seems to be the only effective way," and along with the other employees, and the terrified paying customers they herded them all into the exhibition area under armed guard.

"You are now prisoners of war, and are therefore the property of the Zradian Republic. Long live the President!" said the Leader Pair.

And so, against the splendid backdrop of the sweep of Salisbury Plain and the magnificent standing stones of Britain's most famous ancient monument, the Zradian forces began the invasion of Europe.

The President of the United States looked at his Vice President and smiled.

"I am sorry Denise but yo' all cain't ask me to be-lieve that. Ah can concede we might be attacked." Pause significantly. "But by Aliens?"

"I'm sorry Horace, but the report says that's what is happening," she replied with a sigh knowing that their aides had worked hard on the information aware of the President's reluctance to believe amateurs and the British. "Our own people say the same."

"They are always damn well stoned," he retorted. "I'm more interested in what the Indians and the Chinese are doing."

"Yeah, well soon they won't be doing nothing," she said, aware her grammar was falling apart.

"What do you mean?"

"The Army have decided that as the prospect of invasion is immanent they are not willing to supply information to India, nor are they willing to continue doing the same for the Chinese. The army apologise for the double dealing but the American economy needs the funds. They said. The satellite system is more use against the invaders."

The President looked at her with unconcealed hatred.

She smiled knowing he was having a hard time coping with the fact that she had knowledge she was not supposed to have. He also had to cope with the fact that she was getting more popular as his term progressed. The American public were ready for another woman President, although whether or not they were ready for a black lesbian was yet to be proved. She hoped they were. Somehow during the last two years Horace Revere had decided he didn't like his running mate after all and she knew it. The feeling was mutual. Right now she had to convince President Horace Revere that invasion of Earth by aliens was about to happen.

"I don't believe it because there are no invading armies; no space ships flying around and I have no warning from my own staff," said the President.

Denise Walker smiled at him. "I'm sorry sir but the reason I am here is to let you know that an alien force has just landed in the Nevada testing area. Sorry but that sort of stuffs your ideas up completely doesn't it?"

"Well then why isn't something being done about it then?" exploded the President.

"I guess they are waiting for you to give them the go ahead," she said, calmly.

"They don't need my say so, God help me!" shouted the President.

"No sir, but they do think you should be totally informed, and if you hadn't interrupted me I could have easily explained what has happened so far but I think I'll leave that up to your military advisers to do that. I have to see a few people about an election campaign. See you."

She walked out of the Oval office with her nose in the air leaving the President red faced and fuming to read the report himself. Instead he picked up the phone and when the voice answered he yelled angrily.

"For chrissake will some motherfucker tell me what's going on in this parish?"

The desert crawled with Pairs and vehicles. Stores of food and arms were stacked on the support wagons and troops piled on board the huge battle wagons. The flimsy structures protecting the

Transfer Ports fluttered in the sandy breeze. Wagons dropped the last few hundred millimetres onto the sand and slid out onto the desert to be checked and run up before joining the line. Pairs gathered together in their troops sometimes milling around when some of their number failed to appear, and at others forming into more or less organised groups. Thus the Zradian Invasion Force came together and began its inexorable move on the continent of America. The Supreme Leader Pair gave the order to move, and like the fingers of spilt fluid on a polished floor the soldiers spread out over the desert.

The first American forces they met up with had no idea how many Zradian troops there were, nor did they know that the Zradians had landed. They were busy checking the radiation monitors scattered throughout the area. The task would be much easier the Lieutenant said, somewhat acidly, if local marksmen didn't use them as target practice. When the patrol made contact with the Zradian invaders that was exactly what the lieutenant and his patrol became, target practice for the Zradian laser cannons.

There were no survivors.

When the patrol failed to report in at the allotted time the commanding officer dispatched a helicopter patrol to find them. It never came back and the Colonel in turn alerted her Brigadier. The twenty third Army division sent a full scale probe complete with back up air support, and at approximately one hundred kilometres north of Las Vegas they met the Zradians heading south. The battalion recoiled and staggered back bewildered and scared. Headquarters had warned them there was something out there doing something but they had not expected a full scale invasion. Their sceptical officers assured them it was the top brass having kittens over nothing.

When the rank and file soldiers got a vicious mauling from the invading army they heartily cursed their officers as 'a load of useless faggots with as much idea of what's what as a dead skunk stinking in the middle of the road', and refused to fight unless somebody identified what it was they were fighting.

The airwaves were busy with to and fro insults for a short frustrating time until a harassed Lieutenant Colonel demanded the High Command get off their fat butts and use the satellites.

When the High Command saw the results, and had passed the buck until somebody was brave enough to tell the President, Las Vegas was already under siege, and the United States was fighting its first war on home soil since its last battles with the almost extinct indigenous peoples. And, if the Pentagon was anything to go by, it didn't much like the idea.

It was more or less at this point that the mathematics explaining the Doomsday Bomb arrived on the international communications systems. Internet users and Bubblenet subscribers downloaded the equations, and before the scientific community had a chance to report to their governments and give them the opportunity to fudge the answers the news of the Doomsday Bomb spread around the world.

The communiqué was accompanied by a message that puzzled Americans and non-Americans alike.

"Do not be afraid of the Rodents - I told him - Julie don't go! beware the Ides of March - do not be afraid of the Whiter Shades of Pail - 1812 and cannons!"

"What is this shit?" asked President Revere.

"I'm sorry sir, we don't understand it either but it comes from a location in South America - in the Amazon, sir." Replied an aide, hastily.

The President glanced at him angrily.

Gambling is a sin - and the wages of sin...

General Schwarzkopf slumped in his seat. The enemy were winning. All efforts to contain them failed. General Wiseman, in the North was having no more success and, according to the Sat-Nav read-outs the enemy was pushing East heading all the way to the Mississippi.

His own forces were stuck trying to hold a line long enough to ensure the smooth evacuation of Las Vegas. Stupidly the organised crime syndicates refused to move but the President had decreed that all citizens should be protected. And that was his problem. Did he stay and evacuate them by force or did he let them die? He had enough trucks and troops to help those without transport to head south for Boulder. His commanders were spread out now searching for refugees. He felt let down when his officers reported that some of the major casino owners had decided to stay put. Nobody, they insisted, was going to move in on their turf.

"The President of the United States insists that all personnel be evacuated for their own safety," explained one harassed Major.

"Yeah and let you move in on us you black assed bitch," came the suspicious reply.

She called headquarters and was told to try again.

"I repeat, there is an invasion by enemy forces. The President of the US of A himself insists all personnel be evacuated. We are not interested in your assets, only your personal safety at this time. We have to ask you to cooperate."

The reply to her appeal was a series of rifle and pistol shots.

"This is how we cooperate nigger!"

"Motherfuckers," swore the Major ducking behind a riot shield. "Sergeant, return their fire and let's haul ass."

She watched the tracer bullets rattle on the gatehouse and smiled with satisfaction when a couple of well aimed rockets ripped the gate to bits. There was no return fire. Why did they bother, she asked herself, let the suckers rot. White shit, she thought, angrily and spat on the dusty road.

Major Frances Calhoun ordered her troops onto the next mansion and was not surprised when she received similar replies.

"Sergeant, tell the rest of the company to can the exercise. The General can go spit. If these assholes want to stay here and get fried then let them. We will go find some real people."

"Yes Ma'am," replied the Sergeant, sounding relieved.

General Schwarzkopf listened to the reports and slowly tore up his jottings.

"You sure all friendly civilians are on their way?"

His Aide nodded. "All units report similar status Sir."

"Gerry, you're a pompous ass."

"Yes sir."

"Send the order to fall back."

"Sir."

The General watched his Aide dash off to the radio truck and shook his head. It was a pity, he thought, that Gerry was such a prize jerk; he was still shaking his head when he climbed into his truck. "What are we going to do Sir?" asked the driver.

"We fall back, so go steady and ignore the mansions. We head for the hills and let's hope that is as far as we go," he said as he settled into his seat.

They drove out of the city and took up a position well south on a low ridge watching the troops reform. In addition to the troops a long line of army and commandeered vehicles carried the citizens of Las Vegas south to Boulder City and beyond.

"Tell them to keep going on down to Needles if they have to," he said.

"What everybody?" Asked his adjutant.

"Unless they want to head west to California or go east to New Mexico, as long as they scram out of here," he said.

The General watched them go and shook his head. It was a sad sight, he thought, Americans dispossessed in their own land, and for a brief moment he had the uncomfortable thought that this had all happened before. To the north black columns of smoke rose into the sky and drifted in the wind creating a haze that seemed to roll down on Las Vegas. The city was lost and they had to move on. Retreat was a bitter pill for the general to swallow and he hesitated before picking up the microphone.

"Advise General Headquarters we have abandoned Las Vegas to its fate and that all responsible citizens have been evacuated. Tell them we are digging in until they are clear and request air strikes on call."

"Yes sir. I'll relay as soon as sir."

The General sighed. He hated retreats. What's more he hated the idea of fighting and losing on American soil. More than that he hated the idea of another nation offering to pay for it all. If the Japanese put money and weapons up front, he thought, they would want Uncle Sam's arms and legs as repayment. The President was right. We do it the American Way and Goddamn the Nipponese! All American armies fighting to save American Soil, American Women and Children and the American Way Of Life!

"Long Live America!" he demanded.

"Yes Sir!" reiterated the driver.

He watched the last of the trucks roll out onto the road and gave the order for his own to move out. He intended to make a stand beyond Boulder using the hills as a defensive line. His soldiers would give a good account of themselves at least. He was sure of that, but first they needed somewhere from which to fight.

"Orders from headquarters sir. They say remove all citizens, repeat all, from Vegas sir."

"Tell them we have, sparks."

"Yes sir."

General Schwarzkopf smiled to himself. Two birds with one stone, he thought, get rid of the casinos and their owners. Good, good, neither are useful to America. Against God's laws, he thought, gambling is a sin and the wages of sin are death.

Much later on the hills above a long plain he watched the distant spark of explosions flash in the night sky. Las Vegas, he assumed, was burning. After their meal he called the officers to the Field Headquarters and explained what he wanted from them. Each officer went away with their duty settled and a fair idea of their resources and support. All they had to do now was organise and await events. A calm settled on the positions as sentries and lookouts took up positions. As a precaution he sent patrols out back toward the city and retired to his bunk to sleep.

General Schwarzkopf slept deeply, dreaming soldiering dreams and woke refreshed and ready for action.

Zradian Army High Leader Pair Zrat and Traz ordered their wagon to halt on the edge of the Earth city. He surveyed the empty streets and the abandoned buildings with a satisfied smile.

"Messy place," said Zrat.

"Not laid out at all well," agreed Traz.

"We move on?" said Zrat.

"Yes and see what we can find," replied Traz.

"Driver Pair move on," said Zrat.

The wagon moved steadily along the wide streets pushing abandoned vehicles aside and stopping now and then when Traz and Zrat wanted to look at a building, or examine something else that took their fancy. Behind them other wagons fanned out into the city stopping now and then to let troops out to forage. The inner city was empty although the lighting and the fountains still worked. On the outskirts of the city they were surprised when missiles hurtled at them from the perimeters and roofs of large dwellings. A few Pairs were wounded before they dropped the hatches. Zrat and Traz flicked the radar and the heat seekers on looking for the source.

Enemy ensconced in the buildings. The Leader Pair called on the Comsec.

"Shall we deal with them?"

"Try one wagon at first. If that doesn't work give them Bulgers breath."

A few short periods later a huge column of black smoke rose into the air and the wagon rocked on its cushion.

"Sorry Your Honour. The inmates resisted so we retaliated. The laser cannon destroyed the whole building. Shall we continue and eliminate the rest?"

"Of course. We have an Army to fight but why put up with an enemy in our back yard?"

There was a satisfied chuckle and a few periods later another column appeared rising darkly into the sky. Within a half day the fortressed families of organised crime were wiped from the face of Las Vegas leaving their casinos and strip joints to their uncaring usurpers, the Zradian invaders. That evening, after eating their nutritional sausage, the battle wagon commanders used the large, ugly buildings of Las Vegas for target practice.

In the morning the sun rose to reveal a smoking pile of rubble.

"Right," said Traz. "It is time we moved on."

The Zradian army left the ruins of Las Vegas to the rats and cats to squabble over and headed south.

General Schwarzkopf gazed out over the plain and drew air in through his lips with a low whistle. A column of vehicles were backed up at the barrier halted by the soldiers. He used his binoculars and saw that the lead vehicles anyway were loaded up with people, pets and belongings. The officer was arguing with some of the people.

"Get me the officer will you?" He asked.

Moments later she replied.

"Major Calhoun here sir."

"What's happening soldier?"

"I'm trying to explain that there is no road through Vegas sir."

"Tell them to turn back."

"I tried that sir but they say they want to go west."

"Send the assholes along 95 and tell them to sort it out from there. Why the panic?"

"There's a rumour around that the government is planning on nuking the city sir."

"Holy shit why haven't they told me?"

"A local radio DJ heard it so the lead asshole says."

"Tell the asshole to get down 95 or turn the rest back and do it now Major."

"Yes sir, with pleasure sir!" She said and he watched her giving orders to her troops who immediately aimed their weapons at the drivers and the mob. Four armoured vehicles blocked the road and aimed their weapons at the mob.

Major Calhoun called on her sergeant.

"Sergeant, why are people so thick headed?" she asked.

"They is frightened I guess and I'm sure that being called a 'fuckin' nigger bitch' is not what you want to hear at this hour ma'am?" the Sergeant replied.

"True, but our orders are to look after the people."

"If theys too stubborn to obey orders they ain't people ma'am."

"Samuel we will try not to shoot them but soon we gotta go and the sooner they are gone the better. Let's move 'em on!"

The leader and spokesman of the group stood belligerently staring at the soldiers. He still held his rifle at the ready but he looked nervous now that her troops had taken up positions. Her odder to block the road came too late for a crowd of men in pick-ups who had barrelled into Vegas fully armed intent on shooting the invaders.

Twenty vehicles had driven along the Parkway and so far none had returned. Her orders didn't include chasing after idiots. This one was about to lead his friends and neighbours to their deaths.

"Mister, my General suggests you and your people take highway 95 and keep going. Now, which one of you is the radio man?"

The big man pointed at a young man dressed in shorts and tee shirt with a baseball cap turned the wrong way on his head.

"Him, he heard it and tole us all to git outta here. We figured he was right. Your friggin' general ordered us out and the TV tells us to go but nobody tole us about the nuke until Harris here give us the news. We figgered going west was best. The eastern roads is blocked with traffic."

"So, you go south instead mister."

"Shoot, that ain't where we want to go."

"My army says you do," she said and drew her side arm. Cocking it she pointed it at the man.

He raised his rifle.

His companions backed away leaving him on his own.

"It's either my pistol shot, my men's rifle shots or you change your stupid mind and get going down 95 mister. Your choice."

In the tense silence she heard the click of the rifle's safety catch and watched as the big man lowered it.

Sweat poured down his face and his hands shook as he ejected the shell. He looked at her with fear and like his friend he backed away.

"Yes ma'am, we will take 95," he said.

"Good, I am glad we can agree," she said. Behind her Samuel laughed. "Now, you, young Harris you better go with the soldiers and talk to my General."

She watched as the vehicles turned onto the ramp to 95 anxious to make sure they all followed. It took over an hour for the road to clear which gave her sappers time to set the charges and blow the highway.

Major Calhoun looked back along the road and saw the columns of smoke rising from Las Vegas. Her own contribution could not be seen but at least she was on her way.

"At least the rubble will stop any citizens going north," she said.

"Yes ma'am but I don't think it will stop the invaders for long," said the sergeant.

Their car was in the middle of the column and she was glad to see that other than military vehicles the road was empty. They arrived at the halt and she alighted to report the General.

She saluted and was about to give a verbal report when General Schwarzkopf, grim faced, cut her off.

"Bad news Major, grab some food on the move and we move out."

"The nuke sir?"

"You got it soldier, the nuke, so God help me!"

Zrat and Traz gazed through the scope at the hills ahead. They were glad of the bright sunlight; nights on Earth were dark; too dark to see anything, and there was not enough infra-red detectors to serve the whole army. He cursed C&D Munitions that was supposed to supply the wagons with them for not giving them the best knowing that the the contract was pared to the bone because the bribes were too heavy, and what money was needed for the equipment was spent on greasing palms. He ought to know that because he received a fair share of it for himself. Not only that but their communications were interrupted by strange messages and a tune that played at regular intervals, and whatever they tried to do they could not get rid of the interference. The army ground to a halt spreading across the road resting while their engineers tried to sort out the problem. About mid day Earth time they were surprised by a group of speeding vehicles that spilled over the brow of the hill from the south and stopped, disgorging a horde of scruffy Earth men. Missiles rattled against the armoured sides of the wagons and some Pairs and Half Pairs fell wounded yelling in agony.

"Wimps," said Traz. "Give the order to open fire."

The lasers homed in on their attackers pouring lines of fire at them cutting them down before many of them could turn and run. They burned like lizards on a rock and the attack was all over.

"What was all that about?" asked Traz.

"Bulgers if I know," replied his twin.

But the enemy on the hills above were different. They had real weapons and knew what to do. Not only that but they were in a good defensive position. Zrat and Traz's orders were explicit. Neutralise all ground forces. The task would be a Nong's sight easier if the communications system didn't keep fouling up. Transfer and supplies, slowed down and then as suddenly as the crazy enemy attack had occurred the Comsec cleared and they were on the move again.

"We will have to fan out and attack on a wide front," said Traz.

"We should begin now I think, but first we should call HQ and ask for clearance?"

"Confirmed, I will deal with it," said Traz.

He spoke into the pod and explained their situation. The computer screen flashed a modified plan and for a few small periods they examined it, finally passing on their orders to the Leader Pairs. With concentration Traz and Zrat directed the assault against General Schwarzkopf's forces and so began the battle of Boulder.

Before them on their screens the enemy plan unfolded and piece by piece the Zradian army attacked each point. Traz and Zrat's wagon was protected by an electronic carapace which deflected incoming missiles yet allowed them to have a visual view of the enemy positions. The enemy air strikes unnerved them but the Pairs on the lasers retaliated and drove the first wave off. Wave two was more cautious but by this time the soldiers were ready for them. It was during the third of a series of strikes that Zrat noted the supply figures were dropping.

"Looks like we are running down on gear," he said. "Call for replenishment."

An aide Pair made the call and a few short periods later grovelled before them with a flimsy clutched in their hands.

"We have a problem your Honour," he said.

"Go on."

"HQ are having trouble seeding Transfer ports. They will have to bring supplies in by wagon your Honour."

"Well tell them to get on with it."

"Er, there is also a strange addendum to the message your Honour."

"And what is that?"

"They urge us not to be afraid of the rodents

"Bulgers - the idiots."

The Pair scuttled back to their station and tapped at the keyboard rapidly.

"Conserve fire and make every laser count," said Traz.

"Conserve fire and make every rocket count," ordered General Schwarzkopf. "Supplies are getting short and High Command don't seem to be answering our calls. I am worried. We may have to withdraw. Tell the liaison officer to warn the citizens of Boulder. I am afraid we will have to evacuate again. I hope Mexico is willing to take us."

The General slipped out of the vehicle and slid down between two rocks close to the edge of the cliff. Kneeling to keep a low profile he swept the plain below with his binoculars grunting occasionally muttering angrily. "Bloody headquarters..."

The skinny DJ had frightened him.

"Well boy?"

"I...I picked up a message on another station. They said the President was planning a nuclear strike on the enemy sir," he said and handed him a message sheet. "My producer verified it."

The General read it, his face getting angrier by the second until at last he looked up at the sweating DJ.

"I thought you might want to know."

"Damn right I want to know! Is all the city on the move?"

"Yes sir."

"Thank you. Staff!" He shouted the last word, and ran to the truck.

Stiffly he informed them of the Radio message and ordered a complete and rapid withdrawal.

"Fair on down to Mexico and pick up civilians on the way all the way down route ninety-five!"

The General ordered a small force to keep up a harassing fire and ordered the rest to prepare to move. Within the hour they were ready and he gave the final orders sending the bulk of the forces off behind the civilians and stayed behind to move off with the rearguard. On the heights above their position he halted to take a last look back. He sat with the truck facing the north and for another ten minutes gazed through the protective slats over the heights. The last of his force rolled past and with a shrug he ordered the driver to move on. The airstrikes he ordered had done enough, and when he had given the order to move out he called the airforce. "Listen, Colonel, we won't be able to sight for your targets, I suggest you stop the missions and back off, er, you also need to know what else as well," He said and when the Colonel agreed he told him.

Horace Revere's hand shook. The invaders were rolling up his forces and American citizens were being driven from their homes. American citizens were dying on American soil. If his armies didn't stop the invader he was in dead trouble. That lesbian Walker would have him by the balls if he failed. He had to do something. He hesitated and let his hand drop to his side. He wished it wouldn't shake so much. He needed a drink. He thought about the options and knew which one he would have to choose. The Pentagon scenario was clear. The main enemy forces were in two areas and neither were close enough to major centres to cause horrendous problems. The percentage local kill, his advisers said, was low. The effect on the enemy would be devastating. He hoped. He picked up the telephone and a voice answered.

"Yes sir?"

"We will take the Red option Miles," he said, and gulped. "I will confirm electronically immediately. I expect you will warn general Schwarzkopf?"

"Yes sir we are doing that now sir."

Good, good and God bless America," Horace Revere said, and put the telephone down.

He steadied himself and walked across to the console. It was already activated, and all he had to do was place his palm on the pad and gaze at the check lens for thirty seconds while it checked his iris pattern. He followed the prompts and pressed the buttons on the keyboard in the correct sequence and sat in the seat and waited. Thirty seconds later he responded to the confirmation signal and placed his key in the slot, and again he waited. The screen remained blank, and then with a dull musical tone a message appeared. With a deep breath he counted the numbers down and turned his key. The message changed again and remained like that for one minute. He turned the key again and the screen flickered and showed a message.

Red Option Activated.

And like it or not he was committed.

In the Pentagon an operator, chosen at random from the staff on duty, palmed her pad and ran through the sequence in time with the President. The only difference between what the President had done and what she did was that the operator actually fired the missiles.

In fact, although the President himself had actually, by turning his key the second time, begun the sequence and was under the impression he had already fired the missiles there was still much to do before they took off for their targets. In the operations room Lieutenant Madeleine Orams palmed the pad and waited for confirmation. The sequence took two minutes and with a slight shift of her head she moved so that the check lens could read her eyes. Five minutes later the screen glowed with the simple message.

Cleared to begin sequence.

She concentrated on following the sequence and when the screen finally cleared and the page was replaced with the simple path options she called out to her superior officer.

"Waiting clearance sir!"

"Clearance denied. We still haven't contacted Schwarzkopf. We cannot at the moment get through. It seems there is a block on communications to that area. Repeat sequence in hours two."

Madeleine Orams relaxed and picked up her book. All she was required to do now was to sit and wait. Standing by was the term. Sitting down was standing by.

Two hours and several chapters later she began the sequence again.

"Clearance still denied."

Three more times she went through the procedure and eventually she was told to wait for another hour.

"We are in contact with a local radio station. The general's communication system is blocked – we are awaiting confirmation."

She tried an hour later and this time when she reached the critical path she was ordered to continue. With a dry mouth she pressed button Y and watched the red panel glow, and a line of figures roll out underneath it. They stopped at zero at exactly 11: 21:32 EST and below the time figure a command.

<LOGOUT>

She pressed the escape button and sat back in her seat.

"All over," she said. "Missiles away. Er, what did General Schwarzkopf say sir?"

"Nothing," said the Brigadier. "We couldn't locate him so we went ahead anyway."

Madeleine Orams gasped and paled.

"We ... we've killed our own ..." she began and dropped her head into her hands.

"Maybe, maybe not. He's either a dead hero and due a medal or he will collect one himself from the President. Either way is okay with us."

"Bastards," she said, softly.

"Yeah, sad ain't it?"

General Schwarzkopf asked the driver to stop on the top of the rise. They were a long way from Boulder and behind them on the road was the rearguard of One Mobile Company and that was it. He could see them winding their way up the road several kilometres away. Beyond them were columns of smoke that told him the enemy had reached Boulder.

One Mobile crested the ridge and filtered through the lines and the general waited until they had passed before moving on.

"Okay driver move on," he said, and as the truck rolled down the steep slope he turned to look and what he saw made him gasp.

"Stop the fucking truck!" he yelled.

In the sky falling like a dying signal rocket was a pink light and hastily he donned his thick protective glasses. He watched the weapon drop and explode at ground level and yelled to the driver to move. They dropped over the ridge and down the road as a huge blast rattled the rocks around them and a mushroom cloud rose high above. Their radio communications crackled and ceased altogether.

The radio silence was profound. There were no crackles, no hissing, no spurious beeps that happened when communications began to break down, and no satellite indicator. The system had completely broken down. This, he knew, was the direct result of a nuclear explosion. The short hairs on the back of his neck stiffened as his fear level increased.

General Schwarzkopf shuddered and swore. He swore long and profoundly, and wiped imaginary sweat from his brow. That was close, he thought. If an alert DJ in a hick radio station hadn't picked up the news General Barry Schwarzkopf would be frying on the edge of a nuclear crater by now. He had planned to go down into the valley and take the war to the enemy.

"Shit, that was close," he said. "Too damn close."

Tzu

Tzu slipped sideways and kicked out high, spinning with controlled energy and striking with both hands before taking the wrist of his attacker and flipping his body in an arc onto the mat. He controlled his own fall and stood up immediately, and faced the young man poised ready for his next move.

"Good attack Gerry," he said. "And good recovery."

Gerry bowed politely and smiled.

"Thank you Master," he said. "I worked hard to learn it."

"Now defend from the same move," said Tzu, attacking hard and fast. The young man missed his footing and dropped to the floor and Tzu instantly locked his arms in a back scissors hold and sat grinning as the young man swivelled his head to look up at Tzu puzzled.

"What happened?" he gasped.

"You never learn proper move," said Tzu. "Too bloody cocky."

He helped the younger man up and stood smiling benevolently.

"Lesson number one to three hundred - never believe you have mastered anything."

"Yes Master," Gerry said and smiled. "Too bloody cocky."

They both laughed grasping hands and slapping each other affectionately.

"You a very good student," said Tzu.

"You a very good teacher," said Gerry.

"Thank you," said Tzu. "After training you wanted to talk to me?"

"Yes, if you don't mind I may as well ask you now," Gerry said, his face serious.

"Go ahead."

"As you know I am Julian Renfrew's probation officer."

Tzu nodded.

"The police have asked me if I have any idea of his whereabouts. I promised to ask you if you knew where he is. I'm sorry I have to ask but the police want to find him and they know he was coming here for training."

Tzu looked thoughtful judging that Gerry was actually embarrassed and took his time answering. "I have not seen him since the day I left Mister Byrde's factory. If I had him with me I would give him up. Cannot afford bad reputation," he said.

"Thank you Master I will tell them," Gerry said.

In his room much later Tzu thought of Gerry and let his speculation drift to Julian. He relaxed in his chair and went through the events of the last few weeks in his mind. He began with the increase in orders for plastic tokens. The token order was huge, nearly double and he hoped Byrde's factory could keep up with production. Then there was the need to increase his franchised factories for other goods. His business set up required a strong hand at the helm he had decided and handed over the cleaning contract of Byrde's factory to his nephew. That same day his car was torched by rivals? Or aliens? Was the attack meant for him or Byrde? Then there was Julian Renfrew's disappearance after his escape from custody. He smiled, thinking of the naked fireman. Then there was the explosion at the Bywater Road allotments. He would think about that one later. Tzu sat thinking about all these facts for a long time quietly controlling his breathing and letting the information slot into his mind to interact with the myriad of tiny bits of related and unrelated news he absorbed each day. He was still sitting and thinking when his niece knocked gently and walked in and placed a tray of food on his desk.

"Aunty says you need something to eat," she said.

He reached out a hand and covered hers.

"Tell her she is too kind," he said.

She bowed politely and went out.

"Too kind," he echoed as she closed the door.

He switched on the television and watched the news amused when he listened to Prime minister Smith announcing he was about to meet the Aliens, Dart and Drat from Zrad. "Silly bugger," he said when Smith made some politically pompous remarks, and switched the television off.

Tzu picked up the telephone and punched Byrde's number. Thinking about his business and Richard Byrde's part in it had created many questions in his mind. Byrde, he thought, might know the answers to some of them. Or he might not. After six rings Byrde's answer phone cut in.

"I am not home for an unspecified period - if you have an urgent message please call my office or, if this is Tzu or Arthur, you have Emily's mother's number. I will call you as soon as I get home." Click.

"Richard - I want to talk to you - not urgently but soon please," he said.

Next he made a call to Arthur's university number and when a strange voice answered he was wary.

"The Professor is not here but his lady friend is. You can talk to her," said the voice.

Marjorie took over and tearfully she explained what had happened.

"Colin and his men are not to blame, we were taken completely by surprise. We think the aliens have taken him. I'm going crazy thinking about him Tzu."

"Ah, so Dart and Drat are trying to help?"

"Yes, yes, they are. I have no idea what to do and, and you can imagine how I am feeling," she said. He could hear the worry in her voice.

"We must try and find him," he said and listened to her as she let out her fears finally saying pleasant words before she cut the connection too overcome to speak.

Tzu hung up and switched on the radio.

The tune A Whiter Shade of Pale drifted and with a sigh Tzu listened to the song until it ended. "I am beginning to dislike that song," he said. But he did not turn off the radio. He was disturbed because of Arthur's disappearance and not being able to telephone Byrde. And what about that young Renfrew, he thought, where on Earth has he got to? Mixed in with that thought was the echo of the reason why Richard Byrde Senior had employed him in the first place – he smiled – one day he would have to tell Byrde the story. His thoughts were interrupted by a light knock of his door and the entrance of his daughter.

"Father," she began. "We must make plans for your birthday."

He smiled gently. "We must make plans? You tell me what you want to do and I will approve. I am sure you and your mother have everything in hand already."

"Father, we need to know where you want the party to take place and who you would especially like to come," she said, and bowed her head. "It is a special day for all of us Father."

"Sue, my daughter, you and your mother make it a special day. I will honour that and enjoy it. Invite all the family. I will give you a list of people outside the family you can invite. We will hold it in the Villa's reception rooms and let there be no banquet, but we will have a buffet meal and dancing and Mah Jong and cards and singing and... a special Training Day for our Kung Fu Instructors. Invite them too!"

"Yes Father," said Sue. "We will invite them all."

"And we will need extra staff and Portaloos and wash basins and decorations and fireworks ... we must have fireworks!"

Sue giggled. "You see," she said. "We have arranged it all."

Tzu smiled broadly and waved her out of the room.

"Go, my daughter, do your worst," he said.

He watched her close the door on her way out and smiled again. A pity, he thought, that Arthur will not be there nor perhaps Richard.

"I wish I knew what happened to Arthur," he said.

Kord and Krod sat in the darkness clutching each other fearfully. Their every waking moment was filled with fear. Each time they heard a door open or when they heard a footfall outside their room they panicked expecting to be dragged away and tortured. Something the Earth medics gave them calmed them down a little but their inherent terror of the dreaded Polisocs[6] was enough to keep their demented mind filled with horror stories. They kept enough of their senses to want to escape but their fear of the Polisocs was deep and since their sojourn in the cells they had become nervous and twitchy. Sleep, except for naps, was beyond them. There was too much going on. Too much to worry them and during the nights they lay and waited for the day.

Slowly the day came to life. The early morning sun shadowed the bars on the walls. Within the building people stirred and they heard the clatter of trays and instruments. Now and then the everyday noise was punctuated by wild screams and groans and they clutched at each other trembling. They heard the swish of wheels and a key turned in their lock. As one they leapt at the figure who entered carrying a tray and pushed violently past him leaving him sprawling with their breakfast festooned over his uniform. Cackling with maniacal laughter they ran hand in hand the length of the corridor and out into the grounds through a conveniently open door. They raced across the wide lawns heading directly for the high perimeter fence. With no thought for their safety they rushed at it spurred on by the shouts of angry orderlies. Kord reached the fence first and climbed up feeling but ignoring the jolts from the electric charge. Krod paced him and together they clambered over the overhang and dropped to the soft soil below. Ahead there was another fence and quickly they climbed over it still tingling and twitching from the effects of the electricity.

For a moment they paused and risked a glance back at their prison. With a start Kord recognised the naked figure of Ex Fireman Sidney Weddell who was running to and fro excitedly screaming incoherently.

"Look at that madman," said Krod.

---

[6] *Even Dog Squad operatives were subjected to punishment by the Politics if they failed.*

Ex-Fireman Weddell saw they were watching him and with a thrust of his hips he shook his willy at them and yelled.

"Wait for me... aggh!"

A group of orderlies dived at ex-fireman Weddell and he disappeared under a pile of bodies.

Kord and Krod turned their backs on the institution and ran. They ran all day stopping occasionally for brief rests until as the sun was setting they found a barn and snuggled warmly together between stacked bales of hay. They were tired and hungry but for the moment they were free. And that, said Kord, was what mattered.

"We can carry out the second part of our mission now," said Krod. "We will eliminate Tzu Wu."

"Yes my twin," agreed Kord, his eyes, like his twin's glowed with a fanatical gleam. "And Richard Byrde."

Krod chuckled deeply.

Both Half Pairs dribbled spittle out of the sides of their mouths.

Take me to your leader

Joseph Green looked at the two men with amusement mixed with puzzlement and tried to get his head around what they had just said. He was not sure exactly what it was they had said but he had let them in. "Excuse me, say again?" he said, putting his half full glass of red wine down on his coffee table.

"I said; hi Mister Joseph Green, we are aliens from the planet Zrad, and we want you to take us to your leader," said Dart, and smiled politely.

"I thought that is what you said, but er, what do you mean? Is this some kind of joke?" Joseph said.

"No Joke, mister Green, we have come from the planet Zrad which is about to invade your world and we have come to help your government to sort it out. We were given your name as a reliable contact with your employer, Maurice Bannerman of The Examiner. Could we er sit down and have a chat?" said Dart.

"And perhaps a glass of that wine you are drinking, and in the meantime we will try to convince you," said Drat, and smiled gently at Joseph who nodded and in a mild trance did as he was asked. When the three men were settled with a glass of wine each Dart took out his Atlas, and choosing a space on a side wall projected a movie.

"This is our land, this is what is happening, and we will show you what is going on now. Oh, and when we have finished we will also explain what we want to do. Sit back and enjoy," said Dart.

Joseph was vaguely trying to think in terms of calling the police or throwing the men out but whatever it was they had done to him subdued rebellious thoughts and he did as he was asked. Two hours later he called Bannerman at his private residence, apologised for the late call realising it was eleven in the evening, and explained.

"Bring the buggers up in the morning, on the train will you?" Bannerman said.

"Er, sir, this is bigger than a ride on the commuter train, er, a car would be better," Joseph said. "Like now?"

At a half an hour after midnight Joseph escorted Dart and Drat into a limousine and began the most lucrative and momentous encounter that any media baron had ever experienced.

The headlines on the Examiner's electronic placards screamed the news, and Maurice Bannerman magnanimously spread the story to his competitors. His price was reasonable, and with a smile of contentment he mentally calculated how much he was likely to make from the myriad deals his financial section were negotiating. When Dart and Drat explained how they wanted the media contract to work he nearly bent to his knees and worshipped them. The contract was beautiful, absolutely beautiful; tight and tied up the way he liked it and worth millions; beautiful.

"Exclusives, exclusives," he mumbled happily as he went from his office to the studios patting employees on their shoulders in sheer fiscal joy. "My life, am I going to make a fortune?" He gazed at the placard across the street and smiled.

"Take Me to Your Leader - Alien Envoys say to Examiner Correspondent!- Invasion latest - help for world leaders - alien envoys Dart and Drat in summit talks"

Maurice Bannermann sighed with pleasure and turned from gazing out the window and gazed instead at his office screen. The ribbon message wandered across the bottom underneath a timely program promotion that informed his television audience that something greater than history was impending. Maurice Bannermann added a mental Eurodollar figure to the promotion and sighed happily.

"Oh boy," he said. "Oh boy."

He walked with his hands touching at the fingertips and his lips moving as if he were praying. His staff gazed after him in awe and as he passed them in this pious manner they wondered.

"Oh boy," he repeated and quietly recited huge numbers. "Oh boy."

Maurice Bannermann was not a religious man.

His enthusiastic response was as much inspired by the meeting as by what happened afterwards. The contract the Zradian Pair offered him was perfect, and that enthralled him; that his television and media system was chosen made him ecstatic but what had delighted him most of all was when Dart and Drat arrived in his office with Joseph looking like the cat who had found the cream. They were short, stocky and identical except for a scar on one's face that ran from just below his peculiar double pupil eyes to his firm jaw. Apart from that one difference they were exactly alike and they moved as one.

"How can I help you," he said, wishing he could have thought of something better.

They smiled warmly at him and he caught a twinkle of impishness in their eyes as they answered together.

"Take me to your leader."

Maurice stood opened mouthed as the two men collapsed against each other slapping backs and laughing uncontrollably. He flapped his mouth like a fish for a few seconds trying to reply shaking either with laughter or anger, he wasn't sure which. Bastards, he thought, they're taking the mickey. Aliens land on Earth and they take the mickey! My life! Then he began to laugh. The joke, matey, is on me, he thought, I've been had! He caught a glimpse of Joseph standing leaning against the door jamb grinning broadly and stretched an arm out pointing and tried to speak but couldn't. Joseph, the rat, sloped off glancing once over his shoulder smiling hugely. And then the aliens let the laughter die down and politely they introduced themselves.

"We are Dart and Drat of the Zradian Rebel Army political wing," began Dart.

Maurice Bannermann groaned inwardly but did not let his feelings show.

"We call the organisation The New Moral Few or NMF for short sometimes known as the Zradian Freedom Front, a name that appeals to the people. Quite simply we are here to help you. We are liaison officers with a large heap of power. I think you could call us Emissaries or Ambassadors or something."

"You really do want to meet my Leader?" Maurice said, confused.

"We certainly do," said Dart.

"And as soon as possible," assured Drat.

"Convince me," he said.

They spoke for over an hour and Maurice listened intently and when they finished he sent for refreshments. Joseph and two members of the catering staff arrived with food and a cooler of beer and a bottle of his own favourite wine.

"So what is it you want us to do?" said Maurice Bannermann.

"We want publicity on your media system and we want to use it as a means of conducting our campaign against our President," said Drat. "And we come with our own contract offer. If you wait a moment or two your machine will print it out for you."

Drat took a small flat case from his jacket and laid it on the desk top. He stabbed a few buttons and the printer on Maurice's desk began to hum. Seconds later a screed of typed paper appeared and Maurice gathered it up.

"Read it," invited Drat.

They sat quietly and watched as he read nodding encouragingly as occasionally he looked up at them. At last he put the sheets down and sat for a while thinking. His fingers tick-tacked and then stopped. With a large beaming smile he looked at the Pair and let out a large expansive sigh.

"I need a whole department to work this out properly but for now you have my one-hundred percent approval, support and general financial grovelling. This is power and money beyond my wildest expectations." Maurice Bannermann said and clapped his hands.

"I thought you would like that," said Dart.

He had liked it and when his staff had checked it out the contract was watertight legally speaking and when he totted up a rough figure of what he was likely to make out of it he glowed with pleasure. Rich. Really stinking filthy rich. He was going to make a heck of a lot of lovely money.

When the negotiations were over Dart smiled warmly and said: "When can we meet your monarch?"

"The Palace? You want to be taken to the palace?"

"Of course, that is your leader is it not so?" replied Dart, puzzled.

"Er, no, HRH is what you could say was a titular head; sort of nominally in charge. It is the government in parliament and the Prime Minister who is the leader. HRH is a good sounding board for the Prime Minister but that is all."

"Oh, I think you ought to explain to us how it works then," said Drat glancing at his twin.

Maurice took a deep breath and spent the next hour or so giving them a potted history of England and its role in the British Isles, and the world. Eventually the idea sunk in and Dart and Drat agreed that he should speak to Smith, although they looked disappointed.

"We were looking forward to meeting up with a Royal personage," Dart said.

"Maybe you will," replied Maurice.

That was why he spoke to the Prime Minister's minions himself. His staff connected the calls and handled the details but he wanted to be on top of it choosing his team carefully deciding that Sally would be the presenter, and she and Joseph would liaise with the researchers and coordinators. He introduced Colin to Dart and Drat and said: "This gentleman and his friends are employed by Mr Richard Byrde as security, er only at times they have not quite managed to comply with their obligations as well as they would have liked."

"Yes, we cocked it up when Professor Renfrew was kidnapped," Colin said looking miserable.

"Professor Renfrew kidnapped? When did that happen?" asked Dart turning to his twin with a look of concern.

Colin explained and told them about Marjorie, and explained what Byrde's part in it all was. He explained that as far as they were concerned he was missing and nobody had any idea where he was.

"He was the only man on Earth who had any real idea what the satellite was doing orbiting Jupiter and we were going to have him on another program soon to help convince the silly buggers in charge that there was something dreadfully wrong," said Maurice. "Colin was hired to act as security and escort."

Colin who was standing near the door shifted uncomfortably and lowered his eyes. "Yeah and a right cock-up we made of it too," he said. "We were supposed to protect him but we was out smarted like we was ruddy boy scouts."

"Wasn't your fault," interjected Sally. "We were taken by surprise and gassed. If Dart and Drat can find him they will, I'm sure of that."

Dart grinned and looked up at Sally. "I admire your faith," he said. "However we may not be able to work miracles."

"Just try. His girlfriend is going crazy with grief," said Sally, anxiously.

"Pull up a chair and sit down," said Maurice, cheerfully. "And tell Mister Dart and Mister Drat about Professor Renfrew."

"Just Dart and Drat will do," said Dart.

Sally sat in the chair Dart offered surprised at feeling a warm embarrassed glow when he smiled easily at her. She took the glass of wine he proffered and sipped automatically trying not to show her sudden nervousness. Not nervous. Disturbed. There was something about him that thrilled her. She didn't know what she felt. It was so confusing. She almost spilled the wine when he spoke again.

"Now Miss Aitcheson, tell us all you can about how the Professor disappeared," said Dart.

"Er, call me Sally, please," she said.

"Sally," he corrected.

She told him all she knew and waited for him to absorb the information sipping at her refilled glass nervously. Drat the man, she thought, he makes me uncomfortable. I hope I don't have to work with him, she thought, catching her feelings. I'll be on edge all the time.

"So the Professor was abducted, you think, although he had minders?"

"Yes but Colin and his men were out-manoeuvred. I think also that there were others interested in a piece of Professor Renfrew and they didn't help much either. Colin thinks that the fly in the ointment were MI5 people or some other crowd. They all seem to work against each other," she said.

"Polisocs, they sound like our Polisocs," said Dart. "They are the Political and Social Police set up long ago to keep the Citizens in line. At first they were a benevolent bunch but they sort of deteriorated..."

Drat snorted and grinned and leaned forward to explain. "They are about the most evil and contemptuous bunch of Pairs you could ever find anywhere. Their only redeeming features are that they fight amongst themselves and are by and large incompetent. The best kind are dead ones."

"The best thing we can do is ask our Leader Pair to try and trace your Professor. If he is on Zrad I am sure we can find him. We may not be able to do anything for him but ..."

"Just try and I am sure Marjorie Watts will be grateful. She's his friend. She's worried sick about him. She blames herself for not being alert and Colin can do nothing to reassure her. He blames himself as well. You ought to meet her, maybe you can help ... I don't know..." she said, trailing off despondently.

Dart gazed at her and she felt uncomfortable again but unable to draw her gaze away. Suddenly she felt a wave of feeling that was almost physical washing over her. It stretched her nerve ends and sent a warm thrill up her spine and then her mind seemed to be awash with a feeling of reassurance and something else. Compassion and sympathy and inadvertently she found herself inwardly embracing the sensation and adding her own compassion for Marjorie to it. Dart broke the spell by shifting his gaze and she shook her head a little.

"I feel odd," she said.

He looked startled. "An Empathy Wave," he said, "We have them all the time between us but I never expected that Earth people could feel them too."

"Unusual," said Drat.

Dart turned in his seat and spoke to Maurice. "I think we should talk to this Marjorie."

Sally found herself unable to stop from volunteering to arrange the meeting. She blushed bright red when Maurice laughed softly. I wonder what he's thinking, she thought.

Dart was impressed with Colin's innate violence. The moment they met he sensed the big man's undoubted strength and barely controlled fury and liked it. He liked Colin's men too and smiled warmly. His twin sent an empathy wave suggesting the same feelings and as Sally introduced them to Marjorie he sized the men up in his mind and came to a decision.

"I will do my best to help," he said. "In the meantime I could do with some help myself. Mister Bannerman informs me that there will be security involved in our meeting with the Prime Minister. I suggest that you and your men come a long with us and bring Marjorie too?"

"Er, Mister Byrde is paying the bill Guv so we are sort of loyal ter 'im, if you get my drift?" said Colin.

"I am sure that Mister Byrde will be happy to share responsibility. We pay well," he said. He felt Drat shift his empathy from their own twinness onto Colin and waited. He didn't have to wait long before Colin shrugged his huge shoulders and moved from a leaning position to stand with his hands spread out.

"All right mate, me an' the boys 'll start with you as long as we can switch back to the Professor and his bird when we find the old geezer?"

"Done," said Dart. "I suggest we lock up Ms Watts" apartment and go on to our more commodious accommodation. Ms Watts can come with us. There are vehicles waiting outside. If you would like to call Mister Byrde I am sure we can come to some arrangement?"

"I'll give the Ferret a bell when we get wherever we're goin'," said Colin.

On the way Marjorie told them her version of the abduction.

"I'm at my wits end," she said. "I can't bear to think of what might have happened to him. I have no idea whether he is alive or dead. I have no idea where he is. All I can think about is he is far away and I can't be with him. They should have taken both of us."

Her face showed her anguish and Dart sat listening tight lipped until she had finished.

"I'll send a message straight away, as soon as we get to the Examiner. I am sure that we will find him," he said, hopefully.

"Excuse me," said Marjorie. "I find this uncanny. You are aliens aren't you?"

"Yes," said Dart. "We are, why do you ask?"

"Well how come you speak such good English and seem to be familiar with our world?"

Dart smiled. "We have studied your world for a long time. We have a learning system on Zrad which makes it easier for us to assimilate knowledge than merely sitting down and reading. We can speak Japanese, Chinese, French, German and Italian as well as several dialects from Africa and some of the languages of India. England and America are our speciality but, like all our systems, there seems to be something which is not quite right and somehow we seem to make silly mistakes. For example your history suggested that England would be the centre of World Government but we discovered, too late, there was more than one centre. It is a problem that our organisation, called the New Moral Few or NMF; were not aware of. We have a network of information which is mostly complete but as you can imagine the problem is the distances. Can you imagine getting reliable information rapidly when two places are eight and a bit light years apart?"

"I should imagine it isn't easy," said Marjorie.

"No it wasn't until recently. We have a better system now I am glad to say but we still have to catch up. And let me add, Ms Watts, we will do our best to find Professor Renfrew."

"Thank you - thank you," she said smiling weakly.

Dart saw the tear roll down her face and instinctively sent an Empathy Wave across the gap between them. Marjorie cried copiously and helplessly, Dart looked on catching a warning emotion from his twin. He heard the sobs before he realised who was making them and sat deeper in the car seat despairing. Sally was crying openly and his twin began to twitch his leg nervously. Dart felt the same twitch.

"Stop the car!" he cried out. "We need to er, to find a toilet!"

The driver guided the car to the pavement switching lanes expertly and pointed to a low dingy building.

"Over there."

Dart raced across the paving into the building with his twin not far behind hopping rather than running and together they stood by the trough cocking their legs like dogs. The action on their part was natural when emotionally stressed, and although it was usual in the privacy of their work-places to have piddling posts it was not normally done in public, so it was something of a relief to find such a convenient building.

"This is embarrassing. We will have to stop the empathy waves," said Dart.

His twin agreed. "Thank Nong one of these things was handy."

Dart laughed and together they walked out zipping themselves up ignoring the dark looks of passers by. After that the journey was uneventful and soon they had established Colin and his men in rooms close to theirs with Sally and Marjorie sharing another.

"Tomorrow we meet the Prime Minister," said Dart. "I'm looking forward to that."

"I hope he has a better grasp of the situation than his minions and, I wonder if he also drinks gin and tonics?" said Drat, and giggled. He turned the television on and watched with much amusement the dancing rabbits and hopping rats and mice that bobbed and jinked along the bottom of the picture.

He turned away and walked across the room to the refrigerator and extracted a bottle of spirits from inside.

"Anybody for a gin and tonic?" he said and laughed when his twin scowled. "Well, why not, we've paid for them." And as he poured a drink for himself and his twin he hummed the tune A Whiter Shade of Pale and thought of rodents.

The tone of the meeting in Tokyo was solemn, business like and for most of the proceedings very formal. There were more uniformed members than civilian, and the only women present were there to serve the Sake. The men from the Government explained how they were going to arrange the finances and to whom they were to go. The Military representatives listened and offered their solutions to the problems the Civilians had set them. It took a long time and much Sake to resolve all of the problems that concerned both sides but solve them they did.

In effect, the Prime Minister had managed to remove the women from the conference other than those retained as servants, and that put him in an expansive mood. He handled the delegates with skill and expertise that he often lost when the women members were present. Prime Minister Nakamura smiled benevolently, sighed expansively, and relaxed in his chair as the last document was signed.

"Gentlemen, I thank you for your assistance and I am sure that what we have completed today will make Nippon a very rich nation."

The Military leaders and the civilian businessmen smiled back and bowed their heads, and looked even more pleased when Prime Minister Nakamura gave orders for the buffet meal to be served, and the Sake was replaced with servings of fine malt whisky. The gentlemen chatted and laughed and became at first slightly drunk, and as they imbibed a little more of the fine malt, moderately drunk. At the stage before they became increasingly drunk Prime Minister Nakamura spoke into his desk mike and within minutes servants wheeled a Karaoke machine into the room and plugged it in.

"Okay, whoshe going to shing forush first?" said Nakamura.

The unanimous, if somewhat sycophantic, opinion was that the Prime Minister himself should have the honour. With a smile that was not oily nor modest the Prime Minister picked up the microphone and waited for the music to start. With a startled expression on his face that was mirrored more or less according to their sobriety by the remainder of the gentlemen, the Prime Minister sang, in Japanese, the words that went with the tune A Whiter Shade of Pale

The time was twenty minutes to eleven.

With a satisfied sigh in perfect quadraphonic sound Betty/ Anthony/Napoleon stopped on a rocky hill. The mass of rodents swarmed around her/him/it squeaking, fighting and fornicating. Anthony/Betty/Napoleon gazed around the knoll and the clearing in which it stood assessing the nutritional and rest value of the area. Anthony/Betty/Napoleon needed to find a balance between food and numbers. Napoleon/Anthony/Betty counted the breeding pairs, the number of healthy young, the older non-breeders and came to a decision. With extreme patience and precision Napoleon/Anthony/ Betty exterminated the useless mouths until the family of rodents had once again reached the optimum. Betty/Anthony/Napoleon sighed again. Eugenics was nasty, but with such a population as this, necessary.

Now it was time to find Clard and Dracl. And with a cry that was musical, demanding, plaintive and had all the force of an imperative, the robot set off at steady pace.

"Do not be afraid of the rodents!"
"Do not be afraid of the rodents!"

Slowly the robot moved down the hill and into the jungle. Its family of rodents swarmed after it leaving behind them nothing but a few missed bones of their dead. The tune A Whiter Shade of Pale echoed in the trees and wafted out to the knoll and drifted like birdsong in the warm jungle air.

Betty/Anthony/Napoleon was deliriously and electronically happy.

Professor Renfrew pays a visit.

Arthur Renfrew's eyes blinked open and shut again as the strong light played directly on his face. He tried to resist the men who came for him but he could not stop them grabbing his legs and dragging him out of the claustrophobic cell. Two more propped him up between them and half carried half dragged him along dirty corridors, up rough steps, along even more corridors that as they progressed showed signs of order. As they pushed through a door into a well lit passage he was not impressed. It was a grim looking passage and he thought of dungeons and castles and expected at any moment to see Knights in armour or a Princes and a King. Instead he was pushed through a door and grabbed by two more men wearing bright black and red uniforms. They hurried him into a small tiled room and two more men came in with buckets of warm water, sponges and towels. With no ceremony they stripped his clothes from his body and washed him down, rinsed him and towelled him dry. Two more took their places and gave him some clean clothes to wear. He put on the rough underwear and a two piece tunic of soft material and then he was taken from the washroom through yet another corridor and through a low portal. His guards pushed him into a wide space and with gestures urged him forward.

He stood in a large hall which contained rows of double seats arranged in tiers around a half circle of flagstones surrounding a throne. Soldiers stood to rigid attention in menacing rows either side of the throne and at the entrances. At intervals there were grim faced guards standing with their arms at the ready in recesses set into the walls.

For the second time since he woke he blinked.

The man who sat on the throne was dressed in what he could only describe as a bizarre outfit. On his feet he wore pair of blue suede shoes with deep crepe soles and a pair of bright pink socks. If it wasn't for the fact that the man was middle aged and partly bald Arthur could have sworn he had a haircut directly lifted from the 1950s. And the suit. The jacket was a bottle green drape with wide velvet lapels. He wore a bootlace tie around the neck of a white, lace edged, shirt. His trousers were black and tightly fitted his legs barely reaching his ankles. Arthur remembered his grandfather talking about this sort of attire and recalled the name, Teddy boys. The fifties rebellion against authority. Cut-throat razors hidden in the lapels and deep pockets to hide a cosh. Sideburns. And a bad attitude.

The guards pushed him forward, and with some difficulty he walked a few paces and stood on the flagstones in front of the throne. The man in the suit gazed at him for a long time looking him up and down, and with a foppish gesture of one hand beckoned him forward. Arthur took another couple of steps and the man smiled and inclined his head slightly.

"We is pleased to meets you master Renfrew," he said.

"Oh," said Arthur. "You speak my language then?"

"We learns it in our spares time if We wants to. We are very good I thinks?"

"Not bad at all," said Arthur not bothering to correct him.

"Do you like Our suit? We had it made especially for you. Natty do you nit thunk."

Arthur, in spite of his hurts found the dreadful diction and grammar funny and almost burst into laughter. He controlled the urge because he had the feeling that this man was not one to tolerate amusement at his expense. Arthur was aware of the menacing swordsmen lining the walls behind the throne.

"I ... I think it is very interesting," he said.

"You don't like it?"

"I think it is very good. I like it," he made the last observation quickly and added a smile as well which he did not feel but again the swordsmen were on his mind. Somehow he had to survive and get back to Marjorie. Marjorie. Think of her and you will get through this, he told himself.

"We thunks We looks smat," said the suit.

"You do indeed," said Arthur. "Very smart."

The suit beamed.

"We are the President of the Republic of Zrad. You have arrived in Our Grand Palace. What does you thunks off it?"

"It is indeed grand," Arthur said and meant it. The hall was hung with fine drapes and it was painted more for cleanliness than artistry, he thought, but obviously the President was proud of it. The floor was flagstone and the dais on which the throne was mounted was made of fine plastic. The hall was clean except for a large brown stain on the flagstones under foot and although the place was filled with the thin smoke of perfumed sticks that burned in attractive holders on the corner of every seat there was a bad smell. The place stunk of dead meat. Arthur wrinkled his nose and looked around for an explanation. With a shudder he realised what the brown stain on the flagstone floor was. Swords and prisoners. People had been killed here by the swordsmen. Yuk.

"We are proud of Our Great Hall."

The President fell silent and smugly regarded Arthur eyeing him up and down somewhat like a suspicious chicken. Arthur felt like a victim.

"I suppose you wanting to know why is you here?"

"I was wondering," Arthur said, surprised at his calmness.

"You is heres because We wanting you heres. You are the one Earthman what discovers Us and Our peoples and Our glorious Star Station. We needs to ask you some questions and of course you will be only too eager to answer them for Us."

"And if I do not?" asked Arthur, boldly.

"Then We will kill you. Have a gin and tonic." Said the President with a smile and clapped his hands.

Two men rushed in carrying a tray with a cluster of drinks on it and immediately presented the tray to the President. The President took one of the glasses and downed the contents in one draught and picked up another. He barked words at the two men who immediately rushed to Arthur and presented a glass to him. They backed away and stood politely aside.

"Here's to the Rodents," said the President raising his glass.

"To the rodents," echoed Arthur, puzzled.

The drink was good. It tasted like gin and tonic and warmed his belly. The President snapped his fingers and took a third and fourth glass. The men backed away and dashed into a side door to appear seconds later with a full tray. The President meanwhile had slurped the two drinks down and was already snapping his fingers for more. Twice he did that and then at last he looked at Arthur and grimaced.

"You musht usnwur Our questuns or We will slishe you into swizzle sthicks. Sho there." The President swayed in his seat trying to focus and almost fell but clutching the sides with both hands to steady himself managed to remain seated.

Arthur gaped in horror, fear clutching his heart having no idea what to say to this drunken despot and searched in his mind for something to cling to. Then he remembered Julia. Dear totally inebriated Julia. What was it she said whenever the subject of their son came up. "Arthur precious fucking Renfrew you are a bastard. You hate Julian. What do you know about people?" She screamed that at him every time she drank too much which was most days now and he always found a way to fob her off. And that was the answer here.

"I'll tell you all you need to know but in exchange I would like to be housed more comfortably. You see I really do like the way you are dressed and it is kind of you to offer me a drink too. Ask what you wish and I will tell you," Arthur said, and bowed his head slightly.

The President swayed and gazed at him for a long time before speaking.

"WE will find a better place for you but WE wants OUR qushunsink..."

The President gurgled, twisted in his seat and toppled from the throne. Four men rushed out from a side opening and quickly grabbed him before he fell to the floor. Carefully they lifted the President between them and carried him through an archway. Four more men surrounded Arthur and marched him slowly between them.

After a short march through bright corridors he was shown into a small but pleasant room and using hand signs and suggestion they indicated he should lay on a low bunk. They fitted a complicated contraption to his head and signed he should relax and watch a wall screen opposite. They operated switches and the screen glowed. At first Arthur felt the tingle of a mild electrical current followed by a low hum that disappeared as soon as the screen cleared and suddenly presented a 3D picture. As he watched the action he began to understand what was happening. He realised he was beginning to understand what the actors were saying. Just over one tenth later one of the actors asked him a direct question.

"Would you like to watch a short history of Zrad?"

"I would like to view the history of Zrad," he replied.

What he saw fascinated and frightened him. It also made him think. Within the story he was shown there was an answer to his survival. He had no time to think about it because as soon as the story was finished the two Pairs came back in again and uncoupled the Educator.

"Interesting enough Professor?" asked one Pair.

"Yes, I learned a lot," he replied, and noticed the other Pair were smiling.

"What do you think?"

"I think the process is excellent but there are some things I do not understand. For example why is the President a Half Pair?"

"Simple, the other half of his pairing belongs to the people. He had to kill his twin to make him complete. Did you not see that?"

Arthur remembered the graphic scene where a Half Pair was shredded to death by a Pair wearing tight pants and sharp claws on the hands and feet. Watching with a look of relief on his face was a younger version of the President who when the body was lifeless walked away as if nothing had happened. Arthur shuddered. Kill thy brother. The other strange thing that he wanted to ask about was the odd message that inserted itself at intervals into the session. What did it mean? Do not be afraid of the rodents and what was the reference to the Ides of March and Julie baby? Who was the miller and why did the tune keep jingling in his mind? What was it?

"The tune is called A Whiter Shade of Pale and quite frankly we are utterly fed up with it," said one Pair, sadly.

Arthur smiled.

He had found a weak spot. Now all he had to do was find a way to exploit it. Marjorie. He thought of Marjorie. Another thought struck him. He could understand their language.

Professor Renfrew dreamed of Marjorie and woke to the sound of music. He groaned. The dream was better.

"Marjorie, Marjorie," he whispered and wiped salt tears from his cheeks.

He got out of the cot and padded naked to the shower cubicle. The fine spray cleansed his body from all directions and this was followed by warm air that dried him thoroughly. There were towels but generally these were used at the basins or for wiping up mess. He touched the small scar above his ear with his forefinger and shuddered. Two Pairs had come for him two nights before and with no explanation had taken him to the medical rooms.

"What are you going to do?" he demanded trying to back away.

"A small but necessary operation. A minor implant to let us know at all times where you are, it is our way of making sure you don't escape." The medical Pair said with little expression in their voices and placed a puffer against his arm and tapped the end. He slid to the floor unable to stop the darkness enveloping him and when he woke there was the scar. It was uncomfortable and at first it itched. No stitches and a neat healed scar. He could not even feel a lump.

He let his finger drop and walked across the room to the bed. Halfway there the portal opaqued, cleared, and a Pair entered.

"Dort and Trod, why so early?" he turned to face them.

"We have come to take you to his Honour," they said.

"I have yet to shave and eat," the Professor said and moved toward the dispenser.

"So sorry but His Honour must be obeyed immediately. You must come now."

They looked so agitated that he relented. Dort and Trod were a pleasant Pair who gave him much of their time and made his life on Zrad easier. The President's unpredictable mood swings were hard to handle and he dreaded a call from his honour. Trod and Dort were his buffer and mostly the Pair assigned to his examination. He answered their questions willingly and wrote more answers ready for the President on his own screen. He mused on the change that had happened during the last few days, he refused to call them turns, on his terminal. Working late one night he had logged onto an obscure line and was suddenly party to the president's own line.

Odd. But there was something else too; a presence that called itself by three different names. When he replied he was given a code.

"Rodent #4"

Each time he used the code data flashed on the screen which at first seemed confusing but when he followed the procedures outlined in the menu he came to understand it. That was when he discovered the subliminal message program. The program was exclusive to the president's quarters. He translated the messages by simply logging on as Rodent #4. The sender giggled. It was impossible to giggle on a computer. Wasn't it? The sender managed it. Arthur had a disquieting picture of showers and knives and myriad rodent bodies in the back of his mind which he found difficult to shake off and although it wasn't a frightening image, it seemed to emit sympathy, his reaction was to throw up.

He shrugged his shoulders and followed the Pair. It was a short walk along familiar corridors to the president's quarters. As he got nearer the smell of gin and tonic became stronger. As he passed through the portal he smelled puke and the smell of old man as well. He wrinkled his nose and stopped before the president's futon and dropped to his knees. The president lay propped up by pillows and was holding a drink in his hand from which he sipped through a straw, his eyes red and staring like blood marbles against a sheet.

"Good morrow your honour," said Arthur. He had discovered the president liked archaic speech and so he had cultivated a few older words just to please him.

"We are unhappy this day old chaps, We did not sleep well."

No, I don't expect you did, he thought, not with the crazy messages you have been getting lately.

"I'm sorry, your honour," he said, and thought about his own contribution. Knives and showers and eyes sliced through with thin blades. His source had chuckled at that and sent a message. "Well done Rodent#4" and Arthur was pleased.

"We are tired and Our eyes are sore."

The president clicked his fingers and a Pair rushed in carrying a rolled up flimsy sheet. With a flourish they unrolled it and stretched it out so that he could see it. The president pointed at it and waved his finger up and down not speaking but looking at Arthur with a leering glare.

Arthur gazed at the sheet unable to take in what it was at first but when his first shock had passed he read the words under the picture.

"Julian Renfrew - enemy of the true and lawful state - wanted preferably alive - twenty thousand tokens reward for information leading to his capture. This Half Pair has committed grave crimes against Our armies - this scum has committed atrocities of bombing and fire setting that has destroyed Our valuable resources and dreadfully murdered Our Loyal Pairs."

Arthur looked at the picture of his son and smiled. Good on the little ratbag, he thought, I bet he's spitting tacks and scared out of his inadequate wits.

"You know this person?"

Arthur looked at the pale president.

"Yes, he is my son," he said.

The President smirked.

"That's nice," he said. "You must be very proud of him."

Arthur didn't answer.

The President raised one eyebrow and smirked again.

"We don't get on," Arthur said.

"Pity because you see we rather thought you might like to go and find him for Us."

Arthur emitted a nervous laugh.

"I hardly think so," he said and shook his head.

As he did so there was a faint click inside his head and softly the tune A Whiter Shade of Pale began to play. He clapped a hand to his head and held it there looking around wildly but he knew that it was the implant.

"We think you have very little choice in the matter, Professor," said the President and with a kick of his feet under the duvet cover he laughed. "That is why we is havings yous hereing for all these many turns."

Arthur felt his jaw drop again and with sudden clarity realised what it was he was expected to do. "You bastard," he said. "You despicable bastard."

"Yes, aren't I just," said the President and signalled for another drink.

Back in his room Arthur logged on and connected with Rodent #4 and explained to the contact what was happening to him. He passed on as much information as he could and waited when instructed for the contact to reply. The message appeared on the screen spoken by a cartoon squirrel that bounced.

Have absorbed data – will track progress

He sat in the chair and worked again trying to ignore the regular reminder behind his ear that he noticed as time progressed lessened until it disappeared. It was as if the President wanted to let him know that the thing was there but leave him able to think. Clever. He looked out of the observation window meant for the guards to look at him rather than a view, there was none to be seen other than a dull corridor. Nevertheless he was startled to see a large cat-like animal about the size of a large leopard but chunkier with fangs that showed from its upper jaw like a sabre-toothed tiger. It moved purposefully as if it knew where it was going and for a moment he was tempted to call out but thought better of it. He recognised it from the learning program as a carnibeast.

The carnibeast moved steadily through the dark corridors, hiding when it saw Pairs, waiting until they had passed by or quietly took another turn instinctively heading for the open air. The creature seemed to sense the danger from the weapons the Pairs carried and avoided contact. It reached a door and waited in a dark recess patiently, smelling the fresh air outside aware of freedom beyond. The light showing through the slats and windows faded to the soft night time pink and whilst there was no Zradian presence the beast lay and dozed until at last a Group of Pairs marched out of a lighted portal to the door. The door hissed open; the Pairs marched through, and the carnibeast, suddenly alert raced through the opening, ran across the open space to the next gate and leapt at it, scrambled up the structure, poised for a brief moment on the top and jumped to the ground using the roof of a hover wagon to bounce into the scrub. Astonished Pairs cried out, one raising a laser to fire but the beast was gone. In its mind was an image; a vague memory of a place it knew, a place high up where its mother had suckled it, and with a sense of purpose it headed south. It ran fast, killed, ate and travelled to where its instinct sent it and on the fourth turn it smelled its mother, and other smells. It smelled the sweat of Zradian Pairs and another, strange scent as it loped up the slope to where the mother smell wafted across the burning sands. Suddenly it stopped. A creature stood on the ledge where it meant to stop and call. It stopped, crouched, and when the strange creature turned it leapt, snarling angrily, surprised when the space opened out under it. The snarls and the slashes it meted out during the fall and afterwards were its equivalent of "Oh shit!" What happened next was as confusing for the carnibeast as for the creature it attacked, and for a brief moment just as painful.

Lugs Plays his Hand

Richard Byrde strolled casually to his factory as he did every working day. On this day he was accompanied by Oliver Braine, and walking equally as casually was the Ferret and his mate Lugs. The Ferret was sure of himself, and in spite of the ease with which he walked, or the apparent casualness of his demeanour, he was alert and street keen. Lugs, humming a nursery rhyme to himself, was equally alert. Anybody who knew Lugs would know how alert he was when they saw his hands were not in his pockets but moving gently in time to his gait. Oliver Braine walked as if he were under siege.

"Why did we not drive to work?" he asked glancing about him nervously.

"It's healthier than taking the bus and cheaper than a car," he said.

As they approached the factory Byrde slowed regulating his pace and looked at his watch.

"I like to arrive after the staff have started work. I give them a few minutes grace to get going and then I don't catch them loafing around doing nothing or yarning to each other. I hate it when I have to discipline them."

Braine smiled. Since he started work with Byrde he had walked often rather than go by bus or train. It seemed to him as if Byrde was obsessed with not using transport. He didn't mind walking, but this, he thought, was stupid, much safer by car. In these circumstances he thought, hastily. Oliver Braine was also much puzzled by Richard Byrde's way of dealing with Lugs. From the first days when Emily had gone to her mother's, escorted and protected by a couple of Colin's mates, it was as if Byrde had taken on Lugs as a sort of pet. The first night in the Byrde residence Lugs sat around looking bored until Byrde suggested they play cards. Lugs ugly face lit up, and when Byrde produced a pack of Snap cards his face broke into a wide grin.

"Do you want to play as well?" Byrde asked the Ferret and Braine. The Ferret said he would prefer to keep watch, and Braine, seeing that Byrde meant to play Snap, declined and sat watching the television.

It didn't matter how many times Byrde explained the rules, Lugs always had to stop the game and be reminded. Braine noticed that Lugs won most of the games, and when he asked Byrde why he had lost so many all Byrde would say was that Lugs was too good for him. It was the Ferret who explained.

"If Lugs loses too often he gets sort of upset and bashes the winners. Mister Byrde is just being careful."

But although Braine had to admit that walking to the factory was quicker than by car he was worried that Byrde was not being careful enough.

"Actually the car is Emily's really and it is much too small for all of us so we walk. She chose a small electric because even although the Mercedes was a dual power vehicle it was far too big. So she chose a Volkswagen. I like it," Byrde said.

"Okay, I get the point," said Braine.

They walked into the factory compound and strolled to Byrde's office. Most of the morning Lugs and the Ferret spent sitting around in the lounge and occasionally strolled around the factory. Braine sat reading while Byrde worked.

"I have an after lunch appointment," said Byrde. "So let's go to the Drunken Clown and treat Lugs and the Ferret to a beer or two and a feed?"

Braine grinned happily. "Good idea," he said.

In the Drunken Clown they sat around a table chatting. The Ferret explained about his younger brother who wanted to be a racing driver but usually got asked to do getaway jobs instead.

"There ain't no money in it 'cos mostly you get nicked. 'E works as a mechanic and kin get almost any motor to go like the clappers."

"And what about you Lugs?" said Byrde, affably.

"I used ter be a boxer but when they banned it I sort of 'ad nuffin' ter do so I took up bashin' people fer me mate. We useter collect bad debts fer a bloke but 'e got 'is cousin ter do it after a while. One of me mates; we useter fight in the ring. Yeah ole Denny carn't arf lay it on. Cor, 'e's got a left 'ook wot kin lay out an 'ippopotomous," Lugs grinned at them. "'E carn't play cards 'tho."

Braine laughed behind his hand covering his mouth and trying to stifle his amusement as the Ferret glared at him. He glanced at Byrde who mouthed a warning.

It was as he was looking past Byrde trying to control his laughter he saw two men pass by and look inside. He was sure he had seen them once before but he couldn't quite place where. He wasn't surprised when they came sauntering back to enter the Saloon bar. For a few minutes he sat half listening to the others unsure whether to alert Byrde or to keep quiet. He decided to speak when another pair and then a third came in and quietly took seats not far from their table. He surreptitiously looked into the public bar craning his neck a little and yawning and saw another two groups of men in pairs leaning against the bar. Casually he leaned closer to Byrde and spoke almost out of the corner of his mouth letting his gaze slide to the men he saw as the enemy, and back to Byrde.

"Richard, don't look now but there are six guys in the bar and more in the next one who look a bit suss. Let the other two know please. I'm scared," he said.

Byrde smiled at the Ferret and said. "We have unwelcome company I believe." The Ferret continued talking about his brother and how he and Lugs had known each other since they were children and casually took in the scene in the bar.

"Got yer, Mister Byrde, when we finish, me and Lugs will cover while Oliver sees you outside, okay?" the Ferret said this without a break in his conversation and added a laugh at the end as if he were saying something funny. They finished their meal and when Byrde had settled the bill he nodded imperceptibly to the Ferret.

"Okay," said Byrde. "Time we were off."

Byrde got up first and Braine followed as casually as he could. The Ferret stood up, and more casual and relaxed than Braine was he eased between the tables looking for all the world as if he was contemplating his free lunch. He was, but he was also marking where the strangers were and what they were doing. Lugs got up last and lumbered across the floor casually as if he were concentrating on negotiating the gaps between the tables. Two of the men at the bar followed them out and Braine wanted to hurry, get out quick and run. In the street he watched fascinated as Lugs turned quickly and with hardly any effort dropped their followers with two fluid economic moves left and right.

Suddenly pairs of men seemed to flow out from behind everything, and with a roar of anger Lugs ploughed into them backed up by the Ferret who stabbed with his small fists effectively stopping those who threatened his big mate. Lugs was like a whirlwind but there were still too many of them and Braine, trembling with fear, joined in. He landed one blow and felt it crunch home but somebody's fist hit him and he fell on the sidewalk balled up in pain.

Byrde backed against the wall as the wave of attackers poured at them. He used his fists and his feet kicking and punching as hard as he could. He watched Braine disappear under the press of men and he saw that even Lugs and the Ferret were having trouble. Suddenly men were running and the attack fizzled out. Fighting with fists and batons were constables Bates and Fish, sergeant 'Space man' Orange and two of his burly constables. The survivors ran off leaving their unconscious companions behind. Within minutes the uniformed constables and the sergeant had them handcuffed and sitting against the pub wall in a neat row.

Bates and Fish emerged from the aftermath of the fracas rubbing their knuckles and looking pleased with themselves, and grinned at Byrde.

"We been looking for..." said Fish

"... that Renfrew ratbag ..." Bates continued

"... and your secretary said ..." said Fish

"... we could find you here..." Bates said

"... and we saw this lot and ..." said Fish

"... you know us we..." said Bates

"... can't resist a good ..." said Fish

"...scrap," interrupted Byrde, finishing.

"Yeah well..." said Bates, looking annoyed and puzzled.

"I think you should read the papers or your own reports if you are looking for Julian. If I recall it was your sergeant Orange who seems to think he has taken off to outer space," explained Byrde. "I really think I have problems of my own here."

"We are not talking about ..." began Fish

"... the kid. We want to know where ..."said Bates

"... your mate Arthur Renfrew has ..." said Fish

"... got to," finished Bates.

"He's at the University as far as I know. I am supposed to talk with him later this afternoon..."

"He's scarpered..." said Fish.

Byrde stared at him open mouthed and groaned. "What about Colin and his mates... were they not there?" asked Byrde, nigglingly aware of his archaic speech.

"Yes but the Prof's been ..." said Bates

"...kidnapped..." finished Fish.

"Kid ..." began Byrde

"... napped," said Bates.

It took Bates and Fish a few split sentences to explain what happened and when they finished Byrde spread his hands and shook his head.

"I can't help you. This is news to me," he said.

"Oh well we ..." said Fish

"... thought you might know ..." said Bates

"... something useful but ..." said Fish

"... you don't seem to know anymore than ..." said Bates

"... we do," said Fish.

Byrde shook his head.

"Anyway, gotta go. Nice seein' you Lugs..." said Bates

"...yeah and thanks for the invitation... said Fish

"...to the fight," finished Bates.

Byrde watched them go and turned to the Ferret. "Don't either of those two ever say a whole sentence by themselves?" he asked, looking amused and worried.

"Oh that, you get used to it after a while. We got to get you out of here."

"Yes I suppose so but what about poor Arthur."

"We got more than his fate to worry about," said Braine. "Look at that." He pointed up at the large headline screen on the corner of the street and they all read the message that scrolled across it.

"Aliens Invade Earth - Bridgehead Landing in Nevada - Las Vegas Over Run - US Forces - Mobilised - Do not be afraid - British Forces on Europa Alert - of the rodents!"

"Crikey," said Lugs. "That stupid message gets everywhere don't it. I don't mind rats and mice 'cos I had a pet rat once. I like bunny rabbits too."

"Yeah," said Byrde. "I like rabbits too."

"I don't believe this," said Braine. "The Earth is about to be over run by little green men and all you can do is talk about rabbits and rats."

The Ferret grinned at Lugs and nodded his head. "We better get these two home and hide 'em up for a while," he said.

"Rightho Boss," said Lugs and turned to Byrde. "You reckon we can play some more games mister Byrde?"

"Sure," said Byrde. "But first I better explain the rules. You deal out the cards and then you place..."

Braine clasped his forehead in despair and groaned.

It is my pleasure to serve you.

Blard the Barmy examined the flimsy closely looking for hidden meanings but all he found was three mysterious references to rodents. He wondered what the inserts meant and with deliberation he counted the lines and marked them in the margins. He placed the flimsy on the scan sheet and spoke into the pick-up.

"Computer would you be so kind and check source of marked lines and decode them for me please."

He was always polite with computers. He had discovered many four hundreds past that sometimes computers are more apt to work for you if you treat them right. Especially if you want something out of the ordinary. His request could quite easily be done using the basic system paths but this way the computer could feel as if it were a useful and valuable member of his, Blard's, workforce. On the payroll so to speak.

The screen flickered in glowing pink through green. The scanner glowed briefly and a message appeared on the screen.

Please wait - tracing source and multiple destinations - we apologise for the delay - thank you for using our service.

Blard smiled.

"Thank you," he said

It is my pleasure to serve you.

Blard looked at the large type and smiled. The task he had set would be guaranteed but would not override any other task he set it. The next and most important task was to locate and lock on to the Doomsday Bomb.

"I have another more important task for you. Would you mind giving most of your energies and thoughts to this one. It is important for Zrad and Earth." He said and added. "And our survival."

The screen glowed through pink to purple.

Blard placed a new flimsy on the scanner and watched as the screen glowed pink through to purple again.

I will be some time with this task - please wait - approximate delay 5 divs.

"Thank you. I will get on with other tasks myself while you are engaged with this one."

He left the work station and walked a short distance along the corridor to a larger space where a group of Pairs surrounded the

Doomsday Bomb Receiver busily tapping out calculations and taking readings. Looking out of place was Sherman Holmes watching the activity going on around the bench obviously puzzled but when he saw Blard his face lit up.

"What's going on?" he asked.

"The Pairs are measuring the receiver and checking its circuits. They need to make sure it is the right one. The NMF need the data to help them decide what to do," Blard said. "I have come to take you on a tour around the Star Station. You will need to know something about how we operate because soon we will be going on a mission to the enemy Star Station."

Holmes rubbed his hands together and eagerly followed Blard out of the workshop.

Holmes was amazed at the complexity of the Star Station and yet, once the system was explained, it was easy to understand.

"And apart from updated equipment the layout is the same in all of them?" he said.

Blard nodded and led the way to a large oval screen above a curved console.

"This one has all the best gismos you could ask for including this room which is new although it could easily be fitted into Star Station Two. They may have one or they may have their version of it. I want to show you some graphics on the screen and teach you how to use our computer system," Blard said, and at the same time pressing buttons to activate the screen. He called up a floating seat for himself and another for Holmes. "Sit on the pad and watch what I do."

Holmes did as he was told and watched as Blard went through a series of commands and finally spoke into a small floating microphone. Another microphone appeared just below Holmes mouth and turned to face its grille toward him.

"I can't speak the lingo," said Holmes. "And I can't read it either."

"Don't worry, we'll put you on a learning machine later. For now all you have to do is watch me and I will explain as I go. I will also put the information on a small screen which you can look at whenever you need a refresher. Okay?"

"Okay," said Holmes and grinned.

Holmes watched the screen clear and then slowly fill with a 3D image which gradually moved until it stopped on a small spot roughly in the centre.

"You are here," said Blard. "This is the control centre one floor above us, Follow the white pointer and relate it to what you have already seen here. This is a dimensional expanded plan of Star Station Two."

Blard spoke into the microphone and steadily the pointer traced lines on the grid and slowly Holmes became aware of a pattern. It began in the centre and worked its way out in ever expanding circles which were named and numbered and colour coded. Blard explained what each part did. Holmes worked out there was four main sectors each denoted with a colour. Red for administration and control. Green for living quarters designated for the administration and stores staff, quarters for the Leader Pairs and the Polisoc Stormtroopers. Blue for the ordinary soldiers and the workers and yellow for cargo and stores. This last sector was by far the largest and Holmes noticed that although the Station was divided up more or less neatly into separate sectors there were slices of yellow inserted at sixteen other points. He asked about them and Blard grinned.

"Weapons. If we need to we can defend the Star Station from these points. I'll show you." He pressed buttons and the image reduced to a ball and Holmes gasped when he saw how well the yellow slices protected the Star Station. It must be three-hundred and sixty degree defence.

"How is this thing powered?" asked Holmes.

Blard expanded the image again and pointed to the core and the compartments around it. "That there is a Fusion Nuclear power plant. The activity is converted into energy by induced friction and in turn converted to electrical power," Blard explained and looked at Holmes with a grin. "Don't ask me how it happens because I am bulgered if I know. When we first did it we had to sort of flare off the excess energy but we realised that we could make them smaller. We use a lot of induced current, anyway there's a lot of it down there to make this thing go."

"Sort of like one of our nuclear submarines without the steam," Holmes said.

"I suppose so, gives us power for the defences too. Of course if an enemy could use the Transfer Ports then we are stuffed. One or two well placed bombs and its all over," Blard said and grinned. "That is why we have disabled all but the ones we need and have them guarded by armed troops. They have orders to take prisoners or kill attackers. As for us, we will use the Transfer Ports for a slightly different mission."

"What are we going to do?"

"We are going to sabotage Star Station Two. Make a lot of mess and kill a lot of the enemy."

Holmes looked a him and the screen.

"How?"

"I'm not sure yet but the NMF will think of something. Right now I think you need to learn the language and get a handle on our society," Blard said. "Stay on the seat and follow me. You sort of guide it with your arse."

Holmes crashed into the console and several walls before he got the hang of it but at last after much laughter they arrived at a small double cubicle filled with plastic gadgets and a complicated headset that hung from a plastic pillar.

"Looks like the one in the garden shed," said Holmes.

"Sans the gardener," said Blard.

"Yeah, I wonder how he's getting on with his plot," said Holmes.

Blard giggled and lowered the headset onto Holmes shoulders.

"Hold still, I have to adjust this to fit and then you can sit back and enjoy about an hour and a half in your time being educated."

Holmes sat still and relaxed as his floating chair altered its shape and supported his back shifting as he did until he was comfortable. A screen lowered in front of his face and curved its ends to create an almost wrap around picture and with a small plopping sound it activated. He was aware of Blard leaving the room and then he was watching a fascinating documentary style movie. At first he could hardly understand anything that was said and then slowly it began to make sense and he was following the story. Fleetingly he thought of the gardener and Earth and smiled a little at the poor man's frustration.

The dick, he thought, should wait until the fuss is over. Yeah, what a dick.

Bates and Fish listened politely to the gardener and then strolled absentmindedly across to the ruined garden shed. This is where Julian Renfrew was last seen, thought Bates, and according to the gardener, once you got past his complaints about ruined vegetables, was where other people had come and disappeared as well. According to the gardener a whole troop of soldiers had clambered onto the platform and gone poof!

"...and all of 'em tromped all over me gardin and me and everybody else 'ere is bein' arst to grow stuff for the war and all ..." he began, but it was obvious neither Bates nor Fish was listening to him. In fact they were doing what everybody else had done, walking over his plot as if it wasn't there.

"Oy! Get orf me gardin!" he yelled. "Get orf me friggin' gardin' will yer?"

Bates and Fish looked at him and then down at where they were walking.

"Oh don't worry ..." said Fish

"... I'm sure you will fix it up ..." said Bates

"...all right," finished Fish.

The gardener glowered at them from the other side of his plot. In his hand he held a spade with which he had been lovingly piling soil against his potatoes, and as he stared at the crushed plants and deep footprints Bates and Fish had left in his plot he gripped the handle tightly his knuckles white and tense and growled. Spittle dribbled down one side of his chin and he wiped it away with his free hand.

"You blokes is the same as all the rest," he said, hissing the words between his teeth.

Bates and Fish stared at him, and with a toss of their heads turned away and continued to walk to the shed. The gardener gripped the spade with both hands and skirting the plot advanced on their retreating backs.

"Oy! You two, wotyouthinkyoudoingwarkin'awaylikethatwivout sayin' nuffin?" and with a scream of fury he launched himself at them with the spade raised above his head.

Bates and Fish turned.

"Bastards!" he yelled and aimed a blow at Fish.

"Can't have this ..." said Fish and dodged to one side

"... not when we are officers of the law ..." said Bates stepping the opposite way

"... and doing our duty," said Fish moving in again as the gardener spun quickly and took a swing at Bates.

Bates sidestepped and Fish cracked his fist against the gardener's head catching the flying spade as it spun toward him at the end of its haymaking arc.

"What a dick," said Fish as he and Bates clambered up on the platform. "I'll keep this with me in case ..."

"... the silly bugger gets up again," said Bates.

"You sure about this?" Fish said.

"I think so. If Sergeant Orange is right then this thing here is ..." said Bates

"... supposed to do the trick," said Fish.

Bates gave Fish a puzzled look and fiddled with the plastic pillar unsure of what it was while Fish leaned on the spade watching him. He started back when a small red light flashed and then turned green.

"I wonder what that is supposed ..." said Bates

There was a lurch and for a moment the two officers lost sight of one another and then they were standing in a plastic lined cubicle that looked like an elevator cab.

"...to mean," said Fish.

With a soft hum and a click a door slid open to reveal four armed men who looked as if they meant business.

"Cripes Batesy I don't like ..." said Fish

"...the look of this," said Bates.

Fish launched himself at the men using the spade like a sword and Bates followed him ready to batter somebody with his fists. A cloud of gas hit them full in their faces and before they had taken more than two steps they fell twitching to the floor. Casually the Pairs gathered them up and placed them on stretchers. One Half Pair carried the spade and as they eased their burden along the corridor the doors slid softly shut.

Two things surprised Holmes on the first tenth after his education session. One was accidental and that was more from unfamiliarity than incompetence. He pressed the wrong buttons, and instead of activating the 3D plan he flipped into a channel that the computer explained was a narrow restricted band. Holmes threw up his hands and muttered into the microphone.

"I'm from Earth and I am not afraid of the rodents."

The channel cleared and instead of messages on the screen two speakers moved out from their pods and hovered one on either side of his head.

"You are cleared for interaction."

"Eh?"

"Watch the screen."

Holmes watched the screen and his eyebrows shot up in surprise. I've never done that before, he thought, eyebrows in the Holmes family did not shoot up. What made them shoot up was a scene that was obviously the palace of the Zradian President. The President was sitting on his throne dressed in what Holmes could only surmise was a borrowed outfit and he was talking to Richard Byrde's University mate, Professor Arthur Renfrew.

"Cripes," said Holmes. "What ..?"

"Our Glorious President is talking to the Earthman Renfrew. Subject was abducted from Earth at Our Glorious President's express wishes."

"Can you cut out the Our Glorious bit please and tell me where and how you got this information?"

"We learned this from our friend Betty/Anthony/Napoleon and rodents."

"What...?"

"Cyber 123BANRod/Earth/Tempresxscan.3325logon."

"Some sort of address is that?"

"Connecting now - please wait."

Holmes watched the screen, puzzled by the stream of events, and tried to work out what was happening. His eyebrows shot up again when the screen cleared to be replaced with a picture of a robot standing on a hill surrounded by hordes of rodent like animals that looked like a cross between rabbits and rats. It carried a lance which it used every now and then to kill some of the rodents. Music filled the chamber and at intervals it chanted its message.

Do not be afraid of the rodents!

Around what Holmes could only surmise was its waist hung a tatty blue apron with little animals embroidered on it and it looked - happy.

"Good grief," said Holmes. "What is it?"

"Our friend."

Holmes stared at the screen and slowly a chill of realisation began to creep into his mind. This whole operation is being monitored by that, he thought, this, Cyber, robot or whatever you called it had something to do with what was happening on Earth. The message and the tune was the give away. He shuddered. Across the screen a message tumbled in a wave in time to the tune A Whiter Shade of Pale and he groaned.

"Do not be afraid of the rodents mister Holmes"

"Who are you?"

"We are Betty/Anthony/Napoleon, sometimes more Napoleon than anybody else. Do not be afraid of the rodents and in the main we are on your side. We/I/them do not like the naughty President. I will try and help your Professor but in the meantime beware the Ides of March. Do you like Wayne and Shuster Mister Holmes?"

"Never heard of them,"

"My favourite comedians, second only to the Goons, you have heard of them Mister Holmes?"

"Yes, my old man used to rave on about them, his father used to listen to them too, what about them?"

"Quite unique Mister Holmes."

And with incredible clarity and a depth that he had never heard before in music or voice the crazy Goons song began to play, and with almost manic enthusiasm Holmes sang along with it. Each Ying Tong so precise that even he had no trouble hearing all of it. And with a shock he realised that the robot was entirely but cleverly insane.

"Break the connection please," he said, and added with a measure of despair, "We'll all be murdered in our beds." He giggled at the memory of the the weak, bladder shuddering cry of Minnie Bannister, the darling of Roper's Light Horse, and her febrile companion, Henry Crun from The Goon Show.

The second event was when he returned to the main screen and it was interrupted by a sudden image. The plan flickered, changed and then shifted to show a blip on a transfer port.

"What...?"

The screen changed to show the inside of the port and instinctively Holmes said. "Friends..."

"We will care for them."

Holmes gnashed his teeth. Why didn't the computer let him finish what he was saying. He watched as Bates and Fish were gassed and carried to the sick bay and shook his head. Fish was too slow with the spade. He could have downed at least one Pair if he had really tried.

Holmes sat on the floating chair and mentally doodled.

Well, well, he thought, things are getting along.

The Plans of Mice and Men...

The exercise was going well, too well, and Brigadier General Shafte was worried. In all his experience of exercises on Salisbury Plain he had never completed one that didn't end in farce. According to the situation map projected on the screen, group A was, in effect, doing what it was supposed to do. Group B was falling back against its defences and that in its turn was doing what was planned. The air strikes were working properly and the men and women marked as wounded or dead were not as usual buggering around on the battlefield pretending they were reserves and getting in the way. The armour was working properly and all artillery, laser guided rockets and solid shot weapons were scoring electronic hits at a high percentage. Admittedly the conditions were ideal and group A was a dedicated bunch. Besides, the press were watching, and so were the representatives from Europe. The performance had to be good or his job and the jobs of all the officers and career men were on the line. With the Sino – Indian war continuing there was a good chance that the war would finish and they would all be sent to the Indo-Chinese borders on a policing mission. Whatever happened Brigadier General Robert Shafte wanted to be involved. He imagined active service; in the media eye, allowances, promotion and, who knows, an honour, a royal gong. Not that there was much point now with the House of Lords more or less a glorified legislative body run by commoners. Still, he hoped, there will be medals, and knighthoods. He wondered if he would be able to wear his uniform or would it be a penguin suit. He imagined his wife so proud of him and passing herself off as Lady Shafte. He felt a warm glow of anticipated glory and beamed a sunny smile at the messenger who was offering him a telephone.

"Lt Colonel West for you, sir," she said.

He took the telephone from her and greeted West with a grunt.

"Sir, there is a strange troop attacking us from the rear, with all due respects, sir, who the hell are they?"

"There's no other group out there West," said the Brigadier. "Send a messenger and tell them they are not supposed to be there."

"Sir, they are shooting at us with live ammo, er, we have blanks and dummies. Sir, we have to know who the hell they are."

"There are no other armed forces out there West. You were fully briefed on the plan and know that. I assume you are in the right place?"

"We have retreated Sir. My apologies but I must go."

West cut the connection and the Brigadier handed the telephone back and gazed at the situation screens. There was nothing to see. Either West was going crazy or, and the thought suddenly hit him, there was a troop of bored casualties taking the mickey.

"Get me a chopper over there and if West is stuffing me around or somebody else is I'll have their guts for garters. Send somebody to have a look will you?" He said dismissively.

Lt Colonel Gary West cursed and again retreated. Why didn't the blimps take him seriously, he asked himself and swept the opposite hill with his binoculars. That was the trouble with being a young Colonel from what the self styled upper crust called the boondocks. The force across the way were real troops intent on fighting a real battle and he stood no chance against them with his small force. The enemy, he had to assume they were enemy because they had fired on his soldiers, were not going anywhere yet but they looked as if they were getting ready to move out. There were machines and men, and when he had sent a half track over to find out who they were it was shot to bits by something that looked like a hand held rocket gun. The half track cooked like a tank and there were no survivors.

"Pull out!" he had ordered, and as they moved off they had come under fire. Thankfully as soon as they were on the opposite hill the fire had stopped and he had called headquarters. As usual nothing got through to Shafte, and he had cut off the conversation to order a further retreat.

"Shall we bugger off, sir?" said RSM Dane.

"Not before we find out what that lot are about," he said, ordering a small scouting party to quietly watch and report he prepared to retreat. The enemy were not like any troops they had ever seen, and as they watched the group seemed to expand and men and machines moved slowly down the hill toward them. West ordered the retreat when they again came under fire.

"Move out!"

Motors revved and halted on a high point ready to move. West watched the enemy move over the hill they had just left when an army chopper flew overhead and circled the troops. It dropped lower as it passed and he waved to the pilot who waved cheerfully back. And then with mounting horror he watched as fire spouted up from the enemy and engulfed the aircraft which exploded showering them with hot debris.

"Christ! Get me headquarters!" But there was no need.

"Call for you sir."

He took the telephone and spoke curtly into the mouthpiece.

"West."

"Are you drunk or something West. There are none of our troops in your area. Get that? None planned, none scheduled and any you do see are a figment of your imagination. I want to know why you have moved East."

"I am sorry Brigadier but the figments of my imagination have just shot down a solid helicopter and its crew, they have also destroyed one of my half tracks and killed the crew. Presently they are marching up the hill with firepower and mobile weapons that have the ability to shoot the shit out of us," West said, and waited for a reply keeping an eye on developments outside his truck.

"Sir?"

"I repeat, why have you moved East?"

"The same reason I am going to move further East. Sir. And the same reason that I am asking for reinforcements and some real ammunition. Why don't you try SatCam and take a proper look. Remember that we have electronic tracers tuned to the computer in your hut and that the enemy across the way do not." He broke the connection again, and with all speed his troops travelled further East barely escaping injury from the sudden onslaught of the enemy.

"They move slow Sergeant Dane but even so at this rate we will be in London and unable to fire a shot to stop them," he said. "Fan out a bit and head to the low ridge you can see on the horizon. They spent a half hour or more travelling across country to the low ridge and stopped just below the skyline to observe the enemy movement.

"Look sir, I can see Stonehenge," said Dane. "I went there once with my mum." She lifted her binoculars to her eyes and stared at the monument and gasped.

"What is it?"

"I think there are more of them in Stonehenge itself," she said and gripped his sleeve. "Sir, I think we are in trouble."

He used his own binoculars and as he scanned the area his jaw tightened and his mouth described an O. The image he saw was of a crowd of soldiers who milled around in the confines of the monument. There were war machines, he could only describe them as battle wagons, parked in the public car park and he cursed when he saw public vehicles burning.

"Crikey, that's the A303 and the A360 blocked off if that lot don't shift," he said. "Dane, call headquarters, not the Blimp but the real headquarters. Let them know it is urgent."

RSM Dane used the telephone herself and was soon talking urgently to somebody and finally handed it to him with a sigh.

"I have General Morrison sir who seems to understand the situation," she said, and shrugged.

The voice on the other end was calm and sure, and West took trouble to explain what had happened and what he was doing. He made no mention of Shafte's remarks until he was asked, and then with a minimum of censure he related what had happened, and waited for the General to speak again.

"I urge you to hold on as long as you can Colonel," he said. "We will get you what you need. In the meantime even a token resistance might help. Have you any live ammunition?"

"No sir, General Shafte insisted we carry blanks only, for effect, he said. I guess he did not expect us to fight a real enemy. Sir, where do they come from?"

"It seems they are from outer space, Colonel, the first to land on our sceptred isles and you have the dubious privilege of being the first to fight them. Hang in there Colonel and we will be with you. If it is any comfort to you the Americans and the Australians are also under attack."

"An air strike would help but keep the choppers out of range, sir," he said adding the sir as an afterthought.

"I'll see what I can do."

The connection cut, he turned to Dane and with a grin he gave her the telephone, and said. "I think our colonel Blimp is about to cop some flak from Headquarters. In the meantime we are urged to hold on."

"What do we fight them with sir?"

"Oh, I think that when and if there is an air strike we fire all our ammo at them and let us hope that some of the rocket cases will knock them over. In fact I think that is exactly what we should do, fire low and let the metal bits bounce about like cannon balls. Pass the order Dane."

"Shall we shout 'bang' sir?" said Dane without hiding the sarcasm in her voice.

"If it will help," he said, and grinned.

"Yes sir!" she said and saluted which was difficult in the confines of the vehicle and as a result she rapped her knuckles on a steel rib. "Oh fuck."

"Language Dane, pass the orders to Captains Gordon, Marks and Johns and tell them I want to hear their shouts above those of their soldiers," he said, and laughed.

Dane trotted away from the vehicle shaking her head and he wondered why she didn't just call on the communications set instead. He shrugged his shoulders, and to the amusement of his driver and the men in the back of the vehicle he aimed his pistol in the direction of the enemy and yelled "Bang".

It's easier with a pistol, he thought, and giggled when he imagined crying out with enthusiasm and much noise the words 'rat-tat-tat' in rapid fire mode.

The Leader Pair looked with pleasure at the stone structures and approved. He liked monuments, especially big stone ones. In the first few small periods he had the excess vehicles cleared from the parking lot and took charge of the display and tourist centre. His Pairs pushed the Earth people out and herded them onto the plain across the road where they cowered in a ditch afraid to show themselves. He and his twin walked around the site and touched the stones, sat on them and stood back to work out where the sun would appear and what the first beams would strike. He was an expert in this sort of artefact and was looking forward to seeing more. He liked the idea of sacrificing Earth maidens on the stones, and licked his lips when they both thought of the bloodletting that would be theirs once they had conquered this primitive people. His counterpart across the plain informed him, rather snottily he thought, that there was a contingent of soldiers heading his way.

"We will intercept them and wipe them out," Lertz replied, and grinned at his twin. "These Bulgers cannot handle a bunch of peasants, Zertl my twin. We should send a bunch of Pairs off to sort them out and deal with the incoming troops ourselves."

They detailed off a section with four battle wagons to go out and kill the Earth soldiers and got on with the business of organising the incoming forces. The Transfer Ports were located close to the Stonehenge compound, and as more Pairs and wagons arrived he spread them out in formation breaking down the fences and shoving the shuttle cars back into their sheds. Pairs shooed the civilians away, and when they realised they were not going to be murdered on the spot they trudged off down the hills to Salisbury following roads and tracks. The Pairs set up road blocks and as people in vehicles attempted to get past they stopped them and tossed the vehicles aside after ejecting their occupants onto the grass. Stonehenge became surrounded for a while by burning vehicles and lines of trudging civilians fleeing the area.

The Zradians were so busy organising and consolidating their position that they missed the battle with Colonel West's force and were surprised when a bedraggled group of some half dozen Pairs staggered back to the camp and collapsed at their feet.

"What the Bulger happened to you?" Zertl demanded.

"We were beaten up," came the weak reply. "They stole our wagons and our weapons."

"How! You have enough fire power to cook these stones! How the Bulger did you manage that?" yelled Lertz, and a few moments later discovered why.

The four stolen battle wagons accompanied by a line of Earth vehicles and a pack of well disciplined soldiers rushed along the road attacking first the machines and then the Pairs. Two things surprised the Leader Pair and they were the two things he marvelled at during their captivity, both because they took his troops by surprise, and because they worked. The first was that the Earth Troops attacked the wagons and the transfer ports, and the second was that those who were not using captured weapons were yelling 'Bang Bang' for all they were worth, and firing their weapons at the same time. As his Pairs collapsed under the assault and his supplies came to an abrupt halt he realised that the Earth soldiers had no live ammunition. What sorted him out as far as the battle was concerned was that the rocket missiles that spewed almost continuously from the Earth vehicles, accompanied by the joyous shouts of 'Boom' from the enemy soldiers, simply knocked them off their feet. For a reason that neither Lertz nor Zertl could understand his troops failed to respond. An Earth hour later he was lined up with the rest of the Pairs disarmed, surrounded by a small group of grinning soldiers who fingered the buttons of the captured laser cannons they held trained on them. In the distance there was the sound of weapons firing and above them aircraft flew like small rockets across the plain. As each craft let go its load of missiles the soldiers guarding them laughed and chanted variations of 'Bang Bang', 'Rat-a-tat-tat' and 'Boom Boom'.

Much later that day when the trucks came and took them away as prisoners they were treated to the sight of the devastation wreaked on their fellows and were glad they were not part of it. The somewhat scruffy officer who had defeated them separated them from the rest and allowed them to ride on the top of a captured battle wagon.

"Does one of you speak my language?" he said.

"We had to learn it," said Lertz.

"You realise you cocked it up don't you?" said West. "Did you know we had no ammunition except blanks until our people turned up with a couple of wagon loads, so we sort of borrowed yours. Thanks for sending us enough to get started with."

"How did you do it?" asked Zertl.

"Oh, simple really, we surrendered to your blokes as soon as they reached us, and when they all got out to have a go at us we gave them a thumping with our fists and pinched their weapons. We tortured one who showed us how to work the wagons, and another showed us how to work the weapons, and so off we went. The rest of the soldiers just shot off the blanks and the rockets acted like stones and that was it."

"What about all the shouting?" asked Lertz feeling depressed with every small period.

"It's the way we fight," said West. "We are simple people really."

And when West and his companion laughed Lertz and Zertl huddled together and barely controlled the urge to cock their legs and urinate. It was unfair really because in spite of the rain that had started to fall it was quite a pleasant day.

Oops Missed!

Indian troops faced Chinese soldiers across the shattered hillsides unable to do anything more than throw rocks. Or get out of their vehicles and fight hand to hand. The last hand grenade, the last bullet and the last rocket were already spent. Clustered in groups, troops on both sides stared across the gap. Glance met glance and moved into stares. Shouts, meant to be insults, turned to laughter and gestures of anger became waves of frustration. There was nothing except bare hands and sharp blades to fight with. And no officers to give the orders.

Instead of fighting, the opposing forces climbed down from the temporary redoubts and sat in the sun. One Indian Sergeant carefully laid his rifle down on the dirt and walked in the open cautiously, and then with increasing confidence when no shots rang out. He sat on a shattered tree stump and took a cigarette from a packet and lit up. A cautious Chinese Sergeant put his useless rifle on the ground and walked casually across to where the Indian was sitting.

The Indian soldier offered him a cigarette.

The Chinese soldier examined it and put it in his mouth. The Indian soldier lit it for him and together they sat in the sun smoking, content to sit and say nothing. The Chinese soldier, who was young and skinny, looked full into the face of his counterpart and smiled.

"You speak Cantonese?" the young Chinese said.

"What's wrong with English?" said the Indian.

The Chinese soldier grinned.

"Bloody nutting."

"You speak Urdu?," said the Indian.

The Chinese soldier grinned and shook his head.

"Okay, what's going on?" he said.

"No guns. No rockets. No grenades. No fuel. No food. No fight."

"Me same."

"We want to give up and go home."

"Me too and all us soldiers."

"What's happening?"

"Our officers have all gone off to a conference at headquarters. They went this morning, early, and gave us orders to stay where we were and defend the republic. We are asking what with, and they tell us to make do. So we sit and wait. Who is wanting to fight with knives and bare hands. Too bloody messy."

The Indian soldier laughed. "That is what is happening to us. All the officers take off this morning and tell us to wait and defend the line. We all say bugger that, and are sitting down in the sun hoping you will sit tight too."

The two Sergeants grinned and looked at the lines. Other soldiers were emerging from their cover. Cries of greeting echoed across the valley and gradually as the word spread so the opposing forces came out of hiding and talked to each other. They lounged around in the sun chatting and asking questions getting answers and sharing experiences. There was laughter and hand shaking. Men and women showed photographs of families, partners and homes. They shared cigarettes and jokes and relaxed in the hot sun relieved that at last they had no reason to fight.

And suddenly with a series of small farting sounds pairs of fully armed men appeared from nowhere and dropped, fell or stuck out of trees, rocks or the ground. Those that remained on their feet immediately got ready to fight. The men who landed partway stuck through objects screamed, groaned, yelled or simply died. The Indian sergeant was the first to jump up followed closely by the Chinese. Both men drew their short bayonet knives.

"Enemy," said the Indian.

"To both of us," agreed the Chinese.

The newcomers were taken by surprise as hundreds of soldiers, angry at having their impromptu siesta interrupted, attacked them. Within a few minutes the ground was littered with enemy bodies and discarded weapons. The two sergeants picked up the laser weapons and examined them. They tried one each out on some shattered tree stumps and fell silent when they saw the effect.

"Awesome," said the Indian.

"Fantastic," agreed the Chinese.

Shoji Kamasuki stepped out of the aircraft and walked lightly across the tarmac. Lining the perimeter of the military section was an array of smartly presented Marines. Each Marine had a light machine gun clamped to his or her shoulder at the correct angle held there by two gloved hands. The rigid officer barked an order and the Marines pushed the machine guns out in front of them and stepped one step forward and back again. The machine guns flickered back up to shoulders and there was a perfectly coordinated stomp of plastic boots. Two officers and one civilian detached themselves from a waiting knot of people and came forward to meet him. They came to a smart halt at the proper distance and waited politely. He bowed and waited for them to do the same. All three men looked uncomfortable and bowed politely.

A bit overdone, he thought, but nevertheless they tried. The military reception was better. More precise and much more spectacular. Not relaxed but that was the way they did things here.

"Mister Kamasuki, welcome, please come with us to the limousine. The President is waiting for you."

Let him wait. He thought. He can do nothing until I get there anyway so let him wait.

The limousines sat beside the kerb and he allowed them to escort him to his seat in the middle car with the other two filled with security men. He approved of that. Aides fussed around him and one attempted to take his case but with a smile he kept hold of it.

"So sorry but I must have this with me at all times until after I have spoken with your President," he said, and bowed.

As they travelled he looked out of the car window at America. Wide tree lined streets and people rushing. Hot and busy with jackets over their shoulders or on their arms. Just like home, he thought, and smiled. The vehicle hissed to a stop at the end of a wide avenue and a soldier opened his door. He stepped out and followed the Aides into a dark entrance and into an elevator that dropped at least five floors and disgorged them into a plush lobby. Thirty seconds later he was face to face with the President of the United States of America. So help me God, he thought, and smiled.

The President spoke through an interpreter who paid him the courtesy of speaking a fraction behind the President allowing him a brief moment to absorb the content of the President's speech.

"Tell the Secretary that conditions are hardly acceptable unless he is willing to modify his demands to allow us more autonomy. Tell him that the United States will not tolerate a Japanese High Command. Tell him that the United States Armed forces are to be used mostly where the United States believes they should be used. Tell him that we are prepared to deploy them wherever they are needed but our first priority is to our home land. We are willing to join with the common cause but not at the expense of the United States." She said.

Shoji waited until the interpreter had finished and with deliberation he replied in Japanese.

"...And when the Japanese High Command have finished the task they will hand back the authority to the local offices. The objective is to defeat the invaders using the best resources available, and as we have the financial resources we are offering our expertise for the use of all military forces. The conditions we set are the only conditions under which we will operate." The interpreter said in English.

The President looked grave and shook his head.

"Tell the Nip he is an uncompromising yellow bastard and do it politely. Tell him that we cannot accept Japanese personnel in our High Command," the President said, barely holding his anger back.

Shoji kept his face impassive as the interpreter explained that the President was requesting that his military command be made up of Americans with Japanese advisers. He thanked her and replied.

"Explain that the conditions are set and unless they are followed to the letter we will not and repeat not, transfer any funds to the American sector of the war effort. Also explain to him that we estimate he will lose another four or five states and millions of people if the Zradian invasion is successful. We have the means to stop it. Explain to him that if he continues to be intractable we will choose another nation to work with. Europe has already conceded and if things go the way we expect them to Australia and South America seem ripe for development."

The President listened to the interpreter and bit his lip. He took a deep breath and spoke softly and determinedly

"Ah will not be dictated to by anybody," he said. "We maintain autonomy. And that is my final word."

The interpreter lowered her eyes when she replied and looked at Shoji fearfully.

Shoji smiled before he spoke and said in his own language.

"Miss, you will not need to translate my next few words," he said.

She looked at him, surprised and puzzled. She understood when he began his next speech in English addressing the President directly.

"Mister President, this Nip has the authority to negotiate a deal. It is invested in me through my Prime Minister who has the blessing of our Emperor. We have decided on a plan. That plan will enable the armed forces of the world to combat the invader in a coordinated fashion. We have the money and the technology to achieve this. We also have the arms to carry out this coordinated program in spite of any recalcitrant participants. In all, mister President, this Nip, this yellow bastard, is telling you, not asking you, to hand over your armed forces to us for the duration. If you do not we will organise an army that will," he paused, and looked around the table.

Seated as if isolated from the rest, although she wasn't, the Vice President was smiling.

He added. "Dropping Nuclear weapons on your own territory for whatever reason was a stupid and wasteful action. It will not happen again." Shoji watched the President's face change from smug determination to white fear. That will teach him to be a little more careful, he thought, realising he was probably talking to the ex-President of the United States.

"Right in the poo Horace," said the woman. "Mister Secretary, President, Officers, I would request that we call for a discussion and then a vote."

She looked around at all the delegates and smiled.

"I think that if mister Kamasuki would be so kind as to accompany the aides to an ante room where he will be comfortably entertained we can discuss what he has to offer?"

"Shoji smiled at her and said. "Thank you Vice President Walker I would be delighted. Please take as long as you wish. At least give me enough time to enjoy a refreshing drink and a small snack?"

He stood up and left the room bowing politely to the President.

"So sorry," he said. "You should be more polite."

Apart from the rustle of paper and the scrape of chairs his remarks were greeted by a stunned and embarrassed silence.

"Well?" asked the Vice President. "What is your reply to that?"

She looked from one to the other in turn finally letting her gaze rest on the President. He squirmed in his seat and shifted his gaze from hers. "Horace," she said sharply. "You have made a complete cock up. I suggest you step down while we get on with the business in hand. That is saving the United States from annihilation."

The President sat in his chair looking vacantly at the men gathered around the table. Denise Walker was aware that apart from the interpreter, who was looking scared, she was the only woman. This is going to be a long hard uphill battle, she thought. She started the discussion which began slowly with many arguments for and against until one of the men asked a question.

"Excuse me ma'am but what do you think we should do?"

The question came from Vice Admiral Smith, and she noted that the question was aimed directly to her. The Admiral pointedly did not look at the President. Horace, she thought, you have lost it.

"I think we should jump at the offer. As the honourable Secretary said, the autonomy is to be handed over for the duration and not for ever. And to forestall your question I will state that after the war is over and we have hopefully succeeded in driving the invader away then things will be different. We will have to make some fundamental changes anyway, so I suggest we go with it and see what happens. The deal will save a lot of American lives," she said, and looked at all them again. "Rupert?"

Rupert Walowski put his hands together in a steeple and spoke deliberately. "I am opposed to the Japanese High Command taking over our own but I want a solution that will help America survive."

"Johnson?"

"Me also but I want reassurances that the Japanese will leave immediately the emergency is over.."

It was typical of him to call the coming war an emergency, but then Johnson Biggs was a good man to have on your side. Head of the Army Air Forces he carried considerable weight in any discussion about war and where to spend American dollars. In this case, she thought wryly, Japanese Yen and billions of them too. When she was given the figures and a copy of the Japanese determination she was shocked. Despite the massive growth of the Chinese economy, the Japanese trade had burgeoned, and from the figures she was given it was obvious that Japan was in trouble – the curse of over-production. They had over one third of the world's wealth, and it was increasing at such a rate they would have nowhere to spend it and no customers capable of buying any goods either. World War Three, she had to admit as far as the Japanese economy was concerned, was a viable financial option. The Zradian invasion had arrived in the nick of time.

"We all know what we have been offered. All I need to know is if there are any reasonable objections?" she said. "If there are none then I suggest we vote to go ahead."

"Excuse me but what about the President?" asked the Secretary of State. "Surely Horace has the right to call the vote?"

She grinned. "Horace, do we carry out the vote?"

The President nodded.

"Show of hands or ballot?" she asked.

Ballot. All the men agreed.

Aides came in with cards and handed them around. In their own time the delegates marked their cards and folded them. The aides collected them and one sat at a desk and counted the yeses and the noes.

There was eight for yes and three for no.

"Carried?" she asked.

The President sank deeper into his chair and grunted.

"I'll tell mister K myself," she said.

Shoji smiled when Denise Walker came in.

"We accept your government's offer," she said. "Personally I would like to express my thanks to your government, and I am certain the President will formalise his own version of acceptance shortly."

"Ah, then I expect we will be negotiating with you in the future, neh?"

"Probably, but for now let us assume that we are not?" she said. "First the President will have to sell the idea to the American people. After that I expect he will resign."

"I will personally send him my regards," said Shoji. He liked this woman. Lesbian or not he warmed to her personal power and was surprised when he realised that for the first time in his political career he had come to terms with a woman in power as an equal.

He bowed politely and followed her into the room.

He wasted no time and took the documents he was carrying from his briefcase and handed them out.

"The outline is in this document and the detailed version will be sent by electronic means. If you have any issues you wish to discuss I will be here for a period of one week, and then after that the liaison officers will arrive. As soon as possible after that we will begin shipping arms and soldiers."

On star Station Two the Lead Pair in charge of 14 Sector 3 Yellow watched the numbers drop and dwindle away to nothing. With a curse he pressed a button on the console and waited for the message that flickered across it to pass. It did several twists and turns before the screen cleared to be replaced by a digital image of their target area. Dead bodies. Pairs destroyed and filthy Earthmen walking away with the weapons.

"Bulgers! We've lost all of them," said the Lead Pair despairing.

"We strike again?" asked the operator.

"Drop wafer grenades on the Bulgers," said the Lead Pair.

"Will do."

The screen shook and numbers appeared as the operator added the coordinates. A string of figures rolled down the screen and a figure flashed.

"It's shifted! Change number codes!"

The operator frantically adjusted the codes but at the crucial moment the screen was filled with images of romping rodents. Almost as quick as they arrived they disappeared again and the operator cursed loudly.

"Did you send them?" asked the Lead Pair.

"Yes but we are not certain we hit."

The Pairs stared at the screen as it changed to a glowing pink and displayed a message in white lettering edged with purple.

Oops! Missed! Do not be afraid of the rodents!

"Bulgers! Bulgers! We'll never fight a war with this going on!" roared the Lead Pair. "Send everything we've got! Show the Bulgers; Nong's teeth! I want action!"

The operator looked frightened and backed away from the screen.

"What is wrong?" demanded the Lead Pair.

"I...I...I...haven't got anything else left ...see?"

The operator pointed to the screen and the Lead Pair turned from their terrified faces to look. Immediately they began to shake and like the operator backed away in terror.

"What is it?" he gasped.

"I don't know ..."

"Get rid of it," hissed the Lead Pair.

"We can't."

The Lead Pair and the operator backed into a corner and stood clutching each other, sometimes cocking their legs as if to urinate, and sometimes jerking forward to attack the screen image but recoiling at the last moment to fall back to the clutching position. Their relief Pairs found them huddled in the corner staring at the screen seemingly fascinated by the message scrolling continuously across it.

"Bulgers," said the second Lead Pair. "This station is contaminated." He pressed a button and the screen was filled with the image of a kitten playing with a ball of wool.

"Oh, that," he said, and with his eyes averted he reached down to the floor and yanked out the cables. With a small electronic phut the station stopped completely. With a shrug of resignation he pressed the emergency buttons and stood by the portal waiting. His whole body shook and he felt angry, confused, frightened and wanted to run after something. Particularly a cat. He felt his right legs twitch and with a low cry the Pair grasped each other by the hand and stood breathing deeply. He pitied the poor Pairs grovelling in the corner.

Something or somebody somewhere was tapping into a program that was driving Pairs insane and just now they had come pretty close to it themselves. The answer was to call the Polisocs and hope for the best. Death, they thought, came easily enough, but chasing electronic images of cats was not for them. At least not this time anyway. Within a few short periods the Polisocs arrived and their priority was to observe the exact protocol. And that was enough to stabilise any Pair.

Byrde

Silly bugger was what Richard Byrde was thinking when the hover car veered off the road and hurtled across the pavement. Lugs moved first, and took Byrde with him leaving the Ferret to drag Braine out of the way. When the car crashed into a shop front spinning like a top and came to a crunching halt he thought differently about it. The occupants lay slumped against the inflated air bags obviously badly hurt. Lugs pulled the door open and peered at the two men.

"Buggered I reckon," he said. "We better get going boss. These blokes ain't like us."

The four men hurried from the scene pushing past onlookers who tried unsuccessfully to stop them. Lugs' overwhelming presence hushed their protests, and soon they were clear of the press.

"We better watch it after this," said the Ferret. "I think them blokes is on to us."

"It was Byrde's idea we go and check out that stupid garden shed. We haven't even got there yet and already the enemy are attacking us. It's not fair!" wailed Braine.

"Can it Oliver," said Byrde. "We have Lugs and the Ferret to look after us which is better than walking around on our own."

Byrde conveniently ignored the fact that Oliver Braine was accidentally drawn into the plot. He was not as worried about the attack as Braine wanted him to be. What he wanted to do was to find out what had happened to Arthur Renfrew. After the Professor disappeared he had suggested that Emily collect the children in their new car and go down to stay with her mother. Wisely, the Ferret suggested that instead they get his younger brother to drive the family to Devon accompanied by some of Colin's thugs. Byrde saw the sense in that suggestion and so with a few telephone calls the Ferret's Younger Brother arrived with two of Colin's thugs and a vehicle that would carry eight people and luggage.

"Mornin' Mister Byrde," said the Ferret's Younger Brother. "Missus, Gerry and Mal will grab yer gear. Cor, Ferret, I didn't know you knew Colin 'Icks and 'is mates?"

"Not me, it's Mister Braine here wot knows them. They're his mates."

The Ferret's Younger Brother was obviously impressed, and even more impressed when Byrde offered him a deal if they survived the coming troubles that included a contract for racing vintage motorcars.

"D'ye reely mean that?"

"Sure do, and on your way to Devon tell Emily what you want to do and she will sort it out for you," he said, and was rewarded by the warm glow that the Ferret's smile of pleasure gave him. He was also impressed by Braine's modesty when the Ferret's Younger Brother addressed him as "Governor".

Byrde gave Emily a huge hug and smothered her with kisses before she got into the van with the Ferret's Younger Brother, and watched her go, glad that she was with her mother and the children and glad that at least two of Colin's men were with them.

The night before when they talked over the Professor's disappearance the Ferret suggested they go to the Bywater road allotments and check out the garden shed.

"It might be nuthin' but that's where Julian Renfrew disappeared. Maybe we can find some answers there," said the Ferret.

Byrde agreed, and they decided to walk. Now he was not so sure.

"Let's get going," said Byrde. "The allotments are just around the corner."

The Ferret kept moving and the others followed along the street and into the rear entrance of the allotments. As they walked along the grass edged pathways between the plots they heard somebody's radio playing the tune A Whiter Shade of Pale.

"That tune again," said Byrde, cheerfully. "Must be driving everybody mad."

"Are you always so happy?" asked Braine. "I mean, nothing seems to upset you does it? You nearly get killed by two maniacs in a car and casually walk off. You listen to that blasted tune for what must be the hundredth time in a day and you smile and now you want to look at a wrecked shed? Are you crazy?"

"A little, but then aren't we all?" replied Byrde, affably.

They reached the allotments and walked along the pathways to the burnt out shed. Byrde nodded at a gardener working on his plot and said a cheerful 'good day' smiling at the man. The gardener looked up and scowled.

"I hope you ain't goin' ter tread on me gardin,' he said. "Them bleedin' coppers do it all the time. It ain't right ter treat a bloke's plot like that. Stompin' all over it and parking bleedin' motors all over me onions. Bloody ratbags."

"No, no, old chap, all I want to do is look at the old shed. I agree with you, chaps shouldn't stomp on a chap's garden," Byrde said, defensively.

Byrde and his party walked carefully past the garden plot eyeing the gardener warily, and stood gazing at the dirty remains of the toolshed.

"I don't see what we can learn from this place," said Braine. "I can't see anything to help us at all."

"Let's have a good look around at it shall we before we decide anything," said Byrde. He glanced at Braine, annoyed at his negativity but relented a little reasoning that Braine wasn't cut out for excitement. He climbed up onto the wooden floor followed dutifully by Lugs and the Ferret. Braine hopped up behind them and Oliver discovered the pillar of buttons and fondled it idly as he puzzled at what it was doing there.

"Excuse me but what is this thing?" he asked, turning to the others.

"It looks like one of the crane button pods I use in my factory," said Byrde.

"What do you think will happen if I press them?" asked Braine and without waiting for an answer he pushed buttons down. A red light flashed and then changed to green. Byrde gazed at the pod and then looked up at Braine's pained expression.

"Oops," said Braine. "I think I've done something silly..."

The allotments disappeared in a misty film of grey and Braine felt as if his body was being taken apart and put back together again. Before he could remark on the feeling to the others he was slipping down a smooth wall to land on his knees on a soft plastic floor. Confused, he tried to stand but his stomach heaved and he fell again. Thirty seconds later Lugs lifted him to his feet and propelled him from what he thought was an elevator car.

"So that's what happened to Julian," said Byrde

They stood on a carpeted floor in what could only be described as a luxury Hotel foyer. On their right there was a wide flight of stairs going up, and to the left the foyer stretched to the reception desk and a large main entrance. Behind them the elevator door slid shut with a soft hiss. Braine turned unsteadily and watched the door close.

"Where are we?" he asked.

"No idea but wherever we are we may as well keep going. I suggest we take a look outside. This place seems deserted; have a look at the furniture; it's dusty and I think the carpet is covered in sand."

Byrde kicked gently at the carpet and pink dust flew up a little way and settled again. They followed him and a few minutes later they stood at the top of a wide flight of steps gazing at the gardens spread before them. Instead of a well cut lawn of green grass and beds of familiar flowers there was a strange purple, red and blue landscape that stretched to a horizon of low red hills. The nearest gardens were equally divided between yellow, red, blue and green which bordered flagstone walks and fine fountains set in ornate stone lined pools. At the edge of the grounds small shrubs acted as a fence, and beyond that the land was divided up into paddocks with some unrecognisable crop waving in the warm breeze. Beyond the plantation a large animal, similar to a big cat stopped, seemed to sniff the air and as quickly as it had appeared it disappeared. Byrde shuddered. "Did you see that animal?"

"What, the big pussycat," said Lugs.

"Yes, I hope we don't meet many of them," Byrde said. "I like pussycats but that one looked wild and angry."

Lugs nodded and stared out across the landscape. "The place is a bit odd."

"Weird," said the Ferret. "Never seen anything like this before."

"And that ain't all," said Braine. "Take a look up there."

He pointed to the sky.

"Well I'll be blowed," said the Ferret. "Two suns. Now where the heck did they come from?"

"We ain't on Earth boss," said Lugs. "Reckon we'll meet some little green men?"

All three looked at Lugs.

"Bug eyed monsters," he said. "I read about 'em in me comics."

"He's right you know. This is not Earth," said Byrde.

The Ferret looked grim. Braine looked terrified.

"What ... what are we going to do now?" he asked. "I mean, if we're on another world won't there be aliens and, and ... Oh crikey, we'll be killed. We'll die..."

"Stow it Oliver. First thing to do is look for food and water and the next is to find out where we are and make the best of it. We could try to get back home if we knew how we got here in the first place. Now that reminds me, what the heck happened back there?" Byrde said, and looked at Braine.

"I er, pressed the buttons and er, here we are," Braine said, brightly. "I'm sorry."

"That's okay Oliver, don't let it happen again eh?" Byrde said, grinning.

Lugs and the Ferret looked on.

"Reckon we oughter take a look see if we could find some food?" said the Ferret.

"Good idea. Do you think we might find something back in the building?" said Byrde.

"We could try."

They trooped back inside and found a set of stairs leading to a lower floor and Byrde led the way down. Lights flickered on in sidewall panels as they walked, and at the bottom the stair well opened into a large circular area divided into four sections. The colours were divided similarly to the gardens above.

"Spread out and look for food and water. We may be lucky," said Byrde and immediately walked over to the blue section and began to search.

It was Lugs who found the food stacked in section yellow.

"Dog sausage," he said. "This stuff looks and smells like dog sausage but I reckon we oughter try some and 'ope it don't kill us."

He broke the cover on a full roll of sausage and pinched a bit off. Carefully he bit into it and chewed slowly. His Adam's apple bobbed up and down as he swallowed and gulped the small portion down. His face broke into an ugly smile and he tore another piece off and handed it to the Ferret.

"Try it boss, it smells a bit orf but I fink it's orlright."

The Ferret gingerly took a piece and chewed at it swallowing the mouthful bit by bit and finally he nodded.

"Tastes like dog sausage," he said and looked thoughtfully at Byrde.

"How do you know?" asked Byrde.

"Sometimes a man has to do what a man has to do," said the Ferret and grinned broadly. "A man's gotta eat."

"Ugh," said Braine.

Byrde laughed throwing his head back and supporting himself with an outstretched arm against the wall.

They found water, or something like it, and this time Byrde tasted it and handed around the plastic mug which he had filled for them to try.

"At least it is wet and it tastes a little of gin and tonic without the kick," said Byrde. "What do you think Oliver?"

"Yes I agree but what do we do now?"

"We find something to carry the food in and something to put the water in and we bugger off before somebody comes. I have an uncomfortable feeling that we would hardly be welcome."

They found some containers made of some material that felt and acted like plastic and some convenient shaped bags, and with a makeshift pack each they left the service area and tromped back up the stairs. They walked quickly out of the building and down the steps into the gardens crossing the flagstones and into the shrubs. Byrde went in front and behind him came Braine with Lugs and the Ferret bringing up the rear. Byrde was lucky enough to find a track on the other side of the shrubs that led between the paddocks, and with a regular stride he marched on up the steady slope. At the top he called for a short rest and they turned to look back the way they had come. Spread out below them a surprising distance away was the building complex. It consisted of four large circles with a square courtyard in the centre, and a smaller circular building from where they had walked. It was connected to the others by overhead covered walkways in a regular pentagon. The gardens surrounding the building were divided into four sections with plants that were shades of the colour belonging to each section. Namely red, yellow, green and blue. The circles themselves were coloured red, yellow green and blue and where they had left the building was the only place where all four colours came together.

"Where we came out must be the main entrance," said Byrde. "I wonder what the building was? It looks like a resort of some sort."

They stood looking at the building and suddenly Lugs grunted.

"I fink there's some blokes coming outer the place," he said.

There were. A group of black and red clad men dashed out of the entrance in pairs and immediately fanned out in the gardens searching. One pair gazed up at the track and immediately pointed.

"Oh oh we have been spotted," said Byrde. "Let's get moving."

"Oh Christ," said Braine with feeling. "They'll kill us won't they?"

"Not if I can help it," rumbled Lugs cracking his knuckles together.

"Oh bloody hell," groaned Braine.

The track dipped and then climbed again, and so it went on. Up and down and twisting and turning between rocky outcrops and scrubby hillsides. The vegetation thinned out after they left the rural area and the air seemed to be getting hotter with every step. The breeze was a relief when they were in the open but as they dipped into the valleys the suns heat was so strong that every step seemed like a gigantic effort. Yet they had to keep going. Now and then turning back to look Byrde saw the men on the track behind them. They were gaining steadily and Byrde realised that soon his party would be too tired to keep moving. They had to stop soon and hide or find somewhere to set an ambush, or maybe the cavalry will come and rescue them. Hiding somewhere was the best option Byrde thought. What they wanted now was a miracle. They turned a sharp corner and the track steepened cutting between steeper cliffs of vertical stone, and as they marched wearily up the path Byrde decided he had had enough. At the top of the cutting there was a flat space where the path wandered across vegetation and yet another steep cutting. The top of the next one was crowned with ragged pinnacles and as far as he could see overlooked the path below quite clearly. They would make a stand there he decided.

"When we get to the top of that cutting," he said, and pointed at the crags. "We make a stand and sort these buggers out. I don't think we can run for much longer."

They sweated to the top of the cutting and spread out to look back down the track. Not far away their pursuers were jogging up the slopes like a line of happy hikers. Byrde looked down at them and pursed his lips.

"We ambush them here with rocks and Lugs. If we get on top and drop rocks on them Lugs can sneak up behind and give 'em what for and dash back again. We chuck rocks down on them again and Lugs has another go and then we charge. Okay?"

Lugs nodded enthusiastically, the Ferret looked relieved and Braine trembled.

"Do we have to?" he said.

Byrde nodded.

Byrde, Braine and the Ferret gathered piles of sharp heavy rocks and lined them up ready for throwing while Lugs scrambled back down the track and found a hiding place. No sooner was he hidden than the enemy came trotting over the top and onto the open space. Byrde counted twelve men travelling in pairs, and saw with relief that they were only lightly armed. He nodded to the others and smiled encouragingly at Braine who licked his lips and tried to smile back. Good luck, Byrde mouthed and noted that Braine straightened a little as if determined to conquer his fear. The men reached the end of the flat and Byrde dropped his hand as a signal to fire and launched his first rock. It found a target and eagerly he grabbed another. Suddenly he stiffened hearing a noise behind him and with an icy cold fear clutching at his heart he turned and forgot about throwing rocks at people.

"Oh shit," he said.

On the hot flat rocks behind them a large cat-like animal wobbled its rear end like a huge domestic moggie attacking a bird. Before Byrde could warn the others the animal sprang, and with a yell he dived to one side. It was too late. The animal hit him and together they fell over the edge and dropped snarling and yelling on the track below.

"Oh shit!" he said again.

In the dark street the Dog Squad Leader Pair shushed his Pairs and snarled.

"Stand quiet you scum," he said.

The Pair moved to the front of the small column and peered out into the alien street that was lit by lamps but to his eyes it was dark, and for a several small periods they stood waiting for their eyes to adjust to the gloom. As they waited they listened to the noise of the city and absorbed the ambience, and at the same time tried to work out where the Nong they were. The street was dingy and what spaces were not taken up with parked cars were filled with abandoned wrecks, and the cats fought the dogs for the contents of the garbage cans. There was a movement across the street and the Pair sighed with relief, walking casually or perhaps, like them, blindly, was their contact Pair. The Pair crossed the street and walked slowly along the sidewalk to the end of the alleyway where the troop waited.

"Pairs?" said the contact Pair.

"Right beside you," said the Leader Pair, and fended off the drawn knives and gave the password.

"Nong's teeth you Bulgers, why are you so nervous?"

"It's a dangerous place," came the reply.

"Nevertheless you will lead us to where the vehicles are stored and show us what we need to know," said the Leader Pair. The contact Pair, he noticed, spoke as individuals, and with a perverse sense of spite and twinness he made a point of speaking as a twin with that slight delay between the dominant and passive most Pairs adopted when speaking formally.

Within a quarter turn the Pairs were ensconced in a warm shed and shown how to operate the two small vehicles that would get them quickly to their target. They learned the routes to Bywater road by heart and then watched the screens as the contact Pair made them familiar with Richard Byrde's movements.

"The other Earthman is not up to much when it comes to fighting but the little one and his big mate are good. Byrde himself is a scrapper. Sorry, scrapper is a word we learned from listening in to the Earth style Policemen."

"Why are we after these people?"

"It is all part of the invasion plan launched by our Glorious President," said the Leader Pair.

The Dog Squad Leader Pair looked pleased. He liked the thought of being part of his Glorious Leader's master plan.

Later, at about mid morning, the Leader Pair watching the monitor screens saw Byrde and his party walking together through the narrow streets and alleyways and worked out that incredibly the group were heading for the Bywater road allotments.

And so, with the blessing of their contact Pair and the last orders of their Senior Leader Pair echoing in their minds the troop set off to capture Byrde and bring him and his party to Zrad where the Polisocs were waiting to interrogate them. And that, he thought, as the two vehicles weaved in and out of the traffic, was something he was looking forward to.

He only wished that the vehicles were a lot faster and there were not so many people in the way. He, they, closed their eyes when things got too exciting and opened them only to monitor the progress of Byrde and his friends. At one stage in their journey the Leader Pair's troops were tangled in a traffic snarl up that reduced their progress to a crawl and wasted many short periods. The Leader Pair checked his Atlas and saw that the Transfer Station at the

Bywater road had activated, and before some dumb Pair wiped the data from the memory he recorded the code in his personal file.

"Get moving you Pig Fodder!" they yelled, and fell sprawling into their seats as the vehicle lurched forward and hurtled into a side road.

"On our way your Honour," replied the driver Pair, and it was from that moment the terror began. The driver threw the vehicle around as if it were a child's toy and dived in and out of the traffic on the shortest route to the allotments. In the distance and getting closer the sound of sirens wailed and echoed like banshees.

The Leader Pair glanced at the trace and swore.

"Copy the code! For Nong's sake!" He yelled.

Frantically the communications Pair tapped figures into the hand held Comsec unit struggling to hold on as the vehicle lurched past frightened pedestrians. The driver Pair yelled obscenities at the other vehicles and screamed as a huge public transport vehicle swerved to avoid them. The trace beeped and the driver Pair twisted the quadrant to direct the vehicle to the left and along a wide road. The locals panicked and dived out of the way as they hurtled the wrong way down a busy street, and with a series of sickening lurches, violent swerves and the occasional jarring crash they reached the allotment gate and skidded inside. The vehicle behind followed creating its own havoc and together they tumbled into the allotments where the Transfer facility was located. "Okay Pairs, park by the shed," said the Leader Pair.

"Fine but how in Nong's sake do you stop the Bulging thing?"

"Switch the Bulging thing off you stupid Pig Fodder!" screamed the Leader Pair as the vehicles skidded across the soft gardens toward the brick building that loomed large above them.

With greenery and dirt flying in all directions the two vehicles came to a crashing halt against the wall. It was a long time before the six Dog Squad Pairs recovered and crawled groggily from the crashed vehicles. The escorts spent precious time treating the Dog Squad Pairs for concussion and disorientation during which time an irate Earthman with a garden tool raced across the wrecked allotment screaming unintelligibly attacked them swinging the weapon wildly. Perversely, realising the man was crazy, the escort Pairs spent even more time dodging around trying to stop him without killing him. Eventually they knocked him down and dropped him unceremoniously in his messed up garden.

The delay was long enough for the local police to reach them in force and with the bad luck of those in a hurry a line of officers managed to cut the Dog Squad Pairs off from the transfer port.

"Stay where you are!" cried the officer in charge shakily unsure of the nature of the disturbance. His sergeant was already calling up the armed offenders squad and he was considering withdrawing his men when the group of strangely dressed men charged at them. His men drew their batons and began striking out seemingly ignoring the fact that at least half the group were armed.

They lost the fight but their action made it difficult for the Dog Squad Pairs to reach the platform en-masse. As it turned out two of the escort Pairs were forced onto the platform too and if it was not for the Dog Squad Pairs raising their weapons ready to fire and the police officers, realising their danger and backing off rapidly, the Squad would not have made the trip.

"Shoot!" exclaimed the senior officer. "The buggers have disappeared!"

The two escort Pairs and one Dog Squad Pair remaining attempted to run off but at that moment a cat popped over the wall close by and spat at them in surprise. To a Pair they leapt at it yelling Zradian obscenities, tromping over the rising form of the unfortunate gardener who managed to grab one of them by the legs and drag him down onto the soft soil.

"You bastard!" yelled the gardener battering the writhing Zradian Half Pair with his fists. The remaining Half Pairs tried to scramble over the wall after the cat who turned on the first one and scratched his face with the full power of its claws.

"Aaargh!" the Half Pair yelled and fell from his perch to be caught by two police officers. The other two were captured easily, after all one had just seen his twin clawed by a hated feline, and the other was wondering where his twin was. The Dog Squad Pair tried using their gas guns but what with the cat, the crazy gardener and the effect of seeing their mates disappear without them were overwhelmed by the police.

The poor gardener sat astride the beaten Half Pair trying to batter the man even further into the soft soil but two burly officers, one a woman managed to drag him off. He struck out wildly at both of them. The woman officer flattened him with one blow.

"Cor," she said. "I didn't know I could do that."

They left the gardener where he lay and arrested the other men and waited for Sergeant Orange to arrive. The Ambulance crew that had already arrived picked the gardener up and prepared to take him off to the local hospital. The cat sat on a higher wall overlooking the allotments and carefully washed itself.

Having escaped the Earthmen the Dog Squad communication Pair began pressing the buttons using the code under the glowering gaze of the Leader Pair. Lights flickered and suddenly there was the familiar brief feeling of disorientation and they arrived, hopefully, in the same location as their quarry. The six Pairs waited for the door to open. Each Pair drew their gas pistols and the group dashed out of the port and raced outside.

"Spread out Pairs and look for them. Call back when you locate them."

One alert Pair spotted their quarry almost immediately and with angry vigour the Leader Pair led the chase.

Travelling light with only gas guns and knives was a good idea, the Leader Pair thought, but he wished they had lasers as well. Maybe they could call some up after this, and then they would feel like real troopers. They topped the steep cutting expecting to come upon the fugitives along the flat or at least struggling up the next slope, but as yet they were nowhere in sight. The Leader Pair knew from the signs his men were getting tired and soon they would have to stop. He must keep the pressure up and then he would have them. Pig fodder after the interrogators had had their fun. Nong's teeth. Soon they would find out what Earthmen were like. He chuckled with anticipation.

He dived aside when the first rocks fell and yelled a warning as a man and a Carnibeast toppled over the edge of the rocky ridge above them aimed directly for the middle of their column.

They're attacking us with rocks and carnivores, he thought, worrying mostly about the carnivore. But the beast he didn't see was Lugs who hurtled from his hiding place like an express train and launched himself on the Carnibeast. A shower of rocks hit them and with a yell of agony he and his twin rolled over the edge of the track and fell into a storm gully.

Above them all was noise and scuffling and the dread roaring of the Carnibeast and Lugs' terrible cries.

Police vehicles surrounded the gardens and police officers plodded into the compound and gathered like locusts around the abandoned vehicles joining the already confused force. Sergeant Orange saw the unfortunate gardener struggling with the Ambulance men and walked over to the group.

"What's up?"

"The bloke doesn't want to go with us," was the reply.

"Yeah well youse blokes is tramplin' all over me gardin' ain't yer? And I ain't 'aving it, see?" cried the gardener, and so saying scrambled from the stretcher, ran across to where the Inspector was standing listening to the account of the chase, and picked up his fallen rake. "I'll have the bastard! He's standing on me gardin'!"

Sergeant Orange ran after him and as the angry gardener took a long swing at the unsuspecting head of the Inspector he dived headlong and grabbed the man around the knees felling him in what was a perfectly executed rugby tackle, which was surprising because Sergeant Orange had never played rugby in his life.

The Inspector moved out of the way and looked down at the two men, wiping soft greenery from his otherwise pristine uniform. "Orange, watch what you are doing man! My uniform, look at the mess you've made of it!"

"Sorry sir," said Sergeant Orange from his muddy position, allowing two officers to grab hold of the gardener and take him away. The Inspector turned away and as he got up from the ground the sergeant slipped on the greenery and staggered to his feet bumping into his superior.

"Oaf! Get away from me!"

Sergeant Orange walked off dejectedly. "Sometimes I hate this bloody job," he said.

Star Station One

Holmes laughed.

Bates and Fish sat nursing hot drinks looking confused and worried.

"Where the heck are we?" said Fish.

"... yeah," added Bates.

"You are on Star Station One which is currently parked somewhere in space approximately one decimal zero five light years from Earth and approximately four decimal three five light years away from its home planet. We are not exactly certain that we are where we say we are anyway. The bloke in charge has plonked me on the wagon and has actually forbidden the catering staff to serve any of us alcoholic drinks. He says we are to remain sober until the job is over. You two have been co-opted as well. It's called earning your keep. The Zradians are hot on that. You works and you eats," Holmes explained.

"And just what is it are we expected ... began Bates

" ...to do?" finished Fish.

"I think Blard and Bradl want us to help them destroy a Star Station or invade the President's palace or something," said Holmes. "He hasn't told me yet."

Bates looked at Holmes and looked at Fish and back to Holmes again.

"What is it with these ..." he began

"... odd looking buggers?" said Fish.

"What do you mean?"

"They seem to be sort of ..." began Fish

"...like two people in ..." said Bates

"...one and they seem to act and speak ..." said Fish

"...like one person but there is two ..." said Bates

"...of them?" finished Fish.

"They are born in pairs and they call themselves Pairs. You have to talk to two of them as one person. Blard and Bradl are working as one agent and he is my employer. Pays well too," Holmes said adding emphasis to the last and rubbing his hands together. "Won't let me drink."

Bates and Fish grinned and sipped their hot drinks.

Holmes was glad to see them. He had gone down to the medical centre as soon as they recovered from the gas attack and walked into their cell casually as if he had expected them and stood grinning while they tried to speak. When they did it was typical of them to get confused about who was talking for who. And that's why he had laughed. The Pairs had given them a hot healing drink each to get rid of the toxins and ushered him into their cell.

"What ..." said Fish

"...are you do ..." said Bates

"...ing here," finished Fish.

Both men looked puzzled.

Holmes laughed.

"Come with me when you've finished that," he said. "I'll take you to our leader."

Bates and Fish laughed.

"Corny!" they said in unison.

Bates and Fish stood in the centre of the control room gawking like tourists. Blard glanced at his twin, his face a question. Bradl nodded and Holmes noticed a slight change in the way the Pair acted. It was as if they were comfortable, relaxed and familiar as if they found Bates and Fish acceptable. Bates and Fish did a couple of turns and looked admiringly at Holmes and then at the Pair.

"Awesome..." said Fish

"...totally,..." said Bates

"...awesome," said Fish.

"I think we should put these two on the learning machine," said Blard.

"Wassat?" demanded Fish.

Bates took up an aggressive and challenging stance. Holmes noticed that Fish held him back with one arm which Bates gripped lightly. Menacing.

This time Blard and Bradl laughed.

"You will learn the history and the language in one easy lesson," said Holmes. "It's fun."

He watched Bates and Fish walk with the Pairs to the learning room and sighed. Aggressive buggers, he thought fondly, turning back to his work station and began a new program. "Computer give me Star Station Two again pl..." he began

"...ease on its way," finished the computer.

"Don't you start that!" said Holmes, annoyed.

"Sorry, my little joke."

Holmes fumed a little and soon forgot about it when the program flashed up. In the corner of the screen playing happily was a small rodent cartoon and Holmes smiled happily. His friend, Betty/Anthony/Napoleon was watching over him. He was pleased about that.

The signal whispered into the system and moved quickly through the designated channels and waited all of one nano-second to schedule its arrival. Binary equivalents shifted, twisted, changed and reacted and finally recalculated and a screed of information flowed into the crystal memory. The memory bytes left an indicator on the queue and waited to be recalled.

In his cubicle Blard the Barmy and Bradl saw the indicator and tapped the code. The message flashed into life and filled the screen.

Blard read it through once and then printed it out.

"How shall we respond to this one?" he asked Bradl.

"I think we should use our two new recruits and mister Sherman Holmes. I think we had better start training Bates and Fish for the task and give Holmes a bit more information. It might prove useful if he knows a little more about what's going on."

"Okay my twin I will start the program," said Blard.

"You know, it's funny but I think Bates and Fish are more like us than any Earthmen, what do you think?" said Bradl, reflectively and almost to himself.

"I felt that too," agreed Blard. "Strange."

"Really odd," said Bradl.

Sergeant Orange walked slowly along the track. The allotments were almost deserted except for one lone gardener close by the wall. The man was smashing at plants with a hoe. Earth and greenery flew up wetly and splashed onto the grass. He was so absorbed in his self appointed task he took no notice of Sergeant Orange until he was close. With a jerk the man stopped thumping the daylights out of his carrots and glared at him.

"Come to tromp on me gardin' 'ave yer copper?"

"No, the thought never entered my mind. I was wondering what the heck you were doing."

"Bashing me carrots into the ground. Wotsit look like?"

Sergeant Orange looked at the plot, astonished when he saw that all the plants had been bashed into the ground. He realised at the same moment that there was something odd about them too. And then he noticed the plastic shopping bags discarded beside the plot. Odd. Really odd. Then he saw the row of cans. Processed peas. Baked beans. Beetroot and tomatoes. The plot was filled with neat rows of store bought onions, potatoes, carrots, parsnips, turnips, cabbages, cauliflowers, radishes, lettuces and some globe artichokes. The rows were solidly bashed down and Sergeant Orange saw they were all marked with seed packets. There was even one row of scarlet runner beans sticking out of the soil like asparagus. The gardener's eyes shifted rapidly and his tongue flitted in and out like a lizard, spittle dribbled down his chin and the fingers on his free hand twitched. With the other he gripped the hoe tightly. Sergeant Orange leapt aside a split second before the hoe reached him. He felt the muddy blade brush past his face and to avoid the reflex return blow he dodged backwards and turned. Quickly he shifted ready to attack but the man was too far away and the weapon too wildly swinging to catch. He ran a few steps and blundered against the shed floor. The hoe came down at him and instinctively he kicked out knocking it to one side. The gardener howled with rage and raised the hoe above his head. Sergeant Orange leapt out of the way and landed on the shed floor wobbling on his feet as he crouched to duck the swinging blow. It passed but he had to clutch a protruding pillar to keep his balance. Something clicked under his finger and a red light glowed.

What the heck was he doing here? He had only popped down to take another look at the place where Constable Rice had been killed. It was curiosity and a need to sort out in his mind the criticism from the Super, the bloody press, picking things out of what he said and twisting them around and his missus going on at him about being a big mouth and all that. What about her? You could hear her halfway down the ruddy street 'ollering; foghorn voice and cloth ears. He ducked again as the hoe came slicing at him. Something else clicked beneath his clutching fingers and the light flashed.

"Oy mister, watch what you're doing with that bloody garden tool!" he yelled and added "You had better ..."

But he didn't finish what he was going to say. The light changed to green and then there was a sickening stomach wrenching lurch and the Bywater Road allotments and the angry gardener disappeared.

Sergeant Orange crashed to the plastic floor and vomited. He pushed up to all fours and let it all go. God, and the Holy Mother, he felt sick. Then a door opened and two men grabbed him, sprayed something in his face and he just had time to realise that he was no longer on the floor of the burnt out garden shed before he passed out again.

"Who is he?" asked Blard.

"A rather slow thinking copper named Orange, Sergeant Orange, a sometimes Catholic with a marked ability to say the wrong thing a few moments after he has done the wrong thing. A lad of the village," said Holmes to quote a certain fictional character.

"You never did?" said Blard staring at Holmes with disbelief.

"Yep, made a mask and all. Bulldog Drummond was my hero until I joined the cadets and discovered class distinctions for myself. I was definitely them," said Holmes with a large grin. "Now I am 'us' and I like that."

"This lad do what he is asked?"

"If we make it a patriotic duty, yes," said Holmes, and added a wicked grin.

And thus it was that Sergeant Orange found himself strapped to a bed with a large contraption over his head and his eyes watching a screen that seemed to show him a violent, bloody history of some strange and wonderful nation. When they lifted him gently from the bed he explained that all he wanted really was a good feed, a drink of something hot and a few good lads along with him and he would sort out their problems. In double quick time too, no bloody sweat, so help me God.

"We have our extra man for the mission," said Bradl, obviously very pleased.

In the Amazon jungle Betty/Anthony/Napoleon looked at the group of little men and tried to read their minds. The electronic wall around them was working fine. So far no rodents had entered the circle. There were twelve men and one small boy. The men stood staring at he/she/it for a few Earth minutes and then at a word from their leader they knelt and kissed the ground laying their weapons down beside them.

Betty thought, how touching and shed a tear.

They love us. Anthony.

They worship me. Napoleon.

Slowly their language began to make sense and within a few minutes talking with them she/he/it understood all the nuances of their speech and began to talk gently with them explaining how the family of rodents needed to be looked after and fed. Dzxotl explained that the rodents were in fact eating his own family's livelihood and asked, respectfully, if the great God would favour them in return for their inadvertent sacrifice.

It/she/he agreed that there was an injustice done and that every effort should be made to put it right.

"You are permitted to eat most of the rodents," she/he/it said.

Dzxotl bowed low and thanked the great God.

It is no matter. Anthony.

Thank you. Betty.

It is our bounty. Napoleon.

And then there was that mild probe again. The Earthman. The task was a simple one but It/she/he put it on hold for a while; there was a lot to do here first. Idly she/he/it let the requested search happen and let it hide in the lower memory bloc until he/she/it could check it. The answer came back quickly and the data slipped to its allocated spot and stayed there on hold. It/she/he had other problems. Somebody was trying to shift the Doomsday Bomb. No way. Buster. No way. The signal was strong and imperative but after a struggle she/he/it managed to retain stasis. Ah, that's better.

The operator tried again. Nothing. The bomb shifted a few small periods and slipped back again. There was no way the signal could move it but there was movement. The bomb shifted to and fro oscillating on the axis of its present position and refused to move.

"I'm sorry Leader but I cannot move it. We will have to devise another break code to control it. There seems to be a source that wants it to stay where it is. The bomb will not contact with the receiver."

The Leader Pair gazed at the screen and mouthed the figures as he read them. The Pair muttered to each other and then placed one hand on the operator's shoulders.

"Do not worry. Keep track of the bomb and I will go have a chat with the boffins and see what can be done. There has to be a way."

The operator shifted in their seat and looked around over their shoulders and smiled at the Leader Pair. "Thank you your Honour."

"No need. It is our honour to work with you."

The operator swelled with pride. Working for the NMF was much easier and much much better than working for the President. They were glad they had defected. At least their expertise was valued and not taken for granted. Not only that but they had the feeling they were on the winning side at last. The NMF gave them hope.

"It is our honour to work with the NMF."

The Leader Pair bowed and walked out of the bunker stopping once to encourage another Pair and leaving behind a feeling of well being.

The NMF, the working Pairs agreed, were all right.

Bates and Fish sat together watching the screens and Sergeant Orange stood leaning against a pillar. Holmes sat in his usual position on his floating stool with Blard and Bradl. An image of the Doomsday bomb hovered in the centre of the screen and on one side of the image was a row of figures and on the other was a small gambolling rodent. Holmes liked the little creature and when the rest of the party remarked on it and Blard ordered the operator Pair to get rid of it Holmes chuckled. He knew what it meant but kept the knowledge to himself, he knew the code to contact the source but not to get rid of the image.

"Somebody or something has shifted the Doomsday bomb out of effective range of the Earth. What I want to know is do we let the Earth people know or do we keep quiet and use the knowledge against the President?" said Blard.

"I think that we should keep quiet about it," said Holmes.

"And for what reason do you suggest that course of action Holmes?" said Blard.

"I think the less the Zradians know the better but also I suggest that unless we have a really switched on group of people on Earth who will use the knowledge wisely we will create a dangerous situation. I think the President's reaction will be to increase the attacks on the Earth and Bomb or no Bomb I reckon that once the Zradians get going there is not much we can do about it. The only way is to contact a body on Earth who have integrity. I'd rather trust me own grandmother than any government of Earth," replied Holmes, and looked defiantly at Blard and Bradl.

"And if you knew his Granny then you would know what a statement that is," said Sergeant Orange.

"His granny was known," began Fish

"...as Nicker Holmes," continued Bates

"...because she was always," said Sergeant Orange

"...nicking things," finished Bates and Fish looking somewhat peeved.

"But she was not a bad old stick if you kept your eye on her and didn't trust her with the family stainless steel," said Holmes.

"Don't you mean silver?" said Sergeant Orange.

"We couldn't afford silver," replied Holmes.

Only Bates and Fish laughed. Blard shrugged his shoulders and looked at his twin.

"I will put the suggestion to the NMF and see what they want us to do," Blard said, and nodded to the operator Pair who changed the images to home in on an area of Earth.

"Cor, look there's Stonehenge," said Holmes, and did a double take when he saw the mass of soldiers, some shooting and many others running. "Bloody hell the buggers have invaded England!"

Invasion

The Zradians landed in force in Afghanistan, China and Australia. Their ferocity and superior firepower overwhelmed the opposing forces and in all three areas their advance was slowed only by the speed of their supply system. Hampered by minor communications breakdowns the Pairs in charge of supplies on Star Station Two were often forced to guess the location codes. Pairs, equipment and food too often landed out of reach of their intended base. In their control room Pour and Roup watched the data on their screens scroll down, and as the information tumbled before their eyes so they became more and more confused. At the point where Pour discovered his twin had no idea what was going on he asked for a summary. Within a short period the summary appeared on the large screen and they read it grim faced.

*We recommend reinforcing all bridgeheads
with rodents.*

"Bulgers, what's going on?" said Roup.

"I'll call up again my twin," said Pour and pressed keys frantically. The screen blipped and cleared and was suddenly filled with a message.

*"Do not be afraid of the - casualties are rising - rodents
are not casualties - getting paler - we regret the delay - and
apologise for the inconvenience - do no be afraid of the rodents
the President is a drunken fart - good luck Star Station Two!"*

Pour looked at the screen and then at his twin. Roup stared back and with a groan he gripped the edge of the console. The Pair turned away from the screen not wanting to look at the crazy message.

"What in Nong's sake is happening?" asked Pour.

"I don't know...I don't know. How the Nong can we run an invasion with this stuff going on. Call maintenance. We have to fix this!"

His voice rose higher and he turned around desperately looking for the relief post and slowly his leg came up and cocked sideways. Pour held his arm and eased him to the post indicating with a sideways nod to the Aides to come and help.

"Calm down Roup. We will get you something to help. I feel it too but we have to keep trying and yes I will call maintenance and do something. I'll threaten them with Polisoc purges if they fail. How's that?"

Roup let the Aides help him and with a sigh he urinated against the post. Images of chasing small furry animals raced through his thoughts and he shuddered. He looked at his twin and the empathy wave hit him warmly. The small furry animal died in his metaphoric jaws and he felt better.

Pour called maintenance and oilily explained what he had in mind. Two Leader Pairs arrived in the control room and bowed low.

"We are at your service your Honour. What is it you require of us?"

"We require your Pairs to find an alternative channel to control the invasion. We want it set up independently of the rest of the system and we want it now," said Pour.

The Pairs paled and gasped. "We will do our best," they said together and shuffled their feet. "It will take quite a few long periods your Honour."

"How many?"

"At least twenty."

"Do it or die."

"Yes your Honour."

The Pairs backed out of the centre and rushed off along the corridor. The Polisoc guards stared longingly after them until they were out of sight.

"Do you think they will do it?"

"I think they will," said Pour. "I think they will."

Twenty long periods passed and the Pairs came into the control centre escorted by an eager group of Polisoc guards. The guards pushed the Pairs forward and they stood unsteadily waiting for Pour and Roup to speak.

"Progress please. Are we able to have our channel?"

"Your Honour we have achieved the impossible," said one Pair tiredly.

"If your Honour would like to come with us to sector blue level fourteen we will demonstrate. We have a further request," said the second Pair.

"And that is?"

"Get these Bulgers behind us off our backs. We will no longer cooperate with you as long as they are staring over our shoulders."

"And if we don't?"

"Then you and the Star Station can kiss goodbye to the new program. It won't start without our signal and we are not about to reveal that to anybody," the Pair said, and looked first at the Polisoc guards and then at Pour and Roup. "We will die first."

The other Pair nodded.

"And if you die?"

"You lose it." The first Pair replied and looked at Pour and Roup defiantly. "Also if we do not reach level fourteen within the next five short periods you lose the program."

"We could kill each Half Pair slowly until you give us the codes?"

"Kill one and you lose a quarter of the code," the Pair said in a flat tone staring defiantly at Pour. His face changed to a crafty grin. "Get the idea? And after we set the program up for you we have put in a similar fail safe code which will be deactivated immediately we are at the other end of our chosen destination from a Transfer Port, savvy?"

Pour and Roup glared at them showing hatred in his gaze that would have frightened a Bulger to the point of exploding. He felt a twitch of fear in his hearts and wanted desperately to murder these two. Instead he smiled and asked their names.

"Trip and Pirt and this is my co-worker Trap and Prat," said the first Pair. "We have a deal?"

"You have a deal," said Pour.

True to their word the program was clear of rodent messages, and although the space was cramped and the equipment somewhat archaic it worked. Pour and Roup escorted the Pairs to the transfer port and jealously watched them go. The Polisoc guard Leader Pair growled angrily not saying any words but uttering that deep guttural sound which replaced speech when a Pair is too overcome with anger.

"Bye," said the two renegade Pairs as the port door closed. The light flicked red and then green and back to red again. The Pairs were gone. Pour and Roup walked slowly and sadly back to their new control room and sat down at the screens.

Scrolling across them was a simple message.

So long suckers - You are a trapped Prat and we have Tripped you up. We will drink to you in the waste lands - have a good war!

"At least there are no rodents," said Roup, despondently.

The data was slow coming but at least they were able to keep a track of what was going on, and importantly, send orders to the High Leader Pairs with real knowledge of their troop movements. Late in the turn when they were tired and ready for sleep Roup tapped a key to log out and watched a message scroll across the screen and shakily pointed it out to his twin. His mouth remained wide open unable to give voice to his horror.

"L...look," he said.

Pour stared at the screen and his face wrinkled with fear.

PS - we have connected this program to the robot's bomb - if you win the invasion it will explode – if you don't it won't - but that doesn't really matter does it? You are trapped anyway.

"The dirty Bulgers!" said Roup, and stared at the message for a long time but instead of flipping into depression he tightened his lips and pressed the key to close the machine down. Quietly he walked out of the control centre and back to their room. Pour followed and once in their room he sat with his twin and held him close.

"We will have to find a way out," he said."

"I wish I could believe that," Roup said.

"We will have to do something about the Robot's bomb and I think we will have to try and scarper. Will you handle that and leave me to sort the data out?"

Roup looked up at his twin and sighed. "I would like to try," he said. Pour stroked his twin's head with his free hand and sent a wave of empathy that almost swamped Roup's emotions.

Colonel Chin is promoted

The Australian Premier looked at his newly created minister of War and asked his question again. "The High Command refuse to do what?"

"They refuse to accept the Japanese officers are actually in charge, sir," he said, and blushed. He should have called the PM Mike but somehow he couldn't bring himself to do it without feeling self conscious.

"Sack them and promote others who will," said Mike O'Rourke bashing one fist into his palm. "Sack the lot and give the job to some of the younger Generals. And tell them that unless they cooperate their jobs are on the line. Without the High Command knuckling down to it the Nips refuse to give us anything. Savvy?"

David Clegg smiled happily letting his large mouth split his face almost in two.

"It will be my pleasure s...Mike," he said. "My pleasure."

"Where are the enemy?"

"In South Australia and heading for the coast. At this time they are advancing on Adelaide and there is a contingent heading for Perth. They seem to enjoy dry conditions. We have troops trying to hold them back but they outgun us so to speak. Their fire power is enormous."

"What does that mean David?"

"We are losing," he said.

"Then you had better make those new appointments pronto then?"

"Right away."

The effect of their conversation was felt immediately. Colonel Chin looked at his first Lieutenant and grinned.

"We have promotion, both of us, and we are ordered to repair with dispatch to Canberra. I am now a Brigadier and you are a full Colonel. They will be promoting sergeants to generals soon," he said, and handed her a sheaf of papers.

"Why the sudden move?"

"It seems that a certain number of our High Command refuse to work with the Japanese. We are to take their place."

"Strewth," she replied unable to say much else. She too was overwhelmed by her sudden good fortune.

"Okay Colonel, let's go," he said.

"Yes sir," she said and giggled.

The campaign was going well Traz thought. His twin, Zrat, caught the feeling and turned in his seat and grinned."We have them on the run. Ninety kilometres and we hit the city limits. How about supplies?"

"So far so good. One more stop and we can seed another set of transfer ports. After that it is a short hop into town and beat up on the natives.

Zrat's face broke into an even larger grin. "The President will be pleased," he said keeping the sarcasm out of his voice. You couldn't be too careful with Polisoc troopers on their flanks. High Leader Pair Zrat and Traz were Pongos in this command but ranked well above the Stormtrooper Leader Pair and were in charge of bridgehead Five. They were pleased because the Earth troops opposing them were a pushover, and their forces raced to keep up with the retreat. The downside was that the stores and supplies did not always arrive in good condition. Wagons were sometimes wrecked and troops often ended up in the wrong place. The sight of Pairs and Half Pairs protruding through rocks or half buried in the ground was sickening.

Traz looked at the gruesome casualties and ordered his Pongos to salvage whatever they could. In that way they replenished some of their supplies, that was if the ants, lizards and small mammals didn't get there first. At one time they saw a group of locals running from one pile of abandoned equipment and recognising that they were not soldiers let them go. Zrat checked the Atlas and learned that the people were natives of the land, wandering tribal people who at one time owned the land.

"That's interesting my twin," Zrat said showing his twin the screen.

"What is that my fellow trooper?"

"The people we are fighting are capable of genocide, now that is interesting. They call their Aboriginals blacks and shove them into small patches of land or let them live in the cities and systematically rob them blind until they go off drinking and fighting. It says here that the young ones land in jail or commit suicide more than their white or European counterparts. Useful things these Atlases."

"Perhaps but they can't get us extra supplies or get rid of the Pig Farmers," said Traz indicating the Polisocs with a jerk of his thumb.

Their present troubles were made worse by the messages and the irritating tune that interrupted the communications at irregular intervals. The only compensation was that at least for some of the time they couldn't hear the Polisocs. Nevertheless the wagons rolled on and the soldiers advanced steadily fighting pockets of resistance although there was little of it. In two more turns they would be well beyond Adelaide and heading along the coast to the Australian capital city of Canberra. First they would take Adelaide.

The loose column was travelling along a major highway sometimes using the road and sometimes wandering across the paddocks letting the hover wagons ride over the grass and scrub. Ahead, according to the Atlas was a location the Australians called Gawler and it was a little beyond there where they intended to stop and seed the next group of ports. They hit the town at a fast pace and shot through quickly. A trooper Pair watched the screen and counted down the numbers until they were at the coordinates.

"Okay we are right on the spot."

"All wagons assume formation," said Traz.

The trooper repeated the order into the microphone and the wagons sighed to a stop. A group of wagons rode out until they reached specific computerised points and troopers and Pongos piled out with weapons ready and formed a perimeter.

"Seed," said Traz.

Groups of Pairs patterned out from the ring of wagons and laid small boxes on the ground. From above the boxes looked small and grey with red lights flashing in their centre. The pattern they made was a circular grid which allowed a wagon to land with room to move. Zrat activated the coders as soon as the trooper Pair said that all the markers were in place and for a few small periods nothing happened. The lights on the monitor changed to green and the first supply boxes dropped to the ground. They were quickly gathered and stowed and then the wagons arrived. Pairs climbed aboard and drove them to the edges. Now it was time for the extra troopers. With small plopping sounds troopers and Pongos appeared fully armed and kitted out and with precision moved to the allocated troops. The whole process took one full period to complete. Traz and Zrat called for a rest and meal break and for two long periods the Pairs ate, chatted and rested and then it was time to go.

Adelaide was about to be overrun.

The atmosphere in the War Office situation room was tense. The former High command officers were gone leaving only one Brigadier from the old regime to explain the procedure to the newcomers. He had refused to take the rank of Field Marshall deferring to the Japanese Officers who sat at the end of the large computerised plan. The plan was made up of many small screens linked together. A duplicate set hung from the wall, and as the planners shifted the icons on the horizontal screens their positions were also duplicated. The picture looked grim. As the newly elected officers filed in they looked first at the Japanese officers sitting waiting and then at the screen. Brigadier Chin grinned at the row of officers and took his place with some satisfaction. He would prefer to be out in the field with Helen but at least here he could learn what High Command was all about. The Japanese officers nodded to each of the Australians as they entered although, when Brigadier Chin strolled in and took his place they looked surprised.

"Are you an Australian?" Field Marshall Kanawa asked.

"Too bloody right I am," said Chin. "Fair dinkum Aussie from way back. My parents were born here." He grinned again and looked around at the others. One man, a newly promoted Brigadier like himself looked back startled. He knew the officer when he was a Lieutenant and had to remind himself of the officer's name. James Wienck, a Pole or something from Melbourne.

"Jeez, I never realised, you're bloody Chinese ain't yer?"

Chin nodded. "Been one all me life mate," he said.

The Japanese officers laughed.

Well that broke the ice, thought Chin.

"Let's get down to business," said Kanawa.

He got up from his seat and walked to the screen and picked up a laser light which he directed at each icon as he explained what was happening. While he spoke the room fell silent and all that could be heard apart from his voice was the ticking of the clock and shuffling feet or the rustle of clothes. Now and then a sharp intake of breath broke the silence and as Chin listened the story unfolded.

"The Zradian forces are currently moving at a fast pace out of Adelaide through and beyond Murray Bridge in the south and they have stopped at Waikerie. It looks as if they have halted to gather more supplies and troops. We predict they will send some forces along the coast road and others to Ballarat and Bendigo. We want to stop them before they reach Melbourne." He looked at each of them in turn. "We have devised a plan of action which I think you will enjoy,"

"As long as it works," interrupted Chin.

"Oh it will," said Kanawa and smiled broadly. "All we need is your army and airforce to hold them off for now. In two days our ships will arrive in Sydney and Perth with fresh troops and supplies. Now this is what you can do..."

Kanawa explained his plan and asked for suggestions. He got them and Chin left the Situation Room late that day happy that at least their forces could do something useful.

"Getting to grips with the enemy is what it is all about," he said to James.

They walked along the streets to their hotel passing a group of protesters carrying placards and chanting. For a moment Chin was unsure what the people, mostly men, were chanting. The words slowly made sense and with an anxious tug at James' sleeve he began to move away.

"What's the matter?"

"Do you hear what that lot are chanting?" he said.

"No, I'm not really listening."

"They are saying "Nips out, Japs go home", listen."

They stopped and listened to the chant.

"One -two - if you please - we don't want the Japanese!

Three - four and five and six - we don't want the bloody Nips!"

The group finished the chant and yelled in unison "Japs out! Japs out!"

"I think we should turn around and find another way back to the hotel," said Chin.

"Why?"

"Because mate I look too much like a Japanese, see?" he said and put his fingers to his eyes and stretched the skin. "Ah so!"

With hardly a sound Wienck turned and led him into a side road. But by then it was too late. A few of the chanters had seen him.

"Look! A fucking Nip!" somebody yelled and then there were feet running and voices shouting. James and Chin ran. The first rocks came flying out of the air and rattled around them as they dashed around a corner. James flagged a cab down and they managed to get in and get going as the crowd hurtled around the corner behind them.

"Where to mate?" asked the driver.

"Away from them," said Chin, pointing backwards.

The cab driver accelerated and James directed him to their hotel.

Two days later Chin was directing operations on his sector of the front alongside his Japanese counterpart. The protest had turned into a riot and he had had the satisfaction of watching the action on television. The Police in riot gear arrested many and soaked the rest with fire hoses. It seemed that memories were longer than he thought. Silly really, thought Chin, the protestors were citing atrocities from more than seventy years ago. Since then the great Australian Commonwealth had become a Republic trading with Japan and China as well as the USA and India, and trading too with the Vietnamese, another stupid conflict. Chin sighed, sad really.

The Zradian forces had ground to a temporary halt south of Bendigo and a little west of Ballarat. The biggest problem facing the home forces was how to deal with the evacuation, which was made difficult by the incredulity of the people of South Australia and Victoria who doggedly refused to move. Chin discovered a simple answer. He informed them that if they wanted to stay behind then that was fine with him as long as they paid for their own burial. He didn't bother to force them out of their homes. He ordered the soldiers in his command to set up outposts and defence positions and let the residents come to their own conclusions. The Japanese commander in the field told him that by the end of the second day most of the residents were on their way out.

The soldiers laconic remarks and their readiness to do battle was enough to frighten them.

"The conversation went something like this.

"So what's goin' on mate?"

"Digging in cobber."

"Diggin' in fer what?"

"Defences. Gotta stop the Aliens."

Silence while the resident thought about it.

"You're not 'avin me on are yer?"

"Bloody oath no. Wouldn't be 'ere mate if I was.

More silence.

"Waddyer reckon then?"

"Might pay ter scarper."

Even more silence.

"Like fer real?"

"Fer real."

"Jeez."

And usually the resident and family packed as much as they could in their vehicle and scarpered. If they couldn't do that then they climbed on board a waiting wagon or the train and went east and hopefully to safety. Strictly defensive, Chin's operation was directed against the enemy right. To the north other sectors were preparing to meet the Zradians on their left. The centre was supposed to give way and let them fold inwards and theoretically attack the enemy from the sides. Chin's task was to oversee the operation while his Japanese counterpart acted as liaison. He relaxed and lifted his tired eyes from the screen and stretched.

The telephone burbled and he picked it up.

"Chin?"

"Brigadier, there is a meeting at the Sit Room. We have a craft on its way, urgent. Uplift in minutes six. The female voice cut off and he put the telephone down. Why do they always speak in note form? Six minutes later he was climbing into the cab of a rapid hovercraft surprised to find Helen already inside.

"Where we going Colonel?" he asked.

"Sit Rm," she said and laughed.

The weapon lay on the bench, open ready to be loaded. The officers gathered behind the barrier to watch the demonstration. A

Japanese Colonel stood beyond the barrier with a weapon already loaded in his hands. He hefted it to show how light it was and with a short speech he demonstrated how easily it was to load and how it was armed.

"All you need is a light pressure on the trigger... here, and to adjust the power you give this knob a tweak." He showed them the trigger and the knob which were both coloured orange plastic and with a smooth motion aimed at the target and fired. A stream of plasma burst from the end and destroyed the target completely. The Colonel adjusted the knob and the stream died down to a narrow beam. He aimed it at another target and drilled neat holes in it.

One by one the more junior officers tried it, and when it was Chin's turn he couldn't help remembering the fight earlier that year.

"Can we fit a more powerful version to some of our gunships?" he asked.

The Colonel smiled and said. "Watch the vid."

A few minutes later they were watching a video demonstration of an even more devastating weapon. The cannon was fitted to the Mitsubishi Warbird Helicopter and the fixed wing SuperZero, and from what he saw convinced him there was enough firepower to destroy the whole of their armour without any gun wagons.

"How long have you had this weapon?" he asked.

The Colonel smiled again.

"Since mister Kamaguchi discovered how to make one. He copied it from a Zradian model we stole from one of your captives. So sorry."

Chin laughed. "When do we get them?"

"They are on the wharves now. We bring many more for your soldiers. Even up the score a rittle?"

"More than a rittle," said Chin. "But, excuse me, how did you get hold of the captive?"

"It was a rittle complicated. Our embassy heard of your battle with the enemy and put out some feelers. We had an approach from two disgruntled Aborigines whose mates, so they said, left them in the bush. They found this Zradian soldier cowering behind a rock and although he was fully armed he surrendered to them. It seems the two men took pity on him and fed him and cleaned him up and, er, being city dwellers they sussed out that if they handed him over to the police they would get a hiding. Our people had sort of let it be known that we would pay for any information that was useful."

The Colonel looked embarrassed and coughed politely.

"And why were they gathering information?" asked Chin half guessing the truth.

"We were on the point of starting world war three, so sorry, and when the two men produced the soldier and his weapons our staff were so relieved that they sent all three back to Nippon. The captive, much depressed, was very cooperative and your two countrymen are living it up at the expense of the Great Imperial Army. We are verra grateful."

Chin looked at him and started to laugh.

"Colonel whatever your name is I am most impressed. I remember those two, their mates were killed thinking they were after a mob of rogue Abos. Helen will be pleased!"

"Junichi Marayama at your service."

"Junichi san, I thank you," he said, and bowed politely.

"The engineer who examined the gun, Ito Kamaguchi, redesigned it and his company is making millions of them. Nippon taxman will make millions of yen."

Marayama looked pleased, and as they parted company, Chin to go back to the battle zone and the Colonel to his own unit Chin caught sight of the small insignia on the Japanese officer's lapel and realised he was dealing with an officer of the military intelligence service. He shuddered.

The PM takes a fall.

Dart and Drat walked into the Prime Minister's office together pausing at the door taking in the scene. Prime Minister Smith's loud voice dominated and he was using it to let the camera crew know he didn't want them there. "Get out of my bloody office you bloody parasites," he boomed.

"But ...but the agreement was..."

"Bugger your damn agreement! I want you bastards out of here now!"

Dart and Drat walked further into the room and stood quietly waiting to be recognised. Behind them Sally and Joseph shuffled uncomfortably trying not to look conspicuous. The whole situation, thought Dart, was deteriorating and had been from the moment they set out that morning from the hotel. They had left Marjorie in the hotel in the care of the off duty section of Colin's thugs and set off with Sally and Joseph to Number Ten. The trip was fraught with traffic delays and they had to make a diversion on the way and at the gates there was a further delay for the officers to check the vehicles at the entrance to Downing Street. Finally they were admitted and the cars rolled along the short distance to halt at the door.

And that was when they met their first hurdle. Security refused to let Colin's men remain on guard and was emphatically opposed to Colin and Terry going inside. Dart explained that unless they went with them the meeting would take place outside in the street. Dart also explained that he and his twin felt happier with their own men on guard, and when the senior officer explained in his turn that he did not think that a group of known thugs were the right sort of people to have hanging around outside the Prime Minister's residence, Dart said he begged to differ.

"What I mean officer is that these so-called thugs are my employees and I have every confidence in them. They are here to protect my twin and myself and I wish them to earn their fee. Resistance to their inclusion in my party is useless and detrimental to the negotiations. In effect, officer, your physical objections to their presence will be met diligently and firmly," Dart said, and smiled benignly.

"What are you trying to say?" asked the officer.

"They have my permission to punch your lights out," replied Dart maintaining his benign smile.

The man looked at Dart and shuddered.

"All right, if you are determined then I shall have to let them in, but under protest."

"Thank you, now please let us pass."

That hurdle surmounted Colin's men took up positions guarding the door. Their guide, a smart Civil Servant, the PM's Secretary, led them into the inner sanctum. Dart and Drat and Sally and Joseph strolled into the Prime Minister's residence with Colin and Terry behind them and heard somebody shouting at the camera crew.

The sound mixer and the camera operator were hastily retreating before the anger of a large red faced man who was shouting at them belligerently. The couple, a man and a woman, were struggling to salvage the cables and stands that Maurice had said were the best for the job and in the corner cowering from the big man's onslaught was another cameraman with a portable on his shoulder filming the scene while Aides fluffed around unsure what to do.

"Excuse me," said Dart.

The Prime minister continued to rant at the camera crew ignoring Dart and Drat. The crew, a man with the camera and the woman setting up the lighting, backed away intimidated and bumped into Dart.

"Excuse me but what is going on?" said Dart addressing the crew.

"We are being thrown out," replied the woman.

"Stay where you are," said Dart. "I will have a word with him."

He nodded sideways to the Prime Minister who was swearing profusely and abusing his Aide. Dart blocked the language out and spoke gently to the crew.

"Wait in the ante-room please," he said and turned to face the Prime Minister.

"Shut up!" he said, loudly and sharply.

There was a dead silence, and the Prime Minister stepped back open mouthed a look of disbelief on his face. His mouth worked hard to speak but no words came as he stared at the man who had dared to tell him to shut up.

"If you are the Prime Minister of Britain then I suggest you act like one. I am Dart and this is my twin Drat. The agreement with your office was that we have cameras and selected journalists at our negotiations at all times. The camera crew stay." Dart remained relaxed throughout his speech and when he finished he gazed steadily at the Prime Minister and waited for the man to reply.

The Prime Minister jutted his jaw out like a pugilist and tightened his mouth.

"The camera crew are not official, they go."

Dart shook his head slightly and said quietly. "They stay or there is no deal."

The Prime Minister set his jaw even tighter and glared at Dart. His aides backed away and the secretary began to make agitated gestures aimed at Dart and Drat.

"D ...d .. d..don't d...d...do .."

"Shut up Rodney," said the Prime Minister, his voice register a low angry growl.

"Please mister Dart don't provoke ..."

"I said SHUT UP!" shouted the Prime Minister. "Rodney, stuff off!"

Dart stood relaxed and waiting and Drat moved slightly to one side equally relaxed. The Pair glanced at each other and let quick smiles play over their faces. This was about to get interesting, they thought.

The Prime Minister bunched his fists and drew in his breath. Unaware he was making all the moves he glared even more belligerently at Dart and glowered at the hovering aides as they flitted about trying to catch his attention. He saw Colin and Terry in the doorway heading in his direction and the cowering camera crew. He noticed Sally and Joseph hovering at the side of the main door and he saw out of the corners of his vision the selected members of his cabinet standing looking on in disapproval. He registered all that but it was the cheek, the gall of the man standing in front of him that took most of his attention. And his uncontrollable fury.

"Nobody tells me to shut up," he said. "Nobody!"

And with a bellow of anger he struck out at Dart with his right fist and followed it with his left moving his bulky body forward and put a lot of power into the blows. Neither punch landed and the Prime Minister roared in anger as he staggered and recovered to take another lunge. A large figure loomed up before him and before he could defend himself a fist rocketed out from the looming figure and exploded on his nose. He flipped backwards and fell unconscious between two flapping aides.

Colin rubbed his fist in his hands and grinned.

"Cor, who would have thought I would flatten the Prime Minister of England in 'is own 'ouse," Colin said, and glared at the security officers. "You wanna fight? Then I'm for you mateys."

The security officers backed off when aides and ministers got in the way, some to protect the Prime Minister, and others to stop the security men exacting revenge. Their division amused Drat who whispered to his twin that now they knew who was on who's side.

"Sorry mister Dart," said Colin. "But the bastard asked for it."

"That's okay Colin," said Dart, and looked down at the recumbent figure with some satisfaction.

"Bring the camera crew in and film this will you?" he said.

"Already filming," said a voice from the corner of the room, "got the whole sequence."

"Good copy?" said the woman, and glanced happily at Sally.

"Excellent copy," agreed Sally. "What do we do now?"

"Get him on his feet again and explain the deal to him," said Dart. "I think he will have a lot of explaining to do after this."

And that effectively got them over the second hurdle.

Medics were already fussing around the prime minister. The cabinet ministers, the secretary and the aides rushed to the prime minister's side and had to be pushed away by the medics. A police officer hurried in with two constables and stood taking in the scene. The prime minister's secretary crossed immediately to them and smiled.

"It's okay Reginald, the PM fell over. He'll be all right in a few moments. Now run along please."

Reginald made to protest but the secretary gave him a pleading look and Reginald took the hint and left. In the meantime medics lifted the prime minister from the floor into his chair, cleaned his face of blood and made him as comfortable as possible. He slumped in the seat looking bruised and groggy but awake. Aides brought chairs for Dart and his party and wheeled in refreshments on a polished trolley and began to lay them out on the table completing the task by filling glasses with light wine. The aides fussed around them as if they were royalty and while the medics attended to the prime minister the secretary spoke to Dart.

"I am sorry about what happened but he is like that. He played Rugby at Eton," he said, and shrugged his shoulders. "He gets angry sometimes."

"Nevertheless we will insist on the crew staying and my people and we will stick to our part of the deal. He will stick to his. We negotiated this with the government not just one man. If there is no cooperation we will deal only with the Japanese and regard Britain as a low priority. Understand?"

The secretary nodded.

"I think he will understand that now," he replied.

Ten minutes later Dart was explaining exactly what he and his twin were prepared to do. Throughout, the prime minister remained quiet apart from sniffles and the occasional cough and when Dart finished he sat looking resentful and almost defiant. The explanation took nearly an hour and once the prime minister accepted his defeat he asked intelligent questions and got some respectful and intelligent answers.

"Your reaction?" asked Dart.

"We go with it," the prime minister growled.

"Good," said Dart. "I will need a signature."

The prime minister signed without a murmur.

"My journalists wish to ask you some questions, and for the great British public they would like some good footage for the news programs, something for them to chew over. Do you feel up to it?" Drat said, and grinned at Sally.

"I suppose so," the prime minister said.

"It will look good for the image if you and us seem to be friendly," said Drat, "the whole thing would go much better if we were seen shaking hands and relaxing and my journalists were able to question your ministers?"

And so it went. Sally and Joseph asked the questions and at intervals when the PM was unable to answer them waited politely while he consulted his experts. They manipulated him as best as anybody could and at times found themselves manipulated where he was sure of his ground. The only part of the interview he was unsure of was the situation on the Salisbury Plain and for that he had to rely on his military advisers and the newly appointed minister of war.

"Josh, you tell them," he said and grabbed a glass of wine.

"The invaders are heading for London but we are confident we can control them. The first prisoners were taken by a small group, less than a division, in fact it was a more or less mixed up regiment, it was a group devised to show off our arms to the European Commission."

"Were British arms used in the fighting?" asked Sally.

"Well yes, but unfortunately the officer in charge had only blanks and dummy rockets. Quite a story actually. Very proud of him. Get a medal I expect," said Josh almost to himself.

"I think you should tell me about it," Sally said.

Josh did and it was that story Maurice agreed was the better public interest story and although Dart and Drat's meeting with the PM was worldwide news, in Britain it was this story that captured the public imagination.

On the way back to their hotel Colin looked at Dart, his face a picture of concern as if he was making up his mind what to say eventually blurting out his worry. "Look, I don't know much about politics but I got a feeling you just been done. I dunno what it is but I get the idea that old blood and guts is gonna back out. I think we need to get some extra cover. I don't like it boss. We bashed the bugger and I don't think he is gonna forget that in a hurry."

"What do you mean?" asked Dart.

"I think we might need to get ourselves some hard protection," said Colin.

"Such as?" asked Sally not really wanting to hear the answer.

"Shooters," said Colin.

The telephone burbled rather than rang and the hand that lifted the receiver was casual rather than eager. There was only one person who had that number. The man put the receiver to his ear and listened. His answers were monosyllabic and he wrote short cryptic notes on a pad as his caller explained what he wanted. When the call was finished the man sat back in his chair and steepled his fingers touching his nose and gently licking his lips as he thought through the conversation.

"Interesting," he said. "Very interesting."

He doodled on a pad drawing little rodents with musical notes flitting above them and then with a quick decisive movement he picked up another telephone and spoke into it.

"Get me McCord will you. My office at eleven. I have a job for him."

He terminated the call and sat back in his chair again and gazed benignly up at the ceiling.

"Extremely interesting," he said.

This time he stroked his chin.

Harry McCord grabbed the telephone listening carefully and eased himself in his chair before answering. "All right, I will be there." He put the phone down, stretched his body, legs first, trunk and arms and casually showered and dressed. He left the apartment casually and walked casually along the street where the car parking spaces were taken up by abandoned wrecks and the dogs fought the cats for the contents of the garbage cans. He walked to the end and looked for a cab. There was one on the rank and with a quick stride he got in and demanded the driver get moving.

He arrived at the office two minutes early. The cab driver had been a pain in the arse but with a bit of carefully crafted violence he had made the arsehole shift. He walked up the steps and through the main door which opened to admit him into the lobby. He showed his pass to the camera and steeled himself to get into the elevator. He felt the sweat in his palms as the elevator climbed and he felt his testicles tighten. He hated elevators. On the third floor he knocked on the door before pushing it open and walked in and stood on the carpet in front of the desk and waited for the man behind the desk to speak.

"Sit down Harry."

McCord said nothing waiting for the lecture. It didn't come.

"I won't beat about the bush McCord. I have a job for you from a high source. You will be paid handsomely. Read that."

McCord took the sheets and read them. He said nothing but handed them back casually as if he were asked to do a similar job everyday. The rate was high but the job was worth the fee. If he took the job.

"There are conditions."

"Such as?"

"That after the job you retire."

McCord smiled evilly and leaned across the desk.

"I want double the money."

"No."

"Then there is no deal."

"McCord, you are pushing your luck."

"I always push my luck."

"The fee is the best you will get."

"And I am the best there is. I want double for this job."

The man looked at him and he could see the hatred and the distaste in his eyes. They were cold and cruel but he knew that whatever he asked for he would get. On this job. He would need it too. He stood up and started to walk out of the office.

"Leave this room and the guard will kill you."

"Bullshit."

McCord walked out of the room and stood waiting for the elevator. There was no guard on the floor but he assumed that one would be in the elevator. He shifted position to the left side and as the door opened he moved quickly expecting a guard to come out looking for a shot. The elevator was empty and with an instinct born of cunning he turned and ducked. The bullet passed over his head and clattered against the metal elevator wall. He crouched and faced the guard. The next shot would hit.

"Okay, I'll do the job."

The office door opened and his employer came out.

"That's more like it, McCord."

McCord turned on his heel and entered the elevator. The door shut behind him leaving the man standing watching as the indicator chimed the floors. He watched McCord on the screen as he walked out into the street and said quietly.

"Cheapskate."

He looked at the guard and smiled.

"Good shot Samuel."

"But I missed him sir?"

"Yes, of course, but, good shot all the same."

"Yes sir," replied the guard. "Yes sir." He was, as they say, following orders.

On Salisbury Plain the armed forces that were rushed to try and hold back the Zradian invasion were battling for their lives. This time they were using real ammunition and yet they were getting a pasting. Lt Colonel West stopped long enough to drop off his prisoners and the captured wagons and with his men armed with real bullets and real rockets he gathered his full strength and set off for the fray. When he arrived at the battlefield he was appalled to see his fellow soldiers trying stupidly to fight back as if the enemy were a conventional army. It was obvious they were doggedly following orders.

"Sergeant, tell Major Wiseman to take over and get me headquarters will you?" West said.

The sergeant telephoned and passed one instrument to him.

"Headquarters sir, a Major General Colman from the Wiltshire's, sir. He sounds quite keen."

"Sir?" he said, "Colonel West here, I have some advice on fighting these people if you want it."

"Okay West, give."

"They work in pairs, so wound one and the other seems lost. Their firepower and range is much greater than ours and they direct their weapons with lasers as we do but they pour fire down the track. If we dig in we will be fried and high rockets are easy for them to track. We found that ground skimming was best. Horizontal fire from medium range and use air power on the battle wagons but watch how you use them. I suggest you avoid Helicopter Gunships and stick with fixed wing craft, sir," West said, and waited for questions.

"If they can be beaten without live ammo then we can thrash them with it West," Colman said. "Unless you can give me a reason for your comments I suggest you leave the running of the battle to us."

West drew a deep breath and was very polite when he answered.

"Sir, we were lucky and captured some enemy weapons and I suggest, sir, we were fighting low calibre troops. According to our captives the soldiers we are up against are Stormtroopers and these troopers are dedicated and alert. Sir, with all due respect, digging in is not going to work. Sir, you are outgunned and you will be cut to bits. You need wagons similar to theirs to fight them and air strikes," West said and again he waited.

"West, your comments are out of line. Play your part in the battle and follow your orders."

"Yes sir," West said and hung up.

"Sergeant, tell Captain Wiseman to lose our orders and do as I tell him. That goes for all the officers. Will you ask them to call me if they have any questions. We are cavalry and will fight like cavalry."

"Yes sir," said the sergeant and spoke into the telephone.

West gave the order for his force to roll into the fight.

I like cats but...

Richard Byrde tried to protect his face when he and the Carnibeast fell off the cliff. The animal roared angrily and Byrde felt it begin to right itself as they went down. Like Alice he thought the fall took an awful long time but in reality it was only a matter of seconds. He was under the belly of the big cat which, fortunately was so busy coping with the sudden loss of solid ground under its feet it forgot to bite him. Then they hit something soft. The animal jumped and pounced on something behind him and the soft things he fell on collapsed and screamed. He was on his feet and backing away ready to turn and run when something large and noisy leapt into the fray. Bodies were flung left and right and then there was a sudden snarling roar and more screams. In addition stones hurtled down from the cliff top which, judging by the yells of pain, found their marks. Byrde was half blinded by a mixture of hair and blood and confused by a ringing in his ears. He felt sharp stabs of pain from his right shoulder and blood poured from cuts on his chest and his head. Dazed and giddy he dropped backwards and rolled in the dust and rocks gathering a few more minor cuts and bruises, and lay stunned half listening to the sound of battle. There was nothing he could do except stay where he was. Slowly he lifted his hand and winced at the pain but managed to wipe the blood and hair from his eyes. He was in time to see the Carnibeast leap directly at Lugs and Lugs meet it head on. He uttered a hopeless scream of fear and warning. The big animal hesitated for a moment and as it did lugs fetched it a mighty blow alongside its ear. It dropped over the low ridge beside the road and disappeared in cloud of dust. Lugs stood looking down at it and then with wild whoop jumped after it and hit it again. The animal lay still.

Lugs raced to where Byrde was trying to stand and helped him to his feet holding him steady for a moment and then the big man lifted Byrde over his shoulder and carried him to the top of the track.

"Better keep movin' Ferret," said Lugs. "That bloody pussycat ain't dead."

Braine groaned and with steady strides led the way. None of them thought to gather any of the weapons. All they were interested in was getting as far away from the crazy animal as possible. Their pursuers, by comparison, seemed tame.

"There might be more of the animals," said Braine.

"All the more reason to get a move on," said the Ferret.

They kept up a steady pace with Lugs seemingly tireless carrying Byrde like a sack over his back. They had to stop eventually, and with Braine on look out and Lugs resting, the Ferret examined Byrde and did his best to clean up the wounds. The light was fading but before it got too dark the Ferret could see that some of the wounds were already festering. He bit his lip. Soon they would have to get help. But where and what? There was nowhere to go except further into the desert or back the way they came. The idea of going back appealed to him. At least there was a building there and those elevator things that might be useful. Byrde was asleep, and when the Ferret sat down and stretched out so was Lugs. The big man was curled up sucking his thumb like a baby and twitching like a cat dreaming. The Ferret thought about the large animal. It looked and acted like a domestic cat only several times larger. Bigger than a lion in fact. He wondered how Lugs had had the strength to knock it out. The Ferret liked cats but this one was definitely not nice. He tried to sleep but his mind was too busy thinking about what to do next. Braine was not much use in a pinch although he did quite well throwing rocks. Hit some of the geezers too. And he was ready to go down to help Byrde but the Ferret had stopped him.

"Not a good idea Oliver. We can see what's going on up here and Lugs has got things in hand. Them blokes ain't gonna bother us no more."

He hoped the animal woke up before the blokes did.

He made up his mind.

Best thing to do is head back the way they came and find something in the hotel. One day marching. Plus a bit if Lugs got knackered carrying Byrde. He leaned back against a rock and let sleep take over. Braine woke him a few hours later and wearily he took his turn on watch.

"I'll go until mornin' cos Lugs will need 'is beauty sleep if he's gonna carry mister Byrde on 'is back tommorer."

Braine nodded and said. "I can carry Byrde as well if Lugs needs a blow. What shall we do in the morning?"

"Reckon we oughter go back to the hotel and rest up there now them blokes 'as copped their lot. We could walk for ever out 'ere. Besides, mister Byrde has got some infections and we need some medicine."

Braine whistled softly through his teeth and settled down on the sand next to Lugs and Byrde. "Bloody heck." He said and stared dumbly out into the night.

The Leader Pair crawled slowly along the gully and kept crawling until he was far away from the feasting Carnibeast. The animal was eating one of the dead Half Pairs. There were at least another one and a half Pairs alive. He was sure of that. He fondled his gas guns looking at each other knowing that if the Carnibeast, or worse still, its mate came after them they were as good as exploded Bulgers. They whimpered when stones rattled above them on the road and immediately stood up to run. There was a sudden rush and a scared Pair ran in the opposite direction. They looked wildly around and saw only one dead Half Pair and the running Pair. A dark shape loomed up from the track and they too ran. Plasma slapped rocks close by and somebody yelled for them to stop. The Leader Pair turned to face whatever it was that was after them and saw there was no point in running as a hover wagon shot over the ridge and bore down on them rapidly. It whispered to a stop and it was at that point they did something extremely stupid.

With a yell of anger they picked up a rock each and as the wagon door opened they hurled them at the figure who called out to them. Before they sizzled in a burst of plasma they heard the clunk of rock hitting plastic and a foul oath.

"Bulgers!" Shouted D.G. "Idiots!"

Glord sliced them in two with a quick burst of his laser and the driver turned the machine and raced after the other frightened Pair. This Pair were much wiser and stood waiting with their hands above their heads. They climbed into the rear of the wagon and hastily handed over their gas pistols and their knives.

"Anything else?"

"No your Honour."

D.G glowered at them. "Polisocs, eh?"

"Yes your Honour. We serve our master."

The driver turned the hover wagon and started to roll back up the track. In the distance there was a flock of Carnibirds and D.G reasoned that there were dead bodies and probably a Carnibeast as well.

"Take us up to the birds," he said.

The grim feast revealed a scattering of bodies and bones and two Carnibeasts. D.G poked the frightened Pair with his knife and said. "What happened here scum?"

"Obvious, there was a fight. We lost." Replied the Pair and clammed up. D.G looked at the Carnibeasts feeding and then at the Pair and grinned.

"For Nong's sake no!" they chorused.

"I repeat, what happened?"

"We were chasing some escaped prisoners and got attacked by the Carnibeasts. The prisoners got away."

D.G looked at them and fingered his knife.

"Who and where are they now."

"We don't know."

D.G unlatched the door and prodded the Pair to the step.

"Tell me."

The Pair looked desperate.

"We don't know where they are. They attacked us from the cliff. They could be anywhere. They could be dead. Please don't do ..."

There was a double scream of terror as D.G slashed at them with his knife and kicked them both out the door shutting it quickly as they dropped to the ground. The hover wagon moved off up the track past the feeding animals and as they went D.G waved cheerfully at the grovelling Pair.

"Good luck," D.G called out.

"Nasty bastard," said Glord at his side. "But I like you."

D.G chuckled.

He saw the Ferret first who was followed by Braine and Lugs with Byrde draped over his back.

"The prisoners," he said. "Has to be."

The wagon slowed as they approached and D.G called out to the party. "Are you the escaped pri...." he stopped in mid sentence. These were Earthmen not Pairs, and with hardly a break he called out in English. "Earthmen we are friends. Julian Renfrew. I'm a mate of his" The small ferret faced man looked up at the mention of the name and clapped his hands.

"Yeah, good fer you mate, we need a friend. Mister Byrde is in a bad way."

D.G and Glord alighted from the wagon and examined Byrde's puffed up face and where the Carnibeast had cut him on his chest and legs there were great red and yellow suppurating weals.

"We should get him into the wagon where the medics can deal with him," said D.G.

Lugs picked him up in his arms and carried him into the wagon where Glord and D.G cleared a bunk for Lugs to lay him on. The Medic Pair got busy straight way and with Lugs watching their every move undressed him and with great skill opened the wounds and cleaned them. The Ferret explained what had happened and with a grim face Glord ordered the driver Pair to head back to the site of the battle.

"The medics say they will have to do some tests on mister Byrde to find out what will be needed. They say he has blood poisoning. We will have to hurry," said D.G. "What sort of medicine do you give for that on Earth?"

"Oh, antibiotics and once during one of our major conflicts we gave penicillin, it was a fungus derivative so they said," Braine said. "You inject it into the vein in the buttocks with a hypodermic syringe. Naturally we have none."

"Good," said D.G. "We can find out about it and we may have an equivalent. We are on our way back to headquarters to re-arm."

"Please hurry," said Braine. "We are very fond of Mister Byrde."

Nevertheless they rode back past the site of the battle and cheered when they saw a Pair unsuccessfully trying to escape the claws and jaws of a pair of Carnibeasts.

"Like I said mate," said the Ferret. "I like cats but when they're that big and that playful I 'ates 'em."

Kord and Krod made the mistake of turning up at Tzu's house during the preparations for the old man's birthday party. They walked in on a group of young people busily setting up tables and chairs and made another mistake. Tzu himself was supervising; that is he was attempting to tell his niece what she should be doing, and with the blind stupidity of the truly fanatical Kord and Krod launched an attack on him, screaming in their own language that they were going to kill him. What happened next was an interesting mixture of comedy and practical self defence. Tzu spun between them and pushed them forward with one hand on each head and as quickly as they fell two of the young men lifted them to their feet and rolled them back again ready for Tzu to take a wrist of each and throw them into each other crashing their heads painfully together. Tzu punctuated the short but energetic fight with noises lifted directly from the bad Kung Fu movies he delighted in watching.

Kord and Krod lay on the pavement on top of each other at the end of the fight unconscious, and with a grin Tzu placed one foot on the recumbent forms, raised his old face up to the sun and beat his chest with both hands and ululated like a great ape.

His audience, young men, girls and the older men and women working to decorate the hall for Tzu's party looked on in amazement and then with much laughter and giggling cheered and clapped. Tzu turned and bowed to them formally.

"Take them away," he said pointing at Kord and Krod.

The Pair woke up sitting propped against a brick wall where it met a fence in a remote corner of the Bywater Road allotments. Their bodies ached and when they moved new pains struck them with a sharp viciousness that brought tears to their eyes.

"Ouch! Bulgers! I hurt," said Kord and squealed when his bare skin touched tall green plants that stung. "Horrible planet."

Krod groaned and rolled over and gasped as the nettles stung his skin too. His bodily aches and pains cut in and with another groan he rolled away from the nettles and crunched onto a pile of flints and broken bricks.

"Nong's teeth! What happened?"

"We got done over," said Kord.

They sat in miserable silence that was punctuated by groans and the occasional painful curse and slowly, helping each other they got to their knees and then to their feet. Leaning against the brick wall with his hands supporting him trying to calm the shakes that alternatively heated him and cooled him Kord felt too ill to move. His twin hung over the fence throwing up.

"What do we do now?" asked Krod.

"Plan four I think," said Kord.

"Yes. The transfer station and home."

Eventually they were fit enough to walk and realising they were already close to the transfer station they plodded across the gardens to the ruined shed. An Earthman stepped in front of them and glared. He held a garden fork in his hand and he had a fanatical gleam in his eyes.

"Come one step closer me hearties and you will feel the edge of my trusty blade," he said.

He means it, thought Krod. He felt something inside snap and with a loud cry he lunged at the man ignoring the fork and dropped him with a quick blow. Two short periods later they were on the deck frantically trying to operate the switches while the frenzied gardener aimed blows at them with a hoe. There was sudden lurch and a rattle as the transfer system operated. With a shout of joy Kord and Krod leapt out of the port and onto a lobby floor. Krod clutched half a garden hoe and Kord still held the garden fork. They looked at each other and dropped the tools.

With silly smiles on their faces they danced hand in hand out of the lobby into the gardens and gambolled happily up the steep track.

"Home at last fa la la la" sang Krod and smiled happily at his twin who had picked some of the weeds and carried them in his hand like a posy. And thus, demented and deliriously happy, Kord and Krod danced off into the Zradian sunsset.

Betty/Anthony/Napoleon looked benignly on the villagers as they moved reverently past him/her/it. He/it/she stood in the centre of the village surrounded by tokens of worship. Brightly covered spears lay at his/her/its base and its/his/her feeling of pride grew. These people loved it/him/she. The villagers were busy making cages for the best of the rodents and pens for the weaker less well bred. The villagers quickly adapted to their new god and worshipped her/it/him for the gift of food and the gift of protection. The villagers quickly understood what laser cannon meant and with a speed that surprised him/her/it supplied it/her/him with the means to make new plasma for the capsules. The task of making new ones took a lot more learning but soon he/she/it had taught them what they needed to know. The capsules were crude but effective and the plasma

material wasn't quite right but it was good enough. Betty/Anthony/
Napoleon was pleased.

Especially Napoleon.

It/she/he searched their memory banks and extracted the local e-
system and opened up access to the local communications happy
that the strains of a Whiter Shade of Pale gave it a pleasant musical
background. It/She/He carefully processed the data and discovered
a few interesting facts. Not far from the village in a large township a
group of Zradians were negotiating with the local government and
from the radio communications It/he/she discovered that the
Zradians were not part of the invading force and neither were they
rebels. In fact they intended to create a force of their own.

Napoleon approved of that.

Betty worried about it.

Anthony worried about Betty/Napoleon.

It/She/He also found another trace. Clard and Dracl were in the
area. He/she/it must monitor their communications and follow.
Anthony dearly wanted to see his father/brother/nephew/son.
Something would have to be done. In the meantime the villagers
needed instruction and guidance. For that they were grateful. The
headman approached It/She/Him and bowed low.

"All hail the triple god from the sky," intoned the headman.

"Do not be afraid of the rodents."

"Do not be afraid of the rodents," repeated the headman.

"And what can we do for you today my friend?"

"Today we get a message from our kinsmen."

"Relay your message."

"They tell us of a strange group of beings from the sky who teach
their distant kinsmen many things such as you have taught us. They
tell us of two lost kinsmen of these strangers and how they were
found wandering. I have this in mind that these may be the two your
worship is seeking?"

Napoleon/Anthony/Betty grumbled happily.

Could this be?

Clard and Dracl lay on their backs in the hut. Sunlight poured
through the opening that served as a portal but otherwise the hut
was pitch dark. They were wet and hot and small animals crawled all
over them, insects, bugs and something that bit. There was no
escape because their hands and feet were tied tight and ropes
encompassed their waists trapping their arms against their sides.
They were numb and terrified. The dark men who captured them
said nothing apart from short grunts, and whenever either of them
spoke a spear or a knife was poked into their flesh. How long they
lay there unattended they did not know. What frightened them most

was the constant drumming and the stamp of feet. Some sort of ritual? Whatever it was meant no good for them.

"Eek!" said Dracl when a man appeared in the portal.

Clard whimpered.

The man stood gazing down at them and taking a step inside the hut he pushed the point of his spear into Dracl's belly and then when Dracl shrieked he repeated the action with Clard. Satisfied that his victims were still alive the man left the hut and they could hear him calling out to the others.

A few short periods later a group came in and with hardly a word lifted the Pair to their feet and as quickly cut the ropes.

"This way scum," said one of them.

"You speak our language?" asked Dracl and regretted his question immediately. The butt end of a spear hit his ribs and he gasped.

"Shut up." Clard and Dracl said nothing further.

They were carried out into the full sunlight blinking and stumbling as their captors grasping an arm each hurried them along. There was a confusion of images that spun and danced before their eyes. The bright attire of the tribesmen and the crowds of people gathered around a small battered hovercraft contrasted with the disreputable looking group of Pairs sitting on top of it.

Pairs?

Dracl shook his head and his eyes cleared enough to make out what they were. They were Pairs all right and they were armed with lasers and swords. The tribesmen carried them to the craft and Clard and Dracl stood supported by the men and stared at the Leader Pair.

"What?..." began Dracl.

"The name is Draz and Zrad, we changed our names to suit our feelings, and we welcome you to our little community. I hope you like our friends here," he said. "They wanted to sacrifice you to the Gods but we persuaded them you are more useful to us alive."

Clard looked at the Pair and looked around at the tribesmen. There was a lot of them and running away was obviously not going to be the best option, he thought, depends what they want. Clard decided to stall for time and ingratiate themselves with this Pair.

"Pleased to meet you," he said, getting an encouraging empathy wave from his twin.

"No you are not," said the Pair "You are scared witless and so you should be. We know who you are. You are Clard and Dracl of C&D Enterprises and there is a little matter of what happened to some of our mates to settle."

"What the heck are you talking about?"

"The Pairs you used for your experiments during the Star Station Two project."

"Oh them, well you know, we were given orders to use..." Clard stopped and paled when the Pair raised their lasers and aimed them at his belly.

"You killed them."

"It was all in the line of duty ..." Dracl babbled.

"Don't give me that shit. You will pay for that but in the meantime we have another problem which you can help us with if you value your miserable lives. If you solve it you will live but if you don't then it is goodbye, we will let the tribesmen have you."

"What is the other problem," said Clard, small voiced and very very scared.

"A robot, we are having a problem with a crazy robot and a horde of ravenous rodents. We think you will be able to help us out."

"What do you mean?" squeaked Clard.

"We don't know nothing about no robot," said Dracl, panicking.

"Oh yes you do because, my friends, it has been asking for you," said the Pair with a wide grin.

Clard and Dracl slumped in their captors arms in a dead faint.

Sally Aitcheson has her say.

Maurice Bannerman's conference room was crowded. The centre of attention was Maurice himself who balanced the chair on its back legs with his own braced evenly on the floor, his large hands clasped his neck behind his head and now and then to emphasise a point he took one hand and waved it at whoever he was talking to. The production team which included Sally and Joseph listened as he spoke, and included in part of the arrangements more or less as consultants for content there was also Marjorie, Dart and Drat and Colin with some of his men.

"They will pay top dollar for the space I reckon?" Said Joseph. Maurice looked at him and held his gaze.

"I think Joseph has got something there," said Sally. She looked quickly at Dart and then at Joseph and gave her best winning smile to Maurice who laughed and then with a shrug he turned to Dart and spread his hands.

"Putty I am, putty, I'll do as they say, these young ones," he said, and clicked his finger and thumb. "We'll do it our way and bugger the P.M."

The next thirty minutes was all frantic activity. Maurice gave orders and spoke into telephones while the others put together a script. Sally was the first to finish and she stood watching the technicians running through the camera evolutions and workers titivating the set she caught Dart stealing a glance at her. She turned away, blushing and turned back again as if drawn to him by a magnet. Damn, she thought, he's annoying me, drat the man! Drat, an appropriate response. She felt the smile on her lips form and blushed again when he smiled at her. Oh shit, wrong response. But nevertheless when he walked across the studio toward her she was pleased.

"Sally," he began, "er can we talk. I er, want to sort of er, um, sort of like er, sort of get to know you a bit sort of..."

"Better?" she finished for him as his voice hesitated and she saw he was obviously embarrassed. She added a smile and giggled.

"Yes, you're right," he said.

"If you are going to waffle then start now or for ever hold your peace," she said, and blushed deeply realising where the words came from. Oh no, not that!

"Well I was going to ask about you and sort of find out what you are doing here and how you came to work for mister Bannerman and all that sort of thing," he said.

"I'll give you my file," she replied.

"Ah, that's not what I meant."

"No but that's all you really need. What you really want to know is more than that and I am not sure whether I want to tell you, if you get what I mean?" she said aware of his embarrassment and taking a small but niggling delight in watching him recoil.

"I'm sorry I...I ...I guess I'm out of line," he stuttered.

She looked at him and let her eyes lock on his unsure of what she felt and uncertain of what to say. The sounds in the studio dulled and she could hear her heart beating fast. Her palms sweated and she felt her body tingle with a warmth that started in her belly and spread all over. She quickly looked away and then as quickly back again.

"Bugger you," she said, and took his hand in hers. "I wish you hadn't done that."

"Done what?" he said.

"You know, just being here, being you, everything. Shit, now I'm waffling."

He smiled at her and took her other hand gently in his and she raised her face a little knowing her lips had parted wanting his to kiss them. She responded when he did kiss her by almost doing what a girlfriend said she always did when a boy kissed her, she melted, or seemed to and literally fell into his arms. The kiss lasted for ever and when they pulled apart not letting go their hold on each other's hands for fear of losing the moment she giggled.

"What's the matter? What is so funny?" he said.

"Me, I'm the funny one. Of all the men who have ever tried to do that to me I have to fall for an alien. It's out of this world," she said and when Dart laughed she joined in clasping his hand tightly and leaning against him enjoying the strong muscular body pressed against hers. "For God's sake take me out for lunch and let's sort this out."

"Okay," he said and led her past the grinning crew and past Drat and Joseph to where Colin was standing with a big soppy grin on his face.

"Would you be so kind as to provide Miss Aitcheson and myself with a suitable escort while we partake of a lunch?" said Dart, his face reddening.

"Sure mister Dart, I'd be happy to."

Sally was aware of the faces watching them as they left the studio. Oh dear, she thought, oh dear.

President Horace Revere stared at the sheet for at least five minutes. He read the script several times before it sank in and slowly, his face white and his lips tight, he looked up at the impassive Aide. The invitation was worded in such a way as to make him look second best. His vice president was to be the guest speaker.

"By request of the Japanese advisors," he said.

The Aide stood waiting.

"By the request of the Japanese ADVISORS! Goddamn it! Don't they think I know what this means? Don't they think I know what advisor means?" he put the stress on the word advisor and the Aide looked uncomfortable.

"Answer me! What do you think they take me for?"

The Aide wanted to tell him but President Revere was still his employer. Instead he said. "Perhaps they think you will tie the arguments together for them sir."

"Tie the arguments together ... my ass! What do you think I am, a dummy! They want that dyke bitch to speak for the US of A instead of me. I am an afterthought, an also ran, goddamn it man they got me slotted in after some goddamn limey eye fuckin' witness!"

"Late in the program sir when people will be watching. I have it on good authority there will be a conference of heads of government not long after. I believe you will presiding sir. Well the President of the United States will be presiding and ..."

The Aide started back as President Revere almost leapt at him with uncontrolled rage. What stopped the President was the Aide's quick evasion and the large desk that spread between them. The Aide retreated quickly to the door ready to slip out if the president moved. It wasn't necessary, the president slipped on the fine polished mahogany and dropped with a thump on the floor.

The Aide left him laying and walked out.

"Cocksucker," the President muttered as the Aide passed the desk.

"Sir?"

"Just get out will you."

Outside the room the Aide spoke to the President's secretary.

"My resignation Jerry, I will hand in my resignation unless this asshole resigns," he said to the confused and worried secretary. "Go pick the prick up from the floor and wipe his nose, or something."

The Aide stormed out.

Prime Minister Smith was extremely unhappy. Of the many things that had lately made him so unhappy this latest was the worse. Whenever he turned on his radio there was always that damn tune playing and whenever he turned on the telly, even the cable service, there was the stupid rodent message. The tune, he noted, was played on the hour every hour and at twenty past the hour and again at twenty to the hour. He had tried to remember to turn the radio off but whenever he did that the damn tune played on the telly or on the intercom. Or, and this was something that really did get to him, some bastard was playing it on their own radio. Even the newscasts had shifted time slots. It was now news at three minutes after the hour or whenever the damn tune finished playing. The thing that got to him most was the stream of mathematical formulæ that chattered out on the defence department's computers. The boffins put the formulæ into more understandable form for him and his staff and carefully explained what it meant.

"You mean that if we don't give in these buggers will destroy the planet?"

"Yes sir."

"Bastards, we can't let them get away with that, it's morally wrong," he said and glared at the scientist. God, he thought, they turn them out young nowadays, this guy's scarcely more than a kid?

"Moral or not the reality is that if we don't surrender they intend to blow us out of the sky, literally. We have a choice. Do as they ask or try and find a way to neutralise it," the scientific kid said.

"Can we do that?"

The kid looked at him and blinked. Like an owl. Boffin, nerd, horribly intelligent. Smith hated intelligent people, they made him feel uncomfortable. This kid made him feel extremely uncomfortable. Smith remembered what it was like at Eton; he had hated the school but his father had insisted he go. The fees were paid from the family fortune, and as his father stated: "Your Grandfather worked hard to get this going for you, and now we can do it you will go." It was there he had met intelligent people who made him feel like the proletariat child he was, calling him a pleb who should have gone to a state school. This boy was one of them, he was sure of it, or maybe a Harrow boy? Whatever he was Smith hated him.

"We can try and destroy the bomb itself or we could send a nuke fleet to the Star Station and destroy that instead," the kid said, nonchalantly.

The Prime Minister looked surprised, he felt surprised, what was a nuke fleet?

"What do you mean? A nuke fleet? What is that?"

"I thought you knew, er, excuse me I will consult the oracle." The kid said and with a flourish tapped keys on a small computer terminal he had carried in and dropped gently onto the Prime Minister's polished desk. He looked at the screen for a few seconds and smiled as codes and figures flashed at the command of his dashing fingers.

"You're cleared for response," the kid said.

At that moment Prime Minister Smith hated him more than he hated the opposition.

"And what the fuck does that mean?"

"Oh it just means that I can tell you what a nuke fleet is," said the kid and smiled softly. "I thought you might already know."

"Well I don't already know or I wouldn't be asking you would I you dumb cluck!"

The kid smiled again and looked at the Prime Minister knowingly.

"Sorry."

"Tell me."

The Prime Minister placed his hands on the desk and let his fingers twitch impatiently staring directly into the kid's face as he spoke. His voice was quiet and full of menace. The kid replied quietly and confidently as if he were not afraid of the Prime Minister's threat.

"The nuke fleet is a name we gave to the bunch of missiles we designed in case we needed them against the Chinese. It was a sort of last resort to solve the Sino-Indian conflict. The French and the Germans sort of helped a bit. The missiles are currently wandering around in orbit waiting to be used. I believe the Americans named theirs Star Wars when they were allowed to have them. Unfortunately theirs didn't operate all that well so they abandoned the idea. We, er, sort of commandeered them. We could try attacking the bomb but if that doesn't work we have a contingency plan to send a cluster to the Star Station. If neither scenario is successful we can always learn how to work under whips," said the kid and grinned.

The Prime Minister looked at him steadily for long moments saying nothing and the kid, totally unfazed, leaned back in his chair and continued to look affable.

"All right how many will we need?"

"Bomb or Star Station?"

"Both and how long?"

"The Bomb will need at least six and the whole operation will take no more than forty-eight hours to set up and complete. The Star Station will need something like two and a half years. I'm afraid by then we will either not exist or we will all be working on the levee's or picking cotton."

"You are a cheeky bastard aren't you?"

"Am I sir?"

"Yes, what is your name?"

"Wallace G Dunmoe," the kid replied. "It's on the intro sheet and I did show you my pass, sir."

"Well mister Wallace G Dunmoe whenever I see your name come up again in this operation I will request that you be transferred to another location, like central United States or Australia or anywhere. Now thank you and leave me, now!"

The Prime Minister shouted the last word and with a sigh Wallace, who liked to be called Wally, got out of the chair and gathered his computer terminal and his papers. He stuck out his hand for the Prime Minister to shake and withdrew it when it was ignored. Instead he touched his curly forelock and stuck out his lips and bowed slightly.

"Thank you massa bawse," he said and turned on his heel leaving the Prime Minister gazing angrily after him.

"Black bastard," said the Prime Minister.

Wallace G squared his shoulders and marched off whistling the tune 'When Johnny comes marching Home'. Wallace G wished the Prime Minister hadn't called him a bastard. He was a Christian born of Christian parents and they, he knew, would be offended.

The table in Maurice Bannermann's number one interview studio was decorated with flowers. In the centre there was carafe of water and a tray of polished tumblers. On the table in front of each chair was the name of the participant printed on plastic labels and under each label was a folder. In the folders was a number of easily readable sheets updating the events to date. Currently there were seven battle sites and at each of them the local forces were steadily or rapidly being beaten back depending on the ability of the local forces to respond. The picture looked grim, and as far as the Zradian forces were concerned they were winning. Earth could either surrender or be beaten to a standstill. The Zradian Stormtroopers, it seemed, preferred fighting.

The cameras were ready for action and in the make up rooms the participants were undergoing a transformation. Eyes were lined or made neutral, faces were rouged or whitened and the make up artists fussed to get their subjects right.

Maurice Bannermann stalked the monitor room like a father waiting for the birth of his first child and with massive impatience watched the clock. At last the cue called and the studio began to fill with people. Cameras were staffed, sound technicians stopped chanting and exactly on time the program began.

The first televised summit meeting between East, West and Extra terrestrials began.

Appropriately, so Maurice Bannerman thought, it was named "We are Not Afraid of the Rodents, are we?"

Maurice was proud of the title.

"It's just a matter of convenience"

Tzu's smile was so large that it made his face ache. The party was a success. There was dancing for the young folk, food and drink for the older ones and games for the children. In one corner the old men were chatting and playing a never ending game of cards. In another corner the makeshift band played music of all kinds depending on who wanted to jam. Tzu had approved of hiring a proper dance band but there was so many musicians wanting to play that he had told the band to relax and enjoy themselves and let the music go where it would. As a result the variety was marvellous. And, he sighed a big sigh of relief at the thought, nobody wanted to play A Whiter Shade of Pale. He was glad of that. His nieces, nephew's and grandchildren all paid him homage and added to the pile of presents that grew on the gift table. He looked at the pile and his smile, if it were possible, grew even larger. He stroked his beard pulling the grey hair to a sharp point and giggled. All those parcels to open and all those cards to read.

"I will get the little ones to help me," he said.

"Father?" said his eldest son.

"Just speaking my thoughts aloud. I was thinking I might get the children to open the packages for me," he said.

"After we have cut the cake we baked for you and everybody has a piece," said his son.

"Ah yes, the cake. I like this English custom. I reach sixty and I have birthday party. A big cake and lots of candles, ah here it is."

Tzu stopped speaking as the band suddenly struck up a cord and then with a ragged start played the tune Happy Birthday. The people stopped dancing and followed the progress of the massive cake as it was carried by four women into the hall from the kitchen and placed with loving care on the central table. The lights dimmed leaving the candles, all sixty to sparkle. Tzu stepped forward and with great dignity he walked to where the cake gleamed with its encrusted icing and glittering paper decorations. He stood before the cake poised and ready waiting for the song to finish, licking his lips with his tongue and making rolling eyes at the nearest children who turned and giggled coyly. As the strains of the last 'to you' echoed in the hall Tzu bent forward and with a steady and continuous breath he blew all the candles out and stood back smiling. Everybody cheered. Three times. The last Hurrah broke up into laughter as the candles suddenly re-lighted.

"Oh no!" said Tzu. "I have been caught by my own product!"

With great dignity he pinched each candle wick between his thumb and forefinger and one by one the flames went out only to reignite until at last some of the children helped pluck them off the icing crust pinching them to snuff them completely. Someone handed him a knife and with a steady hand he placed it on the top and cut slowly pacing his movement so that all who wanted to could take pictures. He wished his wife could be there to help him but ... His face clouded over a little and he hesitated but with a gentle touch his sister placed her hand on his and moved with him.

"She would liked to have been here brother," she said. "In spirit she is, take heart dear one."

Tzu smiled at her and with renewed energy he cut deep into the magnificent cake and then let his nieces cut it up for distribution. He was sad and pleased when the piece he was given had his wife's favourite cake decoration sitting beside it.

"Thank you my child," he said and squeezed her hand.

Malcolm Wu staggered out into the yard looking for a dark spot. His bladder was screaming for attention and if he didn't relieve himself in the next few seconds he would wet his pants. Too much beer and an incredibly long queue at the inside toilets drove him into the yard to use one of the portaloos but they were all in use. He forced his bladder to close and literally hop footed to a dark corner of the yard aching from the effort, hands shaking as he undid his fly. He was surprised when he saw a cubicle all on its own standing against the far wall. Gratefully he hurried to it and pulled open the door ready to throw out the occupant if he had to. His need was imperative. The cubicle was empty and with a great sigh he lifted the seat and the cover and let the fluid flow. It seemed to take for ever and as he stood there he was surprised to see that in fact it was a flush toilet complete with paper and a long chain from the cistern. It was old but Malcolm was surprised at how clean it was. There was a light globe in a holder in the ceiling shaded by a utility cover. The floor was smooth and tastefully tiled.

Through the fug of inebriation he looked again at the bowl and it was with some surprise he saw that in fact there was two, side by side each with its own flushing chain.

"Odd, peculiar," he said, taken aback.

Behind the pans the pipes were clean and the cobwebs he expected to see were not there. To his left there was a narrow wash basin and a towel rack with a towel hanging from it. He looked up at the cistern looking for a maker's name.

He made out the scrawl cast on to a small panel but couldn't understand the writing and gave up, content to let his bladder empty. At last he stopped and with a deft movement he zipped up and used the hand basin. With a sense of ceremony he flushed the cistern and then he dried his hands on the towel and walked outside shutting the door behind him. He noticed that the light went out.

"Like the 'fridge," he said and staggered back to the house.

It never occurred to him to wonder how a flush toilet came to be in the back yard. His relief was such that he did not think to question the whys and wherefores of such a handy and convenient building. In fact by this time the beer he had drunk was having a soporific effect and all he really wanted now was a place to sleep. He found it. He entered the house by the kitchen door and turned left into the dark pantry area not bothering to look where he was going and finding some sacks filled with vegetables he lay down and fell asleep. He did not notice the door shut on him; he was as one dead, besides, even if he had woken to the sound of the latch dropping he would have done nothing. The room, the world and all that was in it seemed to be spinning the opposite way to what he thought it ought to. The best way to stop it spinning out of control he found was to let it get on with it.

He woke the next morning in the dark aware of the earthy smell of potatoes and the rank stench of onions and cabbage. The thought of eating any sent him straight back to sleep. The cooks found him not long after breakfast and asked two male helpers to carry him to a bedroom. It was late afternoon when he went downstairs on shaky legs to look for his revered uncle.

Tzu stood with Malcolm facing the cubicle; in the evening light he had to admit that unless you were desperate you wouldn't see the thing. He thought that all the portaloos were gone, taken away by the contractors. This one wasn't marked like the others so maybe it was a different contractor. No, he had given the contract to his cousin. All of them should have the distinctive red hand sign on the door.

"And you say it works like any ordinary loo?" asked Tzu.

"Yes, I flushed it when I had finished and it did its thing. There was even a towel supplied. Notice that I also put the seat and the cover down and shut the door when I left," Malcolm said proudly.

"I never knew there was one there. We haven't had one like this in the yard ever. In fact there should be a shrub here not this," said Tzu and waved his hand in its direction.

Malcolm shrugged and looked at Tzu.

"But venerable uncle it is there and I did use it last night. I was drunk but I do remember coming out here and bursting for a ..."

"Yes yes fine so let me have a look eh?"

Tzu walked to the door and unlatched it. In the daylight it looked like a clean toilet and it had all the fittings just as Malcolm described it. There was the cistern and two chains dangling and the finely made bowl and seat. Double and seats, he corrected. On one wall was a sink with a towel hanging below it. There were two mirrors above the sink which Tzu noticed had a double bowl. Tzu slipped inside quietly and smoothly and turned as if he were about to sit on a pan. He turned again and looked in the pan lifting the seat gingerly as he did so. He nodded and with a flourish pulled the chain. Water rushed into the bowl and sizzled in the cistern as it refilled.

Odd, he thought, I have never had a toilet here, never.

He turned around inside and noticed the little block of grey buttons close to the door jamb. He examined them closely and withdrew his hand when a green light glowed steadily. Tzu quickly stepped out of the cubicle and stood facing it looking for signs of change. In the back of his mind something clicked and as he stood watching the light change from green to red and then back to green again he had it.

"Malcolm, go get a clean house brick from the yard near the door and bring it here."

His nephew trotted off and came back quickly with a large clean house brick. Tzu placed it on the seat and from outside he reached in and pressed the button. The light glowed green, red and green again. Almost in the blink of an eye the house brick disappeared.

Tzu grunted and smiled at his nephew.

"Matter Transfer," he said.

Malcolm kept his face impassive and replied. "Yes Uncle."

Tzu snorted and turned from him to contemplate the cubicle. Youth, sceptical and so bloody, or was it bruddy, naive? That must have been how Julian disappeared or they would have found bodies. Not only that but Constable Rice was cut in half when the shed went up. Must have been a shield or something that protected it; something electronic. He thought about the cubicle. Little hands could wander in and use the buttons.

"We must lock this up until we find out what it is all about."

Malcolm nodded and blushed when Tzu glared at him.

"Bulgers! What was that?"

The Pair ducked and pushed arms and hands over their faces to stop the sharp plastic shards hitting them. Even so the plastic flew like blades and some shivered into the soft walls and bounced off their tunics leaving little tears. The heavy object that fell through the window crashed onto the bench and bounced on the floor skidding against the wall behind them. The Leader Pair rushed to the spot and looked down at the spinning house brick.

"From the emplaced port I take it?"

"Looks like it."

"Well then we have a problem. That thing..." the leader Pair pointed at the brick. "Came in from the wrong place. We need to get a monitored receiver box set up. Do it."

"Yes your Honour!"

The work Pair quickly crossed to a telescreen and tapped a code. Faces appeared and with quick efficient instructions they made the arrangements.

"In half a turn the Crew Pairs will have one set up for us. I will begin tracking and realigning immediately. Er what was it that arrived anyway?"

"How the Bulger do I know? A stone? A rock? A crude message block? Who knows?"

The work Pair turned back to their station.

Sometimes the Leader Pair could get a bit excitable.

Tzu examined the lock and with a sense of relief he turned the key and tried the door. Locked and secure. He pocketed the key and took his wallet from his pocket.

"How much I owe you?"

The locksmith wiped his hands on a cloth and looked at his watch.

"I reckon abaht forty five for me work and thirty for the lock. Say seventy all together, mister Tzu."

Tzu looked at him and withdrew four twenties from his wallet and handed them to the locksmith.

"No change, you do a very good job. I employ you again sometime, okay?"

"Thank you sir, I will be delighted but, er, why the lock on the loo?"

"It's a matter of convenience," said Tzu straight-faced delighting inwardly as the man twisted his own face in an effort not to laugh.

Behind him Malcolm giggled and then with guffaws Tzu repeated "its a matter of convenience!" He slapped his thigh and bent double giggling.

The locksmith looked at them and said: "Bloody Chinese, I'll never understand them."

Tzu slapped him on the back and put his arm around the man's shoulders.

"You very good man," he said. "You call around on Monday and I will give you a contract, okay?"

The man looked puzzled.

"You become official locksmith to Wu Enterprises, eh?"

"Yer, I'll do that," he said, and gathered up his tools.

Tzu and Malcolm watched him go and slowly they walked back into the house.

"This Port-a-loo needs some investigation," said Tzu, "we will have to flush out what's behind it. Sort of pull its chain and see what flows into the bowl."

"Yes Uncle, unlock it at our convenience and let whoever it is come out of the closet," said Malcolm.

"Ah so, you are getting better nephew."

Tzu was smiling when he sat down at table and chuckled when he thought of the bemused locksmith. Something was cooking and before things got out of hand he wanted to do a little preparation of his own. The key to the puzzle has to be the sudden increased order for tokens. Nearly double the amount and that meant something was up. He remembered the strange men who arrived on his doorstep when he was a starving lad.

"We will give you what you need if you find a place to make these for us," they said, and showed him a set of injection mould patterns and a range of plastic tokens. They even gave him the polymer composition which helped to persuade Byrde Senior to take on the project. Tzu thought of that meeting and smiled. Most fortuitous meeting, he mused, from cleaning floors to cleaning up a fortune but also a strong friendship with Byrde Senior that lasted until the older man died. One day he would tell Richard why. Perhaps. In the meantime he had plans to make. The men who gave him the first contract were long gone but every now and then a representative arrived on his doorstep with a new contract. Always two and always in a hurry. He had only a vague idea where they came from, or at least that they were not of his own world, he was sure now. His problem was to decide whether he was dealing with an enemy or a friend. The arrival of a Matter Transfer Port in his back yard was a way of finding out.

A most convenient way of flushing out the truth.

He had an idea to call on volunteers to use it and find out what was at the other end. Collect the house brick maybe, he thought, and smiled again. The idea of finding out what might be beyond his own knowledge of the world excited him and with a feeling of determination he decided that for once he would share his thoughts with an outsider. The best person to talk to, he thought, was not his dear friend, the stuffy Arthur Renfrew but Richard Byrde, and with measured steps he walked to his office. He greeted the girls in the front room with his usual smile and when one of his nieces giggled he stopped by her desk and stood looking down at her fondly.

"Explain your giggling child," he said and glanced around the room catching sly amused looks as his staff turned away.

"We are worried, father, that you are so taken with a toilet that you employ a lock master to keep us out of it?" she said and stifled a giggle.

"My dear niece, you girls have enough toilets already, it would be inconvenient to have you traipsing to and from the back yard, I would never get any work done. Perhaps I may put locks on the rest of them and save even more time and money," he said and tried to keep his face impassive.

"Excuse me Father but we would all have to use the public conveniences on the Bywater Road, this office would be empty and you would lose all of your time and money," she said.

"But at least I will be free of giggling relatives," he said. "Now what is it you were really giggling over?"

"It was cousin Malcolm. We locked him in the vegetable shed, he was so drunk. He fell over dancing with cousin Sue and we watched him go into the yard," and she started to giggle again. "He had rubber legs. He was so funny! The toilets were full and he was looking for a bush!"

The other girls giggled when she demonstrated with her hands how Malcolm had staggered to the corner of the yard and Tzu caught the amusement and imagined Malcolm with crossed legs shaking and staggering trying not to wet himself as he looked for a dark spot in the bushes.

As he left them to go into his office he was convinced that the new toilet was planted in his place for a purpose. It was a puzzle and all the more reason to call Richard Byrde.

He sat in his chair and tapped numbers putting the receiver to his ear and listened to the dialling tone. There was a click and a different tone and a male voice answered.

"If your call is for mister Byrde please identify yourself."

"Mister Tzu Wu speaking. I wish to talk with my friend Richard Byrde," he said, and waited for a reply as the man on the other end consulted with somebody else. The voice asked him to wait a few moments and then Emily Byrde spoke.

"Tzu? Do you know where Richard is?" she said.

"No, Emily, I assumed he was at home. Unlike me he does not work on Sunday. I thought he may be with you. I wish to consult him on a rather puzzling matter. Do you not know where he is?"

"No I do not but he packed me off to my mother's with an escort of useful if somewhat pugilistic gentlemen, and the Ferret's younger brother. He was escorted by the Ferret, his mate Lugs and my cousin's son Oliver," she said, "you do know that Arthur has disappeared don't you?" Her voice sounded desperate and Tzu hesitated before answering.

"Ah, in that case I had better start looking for him. Emily, you have my number and if I need to call you I will call your home number and I will be transferred to your number there?"

"Yes, can you really help?"

"I can really help but I cannot promise results. I will do all I can. In the meantime take heart and take care of yourself."

Emily thanked him and rang off.

Tzu sat thinking for a few moments and when he had thought enough he made telephone calls to some of his people calling for assistance to find Richard Byrde, and the two Renfrews and a call to his Kung Fu headquarters to call for volunteers for a special task.

"And what is this special task, revered Uncle?"

"Call it operation Portaloo," he replied and like the girls in the outer office he giggled.

Byrde on Zrad

Richard Byrde opened his eyes and immediately shut them again. The light seared into his head like knives and he groaned. A cool hand touched his forehead and there was a slight puff of air as something warm touched his skin. Seconds later he opened his eyes again and this time they remained open. Two faces looked down at him. One was dark with strange eyes and the other was thin and anxious. The Ferret and a stranger.

"It's all right mister Byrde you bin looked after proper. This bloke is D.G, him and his mate found us out in the desert. You was ill with scept... septi ... blood poisoning but these blokes fixed it. Give it a day or two and you'll be up and about. Just lay down and go orf to sleep. The aliens reckon you was nearly done for. We would never 'ave made it," said the Ferret.

"Where are we Ferret?"

"Rebel army headquarters with the bloke what rescued Julian, its a long story so you better rest fer a while and when you are feeling more like yourself again we'll tell you all about it. Lugs is okay and so is mister Braine," the Ferret said, and placed his hand on Byrde's shoulder. "You did all right mister Byrde."

Byrde lay back on the soft pillow and closed his eyes. The Ferret was right, he was tired but not exhausted, in need of more rest. His body ached but the comfortable bed seemed to be made especially for him and as he moved it supported him in all the right places. He breathed a contented sigh and let sleep come to him.

The Ferret walked the corridors from the medical centre heading for the training grounds. Lugs was in his element learning the sword and knife movements. He was quick and accurate and unlike the many times when the Ferret had tried to teach him elementary arithmetic and card games the fighting arts seemed to come naturally. The Ferret was learning too but he preferred either not fighting or using the laser weapon instead. The Trainer Pairs explained that it was necessary to learn the blades because when it came to hand to hand fighting that was where it was at.

D.G and Glord had laughed at that and showed him and Lugs their form of unarmed combat. Lugs lapped it up and the Ferret found it fascinating. It was like Kung Fu but quiet like, deadly and fast. They had been there for nearly three Earth weeks and the training was a good fill in while they waited for mister Byrde to come out of his coma. It was a close run thing and Glord told them that they had had to send somebody out to get a medicine.

"We have to find the plant and then distil the material to make enough serum to put into your friend's system. We don't know if it will work on him either. Did you know that according to our medics you Earth people are so closely related to us, metabolically speaking, that we could almost be the same species. Weird."[7] Glord said as they watched the medics working on Byrde.

The whole thing was weird, thought the Ferret, the strange layout of the headquarters that looked more like a prison school than anything else. On the surface there was a compound and buildings and a fence surrounding the place with a number of entrances. The place was divided into four colour sections with a separate function and underground the complex was much larger as if it was a bunker for an exiled government in a war. He smiled at the thought, that was what they were, more or less, a government in waiting. He smiled again when he thought of Oliver Braine, who immediately they arrived, had asked D.G to place him in the propaganda section.

"I'm an artist not a fighter and if you teach me your language I will help you with writing and posters and anything else, but if you give me weapons or ask me to fight I will fall apart in a big way. I'd like to be a hero but I just don't have what it takes. I can't fight my way out of a wet paper bag." Braine said, and after a few sessions on the learning machines he was inducted into Glord's counter-intelligence section. For the first time since the adventure had begun Oliver Braine was smiling and looking as if he belonged.

The Ferret turned a corner and climbed a short flight of steps entering the training rooms with a confident manner. Lugs was teaching the Pairs his particular methods, and the Ferret felt a sense of pride when he watched his mate move smoothly and quickly demonstrating a move, explaining it with confidence in his newly learned language to the awestruck Pairs. He watched Lugs work until the period ended and when the big man turned toward him he called out.

"Mister Byrde woke up and the medics reckon he is going to be okay."

Lugs grinned. "I like that. When he gets a bit better I'll go play cards with him and cheer him up," said Lugs as the two men walked out the portal.

"We gonna have dinner boss?"

---

[7] *This revelation could be quite disturbing for those who believe in God and divine providence regarding the conception of the human race. It could also be equal ing disturbing for those who believe in natural evolution. Either way Glord's statement questions the origin of the species.*

"Yes and after that we go and watch some more videos."

"I like that too boss. Them videos is pretty good and I'm beginning to understand 'em now. The only thing I don't get is when them Pairs keep giggling."

"It's a private joke, you know when they first put you into the machine they had to make it bigger and because of that they want us to go in together, to use the capacity of the machine," the Ferret explained.

Lugs grunted and said no more. The Ferret was glad of that, if there was one thing he didn't want to explain to Lugs and that was that the machine had threatened to terminate him. The Pairs explained that the machine couldn't possibly operate that low. It couldn't feed into such a low intellect as Lugs' and still function.

"There has only been one other person the machine couldn't cope with. We had to give it a program in tandem to keep it interested."

When the Ferret found out who it was and why they called him BB he had roared with laughter. He knew Julian as one of a group of petty thieves on Earth and always thought the boy was a tosser. Now he knew. Unfortunately Lugs operated at about half Julian's speed and so he was asked to be the other half of the trainee Pair. The machine rated him at 93, and when the Pairs told him the implications of that he stared at them in disbelief.

"You mean I have a high IQ?"

They nodded and suggested he apply for work with Glord's section.

"I'll think it over," he said.

What he needed to do first was to explain the situation carefully to Lugs in case they had to work apart. What he wanted to do was talk to mister Byrde and get his advice. Byrde seemed to understand Lugs in a way that the Ferret didn't. They reached the canteen and looked for Braine. He was sitting at table with Glord and D.G and when he saw them he called out.

"Good news it seems, our Richard is on the mend."

Lugs and the Ferret sat on the vacant stools and said together. "Yeah we heard."

Oliver Braine touched the send icon with the pointer and waited for the flimsy to rush out of the slot. It amazed him how fast the computers were and yet how slow the delivery of the printed matter. He was used to almost instant printing. The flimsy whispered from the slot and he took it as it dropped in the tray. There was a figure on the top and with a start he realised that his was the master copy of many hundreds. The printer had in fact printed four hundred and ninety in the time it took his own system to print ten.

"Touché," he said and began to read.

The flimsy was the latest field report of the activities of Julian Renfrew and his troop in the women's rebel army.

"Who ever would have thought Julian Renfrew would be such a hero," he said and showed the flimsy to Glord.

"You know this Earthman?"

"I know of him. He is a stupid bloke with a mean streak, totally unreliable and will fall to bits worse than me when it comes to fighting. How on Earth or Zrad he gets to be a hero I have no idea," said Braine.

"Nevertheless he seems to have riled the President enough to have a good price on his head and from what I know of him I would say he is scared to death," Glord said, and laughed. "Can you keep a watch on anything that goes on with him. I think that as he is one of yours you should. Besides, our Leader Pair cannot abide him."

Braine said that he imagined they would have some difficulty relating to him and started a search for more material. Ironic, he thought, how he was about to promote a no-hoper as a hero and a great warrior when there were Pairs like D.G and Glord. He was also annoyed that because of Julian, D.G and Glord were not regarded as heroes by their own leaders and got all the dirty jobs. When they explained what had happened Braine looked at them and said: "So, there was a plot against him, a conspiracy?"

"We believe so," replied D.G, and described the tense time they had in the main hall after the event. "At least he got away and so did Angela, for which I am grateful as I believe they wanted her dead as well. She had ideas above her gender." D.G told Braine about the incident in the stores and the bar and how Angela had helped destroy the ambush patrol. "She is quite a woman."

Braine smiled: "Like her do you?"

D.G coloured up and looked embarrassed. "Er, yes, I do." He said and looked defiant.

"Good, she is all right," Braine replied.

Braine enjoyed the work and had already created two short bulletins mocking the President, and although his work was not as good as Glord's it was good enough to be distributed throughout the Republic. Added to his feeling of usefulness and satisfaction was the good news that Byrde was recovering.

Richard Byrde took his first steps and felt good. He felt the cloth rustle against his scars and he hoped that when anybody asked how he got them he could tell them a large pussycat made them and keep a straight face. He felt weak but at least he could walk and it was thanks to these strange aliens, Arthur Renfrew's little green men. They were good at what they did and while he was resting, the Pair from Education had given him some sessions on the learning machine. The medics insisted that the program be light and when D.G asked him what he would prefer he had suggested learning the language.

"A good choice mister Byrde because we can let you doze while you learn and that will enable us to speed it up. You will speak our language well after the first session and fluently after the second," D.G said, and although he wanted to help he was gently eased away from the bay by the Education Pair and the medics. Byrde noted with amusement that D.G's face registered a mixture of annoyance and resignation.

"You have a bit a problem with mechanical things?" asked Byrde.

"Not that you would notice," said D.G tartly.

"All you need is a good teacher and some practice," Byrde said. "It's a form of dyslexia and lots of people on Earth suffer from it. It can be relieved if not totally cured. It's a well known fact that a video recorder can only be operated correctly by a three year old child."

D.G laughed and shrugged his shoulders.

"Okay guy, I get the message, love ya baby, have a nice day!"

This time it was Byrde's turn to make a wry face.

And as D.G stood looking a little embarrassed Byrde was amused to see that he took a worn Token from his pocket and began flipping it up and down casually but dextrously catching it and flicking it around his head as quickly as a juggler with a series of balls but with no apparent effort. His eye and hand coordination was so good he seemed to know exactly where it would be at all times.

"You seem pretty good at that," Byrde said.

"Oh, yes, it's my lucky Token. I take it with me everywhere, D.G said and flipped it to Byrde who caught it deftly in his left hand as if D.G had intended for him to catch it exactly that way and, opening his hand he looked at it. What he saw surprised him. It was one of his father's originals.

"Where did you get that?"

"Oh, I've had it since I was a small half pair," D.G said. "It was the first one I earned."

Byrde looked at him and grinned. "My father made that."

D.G looked startled and said: "Tell me about it."

Byrde explained how it was that his father had started making plastics and how Tzu, so he had discovered, had arrived with a formula and a proposal, glad that he had employed Holmes to find out for him, and explained how it was that Tzu and his people had controlled the use of them on Earth and sent him the contracts at intervals. "I have no idea what happens to them after we have shipped them," he added and handed the Token back to D.G.

With a lop sided grin D.G said: "We had no idea where they came from, we simply tapped into the supply. Do you realise, mister

Byrde, you have been supplying the Zradian Treasury, and therefore the President, and us with the funds to fight each other and your planet. Inadvertently you are part of the war effort. And I think you will like learning more about our nation."

D.G was right.

He enjoyed the session on the learning machine and insisted that he had more sessions until he knew as much about Zradian society as possible. D.G was right in that he would learn the language fast and it was a great relief to be able to ask questions and discuss the answers with the Education Pair. He was tired after each session but although the food was dull it was nutritious and within a few turns he began to feel stronger and the exercises the medics gave him became easier to do.

When Oliver Braine came from the propaganda department to see him he was fit enough to take walks outside in the compound. Byrde sat on a bench unaware that it was the same one Julian used as a comfort zone to sit and feel sorry for himself.

"Hi Richard may I join you?" said Braine and sat down alongside him.

"Looks like you already have. You look pleased and excited Oliver, what have you got to tell me?"

"This flimsy is about, er, no I will read it instead. It is from one our operatives in First City," Braine said, and held the flimsy up in front of his face so Byrde could not read it for himself. "It says, The Earthman Halfa Ranpoo," the spelling mistakes are not deliberate but we know who he means, anyway its Arthur they are talking about; "is to be sent to find his son Julian. The enemy have implanted him with a code transmitter. His task must be completed in one tenth. Consequences: destruction of Arthur and destruction of Earth – code transmitter is linked to the Doomsday Bomb – suggest Rebel army co-operate." It goes on to say that Arthur will be sent by wagon to a point in the Outlands beyond Sector Yellow. What do you think Richard?"

"Good news that so far Arthur is alive but bad news that he has to try and get Julian to go back with him," said Byrde with a grin, "and we know how much he dislikes him and how little Julian will trust him. Given Julian's attitude I am certain that we may as well kiss the Earth goodbye. Unless of course we can help."

"Don't you care?"

"I do but I think that there is no good getting depressed about it and I am sure that one way or another the thing will get settled," said Byrde affably.

Braine looked at him as if he were mad and his mouth opened and closed like a goldfish in a bowl, and he waved the flimsy in his hand trying to get a grip on Byrde's attitude. Byrde meanwhile sat calmly and waited for Braine to stop his goldfish impersonation. Before Braine could speak again he quietly made his opinion known.

"We will have to help Arthur and Julian to get together and then we will have to go in and help get them out," said Byrde. "Simple really."

"Cripes, Richard you sound so casual about it," said Braine.

"Why not Oliver, it is our destiny to do these things," said Byrde and smiled benignly. "Do I sound like a Maharishi or something?"

"Yes and that scares me, this is not a game."

"I know that but after surviving the effects of a large cat attacking me and finding myself and my companions on a strange planet and being chased by an enemy I had no knowledge of I think I find the prospect of doing whatever comes next sort of mundane." Byrde said and shrugged.

Oliver Braine nodded his head and then shook it from side to side and muttered "I don't know, I just don't know."

"I think I will volunteer my help Oliver, you feel free to do what you wish, I know Julian and I know Arthur and maybe we can do something to winkle them out and save the world. I would like that. It would be nice to be a hero even if nobody knew about it."

Oliver Braine sunk further in the seat and groaned. He knew that wherever Byrde went he would go and that knowledge frightened him.

A trek on the plains.

Professor Renfrew rode in the wagon with an escort of nervous but cheerful ordinary Pongos instead of the Polisoc troopers normally sent to escort prisoners. He had explained to them that he was willing to be left on his own where the President said he should be and they were to turn around and go back if they valued their families. He did promise to mention their names to the Rebel leaders and they almost tumbled over themselves to be the first to put their names and numbers on the flimsy. The Polisoc wagon had left them on the edge of Sector Yellow and the troopers had agreed to take him at least a half day journey into the Outlands. He had insisted that his coming be announced over the orders system belonging to the President knowing instinctively that whatever the President did the Rebels would soon know about it. He explained that he needed all the time he could get to persuade his son to come with him. The President laughed and sent him off with an escort of Polisocs with orders to pick him and Julian up again at the point where they sent him off into the Outlands.

"We will have Our troops monitor your progress," he said. "Oh, by the ways old chaps, the implant will automatically set the bomb off if you try to destroy it. We thinks should you knows."

"Thanks a bunch," Arthur said and did not wave goodbye when he was marched off.

The wagon sped along the dry plain and skidded around a rock and came to a dusty halt. The Pongos handed his pack to him and one gave him a weapon and showed him how to use it.

"There might be Carnibeasts in the area, you may need it."

The Pairs waved cheerfully as they drove off and Arthur watched them go and when they were out of sight he began his trek. The Polisoc Leader Pair had shown him a rough plan and all he had to do was walk to the low hills from the rock roughly in a line extending from the wagon track. One of the Pongos told him about the cacti with the drinkable fluid in it and advised him to fill a water bottle with some as soon as he had a spare.

"If you drink some water and then some of the cactus water you will get energy but be careful because it makes you as tiddly as the President," the Half Pair said, and his twin nodded with a broad grin. "Well maybe not as tiddly but it can make you drunk."

He thanked them for their advice and the gun and as he plodded across the sands he thought of Julia and how she treated him. She had got him wrong, he thought, and then changed his mind. No, maybe he had got her wrong? She was unhappy and he had failed to make her life a happy one. Since the birth of Julian she had become a drunk and a depressive. He realised that what had happened to her was post natal depression that was actually unresolved and in part he was to blame. He remembered the time not long after Julian was born when he had taken on the deputy head of department's job and how, as a youngish PhD he had had to fight to make his way. His appointment as research fellow a few years later had led to his Professorship and that had entailed many long nights at home and at the faculty working on his published works. The two books he had published cost him much late night work and as a consequence he had no time to spare for Julian and Julia.

He reckoned that right now he was about to regret that lapse. He thought of Julia again at home and wondered how much she knew about him and Marjorie. She may be a horrendous drunk but at least she was a human being, a woman and aware of what was going on around her household. She knew of Marjorie and as he plodded steadily toward the hills he smiled to himself and to the purple lizards that scuttled out from under his feet. He recalled the night he had found the new satellite around Jupiter and arrived home late after using the computer at the Observatory to check his findings and send out questions on the net to other Astronomers. It was past two o'clock when he arrived home in a taxi. Unfortunately the taxi driver was a woman with dark hair like Marjorie's and she was a friendly woman who gave him a cheerful 'good night' as he headed from the street to his door. He waved back as she drove off and before he unlocked the door he watched the car disappear around the corner. He opened his door and almost before he had shut it behind him Julia had rushed into the hallway from the dining room with a saucepan in her hand. He sidestepped her blow easily and dodged the sudden swing that only Julia in her drunken state was capable of delivering. He grabbed her and took the saucepan from her hands and pushed her into the lounge onto a settee.

"Fuck you Arthur fucking Renfrew! Fuck you and that painted up university slut! I know where you've been you dirty bastard! You've been sticking your dick in that tart's twat! Fuck you! Fuck you!" she yelled and attempted to hit him and succeeded in getting one in on his shoulder and a sharp kick on his shin.

"Julia, calm down, I have been at the Observatory looking at Jupiter..." he began but she was not listening and shouted more obscenities.

"You've been fucking that bloody scrubber. Ob-fucking-servatory my bloody arse! Shag her on the bloody lectern do you? You're a fucking wanker, Renfrew, a slut shagging wanker! Ow!"

He slapped her face and she collapsed on the settee and curled up screaming that he had killed her and then she burst into tears. Gently he gathered her in his arms and with a clean handkerchief he dabbed her face and cooed to her until she was calmer. She lapsed into incoherence and he realised that she had mustered all her resources to attack him and with hardly any resistance from her he put her to bed. The next morning she was hungover and grumpy and when he saw how much gin she had drunk the night before he understood why. Julia was easily able to drink a bottle of gin a day when she was depressed and that night she had drunk most of two. He sent for the doctor and waited for him to arrive and examine her.

"She needs treatment Professor," the doctor said, "if you wish I will start proceedings to book her in. All you have to do is persuade her. Good luck."

He had tried but there was no way she would listen to his pleas. He had told Marjorie on the day he had left home for good and she had sympathised with him but chastised him for letting the situation go on for so long. He blushed to think of how callous he must have seemed but then living with Julia was not easy. Marjorie had given him an insight into the way Julia felt, but at least she had not condemned him for his actions, only at the way he had let things go.

"If I ever get out of this mess I will sort things out with Julia and try and tell her why and maybe I will get on better with Julian," he said to a large purple, red and orange bush. The bush remained uncommitted and offered him no advice. In fact he thought it might be responding to his voice but when it started to look attractive he broke the imagined eye contact and moved on feeling the sense of disappointment that emanated from it. He recognised a Carnibush and shuddered, realising that it was easy to become seduced by the perfume and the undulating tendrils that would eventually ensnare him.

"And you can do without me for a meal."

He walked on, and as the day wore on he became anxious. He knew that not far from where the Pongos had dropped him was a look out post that although it moved location there would be people watching for him. The Pongo Leader Pair had said that whenever anybody wanted to defect all they did was head for the hills and they would be picked up. Arthur assumed that he would be picked up in twilight and so, with resignation he plodded on. At least, he thought, it was a chance to study a whole new flora and fauna. If that study was somewhat cursory then maybe if the rebels won and he survived then he might have a chance to study the people too. You never knew your luck in a big city, he thought, and felt embarrassed using such a banal saying.

The terrain was rough but not so that he could not pick a straight path to the hills. He climbed a low rocky outcrop and was surprised when he reached the top to see a rolling plain of grassland before him dotted here and there with rocky formations festooned with trees and shrubs. There were no grazing animals in sight but he knew that sometime or another he would see some and hoped there were no Carnibeasts around. He breasted the crest of the low hill and took a deep breath and stepped onto the grass. It was peculiar stuff, stiff and spiky but as wavy in the wind as grass on Earth. He headed for a rocky outcrop and although it looked quite near it took him a long time to reach it. He sat in the shade of a large rock and examined his rations discovering the mess tin, and food that needed cooking. The twin suns were descending in the east and it was time to make a camp. With the laser slung over his shoulder he searched for dry material and made a pile of dried dung and dropped branches. He lit his fire as the suns set and arranged his pack so that he could pick it up if he had to move quickly, and set about cooking some of the food in the mess tin. He added some bits of cactus and poured some of the liquid into the pan for moisture and let it heat up until it smelled right. It tasted fine and by the time the suns had finally set and the Zradian night began he was rested with a full belly. He sat and watched the stars appear knowing that only the brighter ones could be seen and tried to pick out familiar stars but gave it up as hopeless and concentrated on putting those he could see into patterns. He dozed off watching them and as he dozed he became aware of the sound of vehicles and to his embarrassment he was not ready when a semi-circle of small battle wagons hissed to a halt a few metres from his camp. He grabbed the laser and stood up. Somebody called out to him to come forward and then a light shone directly in his face.

"Lay down the weapon."

He laid it on the ground and heard footsteps approaching him and was glad when the light dimmed. His vision came back after a few seconds and he watched as a woman soldier picked up his laser from the ground and more stood with weapons pointed at him and then he heard a familiar voice and grinned.

"Fucking arseholes, it's me old man, what the fuck is he doing here?"

"Hello Julian," said Arthur. "I think we need to talk."

Arthur Renfrew sat in the rear of the wagon with Glorida and Glorid and Julian and as concisely as he could he told them what had happened to him. He saw Glorida holding Julian's hand and was pleased, he saw the rapport between them and liked it, and hoped that the relationship and the emotion that went with it would help.

"So, what are you doing here?" asked Julian suspiciously. "I mean, the President don't jest let people go you know."

"It is all about you Julian. You have become quite a hero and the President is frightened by what you are doing. People are talking of you Julian and from what I have heard I am proud of you. You are a thorn in the side of the President and I think he is scared of you," Arthur said.

"Yeah all right but cut the bullshit and get on with it, what the heck does he want?" said Julian and glanced at Glorida. "We jest been on a scary mission to First City and we done all right didn't we?"

"Yes Julian we did. We took out the number three and four battle wagon factory and its store in Sector Yellow. Julian's bombs wrecked the place," Glorida said, and Arthur heard the pride in her voice. "And this time he didn't fall to bits with fear and funk when we had to fight our way out."

Julian scowled at her and Glorid giggled.

"Yeah well, I'm getting used to fighting now ain't I?" Julian said defensively, "Anyway, you still ain't answered me question Dad."

Arthur drew a deep breath and told him.

Julian's face drained of blood and he looked aghast at his father and with a shaky, scared voice that was bare of any bravado he said. "Bugger that," and fainted.

On the back foot.

Lt Colonel West was not surprised when a message came from headquarters ordering him to dig in and stop the invaders. He called his Majors and Captains to a brief conference.

"Our orders from headquarters are to dig in but as you have seen that will not work," he said after explaining the details. "What I suggest is something entirely different, so listen up and afterwards I want your comments." He outlined his plan and for a few moments they were silent each officer thinking over their part and coming to a conclusion.

"Sir, we will be court martialled for this," said Captain Green.

"Not so Ronnie, I will be but you will not; I will carry the can. We are not digging in and we are not going to make a frontal attack. What I propose is we make sorties as we retreat and try and take wagons from them. Those of your drivers and gunners who know how to operate their wagons can teach the others so when we get one we use it to capture others. Okay?"

"It's very risky sir."

"Without air support it is the only way. Give them everything we have and under cover of night we grab wagons and weapons, okay?"

The officers looked enthusiastic and with a flurry of salutes they chorused agreement.

"Yes, Sir!"

The British main force was bogged down and it seemed that the Zradians were taking great delight in decimating it. The British main army group retreated in a rout until somebody with a bit of nous took control and stemmed the flood using armour to force the Zradians to fight for lost ground. This suited West and with his troops hidden in whatever cover they could find he let the Zradian forces go past. Their destination was obviously London and so with caution he followed them up keeping as close to the enemy lines as he dared.

West was surprised when as soon as darkness fell the enemy stopped moving. Using the infra red system radar his wagons moved into position to attack. West sat in his command car drumming his fingers on the seat surround and waited for the first reports. He saw nothing and heard nothing but the wind over the land and his sergeant breathing into the microphone as he too waited anxiously. A half hour went by and then another and with a sudden crackle that cleared quickly West heard the reports coming in.

"Sir, two wagons reported captured, sorry three more and squadron four says that sections two and three are engaging. Keep you posted sir?"

"Log it all but only if there are difficulties. I want the wagons and our own vehicles back here ready to move. Swap with mechanics as they come in, okay?"

"Yes sir."

West liked his command car to be free of officers and relied on the RSM to do the work and so far the system worked. He still held to the chain of command and there was no way he would relinquish that but he liked to think when he was in action and that little delay before the officers barged in and asked for directions served two purposes. It gave them the chance to think things out before acting and kept them on task because they were required to pass on the orders to their men with a certain amount of clarity.

"Bring the wagons back here and for Christ's sake keep a watch on the enemy movements. They may have infra-red too. Tell the cutting out parties to find some moments to rest; I intend to fight back early in the morning. We use the captured wagons and back them up with our own. In and out quick lads."

The RSM grinned and relayed the orders and took the liberty of reporting the comments.

"I detect a lot of enthusiasm from the Captains, sir. They say the men are enjoying themselves," he said. "Lieutenant Davis said that her squadron can replace all four vehicles sir."

"Well done, tell her well done," West said and chuckled. Davis was a cheeky baggage and a very good officer. She was one of the troop who had taken to firing the blank rockets at ground level and was the first to suss out the workings of the Zradian wagons. He wrote her name down in his book to be recommended for promotion. Throughout the evening reports came back from the squadrons of captured machines and fortunately of low casualties. Captain Green called him and reported that all his machines were now replaced with wagons.

"Sir, we only need two to operate them, can we have the left over personnel to help the mechanics?" he said.

"Why not and put some of the footies in with them as well to help out. Tell the infantry what you need and get that sorted before three ack emma, okay?" West said and turned to the RSM. "Pass that on to the others."

"Yes sir."

The sergeant led his squad from their parked hover wagon to the enemy laager. They had light weapons but their instructions were to use hand to hand and knives. He and the corporal had infra-red sensors in their helmets and the squaddies knew how to follow and stop them from going too far. The squad consisted of two drivers, gunners and the unarmed combat specialists, the Commandos.

The men kept low and using the cover they moved steadily toward the parked vehicles. As they drew near so they became more alert and each soldier took care to keep their night sight clear - it was up to them to follow the two nom-coms. At last they reached the perimeter and stopped for a while to check the squad was all there and ready.

They watched the nom-coms who eventually gave the signal to move forward. One group followed the sergeant and the other followed the corporal - their targets - two enemy fire wagons.

Softly yet swiftly the two groups reached their targets, crept around to the side step and quietly mounted the rim. The enemy wagons had an open cab where the command Pair stood to guide the wagon. At night the Pairs took turns on guard. It was a useless exercise because their eyesight was such that the night on Earth was too dark, and they had learned that lights only called down night attacks from the air.

The Commandos slipped into the cab and with no more fuss than a slight rustle of fabric, a low almost inaudible gasp from the victims, the guards were eliminated.

The men slipped down into the wagon and it was short work to deal with the inmates. The driver entered and, directed by the corporal the others took up fighting positions. The driver switched on, he was familiar with the wagons having learned from the previously captured models.

"Right soldier, as soon as you can, let's go," he said and grinned as she answered by starting the motor.

The vehicle moved off slowly easing its way back toward the parked assault craft. It was followed by the one the sergeant's squad had stolen. The two wagons passed the assault craft and that was the signal for two of the four to move up and fire a salvo of rockets into the laager.

The assault lasted for a minute or so and the two attacking craft raced to catch up with the others. One more successful raid that would definitely annoy the Zradians.

The Zradian Leader Pair was angry. His Pairs were slow in reporting losses and mostly he realised those losses happened in the ranks of the Stormtroopers. The Pongos had fudged the issue by not running the messages as they should have. It seemed that the ordinary Pairs were afraid to tell him what was happening. It had a lot to do with the Polisoc Troopers they had with them and with a sigh and a Twin conflab he decided to promise messengers immunity from the Polisocs if they brought bad news. The Polisoc Leader Pair strongly objected but, with the simple expedient of a summary execution, their objection was overruled.

"Tell the Polisoc 2IC that if he has any objections to the change in leadership policy he can come unarmed and object properly," said the dominant twin to their subordinates. "Tell him that this is a Stormtrooper affair - an ordinary loyalist fight as directed by the written orders. Remind him that there are thousands of us and a whole division of bloody Pongos to direct and that I outrank him by a long way."

The comment was passed on and as there were only two hundred Polisoc Pairs in the complement there was no further objections. From that time on the reports came in with regularity and that was what made him angry. The enemy were stealing their wagons and weapons and had been doing so since the filthy Earth night had fallen.

"Flood the compound with lights, get Pairs out there with weapons and kill them! In the light we will seek out these swine and deal with them," the Pair said and failed to notice that all cutting out actions had stopped. Instead there were a series of night attacks on their temporary compound that kept him awake and angry all night.

In fact the Pair got no sleep at all for when they were about to fall asleep at just after three ten that morning their world was shattered by a sudden alarm.

"Enemy attack!"

"For Nong's sake destroy them! You don't need us to tell you what to do! Section Leaders, get off your butts and kill the Bulgers," the Pair yelled back at the messenger Pair and cursed under their breaths as the scribes wrote everything down. Nevertheless they set up the situation screen to find out what was happening. The result was not what they expected.

The screen showed a mess of burning vehicles and pinpricks of energy flows that indicated where the enemy were using stolen wagons.

"Attack those points for Nong's sake! There are only a few of them, go for it. What's the matter with you? If they are not gone within the next period then some Pairs are going to feel the execution knife, understand!?" the Pair said, and made certain that all sections confirmed receipt of the message.

"Yes your Honour!"

The Section Leaders sent off squads of three wagons with twenty Pairs each to attack the hot spots and watched in anticipation as the markers closed on the enemy. The hot spots disappeared and the Section Leaders cheered.

"Bring the squads back and get another group ready," Ordered the Leader Pair.

There was an ominous silence.

"I said bring them back, report status at once!"

The first strangled reply came from section green four and the news was bad; there was no response, and that meant no survivors. Within a few short periods all sixteen Section Leaders reported the same fate for their squads and the Leader Pair sat in their command wagon puzzling the mystery. And with a suddenness that scared them more hot points reappeared and again the Leader Pairs sent out squadrons with the same result; which despite their re-organisation to resist chasing after them the Zradian leaders had to respond. If they made no effort the losses were greater and even more confusing for them which meant that the invaders spent a restless, puzzled night wondering where the next attack was likely to be. By day break the Zradians were tired and irritable.

"I want them found and destroyed!" demanded the Leader Pair, and allocated a complete Section to do the task. "Search and destroy!"

But he could not remain in the area for long, his orders were to push on to the next Transfer Point and then on to the capital city. The rag-tag enemy troops harassing them would be dealt with. They had better be, the dominant Half Pair thought, and promptly forgot about the problem. What they hadn't taken into account was that West's tactics were simple – the stolen wagons were used as bait and some of his soldiers volunteered to dress as Zradian Troopers to greet the newcomers. By the time the Zradians realised they were enemy soldiers it was too late and another wagon was captured. In the dark it worked quite well.

West was not inclined to take prisoners.

His attitude had a lot to do with the viciousness of the Zradian Stormtroopers and his Commanding officer's assessment of the situation. As he remarked to Lieutenant Davis. "We have to show the blimps that we are prepared to fight and fight hard to get rid of these buggers and leave them in no doubt that our way of waging war works."

She grinned and said: "Yes sir, oh and thanks for the promotion, sir."

"I will pass it on in orders and ask for confirmation when our senior staff see sense," said West. "Carry on."

The salute was enthusiastic and crisp.

The Australian desert suited the Zradians and as they advanced across the semi-arid reaches of South Australia they relished the hot winds and the scrubby terrain. Adelaide was behind them and as they moved east and south they expressed their pleasure by obeying their orders with hardly a complaint. True there was opposition but that is what they wanted and thus far the Australian forces were real opposition. The Leader Pair did not expect them to be very good but the whole point of the exercise was to subdue the locals by violence and give the troops some practice. The real fight would be against the rebels in their own land and once this mob of amateurs was subdued their force could get on with it. The plan was to head for Melbourne and let the northern attack deal with Canberra. The plan seemed to be working judging by the rapid retreat and the columns of refugees on the roads.

As they approached Melbourne the terrain changed from warm desert to cooler forest and as they neared the coast they smelled the salt tang of the southern sea. They expected to reach the outskirts of Melbourne and another transfer point the following morning.

The Leader Pair spoke into the microphone, the dominant twin speaking while the passive twin tapped the orders into the console and relayed them to the slave screens in the other Leader Pair's command wagons.

"We will camp in an hour, that is about two point four periods, and I expect situation reports from all section leaders. Stormtroopers will form a guard and all other Pairs will complete maintenance tasks. Be prepared for transfer tomorrow morning at four periods past daybreak. All Pairs not engaged in maintenance will practice evolutions. We have spoken and in the name of our glorious President let us believe in our mission!"

A few small periods after they had encamped the Polisoc Leader Pair called on their command wagon, saluted stamping to attention.

"Beg to remark that a certain tone of sarcasm is present in your tone. We have no choice but to pass on our remarks, your Honour!" The Polisoc Leader Pair said staring at the Leader Pair meaningfully.

"You wish us to apologise for something we are not guilty of?" replied the Leader Pair formally observing the question and reply protocol and speaking together.

"We are not accusing you but merely offering a caution."

Bulgers, thought Graz, these idiots are giving me the screaming fidgets, but instead he replied allowing his twin to copy his voice just one pace behind and grovelled.

"It is not our intention to disparage our Glorious President, nor is it our intention to sound sarcastic, we were merely pacing our voices to allow the Leader Pairs to pass on the orders immediately to their Pairs. You must be aware that our army group is large and communications can be somewhat fragmented at times. We merely intended to be more efficient. Do it once and do it right. This is a

Zero Defect Army Group," said the Leader Pair with as much dignity as their fear could muster.

Their short speech seemed to work. The Polisoc Leader Pair glared at them, about faced and stomped from the command wagon and clattered down the steps. Outside they dismissed their escort and in typical Polisoc fashion marched off angrily.

Graz and Zrag listened to the retreating footsteps and carefully and deliberately ordered their servant Pair to bring their meal.

"This is going to be a long and politically tricky campaign," said Zrag. Graz nodded his head and suppressed the urge to cock his leg and urinate.

The Zradian forces swept down from Ballarat and pounced on Melbourne. The Australian forces were nearly ready but ready or not the enemy were far too strong. The main concern for the home forces were the civilians. Persuading them to leave their homes and head out east was not easy especially when the locals discovered that the General Officer Commanding their armed forces was a Japanese Field Marshall. Worse still was when they learned his name was Tojo.

"No bloody way mate," said one old timer to the young lieutenant who told him to pack up and leave two days before the Zradians were due. "I'll hook me gun out and shoot the buggers. No bastard is goin' ter bugger me and me bloody shed without a fight. I got forty years of hobby stuff in there mate and I ain't about to let them stuff me life's work up."

"Who, the Zradians?" said the Lieutenant.

"Nah mate, the bloody Nips, me grandfather was in bloody Changi mate. The only good Nip is a dead one. Shoot the bloody lot of 'em."

"Okay mate," said the Lieutenant. "You stay put and when we come back this way we'll give youse a decent burial. Ooroo."

And that was how the recalcitrants were treated, but in spite of this there was a long stream of refugees heading out of the city leaving the Australian armed forces to hold the Zradians back while the people fled. When the enemy came there was no signal, no challenge and no quarter given. The Zradians killed and did not let the Geneva Convention or any other convention get in the way of their lust for blood. They pushed the armed forces back. The old timer who stayed behind to defend his hobby shed saw the armed might of the Zradians roll on along his street and promptly dropped his hunting rifle in the yellowing grass that was once a lawn and dived into his shed. He locked the door behind him and for the first time in his life he prayed. He prayed that the war would pass him by and that he and his shed would survive intact, that his wife and his family were safe and that the enemy would not cut off the electricity. And if they did cut off the power he prayed that he would have time to drink all the beer in his shed fridge before he was slaughtered.

Piously he snapped open the fridge door and took a can from a six pack and snapped the ring pull open and with a long and grateful sigh let the amber liquid slide down his throat.

"Jeez," he said, "now that's what I calls heavenly."

For three days the battle raged and for three days the old timer sat in his shed and took the occasional trip to the house to bring in some tucker and to relieve himself. On the morning of the fourth day all was quiet but by then he had started on the spirits that were left in the house he no longer cared whether the enemy were Japanese, Poms, Americans or little green men and with a feeling of warm friendly fuzzies creeping all over him like a second skin, he lay in the leather seat of his vintage car and tried to sing what he could remember of his national anthem, Advance Australia Fair. To the garbled sounds of Waltzing Matilda and A Whiter Shade of Pale the old timer mumbled the words of his beloved anthem and fell into a long and drunken holy sleep.

The Zradians pushed the Australians back along the Pacific Highway, rounded up the citizenry of Melbourne and put them into temporary compounds like cattle or slaves. The old timer was overlooked and missed out on the humiliation of captivity. The Zradians made no rules yet those people who did not act cooperatively with each other were taken aside and beaten. In a few days the Zradians established control over their captives who had the dubious privilege of becoming the first Australians to be turned into Zradian slaves, and while their compatriots continued defeating the Australian armed forces, the Polisocs began to process the inhabitants and categorise them for future work.

The old timer didn't see all that as he lay in his shed trying to come to terms with the fact that Australia, as far as the citizens of Melbourne was concerned, was buggered. He took to creeping around the houses and gathering foodstuffs to hoard in his shed fridge and was surprised at the eating habits of his neighbours. He dare not cook anything nor dare he show a light at night and so he lived like a hermit in his shed and watched as sneakily as he could what went on in his beloved city. The day of the Melbourne Cup races came and went and that depressed him; so too did the fact that the last of the footy games would obviously have to be cancelled. He thought too that at the rate that the invaders were clobbering the Army the first Test match against the Indian eleven had no chance of getting under way. And as for the Sydney to Hobart race and Bathhurst there was likely to no bloody sport on the telly this side of bloody Easter. And that thought made him so depressed he drank his neighbour's last 750ml bottle of Jack Daniels.

"Strewth, Christmas is gonna be a bit of a bummer," he said and drifted into an all time low. As a result he missed the air attack and the sudden appearance of Australian troops led by Japanese officers.

He was drunk when the tanks and armoured cars rolled down his street and surged out into the suburbs to take up positions that encompassed his shed. He had a vague idea that something important was happening but dismissed it as 'nothing to do with him' and dropped into a drunken sleep.

"Jeez, I'm pissed," he said, and for the first time for many years he thought of his mother. "Bloody old tart."

It is a wise decision

Professor Renfrew stood up to speak and there was a hush in the room as all eyes gazed at him. Here, the Pairs whispered, was the father of the great bomber. Since he arrived in the camp with Glorida's troop the women had fussed around him giving him the attention he enjoyed at the University. Noticeably Julian was absent from the discussion and as the morning progressed it was obvious he was deliberately avoiding him. The Leader Pair outlined to the troop leaders what was expected of him and Julian and when she had finished she asked him to speak.

"Ladies," he said, and waited for the giggles to subside, "As your Leader Pair told you I have an implant in my neck just below my ear that is code linked to the Doomsday Bomb. You are aware that the conditions are that I return with Julian to the presidential palace and surrender him to the Polisocs. I am aware that he cannot be forced and so, in the interests of saving his own planet and my people, he must be persuaded. I have tried to do that but he will not speak to me and so I must ask for your help. I also approve of using our return as an opportunity to do some damage to the president's cause. Just how you do that is up to you and the least said the better so that neither Julian nor I can give away any vital plans. For my part if my death means that we save Earth and your good people then I have done all I can, but Julian's wishes should be respected. He may not want to die for his home world."

The Pairs laughed and nodded to each other and he heard many comments about Julian's heroism and wondered how his son became such a wanted man. Glorid and Glorida were the only Pair not laughing. Glorida was glowering at the other Pairs furiously, while Glorid was trying to pacify her. He knew that she was torn between defending him and wanting him to do his duty. Arthur Renfrew wanted his son to do his duty but realised that Julian was so resistant to being ordered around by him and others in authority that he would be a burden. He was about to speak again when Glorida herself stood up and glared at the Pairs in the room, glared at the Leader Pair, and then faced him biting her lip.

"All right, so my Julian is not a fighter," she said, and glared at the Pairs and Half Pairs who made amusing comments, "but he is the best bomber we have, and to me he is a hero. The people of Zrad fear his name and the president has put a huge price on his capture, but he is not one of us, and has no need to fight for us or to willingly die for us."

She paused and looked around at the Pairs and then turned to the Professor, and he could see the anguish on her face as she spoke directly to him.

"But for the wickedness of the president Julian could have stayed with us and carried out his work. Now he is being asked to go with you, Professor, and I can see that you would rather he did not. However as much as I prefer not to, I will help persuade him to go with you. Give me a few short periods and gather the Pairs outside the hall and I will bring him to you. I guarantee he will do as he is asked."

Glorida turned from the end row seat she and her twin were using and walked steadily out of the hall. Glorid smiled weakly and raised her hands shrugging her shoulders, and apologetically addressed Arthur and the Leader Pair.

"I am sorry your Honours but she is in love with Julian and she is upset," she said, and with a concerned look on her face followed her twin from the room.

Arthur followed them out and stood waiting on the stoop with Glorid and the Leader Pair and watched Glorida march to the latrine block where Julian had retreated and refused to come out. He had to make way for the Leader Pairs from the briefing room as they too came out to witness what was about to happen.

Pairs came out into the lanes between the huts, or on the parade square, from the canteen, from the stores and stood, like him, watching as Glorida stormed into the latrines. The Pairs were silent except for the rustle of clothing and the occasional mutter of query or the clink of arms. Birds squawked but their cries were muffled by the stillness, and all eyes were on the latrines and all ears were waiting to catch any sound. According to his watch three minutes passed, and from the latrines came a plaintive wail.

"No Glorida, please don't! No! No-o!"

A scream of agony and then the sound of a flushing cistern, some burbling cries and a long wail and then silence.

"Right scumbag." Came Glorida's voice. "Are you ready?"

"Yes, yes, of course I am, if you say so," Julian said, his voice rising as if she had threatened him again.

Footsteps sounded on wooden boards and Julian emerged, staggering a little, with Glorida behind him cleaning her knife. He walked a few steps in front, and hobbled painfully to the hall, his lank hair dripping wet and blood oozing from cuts on his arms and chest. He walked to where Dorida and Dorid stood on the stoop waiting for him, and stood almost to attention looking like an errant schoolboy. Arthur looked on him pityingly and smiled at him giving what he hoped was encouragement. Glorida caught up with him taking a position beside and slightly behind him. Glorid joined her and stood on the opposite side as she too knew that Julian might try and run.

"Has Julian come to a decision?" said Dorida, and looked at him compassionately while her twin took her hand in support.

Julian said nothing so Glorida gave him a dig with the point of her knife.

"Yes! For Chrissake!" he said, "That bloody hurt you bitch!"

"Language my love," Glorida said, and stuck him again.

"And what decision did you come to Julian," asked Dorida trying not to giggle.

Julian groaned and began to sag and instead of speaking clearly he mumbled his reply. Glorida and Glorid moved in closer and held him firmly. His pasty face and trembling limbs, and his terror was pitiful to see – his mouth moved but it was obvious he was struggling to speak.

When he had finished it was not clear to anybody exactly what he had said.

"I take it you agree to go then?" said Dorida.

Glorida stepped forward slightly, still holding on to Julian, and with a forced smile she replied for him.

"After much deliberation Julian has decided that he will accompany his father to the palace. He does this in the full knowledge of the consequences, willingly and with a desire to do his duty," she said.

The crowd erupted into a mixture of cheers and laughter that continued as Glorida and Glorid dragged Julian to his room.

"That's my boy," said Arthur, and glowed with embarrassment when the Pairs laughed even more loudly.

The wagons halted a kilometre from the dropping off point and a long period later one lone wagon moved off to stop at the place where the Pongos had dropped Arthur Renfrew. It parked for a long time with the door open and nothing happening. Eventually a figure stepped out onto the desert carrying a pack. The figure stood in the shade of the wagon waiting patiently. There was sad cry from within and another figure was ejected and the door slammed shut. Arthur grabbed his son's wrist and dragged him away from the side of the wagon applying a wrist-lock he called Sankyo and held him close until the wagon had turned and moved off.

"This way Julian," said Arthur, and released his son's wrist. "There's no going back now. The pongos will treat you right and when we get there we will have some time before the president will do anything to us. Besides I happen to have a helper who promised to keep a watch on me."

"That doesn't help me," wailed Julian. "Bloody Glorida has gone off and left me and you don't care about me. All you want is your poxy Earth saved and all that crap. I want to go home. This whole place stinks. I hate it!"

"Julian, you cannot go home and you have to help me. There are risks we all have to take, and I do care about you."

"No you don't. You threw me out of the house and made me live in that shitty flat and and …" Julian trailed off as from over the rise a squad of wagons sped towards them. "Help me!"

Arthur grabbed him and held him tightly until the pongos drew the wagons to a stop. He kept close to him as the soldiers marched them into the wagon.

"You helps us?"

Arthur smiled at the Pongo Pair and nodded.

"Everybody's name went in and I hope I can count on you men in First City?" Arthur said, and guided Julian to a seat. Julian sat rigid facing the opposite wall and said nothing.

"We will do what we can Professor. For now we have to take you to your escort. All the best to you and your brave son. We have heard of him and his exploits. Oh yes, the President is very upset. He swears to kill all the rebels who attacked First City and kill them slowly. We are very proud of you Julian, very proud." The Leader Pair said, and the others all smiled and bowed to Julian who cringed against the seat and looked as if he were about to wet himself.

"I think he is a little scared of what might happen next," said Arthur.

"Ah yes, we understand, the President is a very scary Half Pair, unpredictable and he likes torture."

It was more or less at that point that Julian emitted a long drawn out wail and wet himself. Arthur put his arm around his son and held him close, in spite of his own fear Arthur spoke softly and comfortingly to him, and admitted that he too was frightened. He was scared and the constant playing of the tune A Whiter Shade of Pale in his ear did not help matters much, but however scared he felt he knew that Julian's fear was much much greater.

"Julian is giving himself up to save our world," he said, and although he was apologetic he felt more in tune with his son than he had ever done and vowed that whatever happened he would do his best to help him through his present tribulations.

The wagons slowed.

"We join the Polisoc soldiers now who will take us into First City." Said the Leader Pair.

The cavalcade travelled fast but even so it was a long trip. Twice they stopped and everybody was bundled out for a natural break and some food. Arthur and Julian were given food and water by the

Pongos watched by the Polisoc Troopers who stood with their weapons idly aimed in their direction.

Julian was numbed and said very little, and whenever Arthur tried to speak to him all he did was whimper and mutter to himself. And so, it was like this that they arrived at the prisoner's gate of the Palace. The wagon came to a halt and the Pongo Leader Pair opened the door. Eight Polisoc Pairs grabbed Arthur and Julian and frogmarched them through the entrance into the depths of the palace. Julian wailed and struggled but one Polisoc Half Pair showed him his knife and he shut up. Arthur merely allowed them to carry him along and thought nothing of it. He was used to being pushed around everywhere. They hurried along until with a sudden skidding lurch the pair of them were ejected from the corridors and into the great hall through a side entrance and hurried on to the circle where the President sat waiting for them.

The Polisoc guards threw them onto the floor and Arthur hissed a warning to Julian to stay down and wait. They did not have to wait long before the President ordered them to rise, and it was with some trepidation that Arthur stood up and helped Julian to his feet.

Julian stood staring open mouthed at the President and Arthur could understand why. The President was dressed in a bright green jacket, a purple shirt, a yellow tie that was long and wide at the bottom, baggy trousers coloured bright blue with pink flashings at the pockets and paisley patches at the knees. His socks were fluorescent green and he was wearing blue suede shoes with pink shoe laces. His lank hair was dyed a mixture of red and russet with dark brown stripes and he wore a pair of butterfly spectacles.

"We are pleased to see you back again, Professor, and of course We are pleased to see your son. Welcome to Our humble home Julian," said the President, and smirked.

"Bollocks you stupid old fart," said Julian.

The President's smirk vanished, and he stared at Julian disbelieving what he had just heard, and leaned forward menacingly and spoke again.

"What did you say?"

"I said bollocks, cloth ears," said Julian, and stood defiantly with his arms folded and held the President's stare.

Arthur had seen Julian like this before and although this time he was in dreadful danger and likely to be cut down in the next few seconds by the Dog Squad guards he stayed put and faced the President out. Arthur felt proud of him, and as he watched his son make his futile stand he saw himself in Julian and thought, like father like son.

"That's my boy," he said, and laughed.

Incredibly Julian laughed with him.

"No!" shouted the President. "Sheath your weapons, we have plans for this scum!"

"Yeah, sure you do you old wanker," said Julian, and shot a glance at his father. "Does this silly old sod always dress like a poofter?"

"He has a quaint idea of dress sense," said Arthur, and noted his son's puzzled look. "Yes, he always dresses like a poofter, he thinks he is fashionable, or if you like he is a drunken wanker."

Julian looked shocked and stood glaring sullenly at the President who waved his hand effeminately at the Polisoc guards beckoning them forward.

"Take the young man to the cells and take the Professor to the laboratory," he said, and turned to the Professor. "I trust you will behave yourself. If you do not your son will die slowly and horribly while you watch, and while he is still twitching from his tortured death we will start on you. In the meantime We will see how well he stands up to Our methods. Take them away!"

"Your Honour," said Arthur, "May I be permitted to take Julian's place?"

"Very honourable but extremely foolish. No. Let him suffer," the President said.

"You bastard," said Arthur, and shot Julian a sympathetic glance but Julian was aware of what was going to happen and he had already fainted. His bravado, false as it was and defensive, was gone and Arthur knew that as they led them away Julian was going to suffer more than he himself had suffered before.

An hour later he dabbed at the mark on his neck and felt relieved that at last the tune had stopped and that whatever was going to happen at least they had let him back on to the computers. They needed him for that and once they left him to his own devices he tapped into the secret file. The message that appeared on his screen in English and not Zradian was peculiar but comforting.

Aware Prof re son and thee – a rodent hatched plan is in hand – hang in there batman – we are winning the battle of the bomb – nuts – beware the ides of rodents. Arthur me old mate you are in safe paws.

Arthur read the message twice and tapped in two words 'thanks Betty' and switched back to the program and while he was working tried to think of a way to save Julian. Now that the implant was gone he was free to plot against the President and set about trying to contact his Pongo friends.

"Hang on Julian," he said, "I'll do my best to get you out of there."

Clard and Dracl - almost strike back

Betty/Anthony/Napoleon marched to the nearest high point and gazed happily across the bush. It subdued the tune and shut down the passive Betty/Anthony parts of its personality and brushed aside the other small parts that were clamouring for attention. The signal it was looking for came through loud and clear and almost lazily it locked on to it, passed the data through some communications satellites and triangulated the source.

Clard and Dracl with the renegade force.

The signal broke off and inconveniently buzzed fuzzily.

Jamming, and that was not allowed.

The robot attempted an electronic thrust and failed to establish contact discovering only a heat source that meant plasma. It worried that something was about to attack it and its family. It pushed its antenna out to its maximum and activated the visual search on the highest power and saw a column of Zradian wagons moving steadily north. It projected the track and realised that within a period the column would be past. It concentrated the viewer on each wagon in turn and saw the Pair Clard and Dracl sitting in the rear of the third wagon surrounded by armed Pairs.

"Our father. I need them."

The robot checked its data input and found its friends. It gave Arthur a message and began a series of small tasks that it checked and programmed to operate in the background and then it concentrated on the Doomsday Bomb. It struggled to re-establish control and succeeded in shifting it to a larger orbit and locked out the code adding its own protection to the defences. It searched for the receiver and was pleased to note the original was sitting in Star Station One. It found another one and set a trace on it knowing that at sometime it would have to re-locate it or get somebody to shift it. It set a program to monitor that too and began a search for some allies to assist with its destruction.

The tasks completed it sighed an electronic sigh and thought about Clard and Dracl. The solution was simple. Leave its family in the care of the primitives and go and get them. It memorised the possible co-ordinates of the column and trundled down the hill back to the village. It wandered into the compound and waited for the villagers to appear.

"Oh great god, what is your wish?" intoned the headman.

"It is our wish that your people care for our family until our return. We have a quest, a divine mission which we alone must do. It is your destiny to serve your God. It is your God's destiny to punish the evil ones."

The Headman bowed his head and knelt on the ground and drew his ritual marks in the dust. The women sang and the men countered with a deep chant and a great clattering of spears. Each man carried a rodent in a cage and placed it on the ground before him and with much chanting danced around the cages slapping their spears on the ground.

"Charming." Betty.

"Worrying." Anthony.

"It is Our due." Napoleon.

"Why do they do that?" A persistent sub-personality.

The robot allowed them to finish their dance and then with a grand gesture of peace and goodwill to its subjects and worshippers it tested its weapons and moved off steadily. The tribesmen watched it until it had disappeared into the bush and with a deep resonant chant the headman began to walk in a circle around the place where the robot habitually stood and sang the song of parting.

The robot climbed the ridge west of the camp and chose pathways that would lead it in the right direction. Betty/Anthony took control for a while and held Napoleon down but could not stop the strong desire in all three to reunite with Clard and Dracl. The fourth and fifth personalities, one named Gogo and the other named Didi started to argue with each other, and whatever Napoleon said to them they answered that 'nothing was certain' and 'nothing to be done'. Napoleon decided to remain puzzled, and when he searched the memory banks it came against a block that reminded it of Moscow.

"I don't need this," it said but failed to subdue the two new personalities. And what was most disturbing was an image of a hanging tree and a lonely island, both of which were so vivid that its whole frame shuddered. It thought of Professor Renfrew and thought of its parents/brother/servant/son/cousin/visitor/Godot, marching steadily it calculated its route to the nearest decimal point and started another train of thought and explored the Bubblenet listening in to the myriad chattering of the Earth people. It caught a trace of data that was akin to its own and latched onto it with a soft and undetectable probe that blended with the new data stream and monitored the effect. Ah, it thought, so that's how they manage it. The robot hacked into the source, examined the data, analysed it and rearranged streams of it passing on the results to the NMF and to Professor Renfrew's Zradian mailbox and placed an automatic monitoring track on the source. It liked the Bubblenet with its satellite network and the wonderful fibre optic lines the earth people seemed to favour. Maybe they were not so fast as their own system but at least it was easy to trace and not much data was lost. It made tracking the renegade Zradian wagons much easier. It felt better once it had sorted the data and with the return of Betty/Anthony all six of them moved off again humming.

That a series of shipments intended for the Republic of Zradia's treasury went missing and the NMF suddenly discovered their coffers were filling at a prodigious rate, or that Tzu's office system recorded a change in shipment addresses; Pour and Roup's monitors recorded in the myriad transactions a diversion from their transitional transfer ports in the automated regions of Star Station Two's sector yellow did not worry the robot. It was making arrangements to find Clard and Dracl.

The millions of plastic tokens that passed through interstellar space went from the warehouses in London and Albany in New Zealand to Star Station Two, diverted to Star Station One, split into one third for the Republic and two thirds for the NMF and hence on to destinations on Zrad.

The tribesmen piled the cages in the huts and the women fed the animals inside. Life for the primitives returned to normal and as the weeks rolled by the rodents grew fatter and the tribesmen looked at them hungrily. There was a week when the food for the animals was all the tribesmen had and the children and the women began to complain they were hungry. The families ate the food meant for the rodents and the rodents, hungry for a feed ate their way out of the cages and attacked the old, the young and the weak primitives. The strong men and women turned on the rodents and slashed and fought with spears and knives but there were too many rodents and not enough primitives. The fight went the way of the rodents and soon all that was left in the village were the whitened bones of the dead and their goods and chattels. The freed rodents moved as a group across the land and followed in their master's tracks. Snakes and other predators took their toll on the numbers but many survived the onslaught, and although they were distracted from their path by the need to find food, living flesh, they headed generally in the direction the robot had gone. The camp they left behind rotted with neglect and rain and the small animals, always the first to take advantage of human absence, eeked into the compound and ate whatever the emigrating rodents left. Their excreta and their digging opened out the ground to the dormant seeds, and soon, within a week or two of neglect, shoots appeared, to be eaten in their turn by nibbling creatures and caterpillars. The caterpillars and insects were eaten by birds who dropped seeds on the fertile soil and those that were not eaten by worms were dragged down into the soil to germinate and produce shoots. The bones of the primitives nourished the surrounding bushes and they too began to flourish. The little cages that once held the rodent family rotted in their turn and supplied humus to the camp floor and within a month after some heavy rains the encampment was covered in green shoots and bright flowers and the edges that once were so delineated became fuzzy with green plant tendrils, liana vines and exotic flowering vines that, no longer continuously cut back, thrived and sent out feelers searching for purchase on which to grow. The jungle, bereft of its occupants, was claiming its own.

Unaware that their nemesis was in hot pursuit Clard and Dracl miserably endured their captivity and cringed every time one of the coarse Pairs glared at them. The rough looking Leader Pair chose to tell them that they were about to discover how it was to be a used and abused and that was all. The dominant Half Pair laughed and the passive Half Pair quietly explained that the experience would not be pleasant.

"There is a matter of a certain Robot and an order for so-called volunteers that you and your company made to build Star Stations Two and Three," the Half Pair said.

"We did not know what else to do," said Clard, and clutched his twin.

"You could have found a more pleasant way and tried something inanimate. Or you could have designed the thing properly in the first place and did a good job instead of making a Bulger's arse of it," replied the Half Pair.

"It wasn't our fault, we were never given the right materials," said Dracl.

"Nor the right funding either," said Clard.

"Wrong answer, Pair! What you mean is that you spent so much on bribes and graft that you didn't have enough money left to do a proper job. The transfer ports, the most important part of the whole station, are a complete Bulger's arse and if it were not for the fact that we installed the guidance system in the ones we used we would have been shot almost anywhere. Shut up and listen!" the Leader Pair said, when Clard began to answer, and continued. "The system itself is flawed and the parts we had to replace them with were duff too. On top of all that because we are all low level volunteered troops they had us earmarked for the front line. So we said bugger that and here we are."

"What are we supposed to do?" said Dracl.

"What do you want of us?" said Clard, and cringed against his twin who in his turn cringed against him.

"We want you to help us destroy your rogue robot because it is out to get us. We intend to control this area and you will help us, got it?" said the Leader Pair, and both Half Pairs took their knives from their sheaths and showed the double points to Clard and Dracl and chuckled. "We will have some fun if you don't comply."

"We understand," said Clard and Dracl together, and clutched each other tightly.

"Well then you had better start thinking of a way to do it then had you not?"

"We're thinking! We're thinking!" the desperate Pair cried out and cringed even more than before, if that was possible.

The Leader Pair casually sliced Clard and Dracl's arms and as casually called a medic Pair over to tend to their wounds. The medic Pair were not very kind and used a stinging antiseptic to clean them with and stitched up the worst cuts without any local anaesthetic. It was the most painful experience Clard and Dracl had had and they didn't like it at all.

"My twin," moaned Dracl, "we have to escape from these maniacs."

Clard groaned and held his aching arm rocking to and fro and nodded his head in agreement and as the wagon bumped over the rough track they sank lower in their seats and thought desperately of what they were asked to do. There was no solution to the problem except escape, and that is what they concentrated on but tied as they were to the wagon rails by strong chains attached to their ankles and wrists they had no chance.

Life, they thought, was one Bulger's bum and with all their millions there was no way they could buy themselves out of this situation. Nevertheless they had to try.

"We'll give you all a hundred thousand tokens each if you let us go," said Clard hopefully.

"Stick it up your arses," said the Leader Pair and sliced them again.

This time the medic Pair used an even more virulent antiseptic and put stitches where stitches weren't really needed. Clard and Dracl screamed and fainted and with perverse pleasure the medic Pair waited until they recovered before adding more. What annoyed Clard and Dracl most was that as the medic Pair worked they hummed the tune A Whiter Shade of Pale. "I hate that bloody tune," said Dracl and gritted his teeth as another suture was pulled and tied.

"We love it," said the medic Pair and laughed.

Davey Kline babbled into his empty coffee mug and although he was aware that what he was saying made no sense he couldn't stop himself. He pushed switches and listened to the music in the earphones not registering the record and wondering what was actually on the mini-disc that he had slipped into the player. He longed for the comfort of pre-recording and the certainty of being remote from the studio. His boss had decided that all program presenters should play live and that they should be ready to present the news as it came in. And that was why Davey Kline was babbling. The latest report from the newly formed emergency cabinet stated that the invading forces were now approaching west London and had overrun his exclusive luxury home. All his music, his clothes, his videos, his posters and, and everything, gone. He imagined the nasty bug-eyed monsters crawling all over his property, destroying everything they touched or using the house as a giant toilet. Not only that but according to the clock on the studio wall the time was almost twenty to eleven, and as the recording he was playing came to an end he waited for the dreaded inevitable.

Exactly at twenty minutes to eleven his earphones, the studio and the airwaves were filled with the ghastly sound of A Whiter Shade of Pale and Davey Kline collapsed on his arms and cried. His sobs were broadcast as an accompaniment to the tune, the version by Procul Harem, and despite the efforts of the technician in the mixing and monitoring room there was nothing the station could do to stop it.

At sixteen minutes and thirty seconds to eleven two men entered the studio and removed Davey Kline from his chair and handed the earphones to a third person who calmly took his place. As the men carried Davey Kline out through the studio door she read from a sheet she carried in her left hand in a voice that was both firm and solemn.

"We apologise to our listeners but Davey Kline has been taken ill. I am Janey Sims and here is the latest bulletin from the emergency cabinet. The invader has reached Heathrow airport and in spite of heavy fighting is advancing along the M4 and all western approaches toward central London. The recently appointed head of West Force, General West, advises all non-combatants to leave the area immediately if they have not already done so. In the meantime listeners are advised to stay tuned to their radio stations and to remain calm. This is Janey Sims, radio west 99.9FM sitting in for Davey Kline."

With deft movements she flicked the switches and re-started the mini-disc and leaned back in the chair snapping a cigarette from a pack and lighting it almost before it touched her lips. She sucked smoke down into her lungs and ignoring the nasty tickle in her throat she sent two thin streams of smoke up into the ceiling and watched them disappear into the vortex of the extraction fan.

In less than a day, she thought, the Zradian invaders will be upon them, unless that hunky general and his troops can stop them.

General West

The hunky General, the former Colonel West, hunkered down again in a new defence line and watched the Zradians grind to a halt. With no mercy he gave the order to attack and his modified wagons lunged into the enemy ranks and withdrew as quickly as they went in.

"Sergeant, send a general air strike request and order the CO's to call on them as they see fit. I want fast strikes and coordinated attacks here. They know the plan so tell them to see to it," West said and turned to his 2IC. "Tell the lads with the pop-guns to fire a bit afterward just to rattle the enemy and conserve the Zradian stuff."

Across the vast concourse where aircraft were parked, some intact and others wrecked by enemy fire, the Zradian forces were halted, alert and set down under what cover they could find. For some reason that West could not work out the enemy were stopped and unable to go forward. West decided to take advantage of the halt and attack. He realised that his actions would wreck the airport but he rationalised that as he had never liked Heathrow, even the re-built version, the destruction hardly mattered, the idea was to destroy the enemy. He grinned when he saw the effect his troops had on the invaders, and as they withdrew the aircraft came in and poured rocket fire into the enemy. The buildings burned fiercely and the wrecked aircraft were caught in the fire and that in turn spread to the other parked aircraft adding to the blaze.

"Sergeant, order the cutting out actions please. Major! Operation Sting."

West watched the troops rush in and attack selected points cutting out wagons that although they couldn't move were a good source of replenishment for their dwindling stocks of Zradian plasma capsules. Prisoners were shunted to the rear and as they were hurried away their weapons were taken and handed out to his own troops. The captives were shocked and confused and gave in easily as if some fit of depression was gripping them, and although West's soldiers tried to find out what was wrong there was little they could do to solve the problem. Whatever was wrong, West reasoned, it was to their advantage and with only a little thought as to the reason he kept up the attacks until darkness fell.

Heathrow burned and with it so did the Zradian forces, and when dawn broke to the usual dismal rain it revealed an airport that was a total ruin, and where proud buildings once stood to receive their travellers there was only smouldering ruins and wrecked Zradian fighting wagons. A few dishevelled enemy soldiers crawled out from their shelters and gave themselves up. General West personally called the other commanders on the radio system and asked for a situation report. All over the tight battlefront the answer was the same. The Zradians had halted the previous day in the late morning and allowed themselves to be picked off.

"Roll them up as far as you can maintain supply and keep hitting them," said West, and even 'though he knew he was outranked by many of the other commanders he was certain they would be glad to follow his orders. For the moment the Zradian advance on London was halted. With relief he ordered some of the men to stand down and rest.

The Command Leader Pair sitting in the dead wagon on the road leading out of the Heathrow area cursed and frantically tried to call up Star Station Two. While the dominant Half Pair yelled for the messengers the passive Half tried to activate the emergency drive system. Nothing he did worked and with the realisation they were stuck he tugged his twin's sleeve to get his attention.

"My twin?"

"I think we will have to start walking," he said, and sagged into the now defunct bucket seat.

"Nothing works. The weapons are dead, the power source is gone and there is no communication with anybody," said the dominant half feeling subdued and vulnerable.

"What does the Atlas tell us?"

The dominant half gratefully grabbed the Atlas and pressed the keys. He smiled when it activated, and with a trembling hand he touched the emergency contact control. The screen glowed and a message scrolled across it which he read out to his twin in a cold and frightened voice.

"We regret the inconvenience, do not be afraid of the rodents, but all activity in this sector is suspended until further notice. Have a nice day-ee! Repeat, we regret the inconvenience, the rodents regret they are unable to dine today. Nothing to be done."

The dominant half sat silent for a few short periods and then with a sob he gripped his twin's hand and said in a very frightened voice.

"My twin, we are Bulgered."

They sank deeper in their seat and lay staring blankly at the dulled windshield and that is where the messenger Pairs found them when they arrived at the command wagon to tell them that the local forces were on their way. The message made no difference to the Command Leader Pair because when the troopers examined them they were dead. The 2IC took over command and with nervous twitches ordered the troopers out of the wagons with as many provisions and weapons they could carry, and ordered a march to a safer more easily defended place.

The long suffering Pongos laughed to see the elite troopers and the Polisoc Stormtroopers scrambling from their wagons to take to foot slogging and although they too were under threat of their lives they were buoyed up by their compatriot's discomfort. Pity that the Command Leader Pair snuffed it, they said, and pity too that the poor Polisocs and Troopers had to carry so much gear on their weary backs.

"Serves the Bulgers right," one Pongo Leader Pair remarked and his remarks were echoed by the rest. But with the onset of General West's army the Polisoc Stormtroopers and the Troopers consolidated their position on a centre close to Windsor determined to sell their lives dearly. For their part the majority of the Pongos decided that at the first opportunity they would surrender to the local army and to do that they would shoot their Polisoc and Trooper overlords, if necessary in their backs.

From the ruins of their wagon a Pongo Leader Pair, Grit and Trig gathered his disillusioned troops and under cover of darkness led them into the surrounding mixture of parks and suburbs. They slipped through the outer ring of watchers carrying their weapons and moved off in attack file looking determined as if they were about to go into battle. Grit and Trig cleared the way by explaining to a Stormtrooper Leader Pair they were the lead party of a larger foot force. Once clear of the outer rim they led the troops out into the side roads and with a white flag on their guns they found the enemy troops and gratefully surrendered.

General West listened to their request and grinned when he answered.

"We will accept surrender from any Pongo who wishes it," he said and shook the Pair's hands in turn.

Under the cover of the smoke and fire that roared over Heathrow another Pair, this time on their own, crept out of hiding and slipped through the smoke and dust to the darkened roadway leading west. Luck was with them and they found a way through the enemy troops that led into some side roads, but unlike their Pongo counterparts they had no intention of giving in. Their intent was to find the nearest transfer station and disappear. They travelled the remainder of the night and hid during the day in a garden shed too wary to try the house for food or sustenance. They had enough water and some hard rations that they hoped would keep them going, but the day was still traumatic. As they lay on a bed of garden fertiliser and seed bags they drifted in and out of a fitful sleep and woke now and then to grip each other tightly.

"I am thinking of rodents," said Graz.

"I too am thinking of Rodents," replied Zrag and whimpered. "Are we going Half?"

"Not if we get away my twin. We are tired from war and our constant battle to keep these Bulging soldiers in line. The fight with the enemy is always spoiled by the Polisoc Troopers and the reluctance of the Pongos."

"Why can they not be like Stormtroopers? Why there is even talk of desertion!" said Zrag.

"Is that not what we are about?" said Graz.

"Ah, yes but we are not taking troops with us. We are saving our skins," said Zrag and clutched his twin.

"Yes, yes, saving our skins," agreed Graz.

And so they lay until nightfall and set out on a walk that led them close to the Bywater Road allotments. They hid in a broken garage behind a dingy street where the parking spaces were filled with abandoned cars and the cats fought with the dogs for the contents of the garbage cans, and fell into another fitful but hungrier sleep. Late that afternoon they rose from their uncomfortable bed and staggered along the road avoiding the garbage and the dog turds, and by the light of the street lamps they found the transfer station and gratefully clambered aboard.

They stumbled over a recumbent form that they were too weary to eject, gagged a little at the smell of cold chips and batter, and tapped in a code on the transponder. At the first station they rolled the groaning figure out of the port, hurriedly closed the door and tapped the second stage. With a feeling of great relief they stepped out of the cubicle and into the familiar landscape of Zrad. That they were close to the outer edge of First City's sector blue bothered them a little but nevertheless they were out of the fight and whatever happened next was better than being fried alive by the mad Earth soldiers. Although they still wore their Stormtrooper uniforms they were prepared to fit in with the residents of sector blue. They were glad they were not Polisoc troopers, and as a twin they shuddered at the prospect of being treated to the nasty end most Polisoc troopers suffered if they should be so silly as to venture into sector blue alone. They were shocked and unpleasantly surprised when a group of scruffy Pairs and Half Pairs suddenly appeared from the dirty buildings a few metres from the transfer port carrying weapons and called on them to halt.

"We are refugees from the President's army," they cried out raising their hands high above their heads.

"So what?" said a large Half Pair who held an ancient plasma gun levelled at them. "So are the rest of us but you have new uniforms on, Stormtrooper uniforms too. Get your weapons off, now!"

Graz and Zrag hurriedly removed their swords and knives and handed over the gas guns wishing they had not discarded their plasma guns ruefully knowing that they could have fought their way out. They dropped the weapons on the ground and stepped away from them when the Half Pair ordered them to, and watched as a Pair stepped forward and gathered them up. Two more Pairs came forward with thongs and tied their wrists behind their backs and another to their belts by which each Pair pulled them along.

"Walk or get dragged," said the Half Pair, and with a nod to his companions they moved off into the dark streets of sector blue. "And shut up."

They did shut up and were pulled, pushed, kicked and sometimes dragged deep into the maw of the worst quarter of sector blue. When their mutilated, naked bodies were found laying on the paving of a Sector Yellow Square, what with the damage done by the hungry carnibirds, the only means of identifying them was the official Stormtrooper's identity tags that their captors had heated to a high temperature and pressed into the flesh of their ample buttocks.

The method was a form of branding.

Dart and Drat

The Prime Minister looked at Dart and Drat as if they were aliens. They are, he thought, and what they had told him was almost incomprehensible. Sure, he had listened to the Army boffins, seen the mathematics, looked at the charts and tried to grasp the concept but to no avail. What phased him was the presence of the Japanese attaché and his advisors, the Japanese military commander and the common thugs that Dart and Drat insisted on lugging around with them.

"Can you explain that again please in simple terms," he said and tried not to look puzzled, "so that I can tell the masses."

The rest of the emergency cabinet looked at him, some gratefully and others, especially the labour party members and the senior Tories, with a various mixture of smirks and sneers. Up you, he thought, and concentrated on what Dart and Drat were about to say.

"The Doomsday Bomb is not an easy concept, Prime Minister, but roughly what happens is that the bomb has to be taken apart and put back together again within one third of a light second, whereupon it will explode and act like a mini black hole. The whole planet will disappear. The way we can do this is by seeding the target planet with a receiver, say fitted in a public telephone box, and put the bomb in orbit around the planet approximately zero point three, three and zero point three, two five light seconds from the circumferential position of the receiver. If it is positioned under the lower limit the effects are somewhat reduced and the target planet gets blown to bits and lumps fly around everywhere. If it is too far out then the Bomb will either planet fall and land harmlessly or it will not respond," Dart said, and grinned broadly at the men and women sitting around the table.

"Can we get rid of it ourselves?" asked the Prime Minister.

"You can try but I think you will not succeed because it has its own defence system," said Dart.

"Nasty," said the Prime Minister and hoped that Dart could not see his sudden pallor and nervous twitch. He had to get to a telephone and quick. Surreptitiously, as he listened to the First Admiral ask a question he pushed the call button under the lip of the table and waited almost bursting with impatience for the aide to enter the cabinet room. Rodney wafted in as he was apt to do and the Prime Minister pretended to be angry when the aide leaned close and whispered in his ear. He coughed to attract attention and stood up.

"Excuse me ladies and gentlemen but there is an urgent telephone call for me, I will be only a few moments," he said, and followed Rodney's mincing walk out of the room feeling embarrassed.

When he had gone Dart looked around the room and smiled. Sally sat in a chair behind him and to one side taking notes, and Joseph directed the camera operator while Colin and his lads kept watch. Dart turned and looked at Sally.

"The PM is about to try and cancel the nuclear strike that he and the French PM ordered Euro-force to attempt. Perhaps Joseph, you could display the results on the screen I gave you?"

Joseph happily stepped to the far wall and tapped a pad on a hanging screen that looked like a laminated plain sheet of paper. It flashed and glowed and filled with a series of images. A large central image of space with a sparkling point of light held more or less in the centre of the picture and this was surrounded by a read out and a sky plan, and in the bottom left corner a picture of the Prime Minister talking on the telephone in the next room. In the bottom right corner the French Prime Minister was talking animatedly back and gesturing with her hands. Their conversation, translated into verbatim sub-titles, scrolled steadily across the top and all who watched it and read it were in no doubt that their Prime Minister and the French Prime Minister were arguing the finer points of whether or not the planned nuclear attack on the Doomsday Bomb should go ahead or not. The conversation ended more or less at the point when the French Prime Minister explained that the attack was already under way.

"Merde! It is already happen."

And with a gesture of impatient contempt she hung up.

The Prime Minister walked into the room at the exact moment when the combined Euro-force nuclear strike weapons hit the Doomsday Bomb. He stood, gobsmacked, as the trajectories of the weapons coincided with the orbital location of the bomb and exploded. There was a multiple reaction and a sudden explosion of space and Earthbound debris and for a few moments the screen showed nothing but confusion.

"You knew?" he asked.

"Of course, we may be aliens but we are not stupid," said Drat and giggled. "I have been monitoring your activities since we arrived and I must admit that I have had quite a giggle watching you trying it on. You are so transparent."

"Nosy bastard," said the Prime Minister, and clenched his fists glaring at Drat with his jaw jutting out ready for a fight.

Sally giggled and Colin moved from the wall with a look of happy anticipation. Both Sally and Colin were disappointed when the Prime Minister backed down and took his seat obviously angry, embarrassed and frustrated at being unable to have his way. If the PM had steamed from his ears and nostrils nobody would have been surprised, and if he suddenly took off like a rocket from his seat and shot through the cabinet room roof then that would have been quite acceptable. In fact what he did was sit in his chair and glower at everybody as they discussed the options open to them.

In the end he was forced to admit that the plan the Japanese military advisors thrashed out with the help of the British armed forces leaders was a good one and acceptable to the British public. He sat rigid and angry as the roomful of people gazed at Dart's screen display and groaned when he saw the flurry of nukes and the satellite weapons the French and his own people had authorised destroyed as if they were moths in a flame.

"Now you have really annoyed it," said Dart, and the next time anybody attacks it the Bomb will retaliate and attack the source of the weapons. You will be well advised to let other nations and their armed forces know what will happen."

"And if I choose not to?"

"There is no such option. What has happened here today is on file and that particular little cock up will be broadcast in all languages on E-TV, understood?" said Dart acidly.

"That is a breach of national security."

"Bulgers to that," said Dart, and raised his voice a little. "The security and rescue of your whole planet has more value than your poxy little infighting you selfish, backward, bigoted, uncultured political thug. I warn you that any more of your stupid tricks and I will see to it that you will be ruined. I will personally help destroy your political career, and if necessary I will see to it that your citizens tar and feather you and run you on a rail out of this city directly into the waiting claws of the Polisocs. So help me Nong! For a man who was educated at one of your country's finest schools you are a veritable moron."

And such was Dart's anger that the PM signed the orders without any further opposition and almost but not quite apologised to the Japanese envoy. Whatever he thought the PM had no chance of stopping the plans going ahead anyway, for at that moment a messenger was ushered into the cabinet room carrying a sheaf of reports and handed them directly to the Japanese Military Advisor who read them quickly, grunted and handed them to Dart. Dart read them and handed them to the PM. The PM read the reports and while he was reading them the rest of the members of the committee sipped drinks and ate some of the nibbles supplied by the caterers.

Colin and his men drank tea and ate some of the food. Maurice Bannermann's team relaxed and indulged in a small feast.

"A bit of all right this," said Colin, and snatched another sausage roll from a passing tray.

And a bit of all right was what Dart laughingly described the PM's grumpy manner when he signed the orders that enabled the Japanese advisors to pass weapons to the British army and airforce for use against the Zradians. Outside he sat in the seat of the car with Sally and his twin and grinned broadly.

"The PM didn't like the idea of telling the people what was happening did he?" Dart said and chuckled. "With his rugged face as black as thunder he looked as if he was about to cry when I said he was on TV warts and all."

"He is used to having the bulletin's edited and security dictating to the press what should be said. Maurice has always been a thorn in his side because E-TV is the biggest, second only to Auntie Beeb, for the news and current affairs and that really rankles," said Sally and chuckled too. "He looked as if he were about to mess his pants when you told him that the Doomsday Bomb was likely to fight back."

"And so he should, because if there is another attack on it then it will fight back. It is designed to retaliate by sending weapons back to source and being nuclear itself it will calculate what will happen to the target and adapt the system for maximum effect," said Drat solemnly.

"What do you mean?" asked Joseph.

"I mean that if it chose to it could turn your weapons against you and destroy all life on Earth without destroying the planet. To attack the Doomsday Bomb a third time will be like committing suicide. My people will then attempt to clean the radiated portions of the planet and simply walk in," said Drat.

"Then what we need to do is persuade all governments that a strike against the bomb is a definite no-no," said Joseph.

"Yes and that is why we must put the program out in all languages and in particular we must prevent any further nuclear strikes against the invaders," said Drat. "So as soon as we get to the studio the sooner we can send out the news."

"I understand the Palace has called on the PM to explain," said Sally. "It appears that HRH is definitely not amused. And if you were to meet our monarch I think you will be impressed. HRH has at times expressed opinion, and I believe that is what is happening right now." She grinned broadly.

"Our Old Etonian will be in for a right royal dressing down?" asked Dart. "It's odd but Smith does not seem like the Eton type."

"I think he was the Janitor," said Sally.

"His grandfather was enormously rich," supplied Joseph. "It seems our mister Smith had a few doors opened for him. His family were in scrap metal."[8]

"Oh was he now," said Dart. "Where did he work from?"

"He had a large depot near Romford and used to send truck loads of scrap cross country to steel works and foundries all over," replied Joseph.

"Oh," said Colin. "That Smith! Then me an' him are cousins. Funny old world ain't it?"

Everybody stared at him.

---

[8] *Smith's unlikely attendance at Eton is my joke against the so-called upper crust. Author.*

General Schwarzkopf speaks his mind

In the dense bush of the Amazon jungle the multi-personality that was Clard and Dracl's robot received the E-TV news broadcast as data to be processed, and with a touch of annoyance realised that its family of rodents was threatened by the stupidity of the British Prime Minister. It searched the communications systems of the entire planet and gathered signals from all dangerous sources. It traced the electronic surveillance the Doomsday Bomb was making of the planet and allowed one of its personalities to curse, and with a sigh it linked the data and stopped moving. With another sigh it began to weave a security web around the planet that took a long time and much power. It knew that it was about to have a long regeneration period so it shut down as much of its activity as possible and drew on the power that emanated from Star Station Two. As a result the entire mechanised force of the Zradian invaders was brought to a grinding halt. The robot reconfigured the entire data system, and hours later it sighed with relief when the power module it commandeered was taken off its task of transfer modulation and redirected at neutralising the nuclear strike systems of Earth, and the orbiting weaponry, plus placing a jamming signal on the Doomsday Bomb's defences. The latter, it knew, was likely to be temporary but for the time being the measure would do. Its power somewhat depleted it drew on the module again and let the waves and the power of the sun replenish its own.

For a few hours wherever the forces of Earth were fighting the invader there was a respite. Some took the chance to counter attack and others gathered their shattered armies and their wits and looked for a sensible place to hide.

In the good ole US of A the struggling President gave in to his opponent and cooperated fully with the advisors in an attempt to negate her rising power.

It was a timely action, especially for the Northern states and Canada where the Zradian forces were consolidating. The Zradians realised that the armies attacking the southern states were blocked by the contaminated area around Las Vegas. They concentrated instead on moving north and east. But no longer were they dominant. The forces opposing them grew steadily stronger, more organised and with weapons as good as their own.

"Bulgers, what have these primitives done?" Asked the Leader Pair when reports of the losses arrived on his screen.

"The swine are fighting back," said his 2IC.

"What with?"

"It appears they have copied our weapons and improved on them. They have put some on their flying machines and like the filthy rebels back home are using rockets," explained the 2IC.

The Leader Pair wished they had some rockets but to his regret the Zradian Army had never invested in them. One problem was that when they were transported by the matter transfer system they often exploded. Which effect, the Leader Pair agreed, was not conducive to peace of mind amongst the troops, especially their own precious selves.

"Oh well, we will just have to fight harder for the honour of our glorious President," the Leader Pair said.

"For our Glorious President!" Echoed the 2IC enthusiastically.

In the western states the remnants of the Zradians that had escaped the nuclear bomb were rounded up by General Schwarzkopf's troops and taken prisoner. The General, standing on the dock in San Francisco bay where his soldiers were unloading supplies shipped to them by a sympathetic Mexican government gazed inland and silently cursed the President of the good ole US of A.

The troops watched him with amusement as they worked and waited for the stream of bad language that would burst forth from his lips when the inevitable happened in a few seconds at ten forty. The seconds ticked by and then at exactly ten forty from the numerous radios that were tuned into the local station the strains of A Whiter Shade of Pale began to play. Almost at the same time as the radios were switched off the General began his long string of curses that ended with mildest epithet of his rich vocabulary.

"I hate that fucking tune!"

This is the conclusion of Book II of The Zradian Chronicles. The story finishes in Book III, The Doomsday Bomb in which Julian and Angela play their part.